the day
of the dolphin

A NOVEL BY
ROBERT MERLE

TRANSLATED FROM THE FRENCH BY
HELEN WEAVER

SIMON AND SCHUSTER • NEW YORK

SECOND PRINTING

SBN 671-20182-4
LIBRARY OF CONGRESS CATALOG CARD NUMBER: 73-75865
DESIGNED BY EDITH FOWLER
MANUFACTURED IN THE UNITED STATES OF AMERICA
BY AMERICAN BOOK–STRATFORD PRESS, INC.

To
PAUL BUDKER
AND
RENÉ-GUY BUSNEL

1

March 28, 1970.

Home, please, William, said Mrs. Jameson with the affected politeness she habitually used to talk to her chauffeur (You know, Dorothy, my servants adore me, I never forget their birthdays and I always speak to them politely). William bent his fat, shaved neck—as it happened his name was not William, but to simplify life Mrs. Jameson addressed all the chauffeurs who had worked for her since the death of her husband by this name—placed his two plump hands on the steering wheel, and the Cadillac gave a smooth hum and started off with infinite, cautious slowness.

Mrs. Jameson rested her massive frame against the back seat, which had been custom-made of beautiful English leather, adjusted her glasses, which were trimmed with small but real diamonds, propped her alligator bag on her vast thighs, pivoted her heavy head to the left, dropped her lower lip, opened her gray eyes very wide, and peering at Professor Sevilla, examined him at leisure, in silence, without a trace of embarrassment, as if he were an object. Her first impression was confirmed, dark eyes, dark complexion, coal-black hair, he looks like a gypsy, I'll bet he's just as hairy as poor John, a real ape, hair even on his back and a thatch on his chest, another of those supermasculine red-blooded Latins, always in rut.

Mr. Sevilla, are you of foreign descent, Not at all, I'm a hundred-percent American, but my paternal grandfather was born in Galicia. Galicia? she asked, raising her eyebrows, Sevilla looked at her

7

and smiled courteously, She looks like a fish, she has the hard lower lip and big stupid staring eyes of the grouper. Galicia, Mrs. Jameson, is a Spanish province, How romantic, she said, fiddling with the catch of her bag, she felt depressed, so he really was a kind of gypsy after all, she pivoted her head to the left and took possession of Sevilla again, beautiful hands, dark eyes, black hair graying at the temples, those idiots will be mad about him, anyway it'll only last an hour.

She felt a slight twinge above her right breast and controlled a desire to slip her hand under her blouse and feel under the skin for a little lump the size of a hazelnut whose name might be death, Murphy was reassuring but it was his job to reassure people, It's nothing, Mrs. Jameson, absolutely nothing, the deep voice, the piercing look, the tired but patient manner, she leaned forward and closed her eyes, perspiration trickled down her back, and she heard herself dying, terrified, a few seconds passed, she sat back, raised her eyelids, her steel-gray eyes reappeared like little nervous animals and registered the alligator bag on her lap, the brown leather of the seats, the shaved neck of William, it was all there, Lord, it was not fair, it was not true that Mrs. Jameson, widow of John B. Jameson, could die, John went pale, he looked at her with his bloodshot eyes, inhaled with a horrible sucking noise and fell forward on his plate, dead, there is such a thing as justice, Lord, he drank too much, smoked too much, he was hairy and lustful, Mrs. Jameson was sitting, irreproachable, at the top of a mountain, in a pale blue dress covered with little flowers, the lions licked her Christian feet, she raised her head, thrust her jaw forward to erase her double chin, then she opened her bag, took out a sealed envelope, and grasping it between her thumb and index finger, held it across the entire width of the Cadillac and handed it to Sevilla without a word.

Thank you, said Sevilla, he blushed under his dark complexion, his dark eyes blinked, he resisted a desire to thrust the envelope into his pocket at once, and forced himself to toy with it absent-mindedly, as if it were an object of no importance which he might easily leave behind on the brown leather seat when he got out, Some of our lecturers prefer to be paid in cash, she said in a neutral voice, It really makes no difference, Mrs. Jameson, murmured Sevilla, Marian was costing him a fortune, he was paying her an enormous amount of alimony, My dear, said Marian, showing off

8

her newly decorated home, it's unbelievable, all this money that fell on me by some miracle. But the miracle was Marian in front of the judge, the maximum number of demands and the maximum cunning, she had had her pound of flesh and then some, leave it to the religious to suck your last dollar, Sevilla looked at Mrs. Jameson with resentment, a hundred thousand dollars to spend a year, what does she do with it, a husband who died on the job at the age of sixty to make her wealthy, one life cut short for another life without purpose, two absurdities, Are you married? asked Mrs. Jameson, Divorced, he answered briefly, Any children? Two, She looked at the back of William's neck with an air of disapproval, Don't you think, she said in her throaty voice, that it is a shock for children to see their parents separate, I think, Mrs. Jameson, that it is a much greater shock for children to live in a divided home, and a much more destructive one, because it is repeated every day, I don't think so, said Mrs. Jameson, closing her alligator bag with a click, In that case we do not agree, said Sevilla, William shifted his plump hands on the wheel, glanced in the rearview mirror, his face impassive and serene, and thought, The old bitch, always boring the shit out of people.

How old are you? Sevilla looked at her, Fifty-two, the minute he said it he was furious at himself for answering so submissively, you always make too many concessions to people in the name of politeness, they take advantage of it to misuse you, My husband, said Mrs. Jameson, died at fifty-four, he was an extraordinary man, and we were, thank God, very happily married, I have always had a very strong sense of social obligation and my only regret is that I did not spend more time with him, but John left for the factory very early in the morning and was careful not to wake me, and in the evening when he came home, very late, always very late, poor dear, I was usually out.

Do you enjoy good health? Pretty good, said Sevilla, and he remained on guard, tense and uncomfortable, Mrs. Jameson fell silent, her lower lip drooping a little like that of a fish, her question was pointless and the answer meant nothing to her, she looked like a chicken that has dug up a little piece of glass with its beak and looks at it sideways out of its round eye, there was a silence, she half shut her eyes and forgot Sevilla, he was an object placed on her seat, to be used and then returned to the place where she had found it, she sighed, the Club, the presidency of the Club, the lectures, what a chore, time kept passing, every year another spring, how many springs in a lifetime, the Cadillac slowed down, made a right-angle turn and slowly drove up a driveway bordered with blue cypress trees, the gravel crunched beneath the tires, Professor, may I suggest that you not speak over forty minutes and that you use simple language?

. . .

Mrs. Jameson motioned Sevilla to an enormous wing chair of dark red velvet. He faced the audience. Forty pairs of eyes looked at him, he nodded and sat down. The cushion yielded under him luxuriously until only the top half of his body was visible. He tried to sit up straight but the velvet held him prisoner. He had expected to sit in a straight-backed chair, behind a desk on which he could have arranged his notes. But there was nothing either in front of him or beside him, not even a low table. Surrounded by maroon velvet and almost engulfed by it, he was paralyzed with comfort. He could not even put his forearms on the armrests: He was too low to reach them. Nor was there any question of keeping a piece of paper on the inclined plane of his knees. Sevilla put his hand in his pocket, hesitated, and resigned himself to speaking without notes.

Seated in a semicircle around him, about forty women of all ages were examining him. Sevilla gave them a discreet look and smiled. It was a rather charming smile, candid and young, a smile he knew he could count on. But nobody returned it. The faces opposite him remained impassive. They were considering him without ill will, but without good will either. Obviously the fact that he was the only man in the room conferred no privilege on him. Sevilla looked again at the faces opposite him and was amused. He could almost see how the minds of his listeners worked. The members of the Club met once a week to listen to a lecturer and expose themselves to the world. In view of this lofty aim, the sex of the lecturer was of no importance. The Club did not notice it.

Sevilla became aware that Mrs. Jameson, standing at his right, was telling the story of his life with the help of a typewritten sheet which she was holding in her hand. She had undergone a surprising transformation: She was all sweetness and light toward him. Radiating the Christian virtues, she attributed them to him. She over-

10

flowed with an inspiring optimism. Everything was perfect and pure: America, the state of Florida, the club, the magnificent city that had given birth to it, the members of the club, the president of the club, the lecturer. And the husbands, thought Sevilla, what are they doing while this is going on, poor men? Making money, to give their wives the leisure to improve themselves? But after all, why not? The ladies could do worse. This club, when you thought about it, was all to their credit and even to our credit as a nation.

While Mrs. Jameson overflowed with love for her neighbor, the faces opposite Sevilla gradually took on individuality. Three or four were beautiful: a pretty Irish-American redhead with a milky complexion and green eyes, a fine-looking Jewess, very imposing and statuesque, and a young lady, probably of Southern origin, who had a very delicate oval face, a dark complexion, languorous black eyes, and a slow and seductive way of lowering her eyelids. There were other young women, pretty enough, elegant enough, but drier, more anxious, and exuding dissatisfaction with themselves. Over the age of fifty there was nothing but stoutness, diamond-framed glasses, and permanent waves. Sevilla's gaze lingered. What emptiness, what secret misery. It was never much fun to grow old, but to grow old without a purpose in life, without the sense, after sixty or seventy years, of working, seeking, making progress . . . And this Club, in the last analysis, what a ridiculous pretense! Today someone tells them about dolphins, next week Marcel Proust, the week after that Southeast Asia. Universal culture in forty-minute doses. A little of everything, as in a cafeteria.

Mrs. Jameson stopped talking, dripping tact and perfection. For a moment she remained motionless, massive, chin raised, as if posing for her own statue. The ladies applauded, she acknowledged the applause, lowered her eyes, and sat down on a little low upholstered chair. She could afford to be humble, being at home. This low fireside chair served two purposes: It proclaimed her modesty and it rested her legs.

"We're all ears, Professor," she said knowingly and archly, as if she had invented the expression for the occasion.

Mrs. Jameson was sitting with her back to the club. She no longer held it in the vise of her gray eyes, and Sevilla now sensed in several of his listeners a livelier expression and a more relaxed attitude which belied their initial indifference. To his great relief

11

he felt himself exist again as a man. He looked back at his audience in a friendly way and started off briskly.

"In the past few years the dolphin has been the subject of so many articles, statements, predictions, caricatures, comic strips, and Hollywood scripts, that I feel as if I have nothing to tell you about him. [*Polite protests*] If you disagree with me, if you're not protesting out of politeness [*no, no*], I'll do my best to shed some light on the subject. But I must beg you not to expect anything sensational or amazing. Scientific research proceeds slowly, and delphinology is still in its early stages.

"Americans," Sevilla went on, "have a reputation for loving animals and being passionately interested in learning about them. But there is no denying that in the past ten years no animal has aroused greater interest in this country, for several reasons, than the dolphin. Nor is there any other animal who is studied more extensively. Every year the United States Navy and various government agencies spend considerable sums to finance the work of several teams of investigators, including the one I head. In addition, various private organizations like the Lockheed company of California and the Sperry Gyroscope Company also devote substantial resources to delphinology. Although I can't give you a completely accurate figure, I wouldn't be surprised if the amount spent annually by private and Federal organizations now reaches a grand total of five hundred million dollars." [*Keen interest*]

Sevilla paused to let the magnitude of the figure penetrate his audience.

"Five hundred million dollars," Sevilla continued, "makes a lot of cents, but in my opinion the dolphin deserves it. In simple language and briefly, as your president requests [*amusement*], I am going to try to tell you why the dolphin has become the most expensive and the most widely studied animal in the United States.

"You will forgive me if I begin with a few words about his physiology. The dolphin is not a fish, but a cetacean. He does not have gills, but lungs. Since he breathes the oxygen in the air, he must come to the surface to obtain it. The fish, like all animals improperly described as cold-blooded, adopts the surrounding temperature: cold in the waters of the Antarctic, warm in the Caribbean Sea. The dolphin, on the other hand, is a warm-blooded animal, that is, an animal whose temperature remains constant, regardless

12

of the temperature of the water in which he is immersed: Hence the layer of blubber with which he, like his large cousin, the whale, is covered, in order to resist cold. This layer, which is protected by a glossy skin that looks like rubber, helps to give his body a shape that is curved and streamlined and glides swiftly through the water. The dolphin does not lay eggs like the fish. He is a mammal, and he shares with all mammals, including man, the mode of reproduction with which we are familiar [*keen interest*]: copulation, pregnancy, parturition, and nursing of the young. These processes are picturesque and spectacular in dolphins because they take place in water, but physiologically they are in no way exceptional, and I do not intend to describe them. [*Veiled disappointment*]

"Certain characteristics of his anatomy suggest that at a remote period the dolphin was a land animal and that the sea is an environment to which he has had to adapt. But he has adapted to it magnificently. His swimming speed, to give only one example, is greater than that of most fish.

"Why does American science take such great interest in this marine mammal?" Scvilla went on, raising his voice slightly. "Because he possesses the quality which we humans call intelligence. This means that his intelligence seems close enough to our own so that we can understand his behavior if we reason by analogy."

Sevilla paused for a moment, looked at his listeners, and wondered whether he was losing them.

"All cetaceans are intelligent," he went on. "Why, of all the cetaceans, have we chosen the dolphin as an object of study? Because he is smaller and more manageable, as it were, than his cousins, the whale and the grampus. The *Tursiops truncatus,* or 'bottle-nosed dolphin,' which we prefer to any other species, rarely exceeds ten feet in length. The average specimen measures eight feet two and one-half inches and weighs three hundred and thirty-one pounds. He is, therefore, completely transportable by car or airplane. All he needs is a space about the size of a swimming pool— and although he requires almost constant companionship, the cost of feeding him is not extravagant: two dozen pounds of fish a day.

"But what makes the dolphin an ideal animal for research is his extraordinary friendliness. This friendliness is not weakness. With a single blow of his powerful jaw he is capable of stunning a good-sized shark, if he hits him in the gills. He also possesses a double row

13

of very sharp teeth, eighty-eight in all, with which he could shred to pieces the arms or legs of his captors, if he wanted to. But he has never been known to turn his weapons against our species. Most domestic animals bite or scratch when subjected to a slight degree of pain. The dolphin accepts the pain that is inflicted on him without resisting and without ever becoming dangerous. It is as if he is predisposed to regard mankind with inexhaustible good will. Indeed, from the most remote antiquity he has had a reputation for seeking out the company of human beings, particularly that of children. When captured in his natural habitat he may be tamed with surprising rapidity, and he accepts our caresses with pleasure."

Sevilla paused. He had just noticed a certain tenderness in the eyes of his listeners and being a great lover of animals himself, he savored this emotion and stopped to participate in it. *We are a good people,* he thought with a glow.

"Alpers," he went on after a moment, "tells a very charming story about the friendliness of dolphins. On Christmas Day in 1955 in New Zealand, near a small beach called Opononi, a female dolphin appeared, mingled with the bathers, and to their general amazement began to play with them. She showed a marked preference for the children, and allowed them to handle her without showing any impatience. When someone threw her a ball she would catch it in her teeth, throw it into the air very high and ahead of her, swim very rapidly until she was under it, and would invariably catch it before it touched the water. She also played a game which nobody had taught her. She would wedge the ball under her stomach, dive into the water with it, and release it when she had reached a certain depth. When the ball shot out of the water the dolphin would hurry until she was directly under the point of fall, and just as the ball fell she would strike it vigorously, using her caudal flipper like a baseball bat. When she didn't have a ball she would go and get a beer bottle from the bottom of the sea and balance it on her snout. In short, she not only played with the children, she entertained them.

"Needless to say, the fame of Opo—the nickname the children had given the dolphin—spread throughout New Zealand. People rushed to see her from all parts of the island and from the neighboring islands. Then, according to observers, a curious phenomenon occurred. The friendliness of the animal infected the people. In the afternoon on the beach strangers spoke to each other and did each other favors. Social and racial barriers fell. Opononi became the village of friendship."

In the now rather drowsy mind of Mrs. Jameson the close succession of the words *social* and *racial* set off an alarm signal. She sat up straight on her little low chair, pursed her lips and gave Sevilla a look that was both severe and frightened, as if to warn him of the abyss that yawned at his feet. But Sevilla did not notice. He was lost in his subject.

"I wish," he continued, his dark eyes glowing fondly, "I could tell you more about the lovable characteristics of dolphins, but that is not altogether my purpose. I would like to make it clear that I consider it a great privilege to spend my life studying this splendid animal. He is a delightful companion—intelligent, playful, affectionate. Although you have all seen dolphins," he said, taking a photograph out of his wallet and handing it to Mrs. Jameson, "I have a picture of one of my subjects which I cannot resist the pleasure of showing you. He is playing in the tank with my assistant, Arlette Lafeuille—she is of Canadian origin, hence the French name. The photograph gives you a good idea of the shape of the mouth. The dolphin's, that is [*laughter*]: very wide, sinuous, and turned up at the corners. Its special shape gives it a smiling expression, and the smile is a mischievous one. As a matter of fact," he went on, while the photograph was passed from hand to hand, "this impression, however subjective, is not false: The dolphin is the happiest and most playful animal in creation."

Sevilla waited until the photograph was back in his hands and the murmuring had died down.

"I said that the dolphin was very intelligent, and I would like to explain how we arrive at this conclusion. The first indication is the weight of the brain. Average brain weight is about three and three-quarters pounds in the dolphin, three pounds in man, and three-quarters of a pound in the chimpanzee. This is a fact which augurs well for the capacities of the dolphin, but which is difficult to interpret accurately. The ratio of brain weight to total body weight, which has been used by certain investigators to establish a comparative intellectual classification of man, the dolphin, the monkey and the elephant, seems today to have been abandoned. Anatomical study seems more conclusive. It also suggests the superiority of the

15

dolphin. For his brain, like the human brain, is complex, dense, rich in cells. The resemblance to the human encephalon is particularly striking with respect to the high development of the cerebellum and the cerebral cortex."

Sevilla paused. Cerebellum, cerebral cortex—should he explain these terms? He looked at Mrs. Jameson, but slumped in her chair with her eyes half closed, she seemed to have withdrawn into a region of herself where the simplicity of the lecturer's vocabulary no longer concerned her.

"Another reason for believing the dolphin to be intelligent," Sevilla went on, "is, of course, his behavior. You are aware of the great popularity of oceanariums all across the United States and their huge success. If you have seen one of these performances you will agree the dolphin's tricks have none of the dreary routine of the circus animal's. The latter is a slave, punished if it performs badly, rewarded if it performs well; it blindly and automatically obeys the man who has trained it, and only him. The dolphin accepts the reward because it is part of the game and refuses all punishment. He is so happy to perform his trick that he will perform it for anyone, as long as he is given the correct signals. Besides, he has fun, he likes to work, he enjoys the applause. The man who shows him these tricks is not a tamer, he is a friend. For example, you can teach him to grasp a ball between his teeth, half raise his body out of the water, and with a powerful movement of the neck send the ball into a basketball net which hangs over the tank. Once the dolphin has grasped what is expected of him you don't have to keep after him to make him practice. He will practice spontaneously, as long as necessary to correct his mistakes. He is not an animal that is trained, but an athlete who trains himself.

"The intelligence of the dolphin is even more evident when he is enjoying himself. You know how fascinating it is to watch young animals play. Seriousness and fun, grace and awkwardness—the mixture is admirable. But the play of the dolphin has another quality.

"A young dolphin discovers by accident that if he drops a pelican feather directly under one of the faucets that supply his tank the current will carry it to the other end of the pool. After this he has only to follow it and catch it. He is delighted at having discovered this diversion, and he does it again, ten, twenty, thirty times. A

16

young female observes the trick and then adds a new twist. Instead of dropping the feather directly below the stream, she releases it in the eddy formed by this stream. When it touches the water the feather begins to turn at the edge of the eddy, and before it is sucked into the center and down by the current, there are two or three seconds during which the female dolphin goes and stations herself in its path and seizes it as it goes by. The male dolphin imitates her. Soon they play together. One goes and places the feather in the eddy while the other waits for it a few yards farther down. It is true that in certain insects we observe some very complex collective activities, but these are stereotyped, non-perfectible activities, and they are not the product of individual initiative. Among dolphins an individual creates a game, others perfect it, and several play it. We have here intelligent creation, teamwork, and a capacity for attention which are very rare in the animal world."

Sevilla paused, and for the first time since he had started speaking let his gaze linger on the two or three pretty faces he had noticed at the beginning. He was as full of his subject as ever, but he felt a need to distract himself before recovering his momentum. That girl, he thought, looking at the Southerner,* has an admirably shaped face. Just then the Southerner turned her head a few degrees to the right and the delicate outline of her face in a three-quarter view stood out against the dark velvet drapes. She threw Sevilla a swift sideways look, then, lowering her eyelids languorously over her black eyes, she seemed to withdraw for the contemplation of secret treasures. The whole thing was admirably planned: the position of the face, the swiftness of the look, and the slowness with which the curtain was dropped. She's a sly one, thought Sevilla with a little thrill of pleasure. The interruption had lasted no more than a second but when he resumed speaking he felt considerably refreshed.

"Surely you have met people who say about their dogs, 'He's so intelligent, he can do everything but talk!' It is quite evident that this statement contains an innocent contradiction. For the fact is

---

* Far from being a native of a Southern state, she was descended from an Italian great-grandfather, a rather stout and very ordinary-looking man who had made a fortune as a wholesale grocer. It was to him, however, that she owed her madonnalike face and pre-Raphaelite neck.

17

that language is the test of true intelligence. Trying to measure the intelligence of the dolphin raises the question of whether he is capable of communicating with his fellows.

"The dolphin does not emit sounds with his mouth but with his spiracle, a small opening located at the back of his forehead which is used for respiration and which closes by means of a valve when he dives underwater. Thus his organs of phonation are different from our own, but even so, they allow for a certain flexibility of use.

"The sounds which the dolphin is capable of modulating are numerous and varied. One can distinguish squeaking—not unlike the noise produced by a rusty hinge—barking, clicking, growling, a great deal of whistling, and finally, some other noises which I would describe as impolite [smiles].

"Are dolphins capable of communicating information to each other by means of sounds? This is the question. By information I mean complex information, which does not include a wounded animal's calls for help to his comrades or, in mating, the violent protest of the male when his companion pretends to swim away from him or to be interested in someone else. For such purposes—translated into human language—a simple growl would be sufficient [laughter].

"It goes without saying that true language presupposes communication on a less elementary level. Researchers today are inclined to believe that dolphins are capable of communication of this kind. Of course, so far we have only theories, but these are already rather impressive, as theories go.

"Here is one of the experiments on which these theories are based. Two dolphins, a male and a female, are separated by a net which is stretched from one end of their tank to the other. In front of each dolphin you put a panel containing three lights of different colors, and under the water, within reach, three levers. When the green light goes on, the dolphin must press the right-hand lever with his snout; when the red light goes on, the left-hand lever, and when the white light goes on, the middle lever. You light the three lights successively in variable order and in series, and if the dolphin does well with his series, you give him a fish.

"A few minutes after you have presented a series to the female you present the same series to the male in his part of the tank, on the panel that is in front of him. You observe that the male antici-

18

pates the lights that are to appear on the panel and pushes the corresponding levers even before they go on. This observation becomes the point of departure for further experiments. You erect an opaque screen between the male and the female so that he cannot see and consequently 'copy' what she did before him. You start the experiment over again. Surprisingly enough, it gives the same result. The male continues to anticipate the questions. It is not by sight, therefore, that the male is informed.

"At this point you push matters further. You erect a sound barrier between the male and the female the entire length of the tank, so as to rule out the possibility of any oral communication between them. For it has been observed that while the female is taking the test she constantly emits sounds. Having done this, you present a series of lights to the female and she responds to it. But now, for the first time, when the male's turn comes, he waits until the lights go on on the panel before reacting.

"You then cut an opening in the sound barrier which allows the couple to communicate by voice. You begin the tests again, and once again the male anticipates the questions. Therefore, it is definitely by means of the sounds emitted by the female that he has been informed [*keen interest*]. It is as if the female said to her husband, who can't see her, as she pushed the different levers, 'I press the left-hand lever, then the right-hand lever, then the middle lever, then the right-hand lever again, and hurry up and do the same, for at the end of the series you'll get a fish.' [*Laughter and tender looks*]

"If such communication exists—and what else are we to conclude?—it includes notions as abstract as right, left, and middle, and implies the vehicle of a true language.

"Other investigators are engaged in collecting the different sounds emitted by dolphins and converting them into luminous shapes which are photographed on plates. If we ever succeed in decoding these plates by analyzing the context of the experiment or the situation being experienced by the animal, we may be on the road to an elementary knowledge of the language of dolphins.

"The second stage, although it may be very presumptuous to think about it this early, would consist of using our knowledge of 'Dolphinese' to teach dolphins the rudiments of human language. This presupposes, of course, that the dolphin is capable of imitating

19

human sounds. This, as you may know, is the position of Dr. Lilly, who is presently attempting to teach his dolphins English.

"However, the transition from Dolphinese to human language implies such a prodigious leap forward for the animal that we really ought to call a halt to the proliferation of 'if's' that has brought us this far, and refuse to go any further along the path of conjecture."

Sevilla stopped, looked at his audience with a smile, bowed his head, and said, "Thank you for your kind attention." [*Prolonged applause*] He added, "I should be happy to answer questions, unless you feel I have already taken too much of your time." [*Protests*]

Mrs. Jameson rose. Exuding sweetness and tact, her fat beringed hands crossed at the solar plexus, she began to thank the lecturer in her throaty voice. The audience looked toward her attentively and immediately stopped listening.

". . . and I am sure," concluded Mrs. Jameson, "that we are all grateful to Professor Sevilla for offering to answer our questions." [*Applause*]

Mrs. Jameson sat down. A silence fell, grew, became embarrassing. There was whispering, a little cough, looks were exchanged. A bony girl sitting in the first row studied Professor Sevilla with an intense expression from behind large tortoiseshell-rimmed glasses.

"Then I'll start the ball rolling myself," said Mrs. Jameson blandly, as if she did not know that everyone was waiting for her to speak first. "Mr. Sevilla," she went on, turning her fish gape toward him, "you mentioned the oceanaria and the success of their shows. You also said that they were springing up all over the country. Am I to assume, then, that they are lucrative enterprises?"

"Very lucrative," said Sevilla with a twinkle in his eye. "Just as an example, I know that this year one of them did an overall business of four million dollars. Of course, the overhead is high, and it takes time and patience to create a program that will draw people. The public gets tired of everything, even dolphins."

The bony girl raised her hand, but the Southerner beat her to it.

"Mr. Sevilla," she said, giving him a three-quarter view of her delightful face and half shutting her eyes, "is it possible to raise a dolphin in a private swimming pool?"

"Certainly, if your pool is heated."

"But what about the fresh water?"

"You can buy sea salt and dissolve it in your pool. It's merely a question of getting the right proportion."

"What is the price of a dolphin?"

"Twelve hundred dollars delivered to New York."

"But that's nothing!" said the Southerner, her astonishment tinged with disapproval.

Sevilla smiled. "The upkeep, however, is rather expensive," he said reassuringly. "In my opinion you must have one full-time person just to take care of the dolphin. Otherwise he gets bored and pines away. Unless you buy a pair."

"Is that possible?"

"Of course. Though if you have children, I should warn you that during mating they may witness some rather violent spectacles."

Mrs. Jameson blinked and the bony girl raised her hand, but the Southerner went on: "Where can you buy a pair of dolphins?"

"There are specialists who capture them."

"Can you give me an address?"

"I . . . I don't have it with me," Sevilla lied.

He uncrossed his legs and went on in a neutral tone: "But if you would care to telephone me tomorrow morning, I'll give you the information. My number is in the phone book."

The Southerner slowly lowered her lids and Mrs. Jameson pursed her thick lips. Those two, practically under her nose, like animals, her lower lip drooped and she shuddered, John had been such a gentleman during their engagement, her hands were cold as she lay on the colonial bed with its white muslin canopy, the dress she had just taken off was white too, he came out of the bathroom looking like a gorilla, Oh, John! John! I hate you, but he's dead, she thought with astonishment, mourning looked well on me, I spent so much money, the house was so depressing, so old-fashioned, I wanted to change everything, Dorian, was that his only name? Mrs. Jameson, this red velvet will lend dignity to your living room, blond hair curling lightly on his neck, long delicate hands, sweet, musical voice, in the pool his smooth chest, his long graceful legs, he revolutionized the house from top to bottom, his prices were mad, mad, absolutely fantastic, Mrs. Jameson, I have an idea, he looked like a poet with his curly hair, so graceful in all his movements, they cost me plenty, those ideas of his, Dear Mrs. Jameson, I'm *so* sorry, I must go, my mother is ill, and after that not a word, not a line, my letters returned, my telegrams unanswered, the damned little swindler, a flood of bitterness burst in her like an abscess, there was a taste of bile in her mouth and a stab of pain over her right breast, the pain ebbed, she straightened her back, looked up, and stared at Sevilla as if she had never seen him before, Animals, she thought contemptuously, all of them.

A lady of about fifty whose hair was a suspicious shade of auburn raised her hand and asked, "Is the dolphin in the process of becoming a domestic animal?"

Sevilla gave his questioner a friendly look. If he had spoken only for her, he would not have wasted his time.

"Your question is very interesting, but before I could answer it we would have to define a domestic animal."

"Well, let's try," said the lady briskly. "Let's say that a domestic animal is an animal that allows itself to be fed by man."

"That won't do," said Sevilla. "Almost all animals in captivity will take food from man, including the lion, the tiger, the boa . . . Personally, I would prefer to say that a species is domestic when it allows itself to be handled by the human species. This is what distinguishes the domestic animal from the animal who is merely tamed. The latter accepts a considerable amount of contact with his tamer, but *only* with him—and it remains a precarious relationship, subject to all the accidents that this precariousness implies. Moreover, there are degrees of domestication. In the bovine species, for example, the female is completely domesticated but the bull remains rather dangerous to handle. And this, it seems to me, is the definition of domestication: the ability to handle an animal without danger."

"It seems to me," said the lady with the auburn hair, "that your definition can also be applied to the tamed animal."

Sevilla thought it over. "The tamed animal is only an individual. Domestication refers to an entire species."

"In that case," said the lady promptly, "the dolphin is not yet a domestic animal, since the majority of dolphins live in a wild state."

"But as soon as they are captured," said Sevilla, looking at her with interest, "they all become very friendly. Anyway," he added after a moment, "the problem may now be seen in terms of the domestication of a new animal species, but if the day comes when men and dolphins communicate in words, it will no longer be possible to regard dolphins as animals, and the relationship will have to be redefined."

"Perhaps, unfortunately, as a master-slave relationship."

"I hope not," said Sevilla with emotion.

She nodded and smiled at him. He smiled back and thought sadly, Nothing is perfect. Under that dyed hair is a good mind. What a shame it hadn't chosen to live in the head of the Southerner. I know that one as if I had already had her, snobbish and conceited, emotionally retarded, just enough narcissistic sensuality to enjoy being petted, my God, why must I be attracted to this bit of flesh without a soul, it doesn't make sense, this thirst in me, this fever, this obsession with the other sex (all the Sevillas were Catholic, Sevilla's mother used to go to Mass every morning with her two boys, they helped the priest in the choir, and meanwhile, her knees aching from the *prie-dieu,* she prayed with hate for the salvation of the soul of her ex-husband, who was living in Miami with a Cuban woman).

The bony girl raised her hand, but the Irish-American was quicker: "You told us that the U.S. Navy was interested in your research. Could the dolphin be put to military use?"

Sevilla's body stiffened imperceptibly, but his face remained smiling: "You should address that question to an admiral," he said facetiously [*smiles*].

"Even so," insisted the Irish girl, "may we not assume that the Navy's interest in dolphins is not completely disinterested?"

"I don't know the Navy's plans," said Sevilla. "I'm a complete outsider. I can only theorize. All I can say is this: The police use dogs; why couldn't the Navy use dolphins?"

"According to everything that you've said, it would be greatly underestimating dolphins to place them in the same category as dogs."

He looked at her. Her eyes were forget-me-not blue, incredibly pure, innocent, and stubborn. You could easily picture her in Nero's Rome in a long white garment, being burned alive on a cross for refusing to deny Jesus.

"You're right," said Sevilla. "We can expect other services from them. But exactly what services I couldn't tell you. It's not my field, and I don't want to indulge in hypotheses."

"I think," said the Irish girl, "that you should concern yourself now with the practical applications of your own research, so that later you will not have to regret having pursued it."

There was some agitation among the listeners, and Mrs. Jameson frowned.

"Let's not exaggerate," said Sevilla with a wave of his hand. "Our gentle dolphins have nothing in common with the hydrogen bomb."

There were some smiles, but the face of the Irish girl remained serious, tense, preoccupied.

"I think," said Mrs. Jameson, "there is someone who has been wanting to speak for a long time. Miss Anderson?"

The bony girl started and her large glasses slipped to the end of her nose. She shoved them back with an immoderately long index finger, thrust her flat chest forward with a sudden movement, and fixed Sevilla with her intense gaze.

"You said," she began with an air of seriousness and concentration, "that the method of reproduction of dolphins was the same as that of mammals. It seems to me, however, that all these operations—copulation, parturition, nursing—cannot take place without great difficulty, since they occur in suspension in water, and sometimes, no doubt, in a heavy swell. Perhaps you could describe—"

Mrs. Jameson rose. "I suggest," she said with the tact of a steamroller, "that we abuse Professor Sevilla's patience no further, and that we all adjourn to the next room for refreshments."

II

The room was hygienically empty, not a magazine, not a scrap of paper, just three armchairs, a small table with an ashtray, and on the painted walls three engravings of full-rigged ships in foul weather, C looked at the ships wearily, he felt a twinge in the vicinity of his stomach, the pain was not sharp but constant, it did not seem to come from the inside of the organs but from their walls, it was more like a painful contraction of the muscles, it radiated downward to the abdomen and upward under the ribs, at times it reached the vertebrae, C felt that if he could just lie down, flex his legs, and relax his muscles his painful organs would return to normal but this was not true, the pain never went away, actually it wasn't a real pain, more of a pressure, vague, diffuse, insistent, unbearable, he could forget it for over an hour at a time if his attention was concentrated, but it returned with disturbing regularity, even at night he could not sleep, everything was breaking down, his nerves were shot, he tired more easily, recovery was slower, C sank into a chair and closed his eyes.

As he did so the blond head of Johnnie rolled against his arm, there was a brief spasm, his lips sucked the air with a convulsive shudder, there was a sudden slackening of the legs and it was all over, they were lying in a rice paddy surrounded by a cloud of mauve mosquitoes, bullets, and mortar fire, behind me a GI said, "He's had it," we had to wait for night so the helicopters could land, the orderly in the copter removed the dog tags from the dead, his eyes met mine, he looked sad and bitter, he shuffled the dog tags

25

in the palm of his hand and said, "They don't take up much space: a dozen Americans."

"Allow me to introduce myself," said a voice, "my name is David Keith Adams, Mr. Lorrimer is waiting for you," a man of about forty, tall, thin, long face, deep-set black eyes, sinuous mouth, "Glad to meet you, Mr. Adams," said C, they walked in silence down a hall that was narrow, painted, and as endless as the corridor of a ship, a door opened, "Glad to meet you, Mr. C," said Lorrimer, "won't you sit down?"

C felt as if he were laying his smile over his face like a mask, "Will you join me?" he said briskly and getting up, he reached across the desk and offered his cigar case to Lorrimer, Lorrimer gave him a quick once-over, baby face, hard eyes, the smile cordial and false, An Upmann! said Lorrimer, the cigars in the case were very tightly packed, he could not get out the one he had selected, C smiled, looked down, and took in the office with a brief professional glance, they must have hidden the mike in the molding of one of the walls, the office itself was innocent of paper, book, memo pad, or pen, a miracle of distinguished vacuity, like the dark, handsome, impassive face of Mr. Lorrimer, the severe elegance, the perfect physique, the black hair with subtle shadings of gray and white at the temples, the dignified wrinkles, the barely aquiline nose, he looked like an actor, still reaching across the desk, C continued to smile at Lorrimer amiably, one of those lousy Boston snobs who pronounce their a's like an Englishman.

"An Upmann," repeated Lorrimer, fingering the cigar in his delicate hands. "Do you order them from Paris, Mr. C?"

"This will surprise you, Mr. Lorrimer, but I get them direct from Havana."

"In that case," said Lorrimer, raising one eyebrow, "our blockade must be ineffective."

"I wouldn't say that. Mr. Adams, an Upmann?"

"No, thanks, I don't smoke."

"My job," said C, "sometimes brings me into contact with people who go to Cuba and who come back."

"I see," said Lorrimer, and his face closed.

C smiled. His blond and babyish face wore that air of serious joviality that had done so much for his career. With a distant and meditative air Lorrimer took a small penknife out of his pocket and

26

began cutting off the round end of the cigar with precise and careful gestures, obviously I wouldn't expect him to bite the end off and spit it out on the rug but this ritual is annoying, he doesn't give a damn about me, he's taking his time, he looks down on me, for him there are two ways of serving your country: the noble way, his way, and the ignoble way, mine, I bet that carved ivory cigar holder comes direct from Hong Kong, and the lighter? Is it made of gold? Of course not, an austere steel utility lighter, a gift from a British friend during the war, the epitome of the glorious souvenir and of respectable poverty, annoyed, C turned his head and looked out the window, under the maple trees rolled the muddy chocolate-colored waters of the Anacostia, it's shit, their famous river, when you come right down to it, and this taste for old things, these cannons with their patina of age, and in the mouth of one, I couldn't believe my eyes, a bird's nest, what a symbol for a damned pacifist, that's what our guns are going to fire at the Chinese: swallows' nests!

"Well, Mr. C," said Lorrimer, taking a puff of his Upmann, "what can I do for you?"

"We have decided," said C, "that it is time we began taking an interest in dolphins in general—and not necessarily in American dolphins, if you see what I mean. . . ."

Lorrimer bowed his head.

"And being an outsider, I have a few questions I would like to ask you on this matter."

"Please proceed," said Lorrimer coldly.

C crossed his legs, his stomach contracted, he felt irritated, he's keeping me at arm's length, the bastard, then suddenly it was as if a danger signal had lighted somewhere, there was a kind of clock in his mind, everything was obliterated, he had learned to control his emotions to the point of suppressing them at will in a fraction of a second, he looked at Lorrimer and his blond, cherubic, competent face smiled in a friendly way.

"First question: Are the Soviets interested in dolphins?"

"Certainly. They publish Russian translations of our studies."

C looked at him, attentive, friendly, just as I thought, the Boston accent, the refined intonation, the precise articulation, the supreme phonetic distinction. "And what stage are they at in their own research?"

"What they publish, and they publish very little, does not seem to indicate that they have made much progress."

C looked at Lorrimer. "If I understand correctly, the Soviets profit from our research but we can't profit from theirs."

Lorrimer smiled. When he smiled the right side of his upper lip swelled and curled, giving his face an air of unutterable superiority. "It's not as disgraceful as it may seem. When it comes to dolphins we are still engaged in basic research. At this stage secrecy would not only be pointless, it would be a disadvantage."

"Why?"

"In the United States we have several groups working on dolphins, some subsidized by government agencies, others by large private enterprises like Lockheed. Research would be impeded if any of these groups failed to publish its results."

"But wouldn't it be possible to restrict the publication of the results to investigators alone?"

"That would be difficult. There are a great many delphinologists in the United States today. In addition, a sizable number of foreign investigators are working for us in their own countries."

C rubbed the side of his nose. "Excuse me for repeating myself, but if all the investigators that we are subsidizing, foreign or American, publish the results of their studies, and the Soviets do not publish theirs, the Soviets are going to catch up with us and, who knows, perhaps even get ahead of us."

"That is out of the question."

"Why?"

Lorrimer raised his handsome head like a monstrance. "We are the only country in the world capable of spending hundreds of millions of dollars annually on dolphins. Better, we are the only country in the world which subsidizes on its own territory one hundred and fifty delphinologists, not to mention the delphinologists we subsidize in allied countries."

He paused and looked at C, his handsome face assumed an austere expression, and he said without raising his voice, "They will never catch up with us."

"Even if we publish everything?"

Lorrimer gave a half smile. "In the United States, as everywhere, there is always a delay between the moment the scientists obtain the results and the moment they publish them."

"You have only half reassured me."

"I shall reassure you completely. It is quite likely that there will come a day when, instead of allowing each laboratory to decide what it should or should not publish, we shall have to impose secrecy."

"And that will be . . . ?"

"When the discoveries of our delphinologists are capable of being applied."

Now it was C's turn to pause and look at Lorrimer: "And this moment has not yet come?"

"No."

Lorrimer had hesitated a fraction of a second, but C was too well trained not to notice it.

"I imagine," he said slowly, "that if you enforce a blackout some-day, it will apply to everybody, including me. On the other hand, I would like to be assured that I will always have sufficient information, and that I will always have it early enough to plan my research in foreign countries."

"You will have it," said Lorrimer drily.

C half closed his eyes and looked at Lorrimer, the handsome austere face, the ten commandments inscribed on every feature, and yet of the two the austere one is not him, it's me, he can still afford the luxury of personal emotions and moral aspirations.

"Mr. Lorrimer," he went on, "I would now like to have a few details which will allow me to give my research a definite direction. For example, I would like to know what aspect of the study of dolphins is of special interest to the armed forces."

Lorrimer smiled, the right side of his upper lip curled, he looked at Adams and said briefly, "The skin."

"The skin?" said C. He looked from Lorrimer to Adams and back to Lorrimer.

"There is a deep mystery in that skin," said Adams, with an air of faint amusement.

C looked from one to the other.

Lorrimer made a vague gesture with his cigar. "Explain, David," he said condescendingly.

"Mr. C," said Adams, "what do you know about the skin of the dolphin?"

"Why, nothing, of course."

"And what about his swimming speed?"

"It is very high, I believe."

"It has been measured, Mr. C. It has been known to reach thirty knots."

"That's remarkable."

"It is astounding."

"And what does the skin have to do with it?" asked C after a moment.

"Well, it is believed that the dolphin owes his speed to certain properties of his skin. There are two theories about this," Adams went on. "Max Kramer—"

"Max Kramer?" C exclaimed. "Did you say Max Kramer? The missile expert?"

Adams glanced at Lorrimer. "The same."

"And what does Max Kramer say?" asked C, immediately recovering his calm.

"That the dolphin actually possesses two skins. A first skin, the inner skin, which covers the layer of blubber, and a second skin, the superficial skin, which overlies little vertical grooves filled with a spongy substance saturated with water. According to Kramer, it is this superficial skin which explains the high swimming speeds of the dolphin. It is very flaccid, very elastic, sensitive to the slightest pressure, and it flattens or ripples when it comes in contact with the turbulence of the water."

C half closed his eyes. "Excuse me for interrupting, but what do you mean by the turbulence of the water?"

"Every moving body in water or in air creates turbulence or, if you prefer, little eddies that reduce its speed. According to Kramer, the superficial skin of the dolphin eliminates these eddies by means of its extraordinary elasticity."

"That's an ingenious explanation."

"There is another. Researchers have observed that the superficial skin of the dolphin is very thoroughly irrigated by a multitude of tiny blood vessels. At high speeds there may be a sudden rush of blood to these vessels which gives off enough calories to warm the superficial layer of water in contact with the epidermis. It is this heat which is said to eliminate turbulence."

Adams stopped, glanced at Lorrimer and went on: "I am sure you see the practical implications of this research."

"Why, no," said C, "excuse me, but I do not see them."

30

Adams looked at Lorrimer and gave a little laugh. "Well, let's say that thanks to dolphins, we now understand better that hydrodynamics and aerodynamics are not simply a question of shape, but of texture. Suppose scientists solve the mystery of the dolphin's skin. They could imitate this skin by an industrial process and use the product to cover objects designed to move through water or air. The gain in speed would be enormous."

"Are you talking about missiles?"

"Not just missiles: airplanes, submarines, torpedoes."

There was a silence and C said, "Is that all?"

"That's all," said Adams.

C looked at Adams and Lorrimer with an innocent expression. "I'm disappointed. I thought you were going to tell me that dolphins are speaking English."

"Mr. C," said Lorrimer, curling his upper lip, "you mustn't believe everything you read in the newspapers."

"So there's no truth to those reports?"

Lorrimer made a movement of the lips which in a less refined person could have passed for a look of disgust. "Go and see Dr. Lilly, Mr. C, he'll tell you about that." He looked at his watch.

"I only have two more questions to ask you," said C with a friendly smile.

"Go right ahead," said Lorrimer, placing the index finger of his right hand on his lips and looking at the ceiling.

"Is it true that the dolphin finds his way through the water with perfect accuracy even when he has no visibility?"

"So I hear."

There was a silence. The bastard, thought C. *So he hears!* "Last question," said C. "Can the dolphin really be tamed?"

"That depends on what you mean by tamed," said Adams.

"Well, for example, if his trainer released him in the open sea and called him after a few minutes, would he come back?"

"To my knowledge," said Lorrimer, "the experiment has not yet been attempted." He rose. "I hope you will excuse me, Mr. C, but I have a meeting now and I am already late."

C rose too. "It is I who should apologize. I have taken up far too much of your valuable time."

"David will show you out," said Lorrimer with a swift smile. "Goodby, Mr. C."

The door closed. The long white-painted corridor.

Adams took C by the arm. "Well," he said, turning his head to the right, "what do you think of the old man?"

"A little stiff."

"With you, you mean?"

"Yes."

"He's that way with everybody." He added, "To be quite frank, he considers your investigation useless."

C stiffened, offended. "Why useless?"

"He told you why. In his opinion it's a waste of time poking our noses into Soviet delphinology. It will never catch up with our own."

"Suppose," said C, "the Russians came up with a genius who made a decisive discovery in the study of dolphins."

Adams opened the door of the elevator and stepped aside so C could get in. "The old man would say that you're behind the times. We've passed the age of geniuses who make sensational discoveries all by themselves with makeshift materials. Nowadays scientific progress requires an enormous investment and numerous teams of investigators: in other words, a lot of money. The problem is quantitative. The richest country will necessarily make the greatest discoveries."

"Do you believe that?"

"Yes."

"If I believed that," said C, "I'd kill myself."

Adams laughed.

"Well," C went on, "thanks for showing me the way. And may I telephone you if I need additional information?"

"Of course," said Adams, giving him a little pat on the shoulder.

As soon as Adams got back to his office Lorrimer sprang to his feet. He still had his dignified manner, but neither his features nor his attitude bore any trace of the stiffness that had bothered C. "Well," he said playfully. "His impressions?"

"You are a little stiff. I am friendlier and more cooperative. Next time he'll deal with me."

He added, "I especially liked the way you tried to convince him that you weren't at all concerned about Soviet delphinology."

"Did I succeed?"

"No, I don't think so. He is not without intuition and he knows more about it than he says he does."

32

"Precisely. Our search people just called. In the first place, C is no run-of-the-mill agent, whatever he pretends. He's a big shot in scientific intelligence."

"Retrospectively, I feel very honored," said Adams, with a thin smile.

"In the second place, C has a degree in physics from Yale . . ."

"And he asked questions about turbulence!"

"That, in my opinion, is how he gave himself away. An uneducated person would have pretended to know."

There was a knock at the door.

"Come in!" shouted Lorrimer.

A man came in, handed Lorrimer a very large photograph, and left.

"Our boys didn't waste time," said Lorrimer. "Come and look, David."

Adams walked around the desk and leaned over his boss's shoulder. "Excellent photograph," he said with a little laugh.

He added after a moment, "That baby face drips phoniness from every pore."

"Oh, you're exaggerating," said Lorrimer. "There are plenty of ordinary Americans who cultivate that jovial style." He threw the still-damp photograph on the desk. "There you are," he said with a sigh. "He's putting us on and we're putting him on. What a farce."

"I wonder," said Adams, "whether he succeeded in learning anything from our conversation."

"I don't think so. But we're going to make sure."

He opened a drawer, a telephone appeared, he picked up the receiver. "Play me the tape. From the beginning."

He leaned way back and picking up the photograph, studied it from a distance with his head on one side.

"What a disgrace, this spying between agencies. What a waste of time! Poor C, when he comes home in the evening he must look at himself through his own keyhole so he can watch himself empty his pockets."

Adams laughed. Just then Lorrimer's voice came out of a cupboard and took possession of the room.

"An Upmann! Do you order them from Paris, Mr. C?"

"This will surprise you, Mr. Lorrimer, but I get them direct from Havana."

"In that case our blockade must be ineffective."

"I wouldn't say that. Mr. Adams, an Upmann?". . .

When the tape was over, Lorrimer got up.

"Well, David, what do you think of our little session?"

Adams smiled. "It was a masterpiece of skin-deep analysis."

•   •   •

Ever since he had got off the plane the California sun had been pounding him on the head, he was lying in bed, damp and naked, in a room on the fifteenth floor of the hotel, fifteen hundred identical rooms, the same enormous lamps with bases in the shape of giant pineapples, the same drapes with big green and yellow flowers, the same shower stall with sliding glass doors—when you took a shower you felt like a fish in an aquarium—C was perspiring on his metallic bed, the beams of this immense dormitory were metallic too, it was maddening if you thought about it, this enormous hive and the insignificant little creatures moving around in each little cell for one brief moment before they died, each in his own little niche, bent on sleep, insomnia, love, money worries, suicide plans, what did it all mean, good God, what a farce. C lay heavily on the bed, inert and damp, what an ass he was, my God, taking two showers in a row, you felt better for five minutes, maybe, and afterwards it was much worse, he was perspiring, he couldn't breathe, but at the same time the cold draft from the air conditioner landed on his head and his still-damp hair, he got up, turned off the air conditioner, tried to open the window, it didn't open, there was no choice, cold air or suffocation, he threw himself on the bed, exhausted, all his nerves quivering, his stomach tense and contracted and the sly, insistent pain spreading under his ribs to the liver, the stomach swollen where he dug his fingers, as if into dough, and massaged himself, he was so lonely that he almost picked up the phone and called Bessie in New York, how ridiculous, what would they have said to each other? what was there left between them? a few smirks, a few words, a lot of silence, not even a child, I don't even touch her any more, her big breasts revolt me, all that flabby meat, what a pleasure it would be to knock off one of those bitches, to empty a cartridge right in her gut, it's been five years since I stopped paying the premium on my life insurance, I'd love to be there after I die to see the look on her face, she'll get married again to the first idiot who

34

comes along, she'll produce more idiots, that's all they're good for, the vermin, to perpetuate the species, nothing to be proud of, he put his hand under his ribs, his liver was painful, he picked up the envelope in which his agent had put a typescript of the conversation between Lorrimer and Adams taken from the magnetic tape he had left on after C had left the office and reread the text from beginning to end, they had taken him for an amateur, those two, what a farce, because of them I have to travel all the way across the United States and go and stick my nose in Point Mugu, my God, even in Saigon, as if it weren't complicated enough already, so many agencies, services, and police forces who spend their time snubbing each other, being jealous of each other, and competing with each other instead of concentrating on the Viets, the Russians make the mistake of overcentralization but we go to the other extreme, we're much too scattered, the waste of resources, the proliferation of agencies, the mania for auto-espionage, we'll all end up in an insane asylum, done in by overwork and electric shock treatments, he picked up the phone and asked to be waked the next day at seven, took two little pills and swallowed them, he couldn't sleep without pills any more, and tomorrow he'd feel so seedy he'd have to take two NoDoz to stay awake at Point Mugu, stimulants in the daytime, sedatives at night, a real drug addict not to mention the bourbon and the cigars, no wonder I have a bad liver, and it will all end in a little box at the bottom of a ditch, so what? I don't give a damn, I don't even care about seeing the look on her face, his arms weighed heavily on the bed, his head stopped moving, a nerve in his leg relaxed, he felt better, he was driving over a road in Florida in a Ford convertible, there was a girl beside him and Johnnie was in the back seat with another girl, who the hell were those cunts anyway, I can't even remember their names, all four of us were drunk, me a little less so, I was driving, I wanted to get back to the cottage we had rented intact, I was driving very slowly, Johnnie sat up in the back seat and said, "Wait, Bill! I'll help you!" and he rowed the air with his arms, laughing like a madman, the girl was hanging on him trying to make him sit down, at the cottage we had a lot of drinks and some food, the air was warm, the sky was dark blue with a round orange moon, Johnnie stood up, "My God," he said, "what the fuck, let's strip! You too, Bill, look at that moon, it looks like an ass!" The girls screamed and I laughed and laughed, tearing off my clothes, "Down with civilization!" said Johnnie, "Everybody strip!" The girls fled squealing and locked themselves in one of the rooms, the next morning I woke up in bed with Johnnie, Johnnie's head was on the pillow next to mine, his arm was flung across my chest, I didn't move, the French doors to the terrace were wide open, the sun was shining, I saw a little section of white plaster wall standing out against the sky, I had never noticed how beautiful it was, the white of that wall against the blue of the sky.

• • •

The circular tank sparkled under the California sun, and in the glittering blue water C watched the dolphin swim. He circled the tank tirelessly, about three feet below the surface, and to catch his breath he had a very elegant way of arching his back without breaking his forward movement, so that only the part of his body containing the spiracle emerged. His caudal fin was not vertical, as it is in fish, but horizontal, and his movements affected not only the fin itself but the whole finely articulated and muscled area in front of it. C watched the dolphin attentively. Fundamentally, it is the horizontality of the caudal fin that explains his skill in moving in the vertical plane, and above all his ability to leap out of the water the height of a room, as I saw them do in Miami. All that's necessary is that the tank is deep enough so that he has room to "stand" on the bottom and shove off with enough force to break the surface. But the most amazing part of the show in Miami was his dance, when he brings his body three-quarters out of the water, balances himself in this position and, by vigorously moving his tail, backs up the entire length of the tank. He looks like a man walking backwards. Come to think of it, it's much more of a feat than a dog walking on his hind legs or even a tightrope walker, for his ability to remain vertical in the air rests solely on the movement of the caudal fin in the water, which implies a muscular strength and control that are truly astonishing.

The dolphin stopped swimming around, came over to C, stopped a yard from the side of the tank, and leaning his big head on one side, looked at him. This was not the round and inexpressive gaze of a fish, but a gaze that was almost human—lively, mischievous, friendly, full of curiosity. The dolphin put his head on the other side and considered C with the other eye, then he opened his mouth slightly; its sinuous shape made him look as if he were giving C a roguish smile.

A few seconds passed. Having finished his inspection and observing that C did not intend either to play with him or pet him, the dolphin turned around, swam away, and started circling again. Obviously only his caudal fin was propulsive. He used the lateral fins only to turn, or to maintain his balance, like the stabilizers that are designed to keep a ship from rolling. As for the large dorsal fin, it must serve the same function as the centerboard on a small sailboat: to keep the boat steady on its course and to permit more rapid turns.

The fluidity, ease, and power of his swimming were impressive. His passage through the water seemed almost to create no eddy at all, or rather, if there was an eddy, it did not appear in his wake, but very slightly, on the surface of the tank, where a few cavitations were visible. This phenomenon was easy to explain, since the caudal fin was horizontal and therefore in the act of propulsion the water was driven upward. But at the level where the dolphin was swimming no disturbance of the water could be seen. Also, the necessity for the dolphin to come to the surface for air by arching his back did not seem to slow his course, so fluid and even was the movement with which he brought his spiracle to the air. The tank was much too small to allow the dolphin to use a tenth of his speed, but even in his most casual swimming you could sense reserves of strength.

"I see you have already met Dash," said a jovial voice behind C.

C turned around.

"M. D. Morley," said the new arrival, offering him a hand that was as red as a ham. "I'll be showing you around here. Welcome to the naval base at Point Mugu, Mr. C," he went on, with mock-serious solemnity. "If you take my advice, you will forget about good manners and remove your jacket."

"With pleasure," said C.

Morley himself was in shirt-sleeves. He had a round face, a round body, round eyes, and short curly hair, the kind of picture of good health and good humor you see on a billboard advertising a famous brand of beer.

"He must be bored all alone," said C, waving his hand in the direction of Dash.

"But he's not alone!" said Morley. "He is connected by telephone, or rather by hydrophone, to Doris, in another tank."

"Do they know each other?"

"They lived in the same tank for a while. They were separated only for the purposes of the experiment: We wanted to record their conversations."

"Do they talk?"

"And how! Like two lovers on the telephone."

"But how do you know it's a real conversation?"

"They never talk at the same time, but one after the other, as if they were having a dialogue."

"Mr. Morley," said C, "I seem to remember that dolphins emit a great variety of sounds—clicks, growls, yelps . . ."

"Yes, but in conversation they rely mainly on whistling sounds, and these whistling sounds vary greatly in duration, loudness, frequency, and modulation. It is possible that Dolphinese is a whistled language," added Morley with a look of contentment on his round face.

"Well, let's decode it," said C in a facetious tone, but his cold eyes watched Morley's face attentively.

"We're trying," said Morley in the same tone. "But first we have to classify the sounds."

There was a silence and C said, "Even at the most optimistic estimate, I suppose success is still a long way off."

"Yes. But you can be assured that we are not just studying the whistling sounds. Actually, we are attacking the problem from every angle."

"For example?"

"For example, we are trying to teach the dolphins English vowels by reproducing them in the frequency and modulation which they use. In other words, we are dolphinizing English to make it accessible to them."

"In short," said C, "you are trying to create a 'dolphin English' comparable to the pidgin English spoken by the natives of the Pacific. Are you succeeding?"

"It's still too early to say. But wait, I want to show you something."

Morley bent down, quickly picked up three objects that were lying next to the outside wall of the tank and threw them into the middle of the water. It was not until after they landed that C identified them: an old yellowish hat of the sombrero type, a red ball, and a short blue stick.*

"Dash," said Morley, rapping lightly several times on the inner wall of the tank to attract the dolphin's attention.

Dash immediately swam toward Morley. When he was about a yard from the edge of the tank, he lifted his head out of the water.

"The hat!" shouted Morley. "Get the hat!"

Without hesitating Dash swam to the sombrero, dove under the water, balanced it on his snout, and brought it to Morley. Morley took it, threw it back into the center of the tank and shouted, "The stick! Get the stick!"

Dash seized the stick in his jaws, and brought it to Morley, who immediately threw it back into play.

"The ball!" shouted Morley. "Get the ball!"

"Bravo," said C. "Does he ever make a mistake?"

"Sometimes. But I almost think he does it on purpose to tease me. Of course the experiment is on a rather elementary level. But its educational usefulness cannot be denied. We are holding Dash's attention, we are teaching him to learn, and we are also familiarizing him with the sounds of human speech. And when we extend the experiment to other objects, it will be very interesting to find out how many English words he can store and recognize."

Morley broke off, looked at his watch, and said, "Come with me, Mr. C. Your timing is really perfect. I am going to show you something rather fascinating."

Walking quickly, he led C to a poured-concrete tank which was separated from the Pacific by a narrow breakwater. Two men dressed in black frogman suits were busy putting a harness on a dolphin.

"I'd like you to meet Bill," said Morley. "He has been given special training. He has been taught to swim toward one of his trainers as soon as the trainer turns on an underwater buzzer. Here is the instrument," he said, taking it from the hands of an assistant who was standing beside a winch. "As you see, the buzzer looks like

---

* These three objects have one common feature which dictated their choice. They are all designated in English by one-syllable words.

a flashlight, it is watertight, and when you turn it on it makes a vibrating ring under the water whose sound waves travel very far. Bill has been trained so that as soon as he hears this sound, he will swim quickly toward the person who is holding the buzzer, whether he is in the water or in a boat. When he gets there he gets a fish as a reward."

"I am impressed by his manageability," said C. "They're fastening his harness and he isn't flinching."

"He is a very engaging animal," said Morley. "He is very well disposed toward us. This is a fact reported by all observers: Dolphins like people. God knows why," he added after a short pause.

The remark was so out of keeping with his good humor and his round, optimistic face that C looked at him.

"After all," said C, "you feed them well and they're not mistreated."

Morley shrugged his plump shoulders. "Believe me, Mr. C, when they learn to talk, they'll have a few things to tell us about the size of their tanks and the solitude we impose on them. . . . When that happens, you'll see, they'll start to organize and maybe we'll have strikes and demands."

C laughed, then turned his attention to the trainers. They were placing the dolphin on a kind of stretcher with two holes to allow for the lateral fins. The stretcher rested on four long feet made of tubing which were connected to the base like parallel bars. The trainers secured the rope of the winch to the arm of the stretcher and signaled their colleagues, and the dolphin began to rise into the air. Then the winch pivoted and the stretcher began to descend toward the open sea. The two trainers climbed out of the tank and quickly walked down some cement steps into the ocean to receive the animal. The water came to about their hips.

"Are they going to let him go?" asked C.

"It certainly looks that way," said Morley, his round red face a little tense.

"Is this the first time?"

"Yes."

Morley looked at the trainers. The dolphin was in the water and out of the stretcher, and the two men were attaching to his harness a cord about five feet long that ended in a little orange buoy the shape of a sausage.

40

"I see that you're taking precautions anyway," said C.

"Yes," said Morley.

Just then the trainers raised their heads and looked at Morley. Their black rubber suits made their short hair look blonder and their eyes lighter. They stood one on either side of the dolphin and with both hands grasping the harness, they held him firmly between them with his head pointed toward the horizon and his mouth slightly open. The open sea must taste good, thought C.

"Now," said Morley, his face tense.

The trainers let go of the harness. The dolphin remained motionless for half a second, then gave a powerful jerk of his tail and took off as if he had been shot from a gun. Swimming about three feet under the water, he made for the open sea. In less than a second C lost sight of his gray steamlined body, but the buoy rose to the surface and marked his progress. Its orange color stood out against the dark blue of the ocean.

"He swims like an arrow," said C.

"He can swim faster than that," said one of the trainers proudly. "The buoy is slowing him down."

Morley said nothing. The buoy danced on the polished sea. With grave eyes and pinched lips he watched it getting farther away from him every second.

"He must be having the time of his life," said C. "If I were in his place I would feel drunk. And if I were you," he added after a second, "I'd be starting to worry."

Morley did not reply.

"Is it time?" asked one of the trainers nervously.

"Yes," said Morley.

The trainer plunged the buzzer into the water and turned it on. A few seconds passed, then the orange buoy slowed down, zigzagged, seemed to hesitate, and made a half turn. Bill was coming back to land.

"We've won," said Morley in a flat voice.

No one spoke. C, Morley, and the two men had their eyes riveted on the orange shape. Fascinated, they watched it bounce over the rippled surface of the sea as the dolphin swam as fast as he could back to the society of men.

Two seconds later Bill's laughing and mischievous face appeared a yard from the trainer, who gave him a fish.

"Bring him back up," said Morley with a sigh. "That's enough for today."

C looked at him. He looked tired and happy.

"Come on," said Morley. "I'll take you to the cafeteria. I could use some refreshment."

"I want to ask you a question," said C, automatically falling into step. "In your opinion, why did he come back? Instead of choosing freedom, which, after all, would be normal for an animal in captivity. I know you're going to tell me that he came back because he has been conditioned by the buzzer and the fish. But in the case of an animal as intelligent as the dolphin that explanation is not completely satisfactory. After all, Bill could very well decide that there are plenty of fish in the sea, and that he doesn't need yours."

Morley looked at C gravely. "I ask myself that same question, Mr. C. And here is my answer: The dolphin is not a loner, he is a social animal. In the sea he lives in a family, and this family belongs to a well-defined group which probably has a marine territory that it does not go beyond, a hierarchy, an organization. Suppose we were to 'lose' Bill a few miles from the coast. Where would he go?"

"He could try to find another group."

"That would not be easy. And we can't be sure that it would accept him."

"I see."

"Whereas here at Point Mugu he belongs, people pay attention to him, they feed him and play with him, he *knows* us."

"You mean he comes back because he has made emotional ties with men?"

"Yes," said Morley. "That's what I believe. We are his family now."

• • •

From Washington to Los Angeles, from Los Angeles to Miami, from Miami to Seattle, what a farce, what an enormous waste of time, energy, money, and gray matter, just because these bastards insist on making a mystery out of everything, a week, a whole week crisscrossing the American continent, jumping from one plane to another, one hotel to another, one research center to another, to piece together information they could have given me in less than an hour, I've had a chance to think about your masterpiece of "skin-

42

deep analysis," gentlemen, and your stupidity is very profound, for now that I have stuck my nose in your business I'm not going to take it out until I find out everything, including the family histories of the investigators whose names you cleverly concealed from me (you thought), they're going to live in glass houses, your darlings, in less than six months I'll know them all intimately, and as for you, the skin-deep analysts, my God, I'll show you, you're going to get it, you're going to be sorry you were born, from now on you won't be able to lift your little finger without my knowing about it, you won't be able to fart without my hearing it or pick up a paperweight without finding me underneath, you're going to be infiltrated, subverted, poisoned, manipulated until you won't even know who's boss, you or me.

"Mr. C?" said a voice behind him, he turned around, "W. D. Hagaman," C shook the outstretched hand, fortyish, very tall, narrow shoulders, an unusually long neck, a long, pale face, so thin he almost seemed two-dimensional, pale blue lifeless eyes, as soon as C had shaken Hagaman's hand it fell back against his body, met the left hand behind his back, clasped it, and remained there.

"Mr. C," Hagaman began at once, as if the pronouncing of his name and the handshake had exhausted the portion he allotted to human relations, "you know what sonar is, don't you?"

C smiled naïvely. "Isn't it that gadget on our ships that detects enemy submarines?"

The naïveté was wasted effort. Hagaman was not looking at him. C was a biped labeled C, nothing more.

"More accurately," said Hagaman, "it is a device that emits sound waves under the water that are above the audible range. The sound waves are sent back as echoes by objects under the water and are picked up by the device. Since the underwater speed of sound is known, a computer immediately determines the distance and shape of the underwater object. Of course this device, including the computer, is heavy and complicated, and the information it provides is sometimes uncertain, due to the presence in the water of sound waves which interfere with the echo."

With his two hands still locked behind his back, always finishing his sentences, however long, Hagaman spoke without moving his hands or his body, without even blinking, his long, impassive face perched high on his neck, his expressionless eyes staring at a spot

43

over C's head, his lips opening just enough to form the sounds, his delivery slow, precise, professorial, polished, the only discernible movement besides that of his lips being the rise and fall of a very prominent Adam's apple almost directly opposite C's eyes.

"That is man-made sonar," said Hagaman. He paused. "The natural sonar of the dolphin," he went on in the same slow, mechanical and impersonal voice, "is greatly superior. It weighs only about a pound, the dolphin carries the whole thing in his head, and it has been shown to be remarkably precise."

He paused again and after a few seconds C realized that this pause had nothing to do with him. Hagaman was not stopping to allow his listener to take in what he was saying or to give him a chance to ask a question. He was stopping because he was about to change the subject. The presence of the human being called C had only an abstract value. C was someone to whom he had been asked to explain the sonar of dolphins, so he was explaining it. He would have explained it in identical terms and with the same pauses to anyone else.

"Nothing is as effective as a demonstration," said Hagaman. "Come with me, Mr. C."

A circular tank as at Point Mugu, bright sunlight, and a dolphin. Standing beside the tank a man in a watertight suit.

"This is Dick. I have trained him to receive a fish under the following conditions: At a point on the circular parapet which I vary each time, I place a bell which is controlled by an underwater lever. I whistle. At this signal, the dolphin must find the lever and press it with his snout. The bell begins to ring and at another point in the tank which I also vary each time, I hold a fish in the water by the tail. The dolphin must find the fish. After training, Dick's score is one hundred percent."

Hagaman paused. "Karl," he went on, "put on the suction cups."

Karl crossed the parapet and plunged into the tank. With two flicks of his caudal fin Dick was upon him, rubbing against him and asking to be petted. Karl stroked him for a few moments and then brought one of the suction cups near his right eye. This suction cup was in the shape of half an egg and was made of some white plastic material. Karl had to demonstrate both patience and skill, for Dick pulled his head away several times before he consented to be temporarily blinded.

44

Finally Karl came out of the tank and changed the position of the bell on the parapet.

"The tank," said Hagaman, "contains a hydrophone which picks up the sounds emitted by the dolphin and transmits them to us in the open air. Listen: As soon as I whistle, Dick will start using his sonar. Are you ready, Karl?"

Karl took a fish out of a pail, stationed himself on the other side of the tank, and stood ready to put it in the water. Hagaman whistled. C heard a series of squeaking noises which were emitted at regular intervals, and at the same time, without a second's hesitation, the blinded dolphin swam straight to the lever and pushed it. The bell went off. At the other end of the pool Karl plunged the fish in the water and held it by the tail. The dolphin made a half turn, the squeaking noises resumed, and without any difficulty, without the slightest deviation or hesitation, the dolphin crossed the entire width of the tank, swam to the fish, and seized it.

"Extraordinary," said C. "It's hard to believe that he can't see."

"Let's go over to Karl," said Hagaman in his impersonal voice. "We're going to conduct a second experiment. This time Karl is going to put two fish in the water at the same time. Look at them closely: They belong to two different species, but their length and shape are almost identical."

"The most you could say is that one is slightly wider than the other."

"Precisely. And as a matter of fact it is the wider one that Dick likes. The other he never touches. Watch closely. I shift the bell to the other end of the parapet, and I whistle."

At the signal Dick turned on his sonar, found and pushed the lever. The bell went off. Karl plunged both fish into the water and held them eight inches apart. Still preceded by his *squeak-squeak-squeak-squeak,* Dick swam straight to the one he liked and swallowed it.

"Does he ever make a mistake?" asked C.

"Never."

"Could he be guided to the fish of his choice by smell?"

"Cetaceans have no sense of smell."

"In that case, it's astounding," said C. "The precision of his sonar is astounding. He sees with his ears."

"More precisely," said Hagaman, in his slow, monotonous voice, "he sees with his spiracle, he sees with his ears, and he sees with the miniature computer which interprets the returning waves picked up by his ears."

With his hands clasped behind his back, his face and body motionless, and his pale eyes staring at a spot over C's head, Hagaman waited. As far as he was concerned his job was finished, but he was perfectly willing to let his visitor ask questions.

"If I understand correctly," said C, "nature has endowed the dolphin with a sonar infinitely superior to ours, and we are trying to discover the secret of its construction."

Hagaman thought this over. "If you wanted to emphasize the practical side of the question, I suppose you could formulate the purpose of our research as you have done."

"But wouldn't it be possible to make direct use of the dolphin's sonar?"

"What do you mean by direct use?"

"Well, for example, by using dolphins for the purpose of detecting submarines."

There was a silence and Hagaman said, "I am not familiar with that aspect of the question."

•   •   •

C's REPORT
KL/256 21, SECRET

(Note by C: I am reporting this interview from memory, since the person whom I call *the informant* urgently requested that it not be put on tape. For the same reasons no photograph was taken of him and it was agreed that I will be the only one to know his name.)

INFORMANT: I decided to look you up as soon as I heard about your interview with Atalanta. But I had a lot of trouble locating you.

C: I know. I appreciate your efforts.

INFORMANT: Frankly, I don't understand why Atalanta turned out to be so uncooperative. This total lack of communication between agencies is unnecessary. Especially since we are working toward the same goal.

C: But are we working toward exactly the same goal? Am I wrong in thinking that the philosophy of certain persons working for Atalanta may not altogether agree with our own?

46

INFORMANT: I understand. Let's say, then, that my personal philosophy is closer to yours.

C: I thought so, but I'm happy to hear you say it. There are far too many doves or near doves among Atalanta's people . . .

INFORMANT: I agree.

C: Would you agree to tell me about them, should the occasion arise?

INFORMANT: It was not for that purpose that I contacted you. In my opinion what should concern us is not the people with whom I work, but the dolphins.

C: The one does not exclude the other. The truth is that we are very much concerned about Atalanta's staff. The matter is much more serious, perhaps, than you think. After all, we cannot dismiss the idea that a third world war may break out in the near future. From this point of view anything you could tell us would be invaluable.

INFORMANT: I had not imagined my role that way. In my opinion it would be rather contemptible to implicate people with whom I work. Just because they do not share my opinions docs not mean I regard them as traitors.

C: In time of war, or impending war, if you will permit me to say so, it is very difficult to determine where treason begins. Are thcse people your friends?

INFORMANT: Oh, no!

C: Well, in that case I don't quite understand your scruples. Especially since there is no question of "implicating" them. I'm simply asking you to help me form an opinion of them.

INFORMANT: But doesn't that amount to the same thing?

C: Oh, there's a slight difference. Consider, for example, the case of Atalanta's right arm. Let's call him Azure, if you like. Do you know whom I mean?

INFORMANT: Yes.

C: Well, I'm a little worried about Azure. I can't seem to pin him down. He seems very elusive. What do you think of him? What category does he belong to?

INFORMANT: In my opinion he's neither fish nor fowl.

C: Well, there you are. That's all I wanted to know. In saying that do you have the feeling that you have "implicated" Azure?

INFORMANT: To tell you the truth, no.

C: I think you will agree that Azure is an opportunist who will always wind up on the winning side.

INFORMANT: With perhaps a slight initial preference for the philosophy we do not share.

47

C: Yes, I think so too. That's it exactly. You've caught the difference perfectly. And I'd be tempted to say the same of Atalanta.

INFORMANT: Oh, Atalanta is another problem. . . . Nobody here knows what goes on in Atalanta's head.

C: Quite frankly, that is why I consider it so important to know the people around him. But let's get to the dolphins. May I ask you some questions?

INFORMANT: That is precisely why I contacted you. In that area I am ready to give you all the help I can.

C: As it happens, I have only one question. How do people like Atalanta and Azure envision the practical utilization of dolphins?

INFORMANT: On that point their thinking is clear. In all underwater activities of construction or destruction in which we now use frogmen it would be much more advantageous to use dolphins.

C: Why?

INFORMANT: The dolphin has a great advantage over the human diver: He is not susceptible to nitrogen poisoning and when he returns to the surface he does not have to undergo decompression. As you know, Sealab used a dolphin named Tuffy to act as a liaison between the men in the underwater house and the ship on the surface. Tuffy brought them the paper, the mail, beer . . .

C: Yes, I remember. I read about it somewhere. It is very remarkable, but it can't, strictly speaking, be regarded as *work*. Aren't you afraid that the fact that the dolphin has no hands will greatly limit his usefulness for underwater work?

INFORMANT: Yes and no. The dolphin is very skillful with his snout. He pushes levers, throws balls, balances things. Furthermore, the skeleton of his lateral fin is that of an atrophied arm ending in a hand, a vestige of the time when he lived on land. These fins are to a certain extent prehensile. Perhaps it will be possible to train and develop them. Meanwhile we will have to use harnesses or special equipment.

C: Precisely. Tell me about these harnesses. Wait, I'll tell you exactly what I want to know: Has there been any question of fastening a mine to this harness, a mine which the dolphin could drop at the entrance to a port or even attach to the hull of a ship?

INFORMANT: Yes. The problem is under study. But I don't know any more about it than you do. What I can tell you is that certain dolphins have already been trained to distinguish friendly ships from enemy ships, even in the dark.

C: How?

INFORMANT: Every friendly ship has a little plate on its prow under the waterline, and this plate is made of a different metal from the hull.

C: And the dolphins can detect the presence of this plate in the dark?

INFORMANT: Yes. Even when it is painted with the same paint as the hull.

C: How do they do it?

INFORMANT: By using their sonar. There must be a slight difference between the echo they pick up from the little plate and the one they get from the rest of the hull.

C: Fantastic. What, in your opinion, would be the role of the dolphin in an offensive and defensive battle?

INFORMANT: I'll tell you the principle that underlies our research: The dolphin is both a non-detectable submarine and an intelligent torpedo.

C: Why non-detectable?

INFORMANT: As far as the enemy's sonar is concerned, he is a fish. In the second place, even if he attacks in broad daylight, he will foil all evasive maneuvers on the part of enemy ships. Remember his extraordinary subaquatic speed. Remember, too, his ability to dive instantaneously to great depths.

C: Tactically speaking, what is the outlook in your agency?

INFORMANT: Let's assume that we succeeded in recruiting and training numerous schools of dolphins and making them patrol the waters of the Pacific or Atlantic. With the help of their sonar they could detect the advance of a fleet of atomic submarines and help us destroy it by sowing mines along its course. They could also attack surface vessels by planting bombs under their waterlines. If the circumstances required, they could even carry atom bombs into the enemy's ports. In this case, obviously, we would have to allow for the sacrifice of the carrier animals.

C: It seems to me that considering the length and cost of their apprenticeship, it would be a serious sacrifice.

INFORMANT: I'm assuming that we would have trained several hundred of these animals. In this case we could select out of this number twenty kamikaze dolphins—unconscious kamikazes, obviously—without any serious diminishing of our resources.

C: All this is of the highest interest.

INFORMANT: But naturally such a complex collaboration presupposes that we succeed in communicating with dolphins by means of a language. This is the necessary condition.

C: Atalanta mentioned Dr. Lilly.

INFORMANT: Dr. Lilly is very intelligent, he has done some excellent things, but he is still far from the goal. In my opinion, Sevilla is much farther along.

C: Sevilla?

INFORMANT: I'll tell you where he stands. Actually, the whole success of Operation Dolphin rests on Sevilla.

C: Does he realize it?

INFORMANT: Far from it! Sevilla is indifferent to the possibilities we've been discussing. Sevilla is an idealist. What interests him is establishing communication between species. He feels that this would be a great conquest for humanity.

C: He wouldn't, by any chance, be one of those . . .

INFORMANT: No. We don't think so. He is politically very ignorant. Very far removed from that sort of thing.

C: Well, I want to thank you. Your cooperation has been invaluable.

INFORMANT: But I haven't told you anything out of the ordinary. You will read much more sensational things from the pens of certain scientific journalists.

C: Yes, but with them you always have to allow for hypothesis, for the imagination. The source of your information guarantees its accuracy.

INFORMANT: Well, I'm glad I could be useful to you. I am completely at your disposal.

C: Thank you. I'm really very grateful. May I return to one point? If you would be good enough to give a little thought from time to time to my interest in Atalanta's staff, you would be doing us a very great service.

INFORMANT: I'll think about it.

III

Mr. C? asked Maggie Miller. She was twenty-nine, short, stocky, red-faced, the corners of her eyes constantly secreted a whitish liquid, there were red splotches on her cheeks, her hair was thin and lusterless, her nose and chin were trying to meet over lips which were thick, red, protruding, and wet with saliva, hastily clad in a pair of skintight blue jeans and a shirt with big red and green checks, she had a passionate and ungovernable air and her face was thrust forward in defense, in a wicked world, of her gods, living or dead: Professor Sevilla, James Dean, Bob Manning, not to mention the minor and temporary gods, How are you, Mr. C? My assistant Jim Foyle, Hello, Mr. Foyle, But isn't there some misunderstanding, Mr. C? According to my calendar your visit was scheduled for five thirty and not (she consulted her big watch of waterproof steel) three thirty, I'm very sorry, Miss Miller, That's quite all right, Mr. C, Unfortunately, Professor Sevilla is not here, but his assistant, Miss Lafeuille, will give you all the necessary information.

There was a silence, Maggie Miller looked down at her engagement pad, asked the Lord to forgive her for lying, and devoted a thought of pure and disinterested hate to Mrs. Ferguson, how can she possibly understand the professor? that snob, let's say it, that whore (forgive the crude language, God), the poor professor, women won't leave him alone and that one, with her sweet manner and her false eyelashes, is the worst of the lot, a completely depraved and cynical creature, she comes right to the laboratory and steals him away from under our noses in the middle of work, I could

51

see that Arlette was furious too, and he, like a big idiot, lets her do it, all she has to do is bat her eyelashes a couple of times and it's all over, he's there beside her in that chic little car of hers, he's a fine sight bent double in that bug, she leads him around by the nose, as Bob Manning says, it's the tyranny of the weak over the strong, but after all, if the strong one were truly strong he wouldn't let himself be bullied by the weak, Mr. C, I'll call Miss Lafeuille, she's in the pool with Ivan, Excuse me? Miss Lafeuille, she's a French Canadian, hence the name, I beg your pardon, I haven't introduced you to Bob Manning, Bob is one of our associates, Bob came forward and C's eye rested on him, a tall, slender, willowy young man, graceful in all his movements, with long, delicate, supple hands, How do you do, Mr. C? said Bob with a ravishing smile.

When Maggie walked out of the prefabricated shed that served as a lab she received the sun and the sea air full on her face and all at once it was as if the warm air of Florida were embracing her, she felt beautiful and rich, she inhaled deeply, she walked rapidly on her stocky little legs, her coarse, ruddy face thrust aggressively forward, Arlette was lying in a bathing suit on one of the two polyester rafts moored at the side of the tank and bending over the dolphin Ivan, her hand in the water, her eyes red, when Maggie walked over she put on her sunglasses, Darling, disaster, the professor has forgotten his appointment with this fellow C, you know, he must be an important person, since theoretically our experiment is top secret, I wonder if he could hurt the professor in any way, I don't like his eyes at all, cold, smiling, and slyly threatening, if you know what I mean, could you possibly see him and explain our work to him and be charming, although he certainly isn't the type a woman can get around, he didn't even look at me, I left them—him and his assistant—with Bob, you know Bob, he's adorable, he could charm a regiment of rattlesnakes, Bring them here, said Arlette with a sigh, I don't want to make a spectacle of myself in the lab in a bathing suit.

Of course, Maggie went on in a hurried and panting voice, as if life were too short to say all she had to say, you know how things are between Bob Manning and me, he's a child, without me he'd be lost, when he looks at me he gets a look on his face that reminds me of James Dean a few months before his death, poor James, he was sitting in Aunt Agatha's old armchair in Denver, holding my hand, suddenly he closed his eyes wearily and said, Without you, Maggie, I'd be lost, you haven't noticed Bob's eyes, Arlette, he's a child, absolutely without defenses, a terribly vulnerable creature, it drives me crazy when I think of the cruel way his father treats him, it's abominable, poor Bob, I think one of these days I'll consent to make him happy by announcing our engagement, he'd be so happy to have a child by me, he hasn't told me so but I sense it, he can't see a child without smiling at it or making faces, of course, she went on with a mysterious air, it presents a lot of problems, I've mentioned it to Sevilla but he hardly listens to me, he's rushed, distracted, and then, you know how much I admire him, but right now he's acting like a child too, Sevilla is old enough to know what he's doing, said Arlette, But no, that's the point, he doesn't, darling, don't forget that I've known him for five years, in certain respects he's a child, you aren't going to tell me he loves that big idiot, it's not possible, with her feather-brain, I'm sure it weighs less than seven ounces, the professor is flattered, that's all, or else it's the magic of sex, she said, thrusting forward her thick red lips, swollen as a wound, Well, go and get them, said Arlette, looking away, I want to get it over with.

I don't know what she can be up to, said Bob Manning, she's very talkative, you know, he was disturbed by the insistent weight of C's eyes on his face, he felt as if those gray-blue pupils were taking possession of him, I'll go and see, he added, blushing, No, thank you, I don't smoke cigars, he left, Bill, said Foyle, turning his innocent boxer's face toward C, what is that tape recorder that keeps turning? Don't worry about it, Jim, it's connected to a hydrophone placed in the tank to pick up underwater sounds emitted by one of their dolphins, I saw the same device three weeks ago in Point Mugu, C bent over Maggie's desk, pulled out her engagement pad, looked at it and put it back, That's what I thought, Jim, that little horror lied, it was for three thirty, misunderstanding my ass, Sevilla simply took off, we'll have to look into the pedigree of this foreigner and of his assistant too, while we're at it, that girl with the French name, Bill, you don't really believe that the Gaullists . . . I don't trust anyone, as Lorrimer put it so well, at night when I go to bed I look at myself through the keyhole to see what I take out of my pockets, oh-oh . . .

Miss Lafeuille is waiting for you beside the tank, said Maggie, if you take my advice, you'll put your hats back on and take off your jackets, there's no shade, Arlette got up and walked the length of the tank, tanned and petite in the sun under the hazy blue sky, C smiled with a false and jovial air, Foyle shook the warm, firm little hand, a flood of gratitude overwhelmed him, he had been expecting another Maggie but this girl was a jewel, short, slender, and ripe, a little round face with a slightly turned-up nose, a smooth complexion, beautiful black eyes, lively, shining, expressive, an adorable mouth, something vivacious, sensual and generous in her expression, she had taken three steps to meet them, they were small steps because she was short, there was no affectation, but her whole ripe, slender body had swayed gently at the hips, she was so round, so soft, and so smooth that she gave the word "baby" new meaning, I want her, thought Foyle, his head throbbing, his throat dry, my God, I want her, she's delectable, and not only that, but she's a nice girl, you can see it in her eyes, not a bitch, not selfish, not boring, a girl in a million, and tomorrow morning I'll be back in Washington.

C smiled at Arlette jovially, Delighted to meet you, Miss Lafeuille, his cold, smiling eyes resting on her face, this little monkey has been crying, there's a tearstain on her cheek.

"If I understand correctly, Miss Lafeuille," said C, "Professor Sevilla is conducting a very original experiment."

Arlette looked at him. He was smiling, but his eyes were cold. This fellow C was annoyed to be dealing with an assistant. She made an effort and gave him a friendly smile.

"The idea is not original, Mr. C, it has already been tried on a chimpanzee, but this is the first time it has been tried on a dolphin."

"Are you alluding to the experiment conducted by the Hayeses with the monkey named Viki?"

"Precisely."

"I know it only by hearsay, Miss Lafeuille. I think I was abroad when the book came out."

"Well, as you know, the Hayeses adopted a little female monkey when it was two days old and raised it like a child."

"A heroic experiment," said Foyle.

"It certainly was! As you can imagine, they didn't have an easy time of it. The curtains, the furniture, the lamps, the dishes—everything suffered. But they felt that the experiment was worth the trouble. The idea was to raise Viki as if she were a human child and, since the vocal apparatus of the chimpanzee is similar to ours, to teach her to talk."

"And it was a failure, wasn't it?"

"Let's say instead that the experiment did not succeed."

C laughed. "What difference do you see between a failure and an experiment that does not succeed?"

"An experiment that does not succeed can teach us many things."

"For example?"

"First of all, this: A chimpanzee cannot voluntarily produce a sound. He emits a certain number of vocalizations, but always as the result of stimuli, never of his own volition. In other words, his vocalizations are no more subject to his will than your reflex movement when the doctor taps you on the knee with a little hammer. So the Hayeses' first task was to teach Viki to produce a sound of her own accord. To obtain her food, Viki had to learn to say *a*."

"And did she succeed?"

"After a great struggle. The Hayeses then went on to the second stage. They were inspired by the methods used in schools where retarded children are taught to speak. When Viki said *a*, Mr. Hayes pressed the little monkey's lips together and released them immediately. In this way, after two weeks of effort, Viki was taught to say *mama*. She was fourteen months old. At two years she learned to say *papa*, at twenty-eight months she learned to say *cup*, and at three years she learned to pronounce the word *up*."

"So Viki's active vocabulary was limited to four words?"

"And even at that she didn't always use them intelligently. These four words, for Viki, were ways of begging. When the Hayeses entertained guests Viki asked them for tidbits by saying *mama* or *papa* indiscriminately. *Cup* was more specialized; Viki used it to ask for something to drink. The conclusion seems to be that the chimpanzee did not associate the word she had learned with the object it designates, or associated it badly."

"And her passive vocabulary?"

"The Hayeses estimated it to be about fifty words. But here again the association between the word and the object was very uncertain. On some days Viki would accurately indicate her nose, her ears, and her eyes when you pronounced the corresponding words in her

55

hearing. On other days she would make mistakes. When Mr. Hayes said 'eyes,' she would point to her nose, and so forth. And finally, when Viki learned new words she tended to forget the ones she already knew."

There was a silence and Foyle murmured, "Four words after three years! That's rather sad, I think."

"Sad for whom?" asked C, looking at him with some mockery and weariness. "For the Hayeses or for Viki? For man or for the chimpanzee?"

"For both," said Arlette, smiling warmly at Foyle. "For the first time in history man made a serious, prolonged, and methodical effort to establish linguistic communication with an animal, and he did not succeed."

"Are you having better luck with your baby dolphin?" asked C, massaging the pit of his stomach.

"He's not a baby any more, Mr. C, he's an adult. And the experiment has not been completed. But with your permission I'll tell you about it from the beginning."

"Couldn't we sit down?" asked C in a toneless voice. "I find standing up in this heat a bit of an ordeal."

"Excuse me, Mr. C," said Arlette, embarrassed. "I should have thought of it myself. Maggie, if you'll stay with Ivan, we'll go back inside the lab."

C heaved a little sigh as he dropped into the canvas folding chair which Arlette indicated.

"Would you like something to drink, Mr. C?" asked Arlette with concern.

"It's nothing," said C, "a touch of overwork. But I *would* like a drink."

Bob came forward, graceful and loose-limbed. "Don't disturb yourself, Arlette," he said in his fluty voice. "I'll play hostess. Perhaps Mr. Foyle would like a drink too?"

Foyle sat down on another canvas chair. "That's too good an offer to refuse," he said with spirit.

Arlette sat down across from them. She was embarrassed to be wearing a bathing suit in the lab, but on the other hand, to leave them to go and change into shorts seemed slightly hypocritical.

"Please go on, Miss Lafeuille," said C, "I feel perfectly all right."

"I should explain first," said Arlette, "that we have two tanks some distance apart. In one we keep a male and two or three females. The other, the one you just saw, enables us to isolate one of our subjects, if necessary. So much for that. Here is how it all began—rather accidentally, as you shall see. Not quite four years ago two of our females gave birth within a few hours of each other. One died after giving birth to a live dolphin and the other gave birth to a stillborn dolphin. The obvious solution was for the surviving female to adopt the motherless baby dolphin, but it didn't work out. She refused. Actually, behavior of this kind is not rare in other animal species. It has been observed that sheep who have lost their young at birth do not necessarily consent to nurse an orphan lamb."

Arlette stopped speaking. Bob had just come in with a tray of bottles and glasses. At once C took a little box out of his pocket and swallowed two pills. Arlette noticed that his hand trembled slightly as he carried the glass of whiskey to his mouth. That man took drugs, it was obvious.

"It was then," she went on after a moment, "that Professor Sevilla conceived the idea of raising the baby dolphin himself. To do this it was necessary to isolate him in the second tank to protect him from the violent struggles of the male, who happened to be in the middle of the mating season. Next, we had to take milk from the surviving female and administer it to the baby dolphin. Stated like this it sounds easy, but actually it presented several problems. The most difficult for us, the team at the lab, was to provide a continuous presence in the water during the first weeks so that the baby dolphin, isolated in his tank, would not succumb to a sense of abandonment. Two at a time, we put on frogman suits and took turns keeping him company. After a month, the professor ordered two polyester rafts on which the dolphin's adoptive parents could station themselves. The dolphin was, of course, connected to the voices of his human family by an underwater loudspeaker, and contact was also maintained by stroking. Ivan had no trouble accepting the elevation of his parents. At night, and even sometimes during the day, for convenience, the two rafts are moored at the end of the tank."

"Why two rafts, Miss Lafeuille?" asked C. "Why not just one?"

"Because the young dolphin has two mothers. A natural mother, as it were, and a voluntary mother who kept the first mother com-

57

pany during her pregnancy, defended her privacy during childbirth, and afterwards helped her protect her infant from the turbulence of the males. Professor Sevilla tried to recreate this situation. When the two rafts were moored at the edge of the tank we always left an empty space between them, and it was there that Ivan almost always chose to remain, at least during the first few months. At night when one of us would put his hand in the water, Ivan would immediately come and put his head under the hand of his 'parent,' even in his sleep."

Foyle smiled. "What a nice animal," he said, shifting the ice in his glass.

"Does Ivan regard you as his family?" asked C. He had recovered his poise, his color, and his shrewd expression.

"I think he regards the team as a whole as his family and Professor Sevilla and myself as his natural mother and his voluntary mother respectively."

"Why?"

"Because we've spent much more time with him than the other members of the team, and above all because from the beginning we were the only ones to feed him, first from the bottle and later with fish."

"Miss Lafeuille," said Foyle, smiling, "since the beginning of this interview you have kept us in suspense. You haven't told us yet whether your dolphin has started talking."

Arlette looked at him, her black eyes sparkling, and he thought, What a smile she has—so open, so good.

"I'm coming to that," said Arlette. "But first I want to emphasize one point. The principle of Professor Sevilla's experiment rests on a phenomenon discovered by Dr. Lilly and later confirmed by other investigators: the fact that the dolphin is capable of spontaneously imitating the human voice. By talking constantly to Ivan, by immersing him from morning to night in what the professor calls the 'familial sound bath,' we hoped he would begin to imitate the sounds with which he was being saturated—at first without understanding them—like the baby who babbles and vocalizes in his crib—but then gradually beginning to grasp their meaning."

Arlette paused, looked from one of the two men to the other, and said with a little laugh of triumph, "And that's exactly what happened."

"So he does talk!" exclaimed C, sitting up in his chair and darting a quick look at Foyle.

Foyle leaned forward, gripped his glass, and said in a flat voice, with controlled excitement, "You have succeeded!"

"Partially," said Arlette, raising her right hand. "In a moment I'll tell you the limits of our success. But first I want to describe the conditions for that success. The dolphin's vocal organ is very different from our own. The dolphin produces sound not with his mouth, which he uses only for eating, but with his spiracle, a respiratory organ which he does not like to have touched and which, therefore, cannot be manipulated the way the Hayeses manipulated Viki's lips. But this procedure turned out to be unnecessary, since from the beginning Ivan demonstrated two advantages over Viki. He is capable of emitting a sound voluntarily, and he can spontaneously imitate the human voice. But his most sensational victory, Mr. C, and one which augurs well for the future, even if for the moment he does not seem to be making progress, is this: Ivan has succeeded in establishing a clear and constant connection between the word which he utters and the thing which this word designates. In other words, Ivan has arrived at the specifically human notion of the word as symbol."

"But that's a fantastic forward leap!" said Foyle.

"I agree," said Arlette, her eyes shining. "Even if Professor Sevilla's experiment stopped there it would represent a turning point in relations between species."

There was a silence. C's eye passed coldly over Arlette's body, how obscene a woman's body is, those big breasts, those hips, everything is so weak, so soft, he half closed his eyes: "a turning point in relations between species," that was pure Sevilla, in love with her boss, naturally they're all the same, always sex, always thinking with their vaginas.

"Miss Lafeuille," he said with an amiable air, "how many words does Ivan have?"

Foyle said at the same time, "Is there much distortion?"

Bob Manning gave a rippling laugh and turned toward Arlette: "We'll have to hand out numbers!"

"I'll answer the first question," said Arlette. She glanced quickly at Bob. The little idiot, I wonder why he's talking so much. She went on: "Ivan's active vocabulary comes to forty words."

"But that's a lot!" said Foyle. "Forty words is ten times as many as Viki learned!"

"Can you give us some examples?" asked C.

"Miss Lafeuille hasn't answered my question about the degree of distortion," said Foyle, looking at C rather indignantly.

Arlette put up her hands like a policeman stopping traffic and said, "Before answering your questions, there is one point I want to stress. Ivan confidently handles the most abstract linguistic symbols. For example, he knows how to say *right, left, in, out,* and he uses them correctly. He uses verbs like *go, come, listen, look, speak,* and he uses them intelligently."

"In that case," said C, "I'm curious about those limits you mentioned."

"I'm coming to them," said Arlette. "And at the same time, I'll answer Mr. Foyle's question."

"At last!" said Foyle.

Arlette smiled at him. "I'll start with the least serious. As might be expected, Ivan 'dolphinizes' human sounds to a large extent. His voice is shrill, nasal and yelping, and he is not always easy to understand. Unfortunately, there is something much more serious than these minor imperfections."

She paused and went on: "The chief limitation is this: Ivan can only say monosyllables. When we try to teach him a two-syllable word he retains only the last syllable, whether the accent falls on it or not. Thus *music* becomes *zick, Ivan* becomes *Fa, listen* becomes *sen.* This is the difficulty which, according to Professor Sevilla, temporarily blocks all progress: Ivan cannot add one syllable to another."

"May I relieve you of your glass, Mr. C?" asked Bob.

"Thank you," said C, throwing him a knowing half-smile but not looking at him.

Bob glided gracefully over and picked up his and Foyle's glasses with a friendly air. This was done with a slight swish of the hips and a flutter of the wrist. Arlette stopped speaking. She was annoyed at the interruption, and also because C did not immediately start up the conversation with a question. Bob had deliberately interrupted her to please C, and C was deliberately prolonging the silence to embarrass her.

Foyle came to her rescue. "You were saying, Miss Lafeuille, that Ivan cannot add one syllable to another."

60

"But there is a more serious difficulty, Mr. Foyle," said Arlette, looking at him gratefully. "Ivan cannot add one word to another. He can pronounce and understand the word *give*. He is capable of understanding and saying the word *fish*, but he has not yet succeeded in saying *give fish*. If he does, the professor believes that Ivan will have crossed an important frontier."

"In other words," said C, "Ivan will know how to talk when he makes the transition from the word to the sentence."

"Exactly."

There was a silence and Foyle said, "It's already amazing that he has come as far as the monosyllable."

"Yes," said Arlette, "I quite agree with you, Mr. Foyle, it's simply amazing."

C got a cigar case out of his pocket, offered it to Foyle, who declined with a wave of his hand, selected an Upmann, and lit it.

"I assume," he said, "that Sevilla has made some attempt to overcome the difficulty you have just described . . ."

His remark could have passed for a harmless question, but somehow he made it sound derogatory to Sevilla.

"Yes," said Arlette, "and I remember exactly how it happened. Professor Sevilla called us together one day in the lab and said—Bob, correct me if I make a mistake—'Suppose I am a prisoner,' he said, 'but a very well-treated prisoner, of an animal species superior to the human species, in a place that is pleasant but confining. My guards present me with a task which requires an enormous effort of mental creativity. I apply myself to it. My living conditions are apparently good. I have all the comfort I could desire, the food is excellent, and I am surrounded by the affection of my guards. However, I am not completely happy, because I am the only one of my species. I need a companion; more precisely, a female companion. Now suppose that my benevolent guards give me this companion, that I like her, that I fall in love with her. Everything changes. My life takes on a new dimension. I receive a powerful psychic stimulus which increases my self-confidence, my spirit of enterprise, and my creative impulse. Don't you think my work will be the first thing to benefit from this change?' "

"Bravo!" Bob Manning said loudly, glancing at C out of the corner of his eye. "A superb imitation of Sevilla's spiel!" He pronounced the word "spiel" with an imperceptible trace of mockery.

Arlette looked at him indignantly. "I thought you agreed with this 'spiel,' as you call it."

"But I do," said Bob, with a sly smile meant for C. "What makes you think I don't?"

C let out a little spluttering laugh which he seemed to regret immediately afterwards. "If I understand correctly," he said with exaggerated gravity, "the professor thought that the company of a female would help Ivan solve his linguistic problems. And after all, why not?" he went on, looking at his listeners with mock innocence. "Why shouldn't there be a connection between philology and sexuality?"

Bob looked at C as if he were suppressing a desire to burst out laughing and repeated emphatically, "Why not?"

Intrigued, Foyle looked from Bob to C, then at Arlette. He observed that she looked mortified and he said briskly, "Miss Lafeuille, please tell us how the experiment turned out."

Arlette smiled at him. "Unexpectedly, to say the least. . . ."

.   .   .

Margaret darling, said Mrs. Ferguson, I'd like you to meet Professor Sevilla, Henry, Mrs. Margaret Mandeville, Come closer, Henry, if you don't mind (the *r*'s pronounced in the back of the mouth and the *o* very open), we're thin, there's room for all three of us in front, the car door slammed, She's playing with me, thought Sevilla furiously, she forces a chaperone on me to go and visit her secluded little beach house, It's an honor to meet you, said Mrs. Mandeville, giving him a fast, expert and extraordinarily impudent glance, she was the same type of woman as Grace Ferguson, tall, thin, long Pre-Raphaelite neck, oval face, bedroom eyes, both so elegant they had managed to persuade nature to spare them breasts, hips, and buttocks and to leave them only an adolescent skeleton on which to hang the asexual dresses of Parisian *haute couture*, Henry, said Grace Ferguson, with the uvular, rolled *r* of a Shakespearean actress, the phrases dropping from her mouth in a slow, melodious, distinguished, barely audible murmur, Margaret Mandeville spoke in the same languid drawl, it was in the most exclusive set at Vassar that they had acquired this voice and this accent, the words articulated in the back of the throat, the phrases very musical but with the minimum volume and dropping from the lips wearily,

Henry was nice enough to let me tear him away from his lab, Margaret darling, his time is so valuable to the country, I feel *so* unpatriotic keeping him from his work, I feel as if I'm stealing him from Washington, Lincoln, and the United States of America, she smiled, slowly lowered her lashes, and dropped the long fingers, bare except for one enormous diamond, on the gearshift, which shot out of the floor, digging into Sevilla's left thigh (after all, you wouldn't expect this kind of car to have the vulgar automatic transmission of a Buick), Sevilla said nothing, surrounded by bare arms and expensive perfume, hemmed in, aroused, furious, what a ridiculous little car, the last word in discomfort, not even enough room for my legs, for a month now she'd been leading him on, he had got nothing, not even a kiss, But see here, Henry dear, we're not going to flirt, that's *so* common, it will be all or nothing, give me time to decide, the eyelids dropping slowly over the promise-filled eyes, but so far it was nothing, the elegant, cool, and inaccessible mannequin that you look at in a shopwindow through an inch of glass, Margaret darling, I beg of you, above all don't ask Henry anything about his dolphins, they are his darlings, he loves them more than he does me, I'm *so* jealous, he never tells me anything about them, on that subject he is an absolute tomb, But it seems to me that he doesn't talk at all, said Mrs. Mandeville, I'm afraid, Grace darling, that he doesn't appreciate my charming presence as much as he should, Not at all, Sevilla muttered between clenched teeth, I am surrounded with charm, it's almost too much for me, Margaret, what did I tell you, he's an adorable man, so witty, *so* European. I love him to distraction, I can't sleep at night, Yes, I feel his charm working on me, said Mrs. Mandeville, it's dreadful, Grace darling, this is going to hurt you deeply, but I'm falling madly in love with the professor, as she spoke, she put her hand on Sevilla's thigh and left it there, Grace smiled, What an awful thing, you, my best friend, betraying me, we are going to be rivals and tear each other to shreds, Sevilla was silent, tense, his body bent double, in everything they said there was an indefinable hint of ridicule and masquerade, as if they were amusing themselves by taking off their tailored dresses for a moment and donning the peasant emotions of other women, their husbands still had contact with real people, company managers, executive secretaries, lawyers, but for them it was all over, they no longer had real relationships with anyone, not

63

even with each other, not even with their servants (the English butler took charge of everything), they withdrew into the power of their money like snails into their shells and from there they looked at the world impersonally and with a faint amusement, they provided their own ineffable value, they did not even have to look down on people any more, they were so far above the human condition, and yet, thought Sevilla furiously, I dare to think that defecation is not a function totally unknown to them.

Margaret darling, here is the key, would you be good enough to open the cottage while I park the car in the garage, the car door slammed, Margaret smoothed her skirt with her hand and left, skipping gracefully over the gravel, Darling, said Grace without starting the car, you didn't open your mouth once during the drive, what is Margaret going to think, you're simply impossible, I should tell you, said Sevilla, shifting away from her and as close as possible to the door, turning, and staring at her with his dark eyes, that the only reason I did not ask you to let me out of the car was precisely to spare you embarrassment in front of your friend, but in any case, you won't have to put up with my bad manners much longer, You mean you're going to reform? I mean that this meeting is our last, she raised her eyebrows, made a face, and said loftily, Oh, really? Yes, really, said Sevilla, she held her disdainful pose, one hand on the steering wheel, the other on the gearshift, eyebrows raised, staring straight ahead, Caliban had dared to rebel and there was only one way to punish him, to pronounce his sentence at once—I'm sorry, Henry, but our relationship is over—but she could not say this because he had said it first, no matter what happened he would have priority, he was not bluffing, what a look he had had in his eyes, dark, proud, and furious, Spanish eyes, he would have cut my throat, something resembling surrender stirred somewhere inside of her, but no, she had to decide, keep a cool head, it's been so pleasant having him dangling from my belt like a charm with his hot eyes drinking in my every movement, I felt as if I were surrounded by warm air, slowly she lowered her lashes and gave him a furtive, sideways look, Henry, she said in a voice that was hoarse, breathless, and musical, you hurt me *so*, you are completely misconstruing Margaret's presence, it doesn't at all mean what you think it means, come, let me clear up this misunderstanding at once, she got out of the car without taking the key out of the ignition, he got out too, Wait for me, she said, giving him a winning smile, she walked away with her feet turned in like a little girl, the cottage was a simple, horribly expensive little affair, of varnished mahogany with a stone foundation, one room with kitchenette, bathroom, outside barbecue, and lean-to garage, practically on the edge of the ocean, its last wave came right to the door to lick the rich man's feet, he saw Grace on the beach talking to Mrs. Mandeville, he dropped into a chair, exasperated, all his nerves quivering, Grace squinted against the glare, Darling, something horrible is happening, Caliban just made a terrible scene, he's a monster, he literally beat me black-and-blue, I'm just as covered with bruises as that poor girl, you know, in the hairy grasp of King Kong on top of the Empire State Building, do you think you could help me? My poor darling, I can, but I don't know whether I should . . . no, no, Grace, I'm joking, of course I understand, it suddenly occurs to me that I have old friends around here, could you possibly lend me your car so I can go and see them, poor dears, the car door slammed, the motor whirred, Sevilla got up and walked toward the door, I lent Margaret the car, said Grace, appearing in the doorway with her dazzling smile and her false eyes, she wants to visit . . . he strode forward and took her in his arms, Henry, you're mussing me, she said, pushing him away, you seem to think everything is going to go like clockwork, she walked by him, her head high, and sat on the couch, her legs crossed high, elegant and superior, he stiffened and stared at her with eyes full of rage, No, he said so violently that his voice drowned out the noise of the surf, no, it's not going to go like clockwork, but I will not be put off any longer, it's either yes or no, and if it's no, I'm leaving now, on foot, Henry, you're terrible, she said, getting up and coming toward him with her eyebrows raised, really, you frighten me, you have the most dreadful manner and all of a sudden, as if her pride were a fragile crust that Sevilla had just broken with a fingernail, she gave in, she let him undress her, he did not say a word, teeth clenched, tense, absolutely without desire, he caressed her, she lay motionless, inert, And so am I, thought Sevilla, humiliated, time passed, he listened to the waves dying on the shore, he could not concentrate his forces, But, Henry, she said, you don't want me, she did not even seem offended, Of course I do, dear, look, you might make some effort yourself, but naturally that too was a failure, she did not know how to do anything, not even that, through the French doors he could see a small strip of sand and the foamy fringe of the sea, Listen, Grace, I don't want to offend you, but you do it very badly, What? she said, annoyed for the first time, but the others never complained, Sevilla raised himself on his elbow, you've been lucky, that's all, and do you think it's the height of tact to talk about "the others" at a time like this? I'm the one who's talking to you, not "the others," as he said the words he thought what an idiotic conversation, how sad this all is when there isn't even friendship, and she, this poor little idiot of a millionaire, what joy can she get out of life, he bent over her and all of a sudden he was able to take her, but badly, quickly, on the corner of the couch, in discomfort, in haste, a bad position, with a complete lack of tenderness, a bad job, a lost cause, without joy and without even real pleasure, he got up, Aren't you going to say thank you? she asked with a roguish smile, he looked at her, it was incredible, and on top of everything else, he was supposed to thank her, what unbelievable lack of humor, Thank you, he said without smiling, Do you want to take a swim? she said as if she were offering him a cup of tea, No, I don't care to, but if you have something besides those spike heels, let's take a walk on the beach, Oh yes, barefoot, said Grace, it's so good for the ankles, they walked side by side for a good half hour, talking, afterwards Sevilla could never remember what they said to each other except for one thing, a remark she made while he was bending over to pick up a shell, Henry, you ought to get your hair cut, it's too long, it's bad form, it was in itself a commonplace, unimportant remark, not even ill-natured, he stood up with the shell in his hand and all of a sudden he was weary and disgusted with her to the marrow of his bones, as nauseated as if he had been walking at her side for ten cold, empty years, and even then, as he smiled at her politely, he knew that his decision was made and that he rejected her from his life.

•   •   •

"In any case," said Arlette, "it was clear that Ivan's solitude was getting harder and harder for him to bear. He was excitable, restless, distracted, he concentrated much less on his vocal exercises; one could even say that he was becoming lazy. And he had made a transference to us, for sometimes he even assumed for us the S-

66

shaped position which is characteristic of the seductive attitude of the dolphin when he is courting a female. More and more often, too, he would rub himself against us, caress our heads with his lateral fins, and nuzzle our arms and legs. This erotic behavior increased in frequency and violence until we reached the point where we no longer dared swim with him, for we were afraid of being wounded by his bites—however pleasant they must be for a female of his species." (Foyle smiled.)

C picked up his cigar. "With whom did he adopt this conduct?"

"I'll answer that question," said Bob with a little laugh and a wink at C. "At first, with almost everybody. After a while, most often with Arlette."

"I can understand that," said Foyle.

Arlette looked at Bob Manning and frowned.

"Go on, Miss Lafeuille," said C.

"So everything led us to believe that the female we were going to give him, whom we had named Mina, would be well received. And so she was. At first, of course, Ivan showed a certain apprehension when a second animal was introduced into a tank which he regarded as his exclusive territory. He stopped moving and observed her for a moment, but his observations must have reassured him, for in a few moments he went from the most watchful caution to the most frenzied courtship. The stroking, rubbing, and biting accelerated, and the nuptial ballet went on all day long in a breathless crescendo. Dolphins generally mate at night and in the wee hours of the morning, so we had no way of knowing whether Mina and Ivan mated; but when day came the behavior of our dolphin toward his companion had completely changed. Not only did he no longer pursue her, but he repelled her advances in the most determined way. As soon as she approached him he snapped his jaws threateningly. Then he turned his back on her and swam off, beating the water violently with his caudal fin. Mina assumed the S position in front of him, but without success, for when she tried to stroke him he hit her with his lateral fins and snapped his jaws again. His attitude toward poor Mina did not improve the following day; in fact, it became more hostile and threatening. When Mina persisted in her advances he even bit her on the tail—a real bite this time— and from that moment on, she no longer dared approach him. When it became obvious that Ivan could not endure Mina, Professor Sevilla feared for her safety and decided to take her out of Ivan's tank. He placed her in the other tank where, by the way, she was immediately adopted by the male and the two females we are raising there."

"What had happened?" asked C.

"We've discussed the matter at length, and we're still discussing it," said Arlette, "but in this area we can only form hypotheses."

"For example?"

"I should explain first," said Arlette, "that the mating of dolphins is a difficult act. It demands a great deal of patience and compliance on the part of the female. Let us assume that Mina was clumsy, that she continued to run away when she should have stood still and that Ivan's attempts resulted in failure. He could have experienced keen disappointment."

"And taken a dislike to her?" asked Foyle, smiling. "She teased him for too long and he held it against her? But that doesn't explain why he did not try again the next day."

"I'd be more inclined to think that when this experiment failed he grew disgusted with females forever," said C.

Arlette smiled. "It may not be as serious as that. Perhaps Mina is simply not Ivan's type."

Foyle burst out laughing. "This time, Miss Lafeuille, I think you're exaggerating!"

"Not at all. Dolphins are just as selective as human beings in their amorous affinities or antipathies. At one point we had two males in one tank who formed a friendship and eventually even presented all the characteristics of homosexual behavior."

"Really?" said C. "And what were those characteristics?"

"Well, they took turns courting each other: stroking, rubbing, biting, it was all there, they even tried to copulate. Then we put a female with them, and they paid no attention to her. In fact, when she tried to approach them to participate in their games, they chased her away. We decided that their homosexuality was already too well established to permit heterosexual relations, and took the female out of the tank. But, some time later, for lack of space, we had to put another female with them. To our great surprise they both welcomed her with the greatest enthusiasm and immediately began courting her."

C crushed out his cigar in the ashtray in front of him. "So you

68

think it is personal antipathy which explains Mina's lack of success with Ivan?"

"Of course, these are only hypotheses."

C went on with veiled irony: "You believe, then, that the therapy which was to help Ivan pass from the word to the sentence has not failed."

"I don't see how anyone could say it has failed," said Arlette with a hint of sharpness. "You can't draw a conclusion like that from a single experiment."

"You mean that Sevilla plans to begin again with another female?"

"He hasn't told me so, but I think he does."

C rose, took his hat, and said with a smile, "Well, he's persistent."

"He has to be," said Arlette with conviction. "Success comes from the refusal to accept failure."

"And where did you get that pretty saying, Miss Lafeuille?" asked C with an acid smile.

"From Sevilla," said Bob Manning in an undertone.

C, who was already hurrying toward the door with Foyle, looked back over his shoulder and smiled at Bob. Arlette stared and when Bob Manning passed, she seized his arm and said in a low angry voice, "Do you think you're smart? You never stopped playing up to that revolting character. What's the matter with you?"

● ● ●

C was damp and naked, he sat down on the bed, ran his hands twice over his round face as if he wished he could erase the tiredness there, my God, he had no feeling in his legs, he was knocked out, he was going to be able to sleep without a pill, what a ridiculous reflex, my God, what the hell difference does it make whether I take a pill or not, what a farce, men of my age giving up tobacco, alcohol, high living, and starting to do push-ups on the rug, what idiots, what's the point of fighting old age, sooner or later they'll be beaten, they'll die by inches, the lungs, the liver, the heart, cancer of the prostate, C laughed, he was full of free-floating hostility and this gave his thinking a verve, a force, an acceleration that pleased him.

They make me laugh, exercise, the outdoor life, hygiene, what are they, after all? a pitiful losing battle, that's all, you fall apart in the end, that is absolutely certain, the only thing that is certain—life or

69

death, what does it matter? the word itself: life, what a mockery, what a hoax, to call these few boring minutes between two voids "life," what a hoax, the whole thing is rigged, fixed in advance, death at the end, what a lot of nonsense they hand us with their "success in life," what life? what success? I believed in success too when I was in college and later, I remember, I told myself I'm nothing but a glorified cop, I could have been a scholar, and even today when that cunt was talking to me—to have a lab, assistants, a creative work like that foreigner, it's all a lot of shit, nobody succeeds in life, there are only failures, all men are failures because they die.

Me too, Johnnie too, well, let them all die, all of them, as fast as possible, I hope they wipe them out with their H-bomb, I hope they burn up a few million and me along with them, what do I care, I never asked to be born, my only joy was to do my job well, if Johnnie had lived I would have recruited him for the agency, we had some good times together, the two of us, it was good to wake up in the morning like medieval barons, boot to boot, spur to spur, that intoxicating freedom, risking your life constantly, Johnnie standing in the sun in that village we'd just taken, his broad shoulders, his legs apart, that athlete's body that seemed indestructible, Do you see that old fart praying in front of his hut, I'll give him heads or tails, tails I don't touch him, heads I wipe him out, he threw the nickel into the air, it whirled, shining in the sun, he caught it in the hollow of his hand and slapped it with the flat of the other hand, Heads! he lost, he said, lifting the safety catch, the old man was scattered in the dust, he died like a squashed flea, at that moment Johnnie was like a god, serene, impersonal, he looked at me, his face immobile, absolutely without expression, he said in an even voice, Today him, tomorrow me, and the day after tomorrow it was him.

My God, I don't care about my job any more, if this keeps up I won't even be able to do it, I really thought I was going to pass out this afternoon in front of that little bitch and her dolphin Ivan, why Ivan, for God's sake? Who the hell stuck a Russian name on an American dolphin? His stomach contracted, he lay down on his back with his legs apart and massaged his stomach vigorously, his fingers dug in and he thought, All this meat, these guts, these nerves, this blood, an animal, nothing more, flabby, sweating,

70

obscene, that foreigner may succeed, anyway he's hot, that's obvious, one more thing Lorrimer concealed from me, you talk if they publish the results, you talk if it's "not secret," you can shove it up your ass, sir, your "not secret," I don't know what kind of measures they're taking, but they aren't going to keep me from taking others, and I'll bet my balls he'll agree to keep an eye on Sevilla for me, the pretty little darling.

The telephone filled the room with a strident sound, Shit, thought C, just as I was getting ready to fall asleep, he picked up the receiver, Bill, it's Keith, I'm sorry to disturb you but I just received an official dispatch, the Soviets have just put a formal ban on dolphin fishing in their waters. Any fisherman who wounds or kills a dolphin will be liable to severe punishment. Well, well, said C, what's the date of the dispatch? March 12. Thanks, Keith, he hung up.

After a moment he got up, no longer sleepy, put on his bedroom slippers, and began to pace up and down the room.

IV

It was the afternoon that character C came to bother us, said Maggie, you remember, with the assistant who looked like a prize-fighter, anyway he looked nicer than his boss, that character C had eyes that gave me the creeps, I remember, said Lisbeth, she was lying on one of the two twin beds in the room she shared with Maggie, it was still hot, the shade barely cut down the light, Lisbeth was in her bra and panties, tall, strong, blond, athletic, with her regular features, broad forehead, and square jaw, she looked like a very handsome, intelligent, and headstrong boy, who at the last moment had been given the wrong sex, even her enormous bosom could not make her look entirely feminine, she was leaning on one elbow inhaling her cigarette with a competent air, her attentive blue eyes were fastened on Maggie, I remember perfectly, she said in her clear voice, Arlette brought them into the lab, she had on a new bathing suit that showed off her pretty little body, and I was with you on the rafts in the tank, Well, that was the day he broke with her, said Maggie, he came in late, very late, he was in one of his quiet moods and he told me, When Mrs. Ferguson telephones again tell her I'm not in, I got up, it was all I could do not to grin from ear to ear and I said, For how long? He raised his eyebrows absent-mindedly, Well, I have to know, I said, is it a temporary order or a permanent order? You'll see, he said, and just from his manner I knew it was over, you can imagine how happy I was, I don't know what she did to him but he was furious, it wasn't until later, when I thought about it, that I began to wonder whether it was so good for him to break off with her, I wonder the same thing, said Lisbeth, frowning, they looked at each other and said nothing, they were not sure whether they were thinking exactly the same thing, they dropped their eyes, several seconds went by, facing each other that way they looked like two wary cats who all of a sudden pull in their claws, tuck their paws under their chests, sit down, and half close their eyes.

That's what Bob thinks too, said Maggie, you know how sharp he is, he knows what I'm thinking before I even open my mouth, it's fantastic, the communication we have, one look is enough, we don't really need words any more, it's exactly like the relationship I had with James Dean, poor James, I can still see him sitting in Aunt Agatha's old leather armchair in Denver staring at me with those sad eyes not saying a word, you remember those eyes of his, you might say they held all the sadness in the world, getting back to Bob, it's not quite the same problem, he's so shy, he has such a horror of showing his feelings that I don't even know whether I'll be able to announce our engagement this summer after all, But, said Lisbeth, raising one eyebrow, has he really . . . ? But, Lisbeth, you don't think he would, said Maggie, thrusting forward her ruddy face and her thick swollen lips, that's not Bob's style at all, he hasn't even tried to kiss me, he's so subtle, not one gesture, he's all delicacy and suggestion, take the other day, we were window-shopping together and he went into raptures at the sight of a little black-and-white striped shirt, Isn't it marvelous, don't you love it, I'd love to buy it, I began to laugh, Oh, Bob, would you wear something like that! my dear, he blushed to the roots of his hair and said very quickly, turning away his head, No, actually, I was thinking of you, I was thinking how well it would look on you, I was speechless, completely overwhelmed, it was his way of alluding to our life together, later, after we're married, I was so moved that I took his hand and pressed it without a word, but even that was too much for Bob, he took his hand away and said in a cold voice, See here, Maggie, are you mad, what's the matter with you? he's adorable, don't you think?

Yes, yes, said Lisbeth, looking down at her cigarette, the sweat stood out on her forehead, between her breasts and under her arms, the rooms were not air-conditioned, she inhaled her mentholated cigarette and thought with a sigh, And now she's going to tell me

73

about James Dean again, and more about Sevilla, and more about Bob, she's obsessed, it's a real sickness, if she weren't such a good girl I'd end up disliking her, and so ugly she almost makes me sick to my stomach, I always want to take my handkerchief and wipe out the corners of her eyes, I think I'll put on my bathing suit and take a dip in the pool, she said, sitting down on the bed, Ivan will bother you, said Maggie, you know he's getting positively indecent, not to mention the way he bites you and hits you with his tail, Oh, I know, he's adorable, so strong, so affectionate, but the other day he took me by the ankle—as you know, he has a slight preference for me—well, he wouldn't let go, I almost got a noseful, I wonder, said Lisbeth, getting up and twisting her right arm behind her back to unhook her bra, whether Sevilla isn't in for a disappointment in expecting a miracle from the new female, after all, if Ivan is having trouble passing from the word to the sentence, I don't see how a successful marriage can help him, it's like assuming that a man will suddenly become more intelligent when he gets married, generally speaking, it's the opposite.

Oh, Lisbeth! said Maggie, looking away, she didn't like the way Lisbeth walked around the room naked, Lisbeth was absolutely without modesty, when she changed her bra she didn't even cover up her breasts, Lisbeth, Maggie went on, that's not it at all, Sevilla never said anything like that, he said that a female would give Ivan self-confidence and increase his creative drive, Well, said Lisbeth, that's an egotistical attitude, as if the female were a tool to help the male in his work after serving his pleasure, you'll see, she went on, now that Sevilla has rejected his woman of the world he won't waste any time falling back on one of us, Arlette, Suzy, me—you (she added "you" because Maggie was looking at her), to increase his creative drive, as he says, I love that euphemism, she said with a short laugh, But look here, said Maggie, in her serious and intense voice, her coarse red girl scout's face glowing with disapproval, it's the woman's instinct to help the man she loves, if I had married Sevilla—you know, of course, that we almost got married a year ago but he could never make up his mind, deep down he's a shy one too, you know, I would have had to take matters into my own hands, but you know me, I'd rather die than force myself on anyone—well, if I had consented to become his wife, believe me, Lisbeth, I would have been only too happy to work for him night and day, You work quite enough as it is, said Lisbeth, and so does Arlette, and Arlette doesn't have your stamina, she lets him exploit her, that's the truth, I worry about her a lot—and about you too, she added after a second's pause, you're both mad, you two, with your Sevilla, and she's so charming, so delicate, she can only be disappointed, You like her very much, don't you? said Maggie suddenly.

Yes, I do, said Lisbeth, with a slight flush on her honest, straight-forward face, she's one of the most attractive girls I've ever met, I don't just mean she's pretty, you know, she has charm, mystery, there was a knock at the door and Bob Manning's voice said, Maggie, may I come in? Of course, he opened the door and stood in the doorway, he never walked into a room, he made his entrance like an actor, tall, svelte, graceful, the dark aristocratic head, the fine, slightly aquiline nose, the beautiful chestnut eyes shifting under the black lashes, the long delicate hands hanging from the willowy arms (he never put his hands in his pockets, he never crossed his legs when he sat down, he was always up on everything, the esoteric novels, the avant-garde films, the newest music, the latest poets), Damn, said Lisbeth with her arm twisted behind her, Need some help? said Bob with a delightful smile, striding into the room, deftly, expertly, he brought the two sides of the bra together and fastened the hook, What a divine bathing suit, he said, putting his head on one side, You know me and compliments, said Lisbeth, he paused, raised his pretty head almost theatrically, and posed there for a moment, loose-limbed and nonchalant, leaning one long arm against the wall, then said in his fluty voice, Listen, my dears, I bear important news, the wife Professor Sevilla has chosen for Ivan has just arrived, we are in the process of introducing her to her future husband, and I thought that out of affection for Ivan and respect for his father Sevilla you might like to attend the ceremony, besides, the professor has been demanding you both rather insistently, Why didn't you say so? said Lisbeth, shrugging her broad shoulders.

• • •

Nervous, anxious, but alert, taking in everything that was going on around her, the female dolphin lay on a stretcher that swayed at the end of a cable which the winch was about to lower into the tank. At the other end of the tank, about two feet under the surface of the water, Ivan lay motionless, attentive, his caudal fin beating the water imperceptibly. His head was raised toward the newcomer and he was turning it from left to right with a supple and powerful gesture so that he could consider her alternately out of each eye. At the same time he was emitting whistling sounds punctuated by pauses which were being broadcast in the open air by the loud-speaker. The female dolphin had not yet made any answering sound, perhaps because her suspended position and the swaying it caused was making her nervous, but her eyelids, which were almost motionless during the pauses, would start to flutter as soon as Ivan's whistling filled the air.

Dressed in white linen slacks and a polo shirt, his body young, his hair raven, his eyes black, keen, and impatient, Sevilla was standing to the right of the winch, flanked by Peter and Michael. The boys, who were both a good head taller than he, were in trunks, Peter blond and Michael brunette but both equally athletic, tanned, relaxed, their short hair shaved at the sides, dimples at the corners of their mouths, candid smiles over perfect teeth, their appearance incredibly healthy, responsible, and well fed.

As soon as Lisbeth and Maggie appeared in the doorway of the dormitory with the long silhouette of Bob standing out behind them Sevilla motioned them with an impatient gesture to approach. Lisbeth and Bob hurried and Maggie began to run. She felt vaguely guilty because she had just seen Suzy and Arlette beside the two boys. The whole team was there.

"I have called you together," said Sevilla, looking from one to the other with his gay, sparkling black eyes, "because I did not want to make the same mistake I made with Mina. You remember, I was so sure that Mina was going to get along with Ivan that I did not think of making arrangements for the couple to be watched from the beginning. You know the result: We have never known what went on between them during the night; in short, the real reason for their divorce escaped us. This time we are going to be more careful, and organize our observation in shifts around the clock. The lights built into the sides of the tank will be turned on as soon as it gets dark. I have divided you into two-man teams. One member of the team will observe the dolphins from the surface, the other through the underwater porthole. The two observers will be able to communicate by phone and each will record his observations on a tape recorder. Each will have a camera. The teams will be relieved every two hours.

"Here is the schedule," went on Sevilla, taking a piece of paper out of his pocket. "Six P.M. to eight P.M.: surface, Suzy; porthole, Peter. Eight P.M. to ten P.M.: surface, Michael; porthole, Lisbeth. Ten P.M. to midnight: surface, Maggie; porthole, Bob. Midnight to two A.M.: surface, Arlette; porthole, myself. Two A.M. to four A.M.: surface, Suzy; porthole, Peter. And so forth. . . . I have scheduled shifts until tomorrow noon, but we may have to extend them beyond that time. Maggie will post the timetable on the bulletin board."

He paused and asked, "Are there any comments?"

Suzy raised her hand. Sevilla looked at her fondly. After Michael and Arlette, she was the third most valuable member of the team. Suzy was a slender blonde with the type of classic profile which is often associated with snobbery and coldness, but which in her, because of the expression in her eyes, gave a pleasant impression of character.

"I assume that refills have been provided for the cameras and tape recorders?" she asked.

"I have asked Peter to take care of that."

"And Peter has taken care of it," said Peter. He looked at Suzy with a smile, which she returned.

There was a silence and Lisbeth said, with a hint of aggressiveness in her voice, "I notice that each team consists of a boy and a girl . . ."

"Why not?" asked Sevilla, raising his thick black brows.

"And that as a rule you have assigned the girl to the surface and the boy to the porthole."

"That is not true in your case, Lisbeth; I assigned you to the porthole."

"But it is true in the case of the three other girls," Lisbeth went on accusingly.

Sevilla glanced at his paper. "Yes, that's true. What about it?"

"Since the porthole post is more important than the surface post, I wonder whether your choice was dictated by antifeminist prejudice."

"Oh, I don't think so," said Sevilla, smiling. "I'm not conscious of harboring any such prejudice. I had to keep the porthole for the

77

boys and for myself because it was a little more strenuous than the surface."

"In that case," said Lisbeth, "why have you assigned me to the porthole?"

"Look here, Lisbeth, you can't accuse me of being an antifeminist because I assigned three of the girls to the surface *and* of being anti-Lisbeth because I assigned you to the porthole. You'll have to choose."

There were smiles and without looking at anybody Lisbeth said, "All right, I choose, and I repeat my question: Why am I the only girl you have assigned to the porthole?"

Sevilla threw up his hands and said impatiently, "I don't know. It was an accident."

"In psychology," said Lisbeth, "there are no accidents, there are only unconscious motives."

"Well," said Arlette vivaciously, "let's say that Mr. Sevilla assigned you to the porthole out of an unconscious respect for your athletic qualities."

There were more smiles. Lisbeth looked at Arlette reproachfully and her eyes filled with tears. She turned her head away and said nothing. Sevilla looked at her attentively for a moment, then he looked at the team and said in a neutral voice, "If you want to make changes among yourselves in the composition of the teams, naturally, I give you complete freedom."

"I have nothing more to say about the composition of the teams," said Lisbeth furiously. "It is a matter of complete indifference to me whether I am with X, Y, or Z."

She turned her back to the group and stared at the dormitory as if she had no interest in what was about to happen in the tank.

There was a silence and Sevilla went on: "Before putting this young lady in the water, I want to say one thing more. Just because your observations are going to be recorded on tape, don't feel obliged to adopt a stiff, formal style of speaking. Express yourselves as freely and naturally as possible. Say absolutely anything you feel like saying. These tapes will never leave the lab. And if we do make a written memorandum of them later, we will make any necessary cuts. After all, we are making a study of behavior, and it is quite possible that a spontaneous remark by one of you will contribute something to our analysis. All right, Michael. It's time to present Ivan with his future wife."

"You haven't told us her name," said Maggie.

"You're right!" said Sevilla, clapping his hands together. He looked around and said with a smile, "Lisbeth, to show you that there's been no conspiracy against your sex or against you, I ask you to name Ivan's wife."

Lisbeth wheeled around and faced him. "You talk as if I were suffering from a persecution complex," she said bitterly.

"Not at all," said Sevilla. "That is not the way I interpreted your remarks."

"Well, how did you interpret them?" she asked defiantly.

Sevilla threw up his hands. "I didn't interpret them at all!"

After a brief pause Maggie thrust her heavy red face forward and said energetically, "Listen, Lisbeth, don't start that again. The poor animal is waiting. Hurry up and give her a name."

"Let's call her Bessie," said Lisbeth gloomily.

*   *   *

TYPEWRITTEN MEMORANDUM OF
OBSERVATIONS OF IVAN AND BESSIE
TAKEN FROM TAPE RECORDINGS, SURFACE AND PORTHOLE,
PRIOR TO PROFESSOR SEVILLA'S EDITING.
MAY 6–7, 1970.

SUZY: Surface here. Six five. The winch is lowering Bessie into the water. Ivan isn't moving. Michael is going into the water and working her lateral fins out of the two holes cut into the canvas stretcher. Bessie is letting him handle her. She seems to have lost her nervousness.

PETER: Porthole here. Six ten. Hello, Suzy, can you hear me?

SUZY: Yes.

PETER: I can see Bessie perfectly well, but where's Ivan? He's not in my field of vision.

SUZY: He's on your right, as far into the corner as he can get. He's not moving. He's looking at Bessie. [A silence] What time do you have?

PETER: Six eleven.

SUZY: I'll set my watch by yours. Do you hear those whistling sounds? He's whistling and she's answering.

PETER: From where I am I can't hear the loudspeaker, but I have a good view of Bessie. She seems slimmer and shorter than Ivan. Except when she arches her back to take a breath, she is absolutely

79

motionless. It's obvious that she's going to let Ivan make the first advances. [*A silence*] Her eye is shining with feminine guile.

SUZY: Oh, Peter! [*She laughs*]

PETER: Six fifteen. I wish he'd make up his mind. What's he doing?

SUZY: He's looking at her first with his right eye and then with his left eye and he's whistling. [*A silence*] He's moving. Six sixteen.

PETER: Ah, I see him! He came within two yards of her. Now he's passing her and swimming around her. She's not moving.

SUZY: His circles are getting smaller and smaller.

PETER: When he gets in front of the porthole I can't see her. Yes, I can, if I bend down. She's not moving, she's watching him out of the corner of her eye. [*A silence*]

SUZY: Six twenty. I'm getting tired of these circles. What formality!

PETER: Six twenty-two. I just took a picture. I hope it will show the way she's looking at him out of the corner of her eye.

SUZY: Look! He's stopped swimming and he's placing himself next to her. They look like two boats moored side by side. Six twenty-five.

PETER: Bessie's body partly conceals Ivan's, but I can see his tail behind hers. Is his head right beside hers?

SUZY: Yes.

PETER: In that case he's considerably bigger than she is. I have a good view of her. She's batting her eyelashes.

SUZY: You're kidding!

PETER: Not at all. I'm telling you what I see: She's batting her eyelashes. What's he doing?

SUZY: He's rubbing the side of his head against hers. I'm going to take a picture. Too late. She's swimming away.

PETER: I can see her perfectly. She's swimming away from him; he isn't moving.

SUZY: He isn't moving, but he's yelping. He's not happy.

PETER: What kind of a yelp?

SUZY: Short, violent, high-pitched. He's calling her back. He seems annoyed. She's coming back. Six thirty. He's placing himself against her, they are side by side.

PETER: I can see them clearly. Ivan is almost touching my porthole. Bessie is on the other side. Ivan is looking at me. I could swear he's winking at me! I'm taking a picture. I wish I could get his expression.

SUZY: They're swimming away together.

80

PETER: I can't see them any more.

SUZY: They're swimming right next to the edge of the tank in a clockwise direction. Six thirty-five.

PETER: There they go.

SUZY: He has placed himself between her and the edge of the tank, perhaps so she won't bump herself against the wall. He must be thinking that she doesn't know the tank as well as he does.

PETER: Yes, I think you're right. He's keeping slightly ahead of her. He seems to be protecting and guiding her.

SUZY: I wonder how long this will go on. I'm turning off my tape recorder.

PETER: So am I.

SUZY: Surface here. Peter, I'm turning on my tape recorder.

PETER: Okay.

SUZY: Six forty-five. They're still swimming around the tank. This could go on indefinitely. What are you doing?

PETER: I'm sitting here smoking, and I'm bored. Are they whistling?

SUZY: Yes, constantly.

PETER: In short, they're having a swim and talking. Is one of them doing more whistling than the other?

SUZY: Yes, Ivan. She whistles rather seldom.

PETER: The conclusion is obvious. He's paying her compliments and she's listening.

SUZY: [She laughs] I'm turning off my tape recorder.

PETER: Me too.

SUZY: Surface here. I'm turning on my tape recorder so I can complain. Seven forty-five.

PETER: So am I. I'm dying of boredom and what's more, I'm hungry. They've been circling the tank for an hour and ten minutes. Is he still whistling?

SUZY: Yes.

PETER: What a line he's handing her!

SUZY: I didn't know the flirting stage would last so long.

PETER: Don't be so impatient.

SUZY: [She laughs] I think I'd better turn off my tape recorder. But you can still talk to me.

PETER: Okay.

SUZY: Surface here. Here's Michael, it's eight o'clock.

PETER: I'll meet you in the dining room as soon as Lisbeth gets here. Hello, Michael, you're going to be disappointed. They've been

81

circling like that for an hour and twenty-five minutes. They're not newlyweds, they're long-distance runners.

MICHAEL: [*He laughs*] Anything interesting?

PETER: Yes, at the beginning. The approach was interesting. Here's Lisbeth. I'll turn you over to her.

LISBETH: Porthole here. What's new?

MICHAEL: Surface here. According to Peter they've been swimming around like this for an hour and twenty-five minutes.

LISBETH: That sounds like fun. [*A silence*]

MICHAEL: They're nice, they seem to like each other.

LISBETH: They make me dizzy. I hope they're not going to keep this up for two hours. [*A silence*] I'm turning off the tape recorder.

MICHAEL: So am I.

LISBETH: Porthole here. Eight twenty-five.

MICHAEL: Surface here.

LISBETH: Ivan just swam ahead and she caught up with him.

MICHAEL: Observation confirmed. They seem a bit restless. Their circling no longer has that quiet, contented quality it had before. [*A silence*] The moon just came out. It's quite a nice evening.

LISBETH: You're lucky.

MICHAEL: If you like, we can change positions. I'll take the porthole and you can take the surface.

LISBETH: I appreciate your tact, but I'm perfectly all right where I am.

MICHAEL: There's no reason to snap at me.

LISBETH: I'm not snapping at you.

MICHAEL: Yes you are. . . . I was just trying to be nice to you.

LISBETH: I don't see any necessity for that.

MICHAEL: Thanks. [*A silence*] Listen, Lisbeth, if you wanted to work with someone else you could have said so. I wouldn't have minded.

LISBETH: Can't you understand that I *have* no preference? I'd just as soon have you as anyone.

MICHAEL: That's nice of you.

LISBETH: I'm sorry, but I find you all exasperating with your insinuations.

MICHAEL: Who are you talking about?

LISBETH: You, Sevilla, the rest. . . . You always bring sex into everything.

MICHAEL: And you don't? Lucky you.

LISBETH: Anyway, I don't see why I should have to team up with a boy to watch dolphins.

MICHAEL: Would you rather work with a girl?

82

LISBETH: Who said that?

MICHAEL: Well, there are only two sexes.

LISBETH: Always sex! This conversation is ridiculous. Let's drop it.

MICHAEL: Surface here. Hello, Lisbeth, I'm turning on my tape recorder. Eight thirty.

LISBETH: So am I.

MICHAEL: I think Ivan just assumed the S position.

LISBETH: I didn't see anything.

MICHAEL: I may have been mistaken. It happened very fast. [A silence] Feeling better?

LISBETH: No, but don't worry about it.

MICHAEL: Look, this time I'm not mistaken.

LISBETH: You're right.

MICHAEL: It must represent a considerable muscular effort for a dolphin to twist his body into an S . . .

LISBETH: I think it's ridiculous.

MICHAEL: No more than a pigeon when he struts in front of a female pigeon.

LISBETH: I wonder how many seconds he's capable of maintaining the pose.

MICHAEL: I just timed him: two and eight-tenths seconds.

LISBETH: I took a picture. I noticed that he folded in his lateral fins.

MICHAEL: I wasn't sure about that. [A silence] I wonder why it's that position rather than another that dolphins consider seductive.

LISBETH: What does the cock do? I don't remember.

MICHAEL: He walks around the hen, spreading one wing and letting it hang down to the ground to show her how well dressed he is.

LISBETH: What a farce! They're starting to circle again. I'm turning off my tape recorder.

MICHAEL: So am I.

LISBETH: Porthole here. Eight forty-five. Can you see Ivan?

MICHAEL: Not too well.

LISBETH: He has just placed himself *under* Bessie with his head near her fins.

MICHAEL: I can't see him. Bessie's in the way.

LISBETH: Michael?

MICHAEL: Yes.

LISBETH: This is very odd. She's stroking his head with her fins.

MICHAEL: Are you sure?

LISBETH: Absolutely. Wait, I'll take a picture. There.

MICHAEL: How is she stroking him?

LISBETH: What do you mean?
MICHAEL: You have a lot to learn: Is she being violent or gentle?
LISBETH: Thanks for the education.
MICHAEL: Well?
LISBETH: Gentle.
MICHAEL: Can you see his eyes?
LISBETH: They're closed. Is he making any noise?
MICHAEL: No, none at all. I moved back and got down on my stomach, and I got a glimpse of her. She's stroking him very gently. I find it rather moving. In a minute he's going to start purring .
LISBETH: You're getting carried away.
MICHAEL: No, but I am surprised. I'll admit I would not have expected so much tenderness on the part of two animals.
LISBETH: I don't see any point in gushing. [*A silence*] They're starting to circle again. I'm turning off my tape recorder.
MICHAEL: So am I.
LISBETH: Porthole here. Nine thirty. I counted three S positions.
MICHAEL: So did I. I timed them: two and four-tenths seconds, two and six-tenths seconds, and three seconds. At nine twenty-five he nibbled her caudal fin.
LISBETH: I missed that. Look! He's placing himself above her.
MICHAEL: I can see them if I bend over, but not very clearly. What's he doing?
LISBETH: The same as before, except that the roles are reversed. This time he's stroking *her* head with his fins.
MICHAEL: There's a method in their madness . . .
LISBETH: I've heard that somewhere.
MICHAEL: *Hamlet.*
LISBETH: She seems rather restless. Oh, I was expecting that, she's swimming away.
MICHAEL: He's following her.
LISBETH: He's stroking her again.
MICHAEL: I didn't quite catch that. What happened?
LISBETH: Just as he caught up with her he swam under her, turned over on his back, and rubbed himself against the whole length of her body. Then he returned to the normal position.
MICHAEL: It seemed like a very acrobatic caress.
LISBETH: Look, she's swimming away again.
MICHAEL: Probably to get him to do it again. I'm going to lean over and see what I can see.
LISBETH: There they go.
MICHAEL: This time I saw it. It's very beautiful, the way he turns over and slides against her. It's very beautiful, very graceful.

LISBETH: I took a picture.

MICHAEL: She's swimming away again. She's beginning to like it.

LISBETH: He's starting again.

MICHAEL: I think the rhythm is accelerating. What energy! They're tireless. Love-making in dolphins is very athletic.

LISBETH: Michael?

MICHAEL: Yes?

LISBETH: Here is Bob.

MICHAEL: Already!

BOB: Can you summarize for me?

MICHAEL: No. Here's Maggie. It's just starting to get interesting.

MAGGIE: Surface here. Bob, I have the correct time. It's ten three.

BOB: I'm setting my watch.

MAGGIE: I want to ask you something. It's very nice of Sevilla to put me on the team, but after all, I'm not a zoologist. Would you mind tipping me off if I miss something?

BOB: But of course.

MAGGIE: What's Ivan doing? I can hardly see him with all the water that's being churned up.

BOB: He has swum under Bessie and is biting her caudal fin. Now he's letting go of that and taking her right lateral fin in his mouth.

MAGGIE: It looks as if Bessie is bending her head around and trying to catch his tail.

BOB: Right. He's letting go of her, he's diving, he's opening his mouth wide. Wait! He's closing his mouth over hers.

MAGGIE: I suppose that's his way of shutting her up. [*She laughs*]

BOB: Is he making any sounds?

MAGGIE: All kinds of sounds: yelps, whistles, squeaks, and sometimes even something that sounds like laughing.

BOB: He's releasing his grip, he's backing away. No, it was only a feint, he's coming back. . . . He's taking her dorsal fin again. Now he's letting go of it and biting her caudal fin.

MAGGIE: This time she's doing the same to him.

BOB: [*He laughs*] Neither one will let go; they're writhing in the water like two wrestlers. Have you ever seen two male dolphins fighting?

MAGGIE: No.

BOB: They use the same holds, but the biting is serious. They inflict terrible wounds; after a little while the water is stained with blood.

MAGGIE: I don't see any blood.

BOB: No, but when they pass close to the porthole I can see tooth marks on their fins. [*A silence*] I suppose that in order to be erotic the bite must be near the threshold of real pain.

MAGGIE: They seem to be calming down. They're swimming around the tank. Bessie's on the inside.

BOB: They're recovering from their bout. [*A silence*] I'm turning off my tape recorder.

MAGGIE: Me too.

BOB: Porthole here. Ten forty-five. Ivan has just slipped under Bessie and is caressing her ventral opening with the end of his fin.

MAGGIE: I note that she has only one ventral opening and he has two.

BOB: In the female, the genitals and the anus are included in a single opening. The male has two ventral openings: one for the anus, the other for the penis. Look! He's moving away. Bessie is catching up with him and placing herself under him. She's nudging Ivan's genital opening with the end of her snout, now she's nibbling it.

MAGGIE: More bites, all over the body. Do we have to describe all this biting again? It's the same as before.

BOB: No. They're starting to circle the tank again. Calm has been restored. The frenzied moments are followed by calm periods.

MAGGIE: Can I take this opportunity to ask you a question?

BOB: Go ahead.

MAGGIE: A question I've always wanted to ask you. Are you Catholic?

BOB: No, not yet; but I'm very much drawn to it.

MAGGIE: What is it about Catholicism that attracts you?

BOB: The discipline and the confession.

MAGGIE: I'm not sure I understand.

BOB: Well, this isn't the time to discuss it.

MAGGIE: But since there's nothing to observe . . .

BOB: Precisely. I'm turning off my tape recorder and I'm going to have a cigarette.

MAGGIE: Surface here. Eleven thirty-five. They're beginning to move around again.

BOB: Yes, I see. Bessie glides under Ivan, Ivan holds still, and she nibbles his ventral opening. He has an erection. I'm taking a picture. This is the first time I've seen one so distinctly and so close up. Very interesting.

MAGGIE: What's interesting?

BOB: What's that?

MAGGIE: You just said it: "Very interesting."

BOB: No I didn't.

MAGGIE: I beg your pardon. Play back your tape, and you'll see.

BOB: Listen, stop bugging me, will you?

MAGGIE: Don't get angry, I'm trying to learn. As I said before, I'm not a zoologist.

BOB: I'm not angry. [*A pause*] And I have no objection to filling you in. As you were able to observe, erection is instantaneous.

MAGGIE: And in other mammals it isn't?

BOB: [*He laughs*] No.

MAGGIE: Why do you laugh?

BOB: I'm not laughing. . . . Do you want me to explain it to you or not?

MAGGIE: Yes.

BOB: The penis of the dolphin has two peculiarities. In the first place, it is not vascular but fibro-elastic. This means that it does not increase either in width or in length. The penis emerges from the ventral opening the way a switchblade jumps out of its case.

MAGGIE: Is that your image?

BOB: No, Sevilla's.

MAGGIE: Well, it's interesting.

BOB: Listen, don't start that again!

MAGGIE: What's the matter with you? How touchy you are! When you laughed just now, *I* didn't take offense.

BOB: I didn't laugh.

MAGGIE: Yes you did!

BOB: I beg your pardon, I did not laugh.

MAGGIE: Well, it doesn't matter. You said there were two peculiarities. What's the other one?

BOB: The other one you can see for yourself. The penis is not rectilinear, but leans about twenty degrees to the left. That is why Ivan is now trying to approach Bessie from her right and perpendicular to the direction she's swimming in, and rolling onto his side a little. See, for him to be able to take her she would have to slow down considerably and turn onto her left side.

MAGGIE: She doesn't seem to understand.

BOB: No. [*A silence*] He missed. Ten forty-five.

MAGGIE: They're starting to circle the tank again. Perhaps she feels that he hasn't courted her enough.

BOB: That's one interpretation.

MAGGIE: [*A silence*] I can't understand how people have managed to bring sin into this sort of thing. It looks so innocent.

BOB: It *is* innocent in dolphins. Not in us.

MAGGIE: Why?

BOB: It would take too long to explain.

87

MAGGIE: You said you were drawn by the Catholic confession. I must admit I don't understand that either.

BOB: In my opinion it is a great thing to be able to say what one is and what one does to someone who pardons you.

MAGGIE: But that's exactly what I find dangerous: the fact that someone pardons you. It's as if you placed your conscience outside yourself.

BOB: You are a puritan. Your god is not God, it's your conscience.

MAGGIE: No, not at all. I am not a puritan.

BOB: Look, this isn't the time to discuss it. We'll come back to it later. [*A silence*] They're calm. I'm going to take the opportunity to turn off my tape recorder and get some cigarettes. I'm all out.

MAGGIE: Okay.

BOB: Porthole here. Eleven fifty. A new round of wrestling, biting, and nibbling. We won't describe it, but I'm going to time it.

MAGGIE: It seems to me that the calm periods are much longer than the violent ones.

BOB: Of course. Otherwise they'd be exhausted. Look at them! What frenzy!

MAGGIE: In a way it's pleasant to watch. They seem so happy! They look as if they're laughing.

BOB: You're interpreting.

MAGGIE: Aren't they even more frenzied than they were before? Isn't it accelerating?

BOB: Yes, I think so, but it's hard to judge.

MAGGIE: What energy! To think that it's midnight and that this session has already gone on for six hours! The vitality of these animals is incredible. Bob, here's Arlette.

ARLETTE: Bob? Can you give me a résumé?

BOB: Excuse me, I'm giving one to Mr. Sevilla.

SEVILLA: Porthole here. Twelve three.

ARLETTE: Surface here. Twelve three.

SEVILLA: The biting has been going on since eleven fifty. An erection at ten forty-five, but no mating. She didn't cooperate.

ARLETTE: Have they started the leaping?

SEVILLA: No, not yet. Only the stroking and the biting. [*A silence*] Are they making any cries?

ARLETTE: Yes, constantly.

SEVILLA: Can you hear any English sounds from Ivan?

ARLETTE: No, none.

SEVILLA: How would you describe their cries?

ARLETTE: Phonetically?

SEVILLA: No, in human terms. By analogy.

ARLETTE: I would say that they are enthusiastic. Of course, that is an interpretation.

SEVILLA: You know my point of view. There is no reason why the anthropomorphic interpretation should be ruled out from the start. It is a mistake to regard man as a creature essentially different from the higher mammal. It is the upstart's pride in man that leads him to think he is. [A silence] Twelve ten. They've calmed down again. The session of struggling and biting lasted twenty minutes.

ARLETTE: What vitality!

SEVILLA: Yes, it's admirable. From this point of view it is man who has degenerated. [A silence] I'll admit I'm a little jittery. I'm afraid it's not going to come off.

ARLETTE: There's no reason why it shouldn't. Ivan will follow his instinct.

SEVILLA: He didn't follow his instinct with Mina. We must remember that Ivan is a dolphin brought up by human beings. He is a Mowgli in reverse. And perhaps he is already too inhibited. I'll never forgive myself for not arranging for his observation when I brought him Mina. I thought success was a foregone conclusion. That was a mistake. The erotic behavior of the dolphin is probably just as complex as that of man. I am convinced of that now.

ARLETTE: If we made a mistake, at least it taught us something. Do I have to remind you that "success comes out of the refusal to accept failure"?

SEVILLA: [He laughs] You're teasing me! . . . They're calming down. I'm turning off my tape recorder.

ARLETTE: Surface here. One five. They're beginning to move around.

SEVILLA: Yes, I see. I think it's going to work.

ARLETTE: Why?

SEVILLA: There's a friendly feeling between the two animals. It's noticeable in the periods of calm.

ARLETTE: They're beginning to get frantic again.

SEVILLA: Yes, he's backing up and pouncing on her as if he were trying to knock his head against hers.

ARLETTE: Isn't that the way they kill sharks?

SEVILLA: Yes. But in mating the dance of death becomes playful. Did you see? At the last moment he swerved and used his momentum to rub his body the length of hers.

ARLETTE: I wonder what would happen if she swerved in the same direction at the same moment.

SEVILLA: There's nothing to fear. This frenzy is admirably controlled. Look! He's starting again.

ARLETTE: It's a very violent caress.

SEVILLA: Yes. It's an attack. A deadly attack that ends in a caress.

ARLETTE: And what a caress! You almost expect to see sparks.

SEVILLA: Observe that at the moment of contact he rolls onto his side. I think the leaping will begin soon.

ARLETTE: Look! Now she's backing up too and rushing to meet him!

SEVILLA: I think she's trying to double the force of the friction.

ARLETTE: Maybe she just wants to feel she's participating more.

SEVILLA: I just took a picture. When the leaping begins, don't forget your camera.

ARLETTE: No. They're preparing for a new attack. [*She laughs*] I like the hypocritically lazy way they retire to their corners before the attack.

SEVILLA: Yes. They're very excited and very relaxed at the same time.

ARLETTE: They're beginning to move again.

SEVILLA: They are literally hurling themselves against each other. You're going to see those sparks before they're through. . . .

ARLETTE: I took a picture.

SEVILLA: They're beginning again. They're retiring to their respective corners like two boxers.

ARLETTE: They're tireless! Oh, look! She's leaping into the air.

SEVILLA: Yes. Just as he was about to reach her she swerved. She leaped out of the water.

ARLETTE: What was the purpose of that?

SEVILLA: It's just a variation. As she fell back, he placed himself under her so he could rub against her as she fell.

ARLETTE: I suppose the stroking is even more violent.

SEVILLA: Especially since he's shoving off from the bottom. They pass each other halfway. It's like a ballet. It's very beautiful.

ARLETTE: I couldn't see because of the splashing. Bessie got me soaking wet.

SEVILLA: Would you like the porthole? I'll take your place at the surface.

ARLETTE: No, no. Take pictures of the underwater ballet. You're a better photographer than I am. And I have an advantage over you. I can hear the cries.

SEVILLA: What are they like?

ARLETTE: Ecstatic.

SEVILLA: They're retiring to their corners.

ARLETTE: I'm setting my camera. [*A silence*] Magnificent! They both leaped that time . . . ooh!

90

SEVILLA: What's the matter?

ARLETTE: They splashed me from head to foot. I'm drenched.

SEVILLA: Run and change your clothes.

ARLETTE: Not for the world! It's very exciting. Can you see them? Can you see their faces? They're laughing. They're beatific. They look so happy, I wish I were in their place.

SEVILLA: I was just thinking the same thing. [A silence] It's one twenty-five. This paroxysm has been going on for twenty minutes now. They have hearts and muscles of steel.

ARLETTE: They're going into the biting stage.

SEVILLA: We're almost in the final phase. It's generally after the most violent leaping and rubbing that mating occurs. Look, she's nibbling his ventral opening. Erection is instantaneous. He's chasing her.

ARLETTE: What an idiot, she doesn't seem to understand that she has to slow down and roll onto her left side.

SEVILLA: Yes she does, she's slowing down.

ARLETTE: But not enough, I think.

SEVILLA: She's slowing down, and she's rolling onto her side.

ARLETTE: He's going to her. Is he making an attempt? I can't see much from here, you know.

SEVILLA: There has been repeated contact, but no intromission.

ARLETTE: They're coming up to the surface for air. I think they're going to start again.

SEVILLA: Yes. The groping is starting again. [A silence] Without success.

ARLETTE: I'm beginning to think that water is not an ideal medium for mating.

SEVILLA: It certainly isn't. They must swim throughout the entire operation, they must occasionally come to the surface for air, they have nothing to support them, and of course they have no hands. Imagine an armless man trying to make love in six feet of water.

ARLETTE: I have one thirty-five on my watch. Have you taken any pictures?

SEVILLA: No, not yet. Would you come here? If intromission occurs I'd like you to time it while I take pictures.

ARLETTE: I'll be right there.

SEVILLA: [A silence] Take my chronometer. Do you know how to use it?

ARLETTE: Yes.

SEVILLA: He's starting again. Again, repeated contact. [A silence] There, at last.

ARLETTE: One forty-six.

91

SEVILLA: I got some good pictures. What was the time on the mating?

ARLETTE: Sixteen and five-tenths seconds.

SEVILLA: That's precision for you. I like the five-tenths! [*He laughs*]

ARLETTE: [*She laughs*] You asked me to time it. One must be precise . . .

SEVILLA: You're quite right. They're starting to circle the tank again, smiling and happy. What animals! I'm more tired than they are.

ARLETTE: So am I!

SEVILLA: And you're soaking wet, too!

ARLETTE: I'll run and change and make you some coffee.

SEVILLA: And I'll wake Peter and Suzy.

ARLETTE: I'm dead. [*She laughs*]

SEVILLA: You're superb. With your hair that way you look like Venus emerging from the waves . . . you know, the one by Botticelli.

ARLETTE: Oh, thank you! What a nice compliment! I have at least one thing in common with her! I'm drenched!

SEVILLA: Run and change. While you're doing that I'll make coffee myself. I could really use a cup of coffee.

ARLETTE: So could I. And besides, I want to talk. . . .

V

On the fourteenth of May, one week after the mating of Ivan and Bessie and eighteen hundred miles from their peaceful tank, some playful and innocuous breezes were wandering aimlessly through a low-pressure area over the Caribbean Sea opposite the Colombian city of Barranquilla.

Without any warning their wandering suddenly ceased to be innocent, they began to whirl at unseemly speeds, not in a circle but in a spiral with an upward, counterclockwise movement, creating by nine o'clock a giant funnel seven miles high and sixty miles wide which was already powerful enough to whip the sea into enormous waves, one of which stove in the steel hull of the Colombian cargo ship *Tiburón,* the water gushed in, the *Tiburón* sent an SOS which was picked up and immediately relayed by a plane of the United States Weather Bureau, the plane went to reconnoiter the hurricane, Henry, said W. D. Dickenson as his airplane began to buck terribly and he pointed its nose up to gain altitude, I'll give you the honor of naming this baby, I'll call her Hannah, said Larski, in memory of my first date, a co-ed from Cleveland Heights High School, he laughed, God, she was a well-built little kid, her family was Italian, her eyes . . . I think, said Dickenson, coming out of the funnel with relief, that Hannah is going to go have a word with Cuba and Castro, unless she misses him by a hair, in which case Florida is going to get it, it was ten thirty-five, Hurricane Hannah, which was already reaching ninety miles an hour, began an intense official existence over the air waves of Central America and the

93

United States as she followed her path of destruction from the southwest to the northwest of the Caribbean Sea, boats made desperately for port, all flights were suspended over the Gulf of Mexico, in Cuba the province of Pinar del Río was put in a state of alert, Radio Miami broadcast alarming bulletins every hour, at twelve o'clock Hannah encountered a Brazilian craft which was smuggling tobacco off the coast of Nicaragua and sank it instantly, at twelve fifty off Puerto Cabezas she came upon a little Mexican coaster and destroyed it and its crew of ten without leaving a trace, at four P.M. she reached the island of Cozumel and sank three fishing boats which were heading back to the Mexican coast, at six P.M. she crossed the Yucatán Channel, skirted the province of Pinar del Río where the Cuban *guajiros,* burrowed in their *varas en tierra,** were already awaiting its terrifying arrival, swerved to the northeast, grazed Key West, swept up the Straits of Florida at an insane speed, and leaving Palm Beach on her left and the Bahamas on her right, disappeared into the Atlantic where she ceased to exist as a hurricane, it was seven thirty P.M., a wisp of wind, a lost child that had broken away from the giant hurricane, lashed the North American coast north of Palm Beach, tore off some roofs and uprooted a few palm trees just for the fun of it, sent waves fifty yards inland for six miles around and suddenly subsided, leaving a torrential rain in her wake, it was seven forty P.M., the road was pitch-black, Sevilla turned on the headlights and windshield wiper of his old Buick, but the water pounded on his car with deafening force, blurred the windshield, streamed onto the sloping road in sheets, the Buick began to skid, he stopped, put her in reverse and, backing slowly to his right, wedged the rear wheel against the edge of the sidewalk, I hope this will be over soon, he said, turning toward Arlette, he stopped the motor and turned on the map light, at once the tiny glow introduced a sense of mystery, warmth, and intimacy into the car, its downward beam shone on Arlette's knees, traced her thighs under the light linen skirt, cast a diffused light above the pale blue blouse on her chin, cheeks, and forehead, leaving her eyes in shadow except for the whites of the eyes, caught a few fine curly locks in the black halo of her hair, Sevilla shifted his gaze to the

---

* Little low huts made of branches, in which the peasants (*guajiros*) hide during hurricanes.

windshield, which was seething like the porthole of a ship cutting through the sea, through the streaming plate glass he could see the glowing circles of the headlights and the water rolling down the asphalt road, as muddy as a river in spate, to his right behind the black windowpane which set off Arlette's profile he could see two or three white spots which were bungalows and the silhouette of a single palm tree, to his left and behind him total blackness, and the rain pounding on the roof of the Buick like drums beating in the jungle, Do you have any idea where we are? asked Sevilla, I was talking, I wasn't watching the road, Yes, said Arlette in a calm, remote voice that was scarcely audible above the din of the water that was lashing the hood and windows, those bungalows to the right belong to that Spanish-style motel, you know the one, we can't be more than ten miles from the lab, But I'm glad I stopped, said Sevilla, here there's enough of a slant so the water runs away, but if I went on I might run into deep water and drown my motor, besides, the windshield is practically opaque, you can't see twenty yards, This is fine, said Arlette, there's nothing to do but wait, he looked at her, he was struck by the extraordinarily easy and feminine way she was sitting, her body completely relaxed, her face calm and smiling, obviously happy to be alive, she was enjoying before his eyes one of those moments of perfect physical euphoria which may be the best and rarest thing that life has to offer, her eyes shone softly in the half-light, her mouth was slightly open, even her breathing seemed slower, so immersed did she seem in languor, she inhaled the rain like a plant, he put out his right hand and ruffled the black hair that seemed to shine like wet leaves in the tropical warmth, she did not move, she looked at him, her eyes were full of good faith, her lips opened, the corners turned up, what a marvelous smile she had, so tender, so trusting, an opening of the soul, a profound generosity, a challenge to everything vile, why is it so late in life that we learn to recognize a look, a smile, how could I not have noticed in Marian's inhuman eyes the neurosis that was to inspire that insane, self-destructive hatred for me, a hatred that corroded her own soul like an acid, dried her out and withered her in less than five years, as if the venom that she carried inside had burned the now useless flesh and left her nothing but a skeleton, which was all she needed to express her terrible passion for hurting, he blinked, he came back to the present, he saw Arlette again, it was almost a shame to erase that smile with a kiss, but the curve of the breast is also destroyed by the hand that caresses it, the pleasures of the senses are not cumulative, each destroys the one that went before, he kept looking at her, his fingers still grasping that admirable fleece, the strange thing was not that she was going to belong to him, but that it had taken so long, he realized how fond of her he had grown in the months they had worked side by side, their understanding was so profound that it had even obscured his desire, he listened to the torrent of water pounding on the car, the downpour cut them off from the world in the dimly lit warmth of the Buick, like a downy nest surrounded by darkness, it was delightful to be alone, invisible to the rest of the world, it was like being in the cabin of a yacht in the middle of an ocean without waves, far from accusing looks, the bitter envy that lurks behind moral condemnation, the resentment of castrated men who have allowed themselves to be dispossessed of their lives, he pressed his lips to hers, he gorged himself on her, he drank her in. In the motel room the decor was determinedly rustic, the ceiling featured false beams, the fireplace fake stone, Sevilla knelt down and got out his lighter, the flame darted out, he turned out the fake candles in the wrought-iron fixtures, they were soaked to the skin, they pushed the bed as close as possible to the fire, they hung their dripping clothes on chairs on either side of the fireplace so they could enjoy the sight of the crackling flames, the rain pattered on the roof, at times the heavy red linen curtains stirred as the wind shivered the two windows in their casements, he laid her head in the hollow of his arm, she closed her eyes, her lower lip protruded, she seemed to withdraw into a deep tranquillity, she looked so young, so childlike, so open, he pressed his cheek to hers, Arlette's hand clasped the sheet, firelight danced in the black hair lying on the pillow, her head with its closed eyes suddenly stopped moving, the hand released the sheet, turned over, and opened, once again Sevilla heard the cataract pounding on the roof as if the sky had burst, he rolled onto his side, he must have fallen asleep for after a moment he felt her behind him, her breasts pressing against his back, her warm lips on the back of his neck, You're not asleep either, she said, No, he said, turning around and again he received full in the face the shock of her gentle eyes and tender smile, happiness is so unfamiliar that it is hard to recognize it when it is there, offered, yours for the asking, between two hecatombs, in the twenty short years that separate world wars,

96

the first from the second and the second from the third, ours, the one that's already knocking at our door, and this one is really the last since afterward there won't be anything left to destroy, but at this moment, in the final paroxysm of the storm, there was no possible doubt, this was happiness, he recognized it by his sense of life throbbing with a triumphant pulse, of life being released, like the torrent that lashed the roof over his head, breaking over the tiles like waves, with hammer blows that shook the frail structure, the casement bolts of the windows trembling constantly in their sheaths, the red curtains lifting and swelling in the sudden gusts like balloons, outside the little bungalow the rain poured and pounded down with such force that he pictured the water tearing it from its foundations and carrying it across meadows transformed into lakes amid floating beams, drowned animals, and lost cars, the regal palm trees emerging with bent trunks, disheveled and horizontal, the beach indistinguishable except for the roofs of the submerged bath-houses, the palm trees drifting toward the sea which sucked them toward its freedom, their little arches still floating, indestructible, sole islands of light and warmth in a chaotic world.

. . .

"It's a failure," said Lisbeth in an imperious voice, pushing away her plate. Sevilla and Arlette had left immediately after the meal but the rest of the team was lingering in the dining room. It was the only air-conditioned room; evening had not brought a breath of air and it was unbearably hot. There was a silence. Lisbeth repeated, "It's a failure." Her muscular thighs filled her short shorts to bursting, the blond curly hair that made her look like a shepherd was short too, her cigarette moved in the corner of her mouth as she spoke, her voluminous bosom, bursting out of a dark-green bra, did not seem to belong to the same person as her broad shoulders and slender waist.

"I'm putting my T-shirt back on," said Peter. "With this air conditioning I don't know whether I'm hot or cold."

He stretched out his long blond legs and propped them on the edge of an empty chair.

"I don't see how you can say it's a failure," he went on. "It's not even two weeks since Bessie came here."

Bob Manning rose and gracefully stretched his long flexible arms. Peter and Michael were in shorts; he was the only one of the boys who was wearing not blue jeans, but pale blue slacks with knife-sharp creases. All the buttons of his shirt were buttoned, the wide Shelley collar framed his graceful neck, his dark head with its aquiline nose was tilted slightly to the right, a precise English-style part divided his glistening hair, which was plastered down with Yardley hair tonic, he was not perspiring, he smelled of lavender, he looked as if he had just stepped out of a bandbox, all freshly scrubbed and ironed.

"I agree with Lisbeth," he said in his fluty voice. "Let's face it: It's a failure. What was the purpose of this marriage? A salutary shock which was supposed to give Ivan new confidence in himself."

"And to increase his creative drive," said Lisbeth sarcastically. "Let's not forget his creative drive. Bessie was supposed to help Ivan cross a decisive frontier and pass from the word to the sentence. The result has been just the opposite."

"The result has not been the opposite," said Suzy, placing her round arm on the back of Peter's chair.

He turned his head to the right and looked at her attentively. What a profile she had, so regular, so classical, so finely chiseled. This profile was the essence of Suzy, her straightness, her integrity—a mama, but a younger mama. Peter had contradicted Lisbeth because he didn't like her tone; actually he was impressed by her attacks, but if Suzy was taking his side against her, that changed everything, then he must be right.

"What do you mean, it hasn't been the opposite?" asked Lisbeth with crushing disdain. "What more proof do you need?"

"Excuse me for having the audacity to contradict you," said Suzy, and Peter gave a little laugh, "but since the mating Ivan has changed in ways that we had foreseen. He is happier, more dynamic, more aggressive—"

She broke off and looked at Maggie, uglier and more red-faced than ever in a dress with big red and yellow flowers. Maggie did not say a word but lowered her eyes. It's strange, Suzy thought, that she has not already jumped into the breach to defend her god Sevilla.

"Yes," said Lisbeth, "so dynamic that he won't even talk any more! Suzy, you can't deny that he hasn't spoken a word of English in two weeks."

"Don't exaggerate," said Peter. "He understood perfectly that we call his wife Bessie, and he calls her *Bi*."

"I've never heard him call her *Bi*."

"I have," said Suzy, "and if you hadn't made up your mind in advance that the experiment has failed, you would have heard him yourself."

"All right, so he calls Bessie 'Bi.' Bravo. What progress! One word. He's spoken one word in two weeks. Before the arrival of Bessie—or of Bi, rather—he used about forty words every day."

"There is something even more upsetting," said Bob, extending his supple arm and leaning it against the wall. "As we have all observed, Ivan now refuses all contact, he won't play any more, he won't even answer when we call his name. And when we try to get in the tank he comes and snaps at our legs."

There was a silence. When Bob spoke there was always a slightly theatrical quality to what he said that embarrassed everyone.

"It seems to me that Ivan's reaction is a normal one," said Michael with a melancholy air, not looking at anyone, his head on his chest.

Suzy gave him a keen look. People said that he looked like Peter because he had the same build, the same manner, the same dimples; but Peter, however lovable, was very resilient. It was as hard for him to get depressed as it was for a cork to go underwater. Michael, on the other hand, thought too much. Suzy looked at him quickly several times, and thought, How astonishing, he is handsome, even handsomer than Peter, more strength of character, certainly, more brilliant, but even so, for me it's been Peter right from the start, Peter is so disarming. Lisbeth wanted to say something but Michael went on, raising his voice: "It's very simple, we must realize one fact: Ivan is jealous."

And what about Michael, thought Suzy, is he jealous? But of whom, that great horse who acts like a basketball star, with her aggressiveness, her sharp tongue, and her bad manners?

"Listen," said Peter, leaning back and rubbing the back of his neck against Suzy's cool arm, "there may be another explanation. I don't know whether Dolphinese comes to a dolphin naturally or whether he has to learn to talk, like a human baby. But can't we say at least that Ivan is rediscovering his own language with Bessie, that this apprenticeship is engaging all his faculties, but that sooner or later he will come back to his human family?"

"What optimism!" said Lisbeth. "When he does come back to us

99

there's a strong probability that he will have completely forgotten the forty words of English we had so much trouble teaching him."

Suzy sat up straight in her chair and said with a trace of polite annoyance, "In any case, it seems very unscientific to make hypotheses about the future."

"Well, Peter started it," said Lisbeth coldly. She took the cigarette out of her mouth, squared her shoulders, and looked from one to the other.

Suzy was struck by the effectiveness of her look. Nobody could deny that Lisbeth had a talent for putting people in the wrong.

"Of course," she said, "everyone is entitled to his own opinion. If you don't want to recognize that the experiment has failed, fine. It's a free country. Meanwhile, what are we doing? Nothing. Oh, I'm quite aware," she said with a quiver of hate in her voice, "that there are various ways of doing nothing. One can be very busy, even passionately busy, and at the same time be doing nothing."

A glacial silence fell. What a bitch, thought Suzy, what an incredible bitch! Even Bob Manning looks embarrassed. And what about Maggie? Why isn't Maggie saying anything? An instant later she heard her own voice saying angrily, "Aren't you going to say anything, Maggie?"

Maggie started, looked up, and said, embarrassed, "I have nothing to say."

Michael sat up straight in his chair, hooked both hands in the belt of his shorts, and said, looking at Maggie, "He was my friend, faithful and just to me, but Brutus says he was ambitious, and Brutus is an honorable man."

"Bravo," said Peter.

Bob Manning sat down. He had suddenly retired into his shell. Even his gestures, usually so sweeping, had contracted. He was not looking at anyone. He was making himself invisible.

"Some people," said Lisbeth in the same hostile and aggressive voice, "have a knack for always being on the winning side. Well, that's their business. But nobody can keep me from noticing that for two weeks we've done nothing but watch them make love—I mean Bessie and Ivan," she added in a hissing voice.

"Oh!" said Maggie.

The exclamation hung in the air. Bob Manning stared into space with a sheepish and frightened expression; Maggie's face was inscrutable.

100

"Why don't you shut up?" said Michael suddenly in a controlled voice, staring at Lisbeth with flashing eyes. "I'm fed up with your manners."

Lisbeth stiffened. "If you think . . ."

"Shut up," repeated Michael violently. "Or I'll pick you up and throw you in the tank."

"And I'll help you," said Peter.

Lisbeth looked from one of the two young men to the other: There was no doubt about it, they were itching to carry out their threat. She's backing down, thought Suzy with a shiver of pleasure, she's backing down, now I've seen everything, Lisbeth backing down in front of the boys. A moment later she felt almost sorry for her. Bob and Maggie had deserted her. Lisbeth was sitting there speechless, rigid in her chair, alone against the world, trying to brave the violence of their disapproval.

"You bullies," she said with a rather unsuccessful attempt to sound disdainful.

"No, you're wrong," said Michael with a bitter smile. He leaned over the table and poured the rest of his Coke into his glass. "I'm not a bully, I'm that 'flower of American youth' which the President regrets sending to its death on the battlefields of Vietnam. . . ."

He paused, brandished his glass gravely in front of him as if he were making a toast, and drained it.

"I'm going to bed," said Lisbeth, getting up. "There's a limit to the amount of nonsense I can listen to in one evening."

"Same here," said Maggie, getting up too.

Lisbeth walked toward the door, tall, supple, athletic, followed closely by Maggie, who seemed absurdly short and awkward in her wake.

"Goodby, honorable Brutus," said Michael. He waved the four fingers of his right hand toward the door in a sign of derision.

How could I have been so wrong? thought Suzy with astonishment. He's not in love with her at all. He despises her.

"You talk as if you expected to be drafted next year," said Bob Manning, turning to Michael.

"And you," said Michael, "talk as if you think the war in Southeast Asia would be over in three years . . ."

The intercom buzzed. Peter picked up the receiver, put his hand over the mouthpiece, and said, "Michael, Sevilla wants to see you."

• • •

101

"Michael, will you walk down the road with me a little way?"

"With pleasure."

The road, whose terminal point was the lab, was a stony ribbon winding among rocks. In spite of the nearness of the sea, the air was warm. A big luminous orange moon lying low on the horizon cast spindle-shaped shadows at their feet.

"Michael, I have a favor to ask you. But first I'd like to ask you a question." Sevilla paused. "Here is the question. Do you ever have occasion, inside the lab, to criticize by implication the foreign policy of the United States?"

Michael stopped short and looked at Sevilla. "It happened this evening, just a moment ago." He added rather drily, "But it seems to me that I have the right to express an opinion."

"Not only do you have the right," said Sevilla, "but your right is protected by the Constitution." He went on: "Now, here is the favor I wanted to ask you. Let me make it clear that it is a personal favor. From now on when you are inside the lab, please refrain from expressing criticism of this kind."

"Is that an order?" asked Michael in a tense voice.

"Not at all. In this area I don't give you orders. This is a personal favor I'm asking you."

There was a silence. "Do you mean that the things I said this evening may be repeated and that if they are they may hurt you?"

Sevilla said slowly and distinctly, "They will certainly be repeated, and they will certainly be held against me."

"I don't see how."

"Because I'm the one who hired you."

"I see," said Michael. "Well, I must admit that I'm rather . . ." He went on in a different voice: "If I understand correctly, there is a spy among us?"

Sevilla did not answer.

"I'm sorry," said Michael, "I shouldn't have asked you that question. And yet, I want very much to ask you another."

"I know what it is," said Sevilla. "I won't answer that one either."

There was a silence, and Michael said with forced humor, "Well, that does tend to limit conversation a bit." He went on: "As for what you asked me, I promise."

Sevilla laid his hand on Michael's shoulder.

Patiently, perfidiously, day after day, Marian had stolen his sons, drop by drop she had infected them with the venom that she produced in abundance, little by little she had succeeded in estranging them from him, Well, thought Sevilla, straightening his shoulders, his hand still resting on Michael's shoulder, why confine oneself to a single family? Michael is also my son.

There was a silence. Michael understood what this silence meant and was reassured. "But what about you?" he asked in a slightly strained voice. "What do you think of our Asian policy?"

"Well," said Sevilla, letting his hand drop, "I'm not wild about it, but this is what I tell myself: I helped elect the President of the United States. It's up to him to take care of Vietnam, and it's up to me to take care of my dolphins. Everyone has his job."

"But suppose the President is pursuing a disastrous policy in Asia?"

"In my opinion," said Sevilla after a moment's reflection, "I do not possess the necessary information to make such a judgment. What would you think of the President if he tried to get involved in electronics without preliminary study?"

"It's not that complicated. If you just read the papers carefully there would be many things about the Vietnam situation that would disturb you." Michael put one hand in his pocket and felt ill at ease. Had he gone too far? He seemed to be lecturing to Sevilla and setting himself up as a model.

"Yes, I know," said Sevilla, "that's what you do. And perhaps you're right. But I don't have the time. To tell the truth, I can't afford the luxury of taking an interest in United States foreign policy."

"Even if that policy is leading to World War Three?"

"Oh, you're exaggerating," said Sevilla. "We haven't reached that point yet."

Michael did not answer. He felt discouraged. Even a man like Sevilla. Oh, the world is done for, he thought with rage. We're all ostriches, that's what we are. . . .

"I'm worried about Ivan," said Sevilla after a moment. "I don't know what to do."

Michael felt an irony. Ivan, yes, Ivan was really important; the world is on the edge of destruction and we're interested in the language of dolphins. At the same time he was moved that Sevilla had chosen to confide in him. The simplicity of the admission, the confidence it implied, the total lack of pretense. They were so close to each other emotionally, so far apart politically. Oh, how I would love to convince him, thought Michael with a fresh surge of hope.

"Perhaps we might separate Ivan from Bessie," he said more or less at random, because he felt that Sevilla expected an answer.

Sevilla walked a few steps in silence. "I've thought of that. It's the most obvious solution. But to be quite frank with you, I can't make up my mind to do it."

After a moment he added, "Perhaps you will think this feeling unworthy of a scientist, but it seems so cruel to me."

• • •

The single room of the rented bungalow was not air-conditioned, but it had large bay windows on opposite sides of the room, facing the rocks and the sea, which consisted of mahogany slats that could be adjusted to a parallel or oblique position depending on how much air you wanted to admit. A wide-meshed blue curtain insured privacy, as could easily be verified by going out on the terrace and walking around the house. Curiously, the absence of windowpanes had not satisfied the architect's desire for natural ventilation. None of the four walls was attached to the roof, and there was a sixteen-inch space between the roof and the wall on all four sides. The bungalow was no less revolutionary in its outer construction. It rested on a concrete slab which was in turn supported by H-shaped iron girders that bravely spanned a gap between two rocks. This slab hung about twenty yards over a small rocky creek which was reached by steps carved into the rock. Since the house was midway between the creek and the cliff, when you came from the road you had to leave your car in a makeshift shelter, go through a solid door between two enormous rocks, and walk down a steep path for about a hundred yards. Since this path was the only means of access, the furniture in the bungalow must have been hoisted up by means of pulleys and ropes. The concrete slab was surrounded on all four sides by a metal handrail which made it resemble the deck of a ship. When I think, said Arlette, leaning on the handrail with her shoulder against Sevilla's, that there are twenty yards of space under our feet I get chills down my spine, Don't say that, said Sevilla, I picked this place for weekends because it looks like a fortress, and also

104

because it has no windows, she looked at him, But why didn't you want windows? Oh, he said, laughing, for a very important reason, a gull flew right over their heads, I wonder what she's doing here, he said, she's the only one of her species, there must be an ascending breeze coming from the fault in the cliff, She's coasting, said Arlette, how delightful it must be, she looked up at Sevilla, her face soft and childlike, he took her in his arms, she had an intoxicating way of melting in his embrace, But first let's talk about serious things, he said in a voice that was getting a little hoarse, What do you mean, first? she asked raising her eyebrows, they looked at each other and burst out laughing, Sevilla felt the happiness flow through his body with a force that was almost unbearable, everything about their relationship was delightful, the gaiety, the games, the rapport, the unlimited trust.

Do you still feel the space under the slab? he asked, setting her down on the bed, Yes, but I don't care, we'll fall together, we'll go right through the concrete, we'll end up in the water down there, like Fa and Bi, their voices subsided, the last sound Sevilla heard was the triumphant cry of the gull, she had caught the breeze coming from the fault and was hovering motionless over the bungalow, the tips of her wings barely turned up, rocked by the warm evening wind, as helpless-looking as a dead leaf, and constantly uttering that short strident cry that was like the creaking of a sail against its block, as Sevilla's head touched the pillow he heard it again, he often dreamed about flying, a dream so intense and so frequent that when he woke up he could hardly believe it was not real, he was running on the hard sand of a beach in a high wind, he stretched his arms out to the sides, he pushed off vigorously with his heel, he rose effortlessly, he cleaved the air a few yards over the water, his ears whistled, he soared without moving, he experienced a marvelous sense of lightness and power, he turned and looked at Arlette, she was lying on the bed as if it were a cloud, looking at him with a tender and mischievous expression, he waited impatiently for her smile to appear, she always had that little quiver at the corners of her mouth, they were always ready to turn up, as if her whole face was permeated with joy, and when her smile broke through she surrendered to it entirely, with good will, with tenderness, he raised himself on his elbow and leaned over, There's still a little daylight, he said, thrusting his hand in Arlette's hair, it would be a shame to let it go to waste, she smiled at him, We could go and lie on the chairs on the terrace, No, he said, how about a little exercise, let's walk down to the creek, if we keep on this way we'll turn into centaurs, the top half human and the bottom half in the shape of a Buick, That would be too bad for the bottom half, said Arlette, Sevilla laughed, nowhere, never in his life, no matter how far back in time he went, had he laughed more often or with more real gaiety.

When you sat on the tiny triangle of round pebbles by the creek it was impressive to look up and see the concrete slab of the bungalow straddling the fault in the cliff, seen from below it looked as ridiculously fragile as a sheet of plywood, the surf died three yards from their feet with a rolling of stones, if you closed your eyes it sounded like an enormous dice box in which dozens of dice were knocking against each other before being flung all together by the furious hand of a gambler, I'm worried, said Arlette, I think there's bad feeling in the team, There is, said Sevilla with a shrug, Lisbeth has elected herself leader of His Majesty's Opposition, Maggie is following in her footsteps, they accuse me of inaction, Arlette looked at him, I must say I admire your leniency, if I were in your place I think I'd— Oh no, believe me, he said, that would be a serious mistake, it is often wiser and more truly courageous not to answer an attack, Arlette looked at him, her eyes shone with indignation, I can't understand those two girls, Sevilla threw up his hands, It's very simple, darling, they're jealous, even though they're not jealous of the same person, he looked at Arlette with raised eyebrows, The real problem is Ivan, if I had solved that problem it wouldn't matter what those two idiots did or said, unfortunately I'm not finding a solution, and what's worse, I can't even concentrate, I'm like Ivan, he added with a little laugh, I'm so happy that I don't feel like working any more, oh, I know, it seems very simple, Ivan has stopped talking now that he has Bessie, the obvious conclusion is to take Bessie away from him, but in the first place, he said with a sudden emotion that made his dark eyes shine, I loathe the idea of separating them, since he started to talk my relation to Ivan is no longer the relation of a man to an animal, but a relationship between two people, and in the second place, he went on emphatically, I *sense* that that is not the solution, if I take Bessie away from him it will be very traumatic and what good will it do?

106

At best, he will consent to relearn and use again the forty words he has learned, and we won't be any farther along, there is another solution, but what it is I can't imagine. He paused for a few seconds and went on, looking at Arlette out of the corner of his eye, Lisbeth would say that my creative drive has not been increased, he laughed briefly, but I won't accept such a negative point of view, anyway, what does she know about it, poor girl, she's one of those people who spend their lives wondering what sex they belong to, which means she is condemned by her nature to sacrificial ideologies, but in my opinion it's happiness and nothing else that helps a man develop, never will I believe that there is some kind of magical power in frustration.

They were sitting side by side on the pebbles with their backs leaning against an enormous round rock, Sevilla's arm around Arlette's shoulders, and their heads so close together that they could hear each other easily in spite of the sound of the surf, Did Maggie tell you about Bob? asked Arlette, You mean the problem of setting the date for her engagement? asked Sevilla with a sigh, for five years I've been hearing about that, the only part that changes is the beneficiary, I was one myself, so was James Dean, And to think, said Arlette, that she knew James Dean so well, that has always amazed me, Sevilla sighed, Last year I had occasion to pass through Denver, I can testify that the place exists, the maps of the United States do not lie, Aunt Agatha exists, I had a long talk with her, the old leather armchair exists too, I saw it, I even sat in it, but the truth stops there, I can't believe it! cried Arlette, Sevilla shook his head, A daydream, that's all, poor Maggie, she raises a terrible problem, and one that is all the more terrible because nobody is interested in it, the problem of the ugly girl, after all, an ugly girl has just as much desire as any other for a man to take her in his arms.

There was a silence and Arlette said, I wasn't talking about her engagement, but about an incident that she promised me she would report to you. The day before yesterday I walked into Maggie's office during lunch hour and caught Bob rummaging through her papers, he went pale and it took him a moment before he said that Maggie had sent him to get her scissors, it was a lie, of course, I checked with Maggie immediately, Sevilla frowned, Maggie didn't say anything to me, but even if she had she wouldn't have told me anything I don't know, he went on, I've known what Bob was up to since May fifteenth. He went on after a moment, That day, if you remember, all of us except for the guards left the lab to go on a picnic, and I had told the guards that in our absence they were going to receive a visit from two "electricians," Two electricians? repeated Arlette, he nodded, I know, it sounds like a grade-B spy movie, a Flint or a James Bond, unfortunately, Arlette dear, it's true, James Bondism is becoming the air we breathe, the two experts discovered that all the wiring in *every* room in the lab had been duplicated by equipment invisible to the naked eye which recorded all conversations on a miniature tape recorder installed in the wall behind Bob's bed, That's dreadful, said Arlette, it's even worse than I thought, Don't worry, said Sevilla, Bob isn't a Russian spy, he's a good American, it was for patriotic motives that he agreed to become Mr. C's antenna.

But what about the "electricians"? asked Arlette, stunned, Let's call them the "Blues" and Mr. C's friends the "Greens," said Sevilla, sometimes I wonder whether I can really trust the pebbles we're sitting on, he said, looking around, I suspect concealed microphones everywhere, And you laugh about it! said Arlette, I have to, I'd go out of my mind if I took it all seriously, anyway, the Blues scrupulously respected the wiring of the Greens so that Bob continues to play his role, all they did was copy it with an identical installation which ends in my office so that I can transmit to the Blues the same thing that Bob transmits to the Greens, It's enough to drive you crazy, said Arlette, I feel as if I'm entering a world of madmen, But it's clear as day, said Sevilla, we are being watched by two competing agencies which are spying on each other while they are watching us, But that's absurd, said Arlette, why are they in competition? Sevilla smiled, According to my information, internal competition is the golden rule of all espionage, there is never *one* secret police in a country, there are always several, and sometimes there are even opposing groups within a single police force, police are snakes, because they're coiled upon themselves they end up biting their own tails.

Arlette leaned her head on his shoulder, I don't know whether you ought to be telling me all this, darling, I may be a nasty little spy working for Russia, I can reassure you on that subject, said Sevilla, the Greens made a thorough investigation of you, and of me too, for that matter, the result is two extremely detailed biographies which the Blues have somehow managed to get their hands on, they haven't sent me yours, It's just as well, said Arlette, But they did inform me that the conclusion was completely favorable, Arlette burst out laughing, I don't know whether I should feel reassured, they may be wrong, Never! said Sevilla with bitter irony, they're never wrong, the Blues sent me my own biography, its accuracy and detail are incredible, it even told me some things about my life that I didn't know, it's rather terrifying in a way, I feel as if I've been living in a goldfish bowl, under the eye of an omniscient god, And the conclusion? asked Arlette, Sevilla made a face, Favorable on the whole, but there are still some troublesome little details, my origins, for example, they went to a lot of trouble to find out who my ancestors were and they did not altogether succeed, so they are wondering am I a gypsy, am I part Jewish, am I even part Arab, or am I the good honest Galician that my grandfather claimed to be? And is that so important to them? asked Arlette, laughing, It must be, since they worry about it, another example of the thoroughness of my biographers: in 1936, you know how old I was, I confessed to some students at Columbia University that I believed in free love, and that is bad, it's true, my biographer or biographers hasten to add that I have been married twice since then, Arlette laughed, But that's not the worst, in 1955 in answer to an investigator who asked whether I believed in the immortality of the soul, I replied, *It's not a question of belief but of knowledge,* and that is very bad, Arlette looked up, Why? Because they conclude from this that I am an atheist, and because to be an atheist in this country where everyone pretends to believe in God is to be suspected of having Communist sympathies, however, in 1958, I had a three-month affair (they know the dates almost down to the day) with a Hungarian countess who I did not know was Hungarian or a countess or, above all, an agent of the CIA, this lady provided a very complete analysis of my character, my tastes, my habits, including my sexual habits, How revolting, said Arlette, Oh, said Sevilla, I know that important political figures and atomic scientists are all in the same boat, for me it all began when I became interested in dolphins, from that moment there have been two investigations being conducted simultaneously, I have been observing the dolphins and they have been observing me.

I'm talking about the Blues, Sevilla went on, the Greens became interested in me only recently, after Mr. C's visit, in fact it's a miracle that the Blues succeeded in hiding me from the Greens as long as they did, Let's go back to the Hungarian woman, said Arlette, If you like, she claims, among other things, that I'm not really an atheist, according to her I'm a Catholic who has wandered from the faith but who retains a great deal of nostalgia for it, Is that true? asked Arlette, Not that I know of, but that doesn't mean anything, sometimes I think they know me better than I know myself, but the greatest service the Hungarian woman did me was when she stated categorically that politically speaking I am a kind of illiterate, and that is excellent, Arlette raised her eyebrows, For the Greens a man who is vitally interested in politics without being a politician is already a bit suspect, political innocence is a form of virginity, once you've lost it you can expect the worst, at least that is the attitude of the Greens, according to the Blues.

What I don't understand, said Arlette, is why the Blues sent you your biography, So I could tell them in writing what I think of it, Arlette laughed, That seems so naïve! But it isn't, darling, their psychologists will find all kinds of things in my answers, whether they're sincere or not, there was a silence, I'd like to ask you, is there a difference between the Blues and the Greens in their attitude toward you? Yes, the Blues watch and protect me with a touch of benevolence, the Greens watch and protect me with a touch of antipathy, Antipathy? Oh yes, C can't forgive me for not being a Wasp, for being a foreigner, which means that I'm capable of anything.

I feel dizzy, said Arlette with a sigh, I wonder whether they'll discover that I am descended from slaves, an atheist, politically deflowered, and practicing free love with Professor Sevilla, Oh, they know that already, said Sevilla, What, she cried, horrified, are you sure? Did they tell you so? No, but I assume they know, in fact I imagine they're delighted about it, it makes their work so much simpler, And what about you, said Arlette, do you think you're simplifying the work of these gentlemen by renting a place like this for the weekend? I am subjected to this espionage, said Sevilla, I accept it as necessary, but there's no reason why I should facilitate it, as a matter of fact, I have mistrusted its excesses ever since I found out that the CIA has tape recordings of the diversions of

110

President Sukarno and his wives, Arlette brought her two palms to her cheeks, But that's revolting! Sevilla nodded, And what's more, it's unnecessary, I can't see Sukarno discussing world politics at times like those, getting back to this bungalow, I chose it precisely because of its isolation, its difficulty of access, And don't forget its lack of windows, said Arlette, Sevilla laughed, I'm coming to that, the Greens have a gadget with which you can listen to a conversation going on inside a house from the outside by amplifying the vibrations transmitted to the windowpanes by the voices of the speakers, Yes, I know what you're going to say, it's rather frightening, the old idea of private life no longer exists, we live in glass cages, observed, analyzed, dissected down to the last detail, Arlette took his hand and squeezed it, Don't you sometimes feel like a prisoner? He looked up, I used to, but not since I have you, he paused and looked into her eyes, You are freedom.

VI

"I have called you together for a very definite reason," said Sevilla, his manner cold and reserved. Arlette was sitting at his right, Maggie at his left, Peter, Suzy and Michael opposite him, Bob and Lisbeth to Maggie's left. In the middle of the group was a desk with a tape recorder. Sevilla ran his eye over his listeners. His Majesty's Opposition was grouped on his left. He thought impatiently, What an absurd situation, it would have been so easy for me to be a tyrannical employer, you really had to be very patient to respect your colleagues' freedom of expression even while they were abusing it.

"First of all, I would like to remind you of the rules of absolute discretion under which we operate, rules which you accepted when you came here. As you know, our project receives no publicity, it is subsidized by a government agency, and it is only to that agency that we are to communicate the results of our studies. Any violation of this rule would be a serious breach of our commitments, yours as well as mine. As you also know, I have always tried to give you the greatest possible freedom of expression and criticism. But this freedom does not extend beyond the threshold of the lab. Neither our successes nor our failures should be communicated to persons unfamiliar with our project, however highly placed they may be. I repeat, this is an unbreakable rule."

Sevilla paused, looked around attentively, and thought, Mission accomplished: Bob and Maggie neutralized by their bad consciences, Lisbeth isolated. He did not want to renounce his liberal-

112

ism, but still he wasn't going to let himself be stepped on in the discussion.

He went on: "Today is the third of June. On the sixth of May, three weeks ago, Bessie was introduced into Ivan's tank. The experiment did not produce the results we had anticipated. However, we can say that it already has positive elements. In the first place, we have shown—and this was by no means self-evident—that a baby dolphin raised entirely by man in a human milieu is capable, on reaching adulthood, of entering into communication with a female of his species and of mating with her. Secondly, we have confirmed the fact that the male dolphin, even when raised in total solitude, remains sexually very selective and does not accept just any female as a companion. Thirdly, we have confirmed the dolphin's aptitude for forming deep emotional ties. Although the honeymoon activities have diminished in frequency and violence, Ivan's behavior toward Bessie gives evidence of a passionate devotion. It is at least partly because of this devotion and its exclusive quality that his human family can no longer enter into contact with him. In the fourth place, it seems probable that Ivan and Bessie have exchanged knowledge. We are sure of this in the case of Ivan: He has initiated Bessie into all his human games—ball, rubber ring, stick. Moreover, insofar as we are able to advance this hypothesis, Bessie has taught Ivan Dolphinese. At any rate, it is incontestable that both quantitatively and qualitatively there is a vast difference between the whistling sounds that Ivan made before the sixth of May and those he makes today. When we are farther along in the study of the whistling language of dolphins, the comparison between these two categories of whistling will be of the greatest interest to the investigator."

Peter raised his hand and Sevilla gave him permission to speak.

"If I understand correctly, you think that Ivan's whistling before the sixth of May, that is, before his meeting with Bessie, was comparable to the babbling of infants, and that he has now made a transition from babbling to the language of dolphins."

Sevilla nodded his head. "That's what I assume. Bessie has replaced the mother in the educational task. Let me insist, this is only a hypothesis. But I believe that in three weeks Ivan has learned an enormous number of things from Bessie and that this is one more reason why he refuses all contact with us. His mind is too busy."

113

"I don't see the point of making that kind of hypothesis," said Lisbeth, "since we can't verify it. At the present time we don't even know whether we can talk about a language of dolphins."

"One always has the right to make hypotheses," said Sevilla serenely, "as long as one doesn't offer them as established truths. Besides, if we didn't make hypotheses, we couldn't conduct experiments to verify them."

He paused to allow Lisbeth to answer, but she said nothing.

"To continue," said Sevilla. "Although the experiment does have a certain number of positive elements all of which you may not have noticed . . ." He paused in the middle of the sentence.

"Not all," said Suzy.

Michael, Peter, Arlette and Bob nodded. Lisbeth remained impassive.

"It does, however," said Sevilla, "present one obviously negative aspect. The presence of Bessie has certainly altered Ivan's behavior, he has certainly become happier, more confident, and more dynamic, but—"

"But it has not increased his creative drive," said Lisbeth.

Sevilla looked at her with his dark eyes. "I will give you permission to speak if you wish," he said coldly, "but I cannot allow you to interrupt me."

"I beg your pardon," said Lisbeth.

"It's not serious," said Sevilla.

Michael, Suzy and Peter exchanged looks.

"What we did not foresee," said Sevilla, "is Ivan's complete abandonment of his human family in favor of the female dolphin. In my opinion Ivan has not become mentally inactive, but communication with us no longer interests him. He has reverted to species."

Suzy raised her hand.

"Suzy?"

"Do you feel that there has been regression?"

"Not if we assume, as I said, that there is a language of dolphins and a wisdom that is transmitted by this means from mother to child and, in the present case, from Bessie to Ivan."

Lisbeth raised her hand.

"Lisbeth?"

"Once again, I don't see the purpose of these speculations."

114

"And yet it seems obvious to me," said Sevilla. "We are trying to understand what has happened."

"In my opinion it would be far more worthwhile to recognize that the experiment is a failure."

"The experiment is a failure for the moment, but we have not given it any time limit."

"It has already gone on for three weeks."

"That's nothing. There are experiments that have gone on for years."

"I admire your patience."

"Well, you're in a good position to admire it."

There were smiles. Lisbeth sat up straight in her chair and said, "Do you feel that I am going too far in the discussion?"

Sevilla looked at her, paused to give his answer more force, and said, "Yes, I do."

"I don't agree," said Lisbeth.

"In that case, we will discuss it later. Right now, it is not your behavior that we are studying."

There was a silence. Lisbeth was sitting up straight in her chair, her shoulders squared, her short-cropped head held high. She's like Joan of Arc, thought Sevilla, and what's worse, it looks as if she wants to force me to burn her.

"I am coming to the purpose of our meeting," said Sevilla. "I have a question to ask you, a question that I have been asking myself and that you have all been asking for three weeks. We have lost contact with Ivan: What do you think we should do to restore it?"

There was a rather long silence and Bob raised his hand.

"Bob?"

"I would like to make a suggestion. To tell the truth, it is rather a vague suggestion, but I am talking off the top of my head. When you train an animal you generally use a system of rewards and punishments. This system enables man to influence the animal's behavior and to get what he wants from him. Up to now we have rewarded Ivan by feeding him, by petting him, and by giving him Bessie. We have only used rewards. Wouldn't it be possible to start using punishment?"

"You have a point," said Sevilla, "but your suggestion, translated literally, is not practicable." He paused. "It is impossible to punish

115

a dolphin. The dolphin is an animal of great dignity. He does not accept punishment, and immediately cuts off all communication with you. There is even good reason to wonder whether he regards the fish you give him as a reward. Take seals: They are very greedy, you can make them do anything to get the food they like. But not dolphins. Wood claims that he has seen a dolphin do circus tricks for a whole day without accepting any food. It is out of friendship for you or interest in his work that the dolphin does his tricks. The fish you give him is only a bonus. . . . Any more suggestions?"

There was a silence and Lisbeth raised her hand.

"Lisbeth?"

"In my opinion there is only one solution. We must take Ivan out of the tank and separate him from Bessie."

Sevilla threw her a keen look. "You mean we must take Bessie out of the tank and separate her from Ivan. After all, it's Ivan we're interested in."

"That's what I meant," said Lisbeth. "How stupid of me." She went on—blushing and, for the first time, acting embarrassed—"I'm sorry, I reversed the names."

"It doesn't matter," said Sevilla, still looking at her attentively. "I hope you don't bear poor Ivan any ill will."

"Certainly not," said Lisbeth, "I just misspoke. Let me go on," she continued in a steadier voice. "My suggestion is to separate them, since their cohabitation has not had the anticipated results."

"I have considered that solution," said Sevilla slowly. "I think we've all considered it. But I find it very repugnant. I am afraid such a separation would bring on a serious trauma in Ivan."

"Well," said Lisbeth almost triumphantly, "this trauma is the price he will pay for renewing contact with us."

Sevilla frowned. "You mean it is the price that *we* will make him pay to renew a contact which he does not desire."

For the first time since the beginning of the meeting Sevilla seemed irritated. He added drily, "The trouble with sacrifices is that the people who recommend them almost never have to make them themselves."

"Is that a personal attack?" said Lisbeth, thrusting her chin forward defiantly.

Sevilla threw up his hands impatiently. "No, it is an attack upon a certain concept of sacrifice. And please stop supplying fuel for your own stake, I have no intention of lighting it."

Sevilla felt that this image was clearer to himself than it could be to Lisbeth. But clear or not, it had an unexpected effect. It reduced her to silence.

Sevilla went on: "There is one point that I want to emphasize. The trauma that we may inflict on Ivan by separating him from Bessie may be much more serious than you suppose. In 1954, a young female dolphin named Pauline was captured with the help of a hook that wounded her. She was placed in a tank with an adult male who helped her to remain afloat and who became very fond of her. The wound was treated with penicillin, and from the outside it seemed healed. But a few months later the infection caused an internal abscess which killed her. When she died the male gave frantic indications of despair. He swam around her body constantly, refused all food from then on, and died three days later of a broken heart. Even assuming that Ivan won't go to such extremes, it is hard to imagine that he won't feel some bitterness toward us for depriving him of Bessie, and I can't see how we'll be able to renew any kind of contact with him."

He paused. "Any more suggestions?"

Michael raised his hand.

"Michael?"

"I note that the only link that now remains between us and Ivan is the food we give him. It is when we give him fish twice a day that there is still a slight degree of contact between him and us. Isn't there something we could try from that angle?"

"Excellent," said Sevilla. "With your permission, I will clarify your idea, for it is the same one I had in the back of my mind. Suppose we omit the eleven o'clock feeding, and at the end of the afternoon the six o'clock feeding. We create in Ivan a privation which must force him to seek contact with us and to start a dialogue with us himself, if only to ask us for fish. Naturally, we will give it to him: That will be his reward for asking for it in our language. This brings us back to the system of rewards and punishments advocated by Bob, but in a non-traumatic, indirect form."

Sevilla paused and looked at the others. "Do you think we should try this experiment?"

All acquiesced except Lisbeth.

Sevilla looked at her. He was not going to let her take refuge in sulking. "Lisbeth?"

There was a silence. "Yes," said Lisbeth with effort. "Why not?"

117

Sevilla rose briskly. He looked at Arlette and his face was happy. For the first time in three weeks he was doing something, and the team had closed ranks behind him.

• • •

Maggie? said Bob's voice through the bedroom door, are you alone? She said yes and adjusted her bathrobe, she was lying on her bed, a novel in her hand, Bob came in, Am I disturbing you? Of course you're not, he had on light gray slacks, white linen shoes and a periwinkle-blue shirt, he sat down on Lisbeth's bed, his brows knotted, his knees pressed together and his long delicate hands clasped on his knees, Maggie, he said, as if he were giving an actor his cue in a domestic drama, did you tell Sevilla? Of course not, I promised, and incidentally, I've never regretted a promise so much in my life, it's the first time I've ever kept anything from Sevilla, and it hasn't made me very happy, Then it must be Arlette, he said, because *he knows*, I'm sure of it, you observed his glacial coldness toward me, and if he'd been the only one, but Arlette too, Peter, Michael and even Suzy, they don't even speak to me any more, I've obviously become some sort of pariah, but what can I do? he said extending his long flexible arms as if he were nailed to a cross, I can't very well ask them, for God's sake what do you suspect me of? They'd laugh in my face, how can I defend myself when I don't even know what crime I'm being accused of? All this is tragically absurd, Maggie, you read *The Trial*, well, the situation I'm living in is truly Kafkaesque, he paused, dropped his hands to his sides on the bed, the long spindle-shaped fingers resting elegantly on the bedspread, and lowering his long black lashes over his eyes, said in a low, flat voice, Maggie, I think I am going to kill myself, he looked at Maggie from behind his lashes, she put her book on the night table and said calmly, What madness, you're getting all worked up, nobody's angry at you, not even Sevilla, I know Sevilla better than you do, when he acts cold it means he's up to something, yesterday his main intention was to intimidate Lisbeth, Bob looked up slowly, Then what was the point of his sermon on secrecy? Apparently, said Maggie, he's afraid Lisbeth's criticisms will be repeated outside the lab, the door opened suddenly, Lisbeth appeared in shorts and bra, a towel in her hand and a cigarette between her lips, she slammed the door behind her, Still

118

here! she exclaimed, looking at Bob, What kind of a boy are you, always hanging around women? scram, please, I have to change, Excuse me, said Bob, getting up from the bed all smiles, running his eyes over Lisbeth's bronzed athletic shoulders, Maggie thought with irritation, He who is so sensitive, she can say anything she likes to him, he never gets mad, he even seems to like being bullied by this big horse, Well, are you leaving? Lisbeth went on, throwing her towel on the bed without even looking at it, she crushed out her cigarette in the ashtray and putting her hand behind her back, unhooked her bra, her breasts appeared, enormous and milky, Bob went pale, his cheeks quivered as if he had been slapped and he disappeared so fast that he seemed to be sucked through the door, Oh, Lisbeth, said Maggie with indignation, you're impossible, you shocked him terribly, he's such a prude, This is my room, said Lisbeth arrogantly, pulling off her shorts and her underpants at the same time, Maggie looked away, Lisbeth's manners horrified her, Lisbeth was nude in front of her bedside table, she took a cigarette and lit it expertly, So are you, she said accusingly, looking at Maggie contemptuously, you're a prude, your hypocrisy makes me throw up, if you ask me, it all comes from attaching too much importance to sex, well, I don't give a damn about sex, mine or anybody else's, it leaves me absolutely cold, she added, holding her head high, she threw on a bathrobe and flung herself face down on the bed, After all, said Maggie, it's not Bob's fault if he's old-fashioned and a little afraid of girls, he hasn't any sisters and he lost his mother at the age of twelve, his father is a sadistic puritan who terrorizes him, he was brought up in a boarding school without any women around, that's why he didn't develop, Bob is a child, I've always said so, Well, marry him, said Lisbeth wearily, go be his mama, Unfortunately, said Maggie as if she had not heard the second half of the remark, I've been meaning to tell you, Lisbeth, everything is up in the air, I don't even know if I'll be able to announce our engagement this summer as I've been intending to, there's a serious difference between us, Lisbeth, I must tell you about it, Bob wants children desperately and I don't want them, Lisbeth rolled over onto her back, raised herself on one elbow, and looked at Maggie accusingly, Well, that's a new one, since when don't you want children, and why not? Oh, I don't know, said Maggie with embarrassment, I like children when they're eight or ten years old, but I don't really like babies, What a joke, said Lisbeth contemptuously, if there's one female on earth who would adore to mess with a kid and get her hands all covered with shit, it's you, No, I mean it, said Maggie weakly, Oh why don't you be quiet, said Lisbeth, I'm getting fed up with your little stories about mammals, they bore me, she inhaled her cigarette with an economical and boyish gesture, sent a cloud of smoke through her nose, and lay there silently staring at the window shade, I'm not so sure that the subject bores you, said Maggie with ominous sweetness, on the contrary, I have the impression that in your own way you too are capable of being passionately interested, Spare me your brilliant analyses, Lisbeth snapped, she looked away and lowered her voice, I'm sorry if I picked on you, I think I'm a little nervous, they looked at each other, smiled rather reservedly and pulled in their claws, a shadow passed in front of the shade, Lisbeth leaped to her feet, what's the matter? You scared me, said Maggie, It's Arlette, said Lisbeth, I've been watching for her, I have to talk to her, she left slamming the door behind her, Maggie clasped her hands behind her head and lay down again, How tiring she can be with that display of virile aggressiveness, she always seems to want to prove that she's a man, as if she could fool anybody with that obscene chest of hers, Maggie freed her right hand and slipped it discreetly under her bathrobe, they were small and perfect, Arlette and I, we have the same little slim and feminine figure, no wonder Sevilla turned to her when I rejected him, Maggie stretched and closed her eyes, Bob was sitting on the bed in front of her, so elegant, so refined, he never crossed his legs, he was sitting very erect, he was tall, with that distinguished look that long legs give you, he was wearing a suit, his pretty, dark, aristocratic head glowed over his dazzling white shirt front, he gave her his arm, she was surrounded by a cloud of adorable white veils, they walked out of the church, she had had to be converted in order to marry him, Aunt Agatha sat heartbroken in the old leather armchair in Denver and me at her feet trying to console her, Maggie, don't tell me you're going to marry according to the rites of those Papists, Bob and I have been converted together, Father Donovan taught us the catechism, he was a nice Irishman with blue eyes and big white badly spaced teeth, the church is new, dazzlingly white, I walk out of the church, petite and slim in my white veils, Bob is beside me, so handsome, so svelte,

120

my hand trembles in his, we are terribly moved, the flashbulbs pop, Sevilla walks over to me, he is in tails, graying at the temples and looking like a Castilian lord, Maggie, he says to me in a halting voice, please accept my best wishes for, he can't finish, he bites his lips, tears fill his black eyes, just then Arlette looks at him and understands, in a split second her face crumples and fades, ravaged by age and vulgarity, I feel great pity for her, I press Sevilla's hand and whisper in his ear, "*Amigo,* if you love me, think of her."

Arlette got up, Sit down, Lisbeth, she said, pointing to a chair, sitting down across from Lisbeth with a patient and reserved air, Lisbeth looked at Arlette, she felt intimidated, she was always intimidated by grace, there was in Arlette a perfection so rare in every curve, she was so small and so pretty that you wanted to take her on your lap like a child, like a child, too, she radiated the charm of inaccessibility, she looked at you with her serene eyes and said nothing, even her silences were part of her mystery, she was so sweet and so simple that she seemed easy to know, but she wasn't, she was surrounded by a fortress of silence, but there was more to it than that, Lisbeth felt that she would never get to her, she felt as if they were separated by enormous ramparts behind which Arlette lived with her smile, her eyes, and her pretty body in the crude world of men, Arlette, said Lisbeth in a low, trembling voice, I hate to intrude in other people's business but you know how fond of you I am, we're friends, I must talk to you, I wouldn't be doing my duty if I saw you starting down a dangerous path and didn't warn you, you must realize that the road you are taking is a dead end, it's not as if it were someone your own age like Michael or Peter, do you realize that he is twenty-five years older than you, when you're forty he'll be sixty-five, when you're fifty he'll be seventy-five, it's madness, the figures alone prove it, Arlette raised her eyebrows, Oh, I know, said Lisbeth, you're going to give me examples from the Bible, you're going to tell me that at fifty you won't be so young yourself and that anyway a woman ages faster than a man, but you can't beat arithmetic, Arlette, such an enormous difference in age dooms the affair to failure from the start, I beg you to listen to me, Arlette, it's really scandalous, he's old enough to be your father, you're going to tell me that the point is that he isn't, but that doesn't make it any less shocking, excuse me, I'm not a prude, but I find it absolutely disgusting, no, Arlette, you'll never make me be-

121

lieve that you can *love* a man his age, you don't know what love is, you can smile all you like, Arlette, you don't know, you can't know, believe me, for the past two weeks I've been worrying about you constantly, I can't sleep any more, it breaks my heart to see you giving the best years of your life for nothing, you're throwing yourself away, that's the truth, and he's playing with your life, if only it were a serious thing with him, but he's a Latin, a ladies' man, he suffers from a Don Juan complex, his interest in a woman can't sustain itself more than a few weeks, remember Mrs. Ferguson, how infatuated he was with her and how cruelly he dropped her, the poor woman called every day, you'll suffer the same fate, Arlette, it's quite obvious, you ought to realize yourself that you'll never be anything more to him than a number in a series, Arlette, I beg of you, pull yourself together, open your eyes, and admit to yourself that you're simply a new toy which he'll break and throw away when he has exhausted its novelty, he'll find himself other toys to increase his creative drive, as he puts it, don't tell me you can respect a man like that, I'd never believe a girl as fine as you can admire someone so frivolous, so weak, so lazy, even if he does manage to cover up his character faults with an impressive manner, Arlette glanced at her watch, looked at Lisbeth, and said in an even voice as she rose, It is almost eight o'clock, if you will excuse me, I must dress for dinner, You haven't listened to me, cried Lisbeth in a choked voice, On the contrary, said Arlette, I have listened with a great deal of attention, you have used two arguments that cancel each other out, What do you mean cancel each other out? It's quite clear, Arlette went on crisply, if I am to be discarded like a broken toy in a few months, or even in a few weeks, you will certainly admit that the problem of excessive seniority will not arise, but if, on the other hand, the present state of things still exists when I am fifty, then the question of sexual instability will not have arisen, Ah, you argue like him already, cried Lisbeth, rushing out of the room with eyes full of despair.

•   •   •

EXPERIMENT OF JUNE 5, 1970
(Report dictated by Professor Sevilla)

Ivan and Bessie have not been fed either at eleven o'clock or at six o'clock and the tank is off bounds for the rest of the day: Nobody is to be seen by the dolphins. However, by means of a one-way mirror previously applied to the porthole, observation of the couple continues without their being able to see the observer. Moreover, the different sounds emitted under the water as well as in the air continue to be recorded.

At noon Ivan and Bessie show signs of agitation. At twelve ten Ivan puts his head out of the water and calls "Pa" several times energetically. At twelve thirty he emerges three-quarters out of the water and, moving backwards in this position with the help of powerful movements of his caudal fin, looks all around, obviously in the hope of seeing some member of the team around the tank. I observe him through binoculars behind the Venetian blind in my office. He cries "Fish!" five times vigorously. At one o'clock he appears again in the same position, but after looking in every direction he disappears beneath the water. No doubt he feels that there is no point in speaking since he does not see anyone.

From eleven o'clock to one Bessie exchanges a series of very animated whistles with Ivan, but makes no appearance outside the water. Of the two, it is Ivan who is responsible for relations with men. Bessie is not unfriendly but very reserved, and in three weeks we have made no progress in our efforts to bring her closer to her human family.

From one o'clock to six o'clock Ivan and Bessie resume their customary games.

At six P.M., the hour for the second feeding, the agitation resumes. Three times—at six eleven, six twenty-six, and six forty-five—Ivan emerges from the water as previously, looks around in all directions, but says nothing. At six fifty-two he appears again and cries in a very piercing and strident voice, "Pa!"

I decide to appear. He sees me before I even reach the tank and cries, "Fish!" I approach. Here is the dialogue:

SEVILLA: Fa, what do you want?
IVAN: Fish!
SEVILLA: Listen!
IVAN: Sen!
SEVILLA: Pa give fish tonight.
IVAN: Night!
SEVILLA: Yes. Pa give fish tonight.
IVAN: Kay! [For Okay]

Then I try to start a game. I throw him a ball and say, "Fa, fetch ball!"

But he immediately disappears under the water and rejoins Bessie. He has my promise and that is enough for him. However, there is an animated exchange of whistles between him and Bessie.

123

No doubt he is informing her that they will be fed when the sun goes down.

At dusk I appear with a pail of fish and sit down on one of the rafts. Ivan swims over immediately. Enthusiastic whistling and varied sounds. Bessie swims over too, but remains about two yards away. I pick up a fish and say, "Fa give fish Bi!"

He says, "Bi!" He receives the fish and takes it to Bessie. I pick up another fish and I show it to him. "Fish for Fa!"

He repeats "Fa!" and takes the fish and swallows it.

I continue alternately giving him a fish for Bi and a fish for himself. Then I pretend to make a mistake and I give Fa two fish in a row. He corrects me at once, vigorously crying "Bi!" and giving the fish to Bessie.

When the feeding is over I ask Arlette to hand me her transistor radio. I show it to Ivan and say to him, "Fa wants music?"

(Before the sixth of May, whenever he saw one of us holding a transistor he would cry, "Zick!")

But he refuses to let himself be seduced. He dives into the water and begins playing with Bessie again. She has saved her last fish and they pretend to fight over it. I call him several times without success.

Discussion:

As anticipated, the fast created a need for contact. At least one encouraging conclusion can be drawn from the experiment: Ivan has not lost his English. He understood everything I said to him, and he uttered seven words: Pa, fish, sen (for listen), night (for tonight), kay (for okay), Bi (for Bessie), Fa (for Ivan). On the other hand, something else emerges that is much less satisfactory: Ivan voluntarily limited his contact with us to what was strictly necessary. Perhaps he understood that the fast was a kind of blackmail to induce him to resume the dialogue. In this case, he conned us: He obtained his fish with a minimum of words. Perhaps we ought to change our mental habits where he is concerned, treat Ivan more like a person, and try to persuade him to speak to us instead of trying to force him to do it by mechanical means.

The experiment will have to be repeated in order to confirm or invalidate the above remarks; but I expect only limited results.

• • •

"Don't misunderstand me," said Michael, "I'm not a conscientious objector," he was lying face down on the burning sand with

124

his head resting on his forearm and his face turned toward Peter, Suzy was sitting on the other side of Peter, her eyes following the movement of the waves, the surf was gentle, from shore to horizon the ocean was streaked with three parallel bands, whitish, petroleum blue, and purplish red, it was very hot, a fine light gray mist filtered the sun's force, when you went in the water it didn't cool you off, but it was pleasant sitting here with Peter and Mike, listening to Mike discuss his problems, Suzy glanced at him over Peter's head, he's beautiful, he really believes what he's saying, he's passionate, he lives for his ideas, and deep down that may be why I'm not in love with him, it's because he doesn't need me, she looked at the enormous pink clouds that hung over the horizon, not horizontal but banked vertically, like the puffs of an atomic mushroom, to hear Mike talk about the future was far from reassuring, Peter was lying on his back between Suzy and Michael, his left hand protecting his eyes from the whitish glare, the other hand lying on Suzy's, her hand quivered under his like a warm little animal, he tried to pay attention to what Mike was saying but every so often he turned his head and looked at Suzy, she was sitting with her face turned toward the sea, he saw her beautiful profile, her features were chiseled with perfect precision but this precision was reassuring, you only had to look at her to know that it would be impossible for her to betray a friendship, lie about her emotions, or break a promise, every time he looked at her with any insistence he knew she would meet his eyes, she was so different from other girls, she always played straight, she would always forgive him for everything, she would always be at his side, good and dependable, until the end of time, and that won't be tomorrow, poor Mike, always predicting catastrophes, I don't believe a word of it, America is too rich, too strong, and too happy to declare war on anyone and who would dare declare war on us? my God, he looked at Suzy and suddenly he was amazed, she was so much smaller, lighter, and weaker than he and yet, lying there within reach, her little hand under my big hand, she gives me an amazing sense of security.

"I'm not a nonviolent person, either," said Michael, frowning, his voice flat, his dark, pensive head leaning on his shoulder, He has the eyes of a prophet, thought Suzy, and the face of an archangel, always ready to draw his sword and suffer for a just cause.

"A nonviolent person," Michael went on, "does not accept war, and I *do* accept it, I would gladly have fought in the Second World War, at that time the aggressors were Japan and Nazi Germany," Peter raised himself on his elbow, he watched the incoming waves become round and then concave, the outgoing waves made a sucking noise as they retreated from the sandy slope and collided with the incoming waves which rose, swamped them, became a crest, and broke as they fell, white at the edges, blue-green below, Poor old Mike, crazy as ever, the war in Vietnam was really unhinging him, he couldn't think about anything else any more, Peter contracted his back muscles and casually stretched his long blond legs in front of him.

"Anyway," he said good-humoredly, "the question is academic, since you work in a lab subsidized by a Federal agency."

There was a silence and Michael said, "I'm thinking of turning in my resignation to the lab and making a public issue by refusing to be drafted."

Peter turned to him and said energetically, "Your resignation! But that's crazy! What we're doing here is fascinating!"

Michael shook his head. "It's fascinating in itself, but we're working for the war."

"For the war?" said Suzy.

Michael looked at her and smiled.

"Dolphins can be used for peaceful purposes," said Suzy.

Michael nodded. "Among other purposes, yes." He went on: "Suzy, I see you haven't noticed the relationship between certain experiments with which you are just as familiar as I am. At Point Mugu they put a harness on a dolphin and train him to swim in the open sea and return to his trainers. At China Lake they teach a dolphin to distinguish between a copper plate and an aluminum plate on the hull of a ship. And we, the keystone of the whole program, are trying to teach Fa to talk. Suppose we succeed, what will that mean? That Fa will do a stint at Point Mugu and another at China Lake to complete his education. After that they'll put a harness on him, and that harness will mean he has become a soldier."

"Well?" said Peter. "What's wrong with that?"

Michael did not answer and Peter repeated, "What's wrong with that?"

"Nothing," said Michael slowly, "if the war for which we plan to use the dolphins is a just war."

"And won't it be?" asked Peter with a smile. "What makes you think it won't?"

"The context."

"What context?"

"Peter," said Michael, looking at him gravely, "your ignorance of the world we live in is nothing short of fantastic. You've never gone beyond the image of a noble America crushing the wicked Nazis and putting down the militarist Japs."

He paused and said with controlled disgust, "This time we are the aggressor. And when I say this time," he went on after a moment, "I am speaking loosely. Actually American expansionism dates from the beginning of the century. I don't need to remind you of our wars of aggression against Mexico and Spain."

"Listen, Mike," said Peter crossly, "I may not be as ignorant of the contemporary context as you think I am. And I'm willing to make a concession: American expansion may well be a form of colonialism, but even if it is, first of all, it's inevitable, and second, better us than the Russians or the Chinese."

"That," said Mike, "is called 'political realism,' and it was in the name of that kind of realism that Hitler tried to conquer Europe."

"You're comparing us to Hitler! Do you realize what you're saying?"

"Yes, I do. What Hitler tried to do with a cynical rhetoric and limited resources we are in the process of accomplishing in the name of morality and with enormous resources."

"That is inevitable," said Peter, taking a handful of sand and letting it run through his fingers. "Our nation is the richest, the most powerful, the best armed, and the most advanced technically."

"That's no excuse," said Suzy in a crisp voice.

There was a silence. Peter looked at Suzy, hesitated, swallowed, and went on: "After all, we're bringing civilization to the peoples whose responsibilities we are assuming."

"We're doing nothing of the sort," said Michael indignantly. "We're saddling them with bloody dictators and keeping them in poverty."

"Poverty?" said Peter ironically. "I had the impression that we were glutting them with dollars."

Michael shrugged. "The dollars go to the leaders and poverty remains the lot of the people. Look at what's going on in the Latin American countries. By buying up their raw materials and flooding

127

them with our products we're condemning these peoples to stagnate in underdevelopment."

There was a rather long silence and Peter said with a short laugh, "Mike, you sound like a Communist."

Michael shrugged, made a gesture of defeat, and said with distaste, "There you are."

Suzy looked at Peter, withdrew her hand from his hands, and knelt on the sand. "You have no right to say that," she said angrily.

Peter frowned and looked away. "I was only kidding," he said, sounding both sheepish and annoyed.

"Precisely," said Suzy. "Couldn't we talk a little more seriously?"

"Fine," said Peter with an offended air. "Let's talk seriously. Who's going to start?"

"I am," said Suzy.

There was a silence. Suzy got up, sat down between the two young men, and encircled her legs with her arms. Peter pressed his lips together and stared at the horizon.

"Mike," said Suzy, "suppose you fail to report when you're called up by the Army. What do you risk?"

"Five years in jail and a ten-thousand-dollar fine."

"In other words, you sacrifice your career as a researcher."

"That's right."

"What's the point?"

"I testify that the war in Vietnam is unjust."

"And in your opinion this testimony is important?"

"Yes, I think it's important. People are always impressed when they see a man willing to go to jail to support his point of view."

"Isn't that a bit melodramatic?" said Peter.

"The melodrama is part of the effectiveness."

Suzy shook her head in irritation. "Let's forget about that aspect of the thing. It's petty and secondary. Mike," she went on, "have you really made up your mind?"

"Yes. I know I'm going to do it, but I'm not sure about the date."

"Why?"

"Because of my job. There'll be a lot of publicity, and I wouldn't want to hurt Sevilla. The best thing would be for him to bring off his experiment with Ivan very soon, for when that happens he'll become so famous and so important that I'll be able to do whatever I like without the scandal reflecting on him."

128

"Have you mentioned your plans to Sevilla?"

"No. Sevilla is not concerned about Vietnam. But I think that once I'm in jail he'll become concerned."

"And that he'll come over to your views?"

"Yes, I hope so. As I said, my purpose in going to jail is to testify, to convince. Not just to convince Sevilla, though I'll admit there's no one I'd rather persuade."

"Why is that?"

"Well, because he's a man with a lot of influence." Michael paused and added softly and rather shyly, "And also because I'm fond of him."

"In your opinion," Suzy went on, "why is Sevilla indifferent to these problems?"

"He's uninformed."

"I suppose," said Peter, "that his ignorance of the world we live in is also nothing short of fantastic."

"Please be quiet, Peter," said Suzy.

"I was quoting Mike. I remember my lesson."

"I wasn't giving you a lesson."

"Oh, yes you were! And with a moral!"

"Peter!" said Suzy.

"Okay," said Peter, looking away. He swallowed and added with feigned indifference, "Since I'm no longer popular here, I'm going for a swim."

He leaped to his feet, covered in a few strides the distance that separated him from the shore, and flung himself furiously into the incoming waves.

A second later he emerged into the air and began to swim toward the open sea. To keep on swimming until his strength was exhausted, to let himself drown, his mouth open, one brief moment of agony and everything would be over, a few minutes earlier he had been so happy and all of a sudden, in a few seconds, with a few words, he had lost everything, oh, he wanted to stop thinking, the water caressed his body, he controlled his breathing, he swam with mechanical perfection but the movement of his body could not erase the pain in his mind, he had lost, lost, he was as alone and abandoned as a dog without a master, he could still see the look in Suzy's eyes when she said, "Be quiet, Peter!" it was as if she had slapped him in the face, he felt the power of his muscles and the speed of his crawl but inside his robust body he felt weak and soft,

129

ashamed, he curbed a terrible desire to cry, he thought, suddenly angry, And what the hell do I have to do with the war in Vietnam, what good would it do for me to go to jail, who am I to buck the United States Government, a poor puppy, they don't even ask his permission to drown him, I've lost her, he thought, she looks down on me, all of a sudden his head felt as if it were splitting in two, the pain was almost beyond his capacity to feel, he was dazed, he stopped swimming and turned around, Michael and Suzy were standing on the beach, Sevilla was beside them, they were waving their arms at him, he felt extraordinarily relieved by the sight of Sevilla, he began to swim for shore as fast as he could, the seconds flew by, someone seized his arm and then his neck, it was Suzy, her face emerged from the water covered with sparkling drops, standing in the water, twenty yards from shore, barely moving his long legs, he held her at arm's length, scrutinizing her features anxiously, Sevilla came to find us, said Suzy, he thinks he's found a solution, he needs us to make a piece of equipment, she looked at him and smiled tenderly and maternally, he put his big blond head against hers and closed his eyes.

* * *

The apparatus visualized by Professor Sevilla would bisect the circular tank where Fa and Bessie lived. Sevilla wanted it to be made of wood, very stout, with a large opening at one end with a sliding door that could be lowered and raised by the winch. The stout wooden beams that formed the armature of the partition had been sunk into the concrete, and the partition itself consisted of a length of waterproof plywood three inches thick screwed and nailed to the beams. As there was no possibility of draining the tank in order to construct the apparatus Peter put on a diving suit to work underwater. This gave Fa the opportunity to play a thousand tricks, his favorite being to swim up to Peter from behind and butt him gently in the rear, just firmly enough to make him lose his balance and fall to the bottom of the tank. At other times, when Fa saw Peter screwing the plywood into position he would seize in his mouth the arm that held the screwdriver and immobilize it, then he would pretend to release his viselike grip, but as soon as Peter tried to wriggle free he would immediately renew his pressure. After ten minutes of these games Fa would go and strut in front of Bessie and

130

exchange joyous whistles with her. Bessie never took part in this teasing herself, but she seemed to look upon it with amusement. According to Suzy, her attitude resembled that of a mother proudly and indulgently observing her son's pranks.

After a full day of this harassment Bob and Michael threw a net into the water and, each holding one end, maneuvered it so as to separate Fa from Peter. Fa entered into the game at once and did everything he could to overcome the obstacle, either by wriggling underneath, in spite of the lead that weighted it, or by leaping over it. He would have won almost every round of the contest if Bessie, at the mere sight of the net, had not taken refuge at the other end of the tank, uttering such frantic cries of distress that eventually Fa rushed over to comfort her. Bessie had stopped in her tracks and was leaning her head to the left, then to the right, barely moving her caudal flipper, and uttering piercing cries. The net undoubtedly reminded her of the circumstances of her capture and judging by her distress, it must have been extremely painful. This helped to explain her abnormal timidity in the presence of human beings.

When the apparatus was set up the door was inserted in its grooves but not dropped into place, the winch holding it in its raised position. Sevilla knew that a dolphin will not voluntarily go through a narrow passageway—some ancestral memory of accidental entrapment between two rocks or disastrous battles in tight quarters. He had allowed for this aversion by giving the opening large dimensions. He had also made sure the partition and the door were padded on both sides with glass wool which was held in place by a plastic cover stapled to the wood here and there. He foresaw that Fa would try to demolish the partition by hitting it with his head or, more accurately, with his chin. He wanted it to be solid enough to resist his terrible battering blows, any one of which could stun a shark, but he also wanted to avoid the possibility that Fa, in his rage, would hurt himself. The partition rose a full two yards above the level of the water to prevent Fa from leaping over it, and the padding on the part located above the water had been made extra thick, for Sevilla foresaw that Fa would certainly hurl himself against the superstructure in his desperate efforts to reach the other side.

Sevilla had overestimated Fa's mistrust. Less than an hour after the partition was completed he swam through the opening that had been provided for him, inspected the other half of the tank, and returned to Bessie. There followed an exchange of loud whistles, as if she were refusing his invitation to follow him and he was annoyed by her refusal. Once again he swam through the opening, turned, and called her, without persuading her to follow him. After this he seemed inclined to be cross with her and circled his half of the tank several times without returning to the half in which she was confined. This maneuver worried Bessie and she began making plaintive cries. But even then she did not succeed in overcoming her timidity.

When Fa continued to sulk Sevilla decided to take advantage of the situation and to begin the experiment immediately. He signaled to Michael, Michael operated the winch, and the door slid smoothly into position and closed off the opening: Fa and Bessie were separated. Sevilla looked at his watch and said aloud, "Two sixteen P.M." Then he elaborated rather solemnly, "June twelfth, nineteen seventy, two sixteen P.M." He looked at his colleagues, who were standing on either side of the tank, tense and silent.

Fa had his back to the opening when the door was lowered. Since the bottom edge of the door was already in the water there was no splash, but a silent glide followed by a dull thud when the bottom of the door struck the groove at the floor of the tank. Fa had not seen the door fall and when he turned around he saw the opening he had been using closed by a wall that looked exactly like the rest of the partition. He froze, swaying his head from side to side to see better, then swam slowly over to the door and inspected it methodically from top to bottom. He did not make a sound. When his inspection was finished he examined the whole of the obstacle from right to left with the same care. Then he backed up, and with three-quarters of his body emerging into the open air, supported by the scull-like movement of his caudal fin, judged the height of the superstructure. When he had done this he swam around his half of the tank several times. At no point had he lost his calm or his self-confidence. A new problem had arisen for him and he was attempting to solve it.

From the first, Bessie's reaction was altogether different. She had been watching the ominous opening through which Fa had disappeared when she saw the door that separated him from her fall shut. Immediately she believed him to be lost forever and, abandoning herself to despair, began swimming around her half of the tank, uttering calls of distress.

These calls had an immediate effect on Fa. He gave several series of reassuring whistles, lifted himself out of the water several times with his caudal fin to try to catch sight of Bessie, and not succeeding, decided to take action. He decided to concentrate his effort on the door, either because he recognized it to be the weakest element or because by bashing it in he meant to restore the passageway through which he had gone. He placed himself at the end of the tank, arched his back to catch his breath, froze, and taking off like a shot, hurled himself chin first against the obstacle. The charge was powerful enough to shake the door in its grooves, but these grooves, which were ample and fastened to the superstructure with strong copper screws, did not budge.

"He's going to try again," said Sevilla in a strangled voice.

Michael looked at him and saw the strain in his face.

"I'm glad I had the door padded," said Sevilla. He noticed that his hands were shaking and put them in his pockets. "As it is, I'm afraid he may hurt himself."

Arlette did not take her eyes off Sevilla. She knew exactly what he was going through and at the moment he had hidden his hands in his pockets she had longed to take his head and hug it to her breast.

"I hope Fa knows how to gauge his blows," said Suzy doubtfully.

"I'm sure he does," said Sevilla. "But there's going to be a very dangerous moment when he realizes that he can't do anything about the partition."

Peter blinked, looked at Suzy and said, "Do you mean that he might kill himself out of despair at losing Suzy?"

"Do you mean Bessie?" asked Arlette with a smile.

"Yes, of course, Bessie. How stupid of me."

"I don't see how I could keep him from killing himself," said Sevilla. "I feel as if I'm playing with his life."

"And it bothers you to play with his life?" Lisbeth asked suddenly, with so much venom in her voice that Sevilla started.

He opened his mouth to speak but changed his mind and stood motionless with both hands in his pockets, his eyes riveted on Ivan.

"You haven't answered my question," said Lisbeth.

"I don't like your tone," said Sevilla, his eyes still fastened on

133

Ivan. "That's why I didn't answer you. And now," he went on wearily, with a little gesture of the hand as if he were chasing away a fly, "I would be grateful if you would keep still. I need all my attention to observe this experiment."

"Are you ordering me to keep still?" asked Lisbeth indignantly.

"That's not what I said," said Sevilla, "but if you want my opinion, it amounts to about the same thing."

There was a silence.

"In that case I have nothing more to do here," said Lisbeth, turning on her heel.

"You are on duty," said Sevilla. He had spoken with the greatest calm and without raising his voice, but there was a little whiplash in his voice.

"I am not on duty," said Lisbeth over her shoulder. "I give you my resignation."

"Until I have accepted it, you are not relieved of your obligations."

"Will you accept it?" said Lisbeth, stopping and staring at Sevilla, her eyes glittering with hatred.

"Submit it to me in writing," said Sevilla coldly. "I will give you my decision."

"What hypocrisy," said Lisbeth.

She turned and left. Sevilla watched her athletic shoulders and heaved a sigh. Exit Lisbeth. It had happened very fast and too soon, but now that it was over, he felt relieved.

Fa stopped swimming around his half of the tank, took a breath, froze, and again hurled himself against the door like a cannon ball. The door shook in its grooves, but that was all. Fa resumed his circling, a few seconds elapsed, and from the other side of the partition Bessie renewed her distress signals. Fa then raised himself on his caudal fin and backed up in this position to the edge of the tank, but he must have decided that it was impossible to leap over the obstacle, for he dropped back into the water and charged the door again, chin first. After this he exchanged a long series of whistles with Bessie and, after what seemed to be a rest interval, battered the door again. By the tenth blow it was clear that he no longer hoped to smash the door in a single blow and that he had decided to break it down a little at a time. It was also clear that he was behaving methodically and without deviating for a second from the most exemplary *sang-froid*.

134

"Three twenty," said Sevilla. "It's over an hour since he started throwing himself at that door, and he doesn't seem to be getting tired. We're going to be here for a while."

Arlette nodded. "One thing strikes me. He has reacted like a reasonable creature, calmly and intelligently, and not at all with the panic of an animal caught in a trap."

"I'll grant you that," said Michael. "But I think you're over-estimating Fa's intelligence. A man would have realized by now that his efforts were useless."

"Fa has no way of realizing that," said Suzy with spirit. "He doesn't know what a door is, he doesn't even know what wood is. He is confronted for the first time in his life by materials that are totally unfamiliar to him. How could he possibly know their degree of resistance?"

Sevilla looked at Suzy. "You're right, Suzy. How could he know the solidity of wood without putting it to the test? But I don't think it will take him long to realize that he can't smash the obstacle."

"And how will we know it?" asked Suzy. "By his panic, by his despair?"

Sevilla shook his head. "That's what I was afraid of, but now I think not. I am very much impressed by his calm. I think we will know that he is abandoning his attempts to smash the partition when he turns to us to solve his problem."

Just then Fa put his head out of the water and cried in a piercing voice, "Pa!"

Sevilla, who was at the other end of Fa's half of the tank, strode rapidly over to Fa and, signaling his colleagues to keep still, leaned over the water.

"Yes, Fa, what do you want?"

There was a pause, and the answer burst forth with extraordinary intensity, the labial exploding loudly and the vowel prolonged like a whistle: "Bi-i-i-i!"

Sevilla motioned again for silence and said nothing, his eyes fastened on Fa. His face was pale under his dark complexion, his features were tense and drawn, and drops of perspiration stood out on his forehead.

Fa tilted his head to the right and to the left to look at Sevilla and repeated with the same powerful explosion of the *B*, "Bi-i-i-i!"

Sevilla said nothing. Fa swam closer by rapidly beating his caudal

135

fin, and as he used to do before Bessie's arrival, he brought his head completely out of the water and laid it on the edge of the tank.

"Pa!"

"Yes, Fa?" said Sevilla, kneeling down and stroking his head.

"Bi-i-i-i!"

Sevilla said nothing.

Fa stared at him with an eye full of astonishment. "Pa!"

"Yes, Fa?"

"Bi-i-i-i!"

Sevilla lifted his brows but did not answer.

Fa said suddenly, "Stand?"

"No," said Sevilla.

Fa looked at him again with astonishment and seemed to think this over. Then he said distinctly, pausing a tenth of a second between words, "Pa give Bi!"

"Good God!" said Sevilla under his breath. The sweat streamed down his body and his hands began shaking again. He repeated, "Pa give Bi?"

"Stand?" asked Fa in a high-pitched voice.

"Yes."

Fa took his head from the edge of the tank and backed up a little way as if to get a better look at his friend.

"Listen, Fa," said Sevilla.

"Sen," said Fa.

Sevilla rested one hand on the edge of the tank and said in a slow, shrill, and explosive voice, as if he were trying to imitate the voice of the dolphin, "Fa speak." He paused. "Pa give Bi night."

"Pa give Bi night!" said Fa, and immediately he repeated with an unprecedented explosion of joy, "Night!"

"Yes, Fa, night."

Fa raised himself out of the water and, turning toward the partition, emitted a whole series of excited whistles. Bessie answered him.

"Listen, Fa," said Sevilla.

"Sen!"

"Fa speak. Pa give Bi night."

"Stand!" said Fa immediately. Then he repeated with an air of joyous exultation, "Fa speak. Pa give Bi night!" He froze. "Stand!" he cried, and violently thrashing his caudal fin, he splashed Sevilla,

136

drenching him from head to foot. "Stand!" he repeated with what looked like a laugh of triumph, leaping into the air.

Sevilla got to his feet. "Good God, good God," he said in a strangled voice. He looked at his colleagues, frozen around him like statues. He was streaming with water, he could hardly speak. "Good God," he said again, tearing each word from his throat, "we've won, he has gone from the word to the sentence!" And turning to Fa, he yelled like a madman, raising both arms to heaven, "Pa give Bi night!"

"Stand!" repeated the dolphin, giving a prodigious leap out of the water.

VII

TAPE RECORDING OF INTERROGATION
OF SEVILLA BY ADAMS,
DECEMBER 26, 1970, ROOM 56–278
3 PHOTOS ATTACHED
CONFIDENTIAL

ADAMS: I apologize for making you come all this way, especially in the middle of winter. Unfortunately, we don't enjoy the same climate as Florida. If you catch the flu I am going to feel responsible. Cigar?

SEVILLA: No, thank you, Mr. Adams, I don't smoke.

ADAMS: Don't call me Mr. Adams. Call me David. I don't see why we need to be so formal. Especially since I am, if you will forgive the liberty, a great admirer of yours. You are probably the most intelligent man I have ever met, and I'm not at all sure that I'm capable of picking your brains.

SEVILLA: Is that why you asked me to come?

ADAMS: Perhaps it wasn't very clever of me to admit it so crudely right at the beginning of our interview.

SEVILLA: I believe that's your job.

ADAMS: Yes. Let's say, to be precise, that I have been given a certain amount of responsibility for the protection of the child of which you are the father.

SEVILLA: Is he in danger?

ADAMS: Yes. [*A silence*] I regret to say that there has been a leak. The Soviets have been informed of some of your results.

SEVILLA: My God, I . . . is it possible? Excuse me . . . this is a shock to me.

138

ADAMS: Calm yourself. I understand your feeling.

SEVILLA: But how is that possible? It doesn't make sense. Exactly what do the Soviets know?

ADAMS: Look, let's proceed in an orderly fashion. Will you allow me to forget about good manners and to ask you blunt questions?

SEVILLA: Of course. Ask all the questions you like. I want to do everything I can to help you.

ADAMS: I wouldn't want you to take offense at my questions. As I said before, I like you very much.

SEVILLA: I am ready to answer you.

ADAMS: Well, let's begin at the beginning. On the twelfth of June you report to Lorrimer that Operation Logos has made an important advance: The dolphin Ivan has gone from the word to the sentence. At the same time you tell us that two of your colleagues, Michael Gilchrist and Elisabeth Dawson, have submitted their resignations and that you have accepted them. Here, if you will allow me to say so, you made a mistake.

SEVILLA: In accepting their resignations?

ADAMS: Yes.

SEVILLA: I don't see why. My contract gives me the right to hire and fire my colleagues as I see fit.

ADAMS: Yes, but it is the spirit of the contract that counts, and not any one article taken out of context. According to the contract, your most important responsibility is the secrecy that must surround the project. If you had reported the two resignations to us before accepting them we could have arranged to have the parties in question watched.

SEVILLA: I'm so sorry, I didn't think of that. Do you suspect one of the two to be the source of the leak?

ADAMS: We suspect everybody.

SEVILLA: You mean, all my colleagues?

ADAMS: All persons who have had knowledge of the progress of Operation Logos, firsthand or from a distance.

SEVILLA: Including myself?

ADAMS: To a certain extent, yes.

SEVILLA: You're joking.

ADAMS: Not at all.

SEVILLA: I . . . I must confess, I wasn't expecting that.

ADAMS: Sit down, please. I wish you would understand that it is my duty to suspect you, regardless of my personal liking for you.

SEVILLA: To hell with your . . . Adams, this is vile! I can't find words to describe . . .

ADAMS: I'm very sorry you're taking it like this. You promised to

139

answer my questions, but if you're too upset to do it we could postpone our interview until tomorrow.

SEVILLA: No, let's get it over with.

ADAMS: Well, since you request it, I'll stop beating around the bush. Let's review the facts: There has been a leak in Operation Logos. First question: Have you, directly or indirectly, encouraged this leak?

SEVILLA: That's a stupid question!

ADAMS: Let me point out that you aren't answering it.

SEVILLA: The answer is no, no, no!*

ADAMS: Sit down, please, and believe me when I say that I deeply regret having to ask you such a question, but it is part of the routine of my job. You know, life is really bizarre. When I entered the university I dreamed of becoming a famous psychologist, not of sitting in an office asking a great scientist unpleasant questions. Will you permit me to continue?

SEVILLA: Certainly. I'm sorry I lost my temper. And I'm going to ask you a favor.

ADAMS: What is it?

SEVILLA: Stop tapping on your desk with the point of your letter opener.

ADAMS: I'm sorry, it's a bad habit of mine. But if it annoys you I'll stop. There. Shall we go on?

SEVILLA: Please.

ADAMS: I would like a more precise answer to my question. I asked you whether you directly or indirectly aided the leak.

SEVILLA: Neither directly nor indirectly.

ADAMS: Perhaps you have answered a little too quickly as far as "indirectly" is concerned.

SEVILLA: I don't understand.

ADAMS: Suppose one of the two people who resigned is the source of the leak. Can't it be said that by letting them leave cold, before we had a chance to arrange for their surveillance, you have indirectly favored the treason?

SEVILLA: It would require a great deal of bad faith to say something like that.

ADAMS: Why?

SEVILLA: Because it would be interpreting as complicity what was merely imprudence.

---

* A series of three photographs taken without the subject's knowledge show him half rising from his chair, his face furious, his eyes popping, the veins in his neck protruding, his right hand extended in a gesture of denial. The voice rises in a passionate crescendo on the three *no*'s.

ADAMS: You mean that by acting in this way you had no intention of shielding them from our surveillance?

SEVILLA: Exactly.

ADAMS: I have an objection. Let's take the case of Michael Gilchrist. Last May twenty-ninth in the course of a conversation with his friends in the dining room of the lab, he criticized our policy in Vietnam. You were listening in in your office. You immediately picked up the phone, asked to see him, and took him for a little walk with you on the road. Why?

SEVILLA: So I could talk to him.

ADAMS: Why on the road? Why not in your office?

SEVILLA: I didn't want that conversation to be recorded.

ADAMS: Why?

SEVILLA: I was afraid of being compromised by Michael's views, since it was I who hired him. I wanted to give him a private warning—

ADAMS: Before our agents got hold of his case.

SEVILLA: Yes, that's about it.

ADAMS: With the exception of Miss Lafeuille, I think I am not mistaken in saying that Michael Gilchrist was your favorite colleague?

SEVILLA: Yes. I was very much disappointed by his resignation.

ADAMS: Let's go back to that conversation on the road with him. I still don't understand why you tried to shield him from our surveillance.

SEVILLA: I just explained that. I was afraid of being compromised by Michael's opinions.

ADAMS: Yes, at least that's what you told him to get him to agree to keep quiet. Actually, your motive was very different. It was not yourself you were trying to protect, it was Michael.

SEVILLA: Oh, I don't know. Perhaps. I wasn't aware of it.

ADAMS: You are a very intelligent man, but I don't know whether you realize the implications of your answer. You have just confessed that you protected a political suspect by trying to conceal his opinions from us.

SEVILLA: Confessed! I have nothing to confess! You are forgetting that at the time of that conversation I had no way of knowing that Michael Gilchrist's views were passionate enough to cause him to resign.

ADAMS: All the more reason to let us decide.

SEVILLA: All this is extremely unpleasant, if you will allow me to say so. You act as if you're putting me in the wrong, and I'm not going to stand for it.

ADAMS: Sit down, please. I am terribly sorry. Please believe that I

141

would far rather talk about cetology. It would be absolutely fascinating. You know, I feel that you have made a fantastic advance for science by being the first person to establish communication with an animal species. Lorrimer was very much impressed by the tape recording you sent us of your latest conversations with Fa.

SEVILLA: Fa has done better since.

ADAMS: Really? And yet it seems to me that since the twelfth of June—it was the twelfth of June, wasn't it, that he went from the word to the sentence?—in six months he has made enormous strides—in vocabulary, syntax, and pronunciation. And according to your latest report, Bi is learning too.

SEVILLA: Bi has caught up to him.

ADAMS: Really! And you say that Fa has improved? You arouse my curiosity. You'll have me believing that you've taught him to read.

SEVILLA: Well, I'm trying.

ADAMS: That's fantastic! I think it's very unfortunate for you that we cannot make these remarkable results public. In twenty-four hours you'd become the most famous man in the United States.

SEVILLA: I have never sought publicity.

ADAMS: Yes, I know. By the way, I would like to ask your opinion of a researcher whose work is very closely related to yours: Edward E. Lorensen.

SEVILLA: Lorensen is very good.

ADAMS: I'm asking you for your confidential opinion.

SEVILLA: And I gave it to you. He is very good.

ADAMS: But?

SEVILLA: There is no "but."

ADAMS: You praise him, but your tone lacks warmth. So there must be some reservation in your mind, and it is precisely this reservation that interests me. Look, you would do me a real service by having more confidence in me. Nothing you say will leave this office, you know.

SEVILLA: I have no reservations. It's just that Lorensen is one type of researcher and I am another.

ADAMS: Well, what type of researcher is Lorensen?

SEVILLA: How should I put it? He would be horrified if he knew how I conducted my experiments with Fa.

ADAMS: Let's say, then, that his attitude of mind is more conventional and yours more artistic.

SEVILLA: Oh, I don't like that word "artistic." Scientifically, Lorensen has a horror of publicity, if you see what I mean.

ADAMS: Yes, I do, and I thank you. All this is of the highest

142

interest, and I am almost ashamed to revert to my bad manners and my unpleasant questions.

SEVILLA: If I understand correctly, you've just given me a little recess.

ADAMS: I admire your sense of humor.

SEVILLA: In that case, we're even. I admire your skill in manipulating people.

ADAMS: I seem to detect a certain amount of bitterness.

SEVILLA: Don't you think it's justified?

ADAMS: Frankly, I do. Let's go back. In spite of the handicap you have imposed on us, we have succeeded in renewing contact with the two persons who resigned, and at the present time I am happy to tell you that they are in our hands.

SEVILLA: They are in jail?

ADAMS: I didn't say they were in jail. I said they were in our hands, or rather, in the hands of people who are giving us the first opportunity to question them.

SEVILLA: An interrogation in a secret place in the absence of a defender: That is akin to inquisition.

ADAMS: See here, Professor! Don't be so bitter. We live in a country in which torture, the arrest of relatives, and execution are not accepted methods.

SEVILLA: I hope not.

ADAMS: Let's get back to our subjects. Perhaps it's time I told you that we actually know who is the source of the leak. It's not Michael Gilchrist, as we had thought at first. It's Elisabeth Dawson.

SEVILLA: Lisbeth! . . . But why did she do a thing like that?

ADAMS: Why did she do it? That's the point. [A silence] She claims that she acted on your instigation.

SEVILLA: What a monstrous slander!

ADAMS: Can you prove that to us?

SEVILLA: How do you expect me to prove my innocence? I'm innocent, that's all. [A silence] My relations with Lisbeth had become very bad, as you know. You have in your possession shorthand reports of all my conversations with her.

ADAMS: We know the conversations that took place in the lab. But we know nothing about interviews you may have had with her on a road or in an inaccessible bungalow.

SEVILLA: Mr. Adams, I wish you would refrain from bringing in that bungalow. It has nothing to do with the business at hand. You are in a good position to know that there is only one person I have taken there.

143

ADAMS: We regard the location of that bungalow as a second attempt on your part to avoid our surveillance.

SEVILLA: Look, you're a human being. You must understand that there are some things in my life that I don't particularly feel like sharing with . . .

ADAMS: Cops. Say the word, it doesn't bother me. Let's get back to Elisabeth Dawson. She claims that actually your quarrels were faked and that her sudden resignation enabled her to get away without being followed. After leaving you she went to Canada where, following your instructions, she immediately got in touch with the Soviet Embassy.

SEVILLA: It's . . . it's diabolical! And what's more, it's stupid! What reason could I have for . . .

ADAMS: According to Lisbeth you were unhappy about the silence that surrounded your work and you wanted to force us, by a calculated indiscretion, to reveal it.

SEVILLA: I'm supposed to have betrayed my country out of vanity! Do you believe that?

ADAMS: No, but you might have another motive. For example, you might be in disagreement with the Government of the United States over the war in Vietnam.

SEVILLA: But I am not in disagreement!

ADAMS: Are you sure?

SEVILLA: Absolutely.

ADAMS: You will forgive me for using your own words against you. At the time of the uprising of the Buddhists of central Vietnam against Ky you said, *"If the Buddhists themselves want no more of us, then all we have to do is leave."*

SEVILLA: I said that? Where? When? To whom?

ADAMS: I don't remember the exact circumstances. But you said it. It's recorded somewhere.

SEVILLA: It's too bad that for once your memory isn't more precise, because I have absolutely no memory of it.

ADAMS: Take my word for it.

SEVILLA: Suppose I do. What of it? I was only repeating something I read in the paper. Actually, you know my position. I feel that foreign policy is none of my business, that only the President knows the facts as they are. Only he can solve these problems, for only he knows the true facts. That's my point of view.

ADAMS: It's the height of common sense. And since you're so frank, I'm going to be frank with you.

SEVILLA: When the head of a security agency tells me he's going to be frank, I begin to get suspicious.

144

ADAMS: You're wrong. This is my confession: I attach no importance to Elisabeth Dawson's revelations.

SEVILLA: Now you tell me!

ADAMS: When I saw her—a few hours after her arrest—she literally pounced on me, she was in such a hurry to talk and to get you in hot water. The diagnosis is clear: She is an unbalanced person. For the sole purpose of harming you she has committed an act of pure folly without weighing the consequences to herself.

SEVILLA: You might have told me that earlier instead of keeping me in suspense for an hour.

ADAMS: Please forgive me, but I had my reasons.

SEVILLA: You had your reasons for playing cat and mouse with me?

ADAMS: Yes, I did.

SEVILLA: And for interrogating me like a criminal?

ADAMS: You're not a criminal, but if you will forgive my saying so, you're a pretty imprudent man. There is no denying that you bear an enormous share of responsibility for what has happened. Once again, we could have prevented the leak if you hadn't accepted that girl's resignation so quickly. I think we are going to offer you a new contract, stipulating that you give us more of a say in the hiring and firing of your colleagues.

SEVILLA: You seem to be punishing me.

ADAMS: Not at all. Please put that idea out of your head. It has no relation to reality. Simply tell yourself that we are freeing you of a minor responsibility at a time when you are making a fantastic advance for the science of your country.

SEVILLA: You're an expert in sugar-coating the pill, I've already noticed that. [A silence] My present contract has not expired. Therefore I have the right to refuse to let it be replaced by a new one.

ADAMS: In that case I regret to say that we would be forced to cut off your funds.

SEVILLA: Ah! There's the iron under the velvet. Well, now I know where I stand. [A silence] If I were to accept your new contract, is there someone among my colleagues whom you intend to ask me to dismiss?

ADAMS: No, no one.

SEVILLA: Do I have your word?

ADAMS: Yes. [A silence] You must agree that this promise puts my proposition in a very different light.

SEVILLA: That's true. Will you give me forty-eight hours to think it over?

145

ADAMS: Gladly.

SEVILLA: This conversation has not been delightful, and I don't want to prolong it unnecessarily, but I would like to ask you a few questions.

ADAMS: I'll answer them if I can.

SEVILLA: Lisbeth contacted the Soviets immediately after her resignation, that is, a little over six months ago. If I understood you correctly, you did not arrest her until recently. Why?

ADAMS: We lost track of her and we hadn't found out that she betrayed you.

SEVILLA: Lisbeth could have told the Soviets only what she herself knew six months ago, that is, that Fa has gone from the word to the sentence. Am I to conclude that the Russians haven't been informed of the fantastic progress Fa has made since then?

ADAMS: No, they haven't.

SEVILLA: So the leak is not as serious as it seemed to you at first.

ADAMS: No, but what is serious, you see, is that the Soviets know something important about our delphinological research, whereas we know next to nothing about theirs.

SEVILLA: I see. [*A silence*] What do you intend to do with Michael?

ADAMS: Well, nobody can accuse you of dropping your friends! . . . You know, I find you rather admirable. After all the trouble he's caused you, you still worry about Michael!

SEVILLA: Can you answer my question?

ADAMS: I think so. [*A silence*] You see, the case of Michael Gilchrist is quite different. The fact that he refuses to go to Vietnam is of absolutely no interest to my agency. What we wish to avoid is his attracting attention and shooting his mouth off about the dolphins. But if we decide to publicize your work ourselves, we would have nothing more against him. His case is in the hands of the law.

SEVILLA: I can't believe my ears. You might decide to lift the secrecy from my work.

ADAMS: Yes, it's not out of the question. It may be the only way to get the Soviets to tell us how far along they are.

• • •

CONCLUSION OF ADAMS' REPORT
ON THE INTERROGATION OF DECEMBER 26
ROOM 56–278. CONFIDENTIAL

. . . It is obvious that the subject's cooperativeness with respect to security turned out to be so limited that the hypothesis of complicity with the source of the leak, however absurd in the light of L.'s special psychology, could not be dismissed *a priori*. On this point the interrogation of the subject removed our last doubts. He revealed a character and personality (which until that time I had known only through the reports of my predecessor) which strike me as utterly incompatible with the cowardly and Machiavellian stratagem L. had ascribed to him. In the course of our interview the subject showed himself by turns angry, aggressive, and sarcastic, but not devious. He never made use of his brilliant dialectical qualities to try to outsmart me or evade my questions. He always tried to answer them with what he believed to be the truth, even when this truth might seem to incriminate him. Far from being a scheming person, he is a straightforward, lively, quick-tempered man who fights openly and takes risks, sometimes even useless risks.

His psychology seems to me to fully account for the errors and imprudences he has committed. In this connection, what he said during our interview about Edward Lorensen can actually be regarded as a very revealing self-portrait. For surely one could never accuse the subject of being "too conventional" or of having a horror of publicity. More than once in his private life he has had occasion to brave public opinion, and he braves it continually in his work, where up to now he has been regarded as an independent. If he has the seemingly unstable and capricious quality of the artist, it is partly because of his extreme sensitivity and also because he is acting in accordance with his own inner logic, without concerning himself with the effect he produces on the world. One is almost tempted to say that there is something feminine about him because he is constantly at the mercy of his own emotions. But although his highly emotional nature may sometimes give him all the outward signs of weakness, he actually commands enormous resources of strength because of his loyalty to himself, his courage, and his integrity. It is obvious that he loves his work better than fame and that he is not interested in money. It is characteristic of his personality that he allows rather considerable sums to lie idle in his bank account without thinking of investing them, even on a short-term basis. Although he is proud and easily offended, his manner is simple, cheerful, and without arrogance. Even during our interview, which was by no means "delightful," as he amusingly observed, the fundamental gaiety of his temperament sometimes came to the surface.

Although the subject is sympathetic on the human level, there are serious drawbacks to his utilization on the level that concerns us. The subject is hard to handle, a complete individualist, unpredictable, and ultimately dangerous, for he is a man who can be

147

neither bought, intimidated, nor even persuaded. He will always do what he has decided to do according to his own lights, without letting himself be swayed and without regard for the danger to himself or the price to be paid. Although in principle he admits the necessity for our surveillance, he tolerates it without really accepting it, he regards it as tyrannical and inquisitorial, and it is probable that he will make further efforts to avoid it, at least in his private life.

Furthermore, he is no longer as politically naïve as he used to be or as he, in good faith, believes himself to be. He disapproves of our methods and he is suspicious of our purposes. In his heart he is a pacifist and he would feel much more at peace with himself if his work had no military application. Since this work is subsidized by a Federal agency, he should have realized from the beginning that such application was inevitable. But on this matter he preferred to adopt an attitude of deliberate blindness which may not last forever, any more than the theoretical confidence he places in the wisdom of the President, a confidence which is already undermined in practice by serious doubts, notably with regard to our policy in Southeast Asia.

It is unfortunate that the subject cannot be replaced as head of Operation Logos because of the long-standing emotional ties he has established with the dolphin Ivan, ties which are necessary to the success of the experiment. I threatened him in veiled terms with the idea of his own resignation by suggesting that we could replace him with Lorensen and lift the secrecy on his work. This would mean, of course, that it would be Lorensen who would receive public acclaim for his labor. This was the maximum pressure that I could bring to bear on him, and I am obliged to say that it had very little effect. Because of his character he is the last man in the world to give in to either threats or promises, and in the present circumstances he is too intelligent not to know himself to be irreplaceable. I even doubt whether he will accept without an argument the alteration of his contract with regard to the recruiting of personnel, although he is aware of the full extent of his own responsibility in the affair of L.

In conclusion, I think that our surveillance must become twice as effective and that when the time comes we will be well advised to erect an impenetrable barrier between the subject and the possible military applications of his experiments.

• • •

Henry! cried Arlette, running to meet him on the terrace of the bungalow, You're early, she threw her arms around him and embraced him passionately, Darling, what happened? Nothing, nothing, he said stiffly, a routine interview, the usual nonsense, will you help me, darling, I have a surprise for us in the old Buick, they climbed the steep path to the log garage, Henry opened the door to the trunk, Well, what do you think of it? Are you strong enough to help me carry the two bags and the outboard motor to the creek? we'll stop for a minute on the terrace so I can change my clothes, the weather was wonderfully warm and fair for the end of December, while he changed she stood motionless in the sun, leaning sideways against the handrail, barefoot, in a bikini, her high, slim waist setting off the roundness of her hips and the delicate curve of her belly, she smiled when she saw him, If you've rested enough, he said, we can take all this down to the creek, Now? said Arlette, looking disappointed, you want to assemble it and put it in the water now, before lunch, *antes de la siesta, señor?* She looked at him, his eyes had dark circles under them, his features were drawn, his mouth tense, I'll tell you what, he said with a burst of enthusiasm that sounded false, do you know what let's do, I want to try this thing out right away, you help me take it down, then you come back up and make us a lunch and get some sweaters, when she got back to the creek he had almost finished assembling the inflatable lifeboat, It's magnificently designed, he muttered with an indefinable hint of derision, it's absolute perfection, no matter how you look at it, they've thought of everything, we are far and away the most industrialized, the most technological, the richest, the most powerful and the most virtuous country in the world, she looked at him without replying, surprised, worried, she did not recognize this bitter tone, launching the boat was easy, there was no surf, he put his hand on the steering handle of the outboard, the boat made for the open sea, he accelerated, the outboard hummed shrilly, But I can't hear you, said Arlette, Come closer, let me whisper in your ear, he said between his teeth, closer, closer, his right hand turned the handle, the motor screamed, and Now, he said with a short laugh, I can tell you everything.

As he spoke he watched the bungalow recede until it was only a white speck on the cliff, like a memory already, like a gull perched there about to fly away, the water was a dark blue that contrasted with the foam and the white glints on the surface, the boat leaped from wave to wave, slapping the hollows, when Sevilla turned

149

toward a little island two or three miles from the coast he took the waves almost broadside and began to roll and drift sideways, The threat is clear, if I don't accept they dismiss me and replace me with Lorensen, Arlette opened her eyes very wide, Lorensen? That tall, pale-faced character we saw at the last conference? oh, I remember, he made a big impression on me, he looked like a pompous candle, Sevilla laughed, No, no, you're confusing him with Hagaman, Lorensen is short, stocky, and bald, he's done some good work on the whistling language, But, Henry, how could they replace you? No one could take your place with Fa, the little island was nothing but sheer cliffs and piled rocks on which the sea broke and whirled, Sevilla half rose from his seat, As soon as I get the wind I'm going to approach, I'd like to know whether this rock really is inaccessible, he went all the way around it without finding a fault or a channel, he started around again, a round rock seemed to zoom toward him, he slowed, swerved, and just missed it, another rock appeared on his right, he passed it, and all of a sudden the water in front of him was calm, clear, and shallow, the propeller gave a sudden jerk, he stopped the motor, lifted the outboard, locked the oars, and felt his way cautiously with a paddle, under an enormous overhanging rock a tiny beach appeared, Sevilla pulled the boat onto dry land, It's wonderful, said Arlette, she felt as if the rocks had closed around her, so perfect was the little circle, half water, half fine sand, the noon sun blazed down and the huge round rocks towered fifteen yards over their heads like protective giants, she smiled, Are you hungry, do you want to eat? Not yet, he said, and scrambled out of his sweater and shorts and dove into the water, turning around, he watched her as she took off her bikini and slipped into the water, curve melted into curve until even the water seemed feminine, it was always a lovely moment when she emerged from her clothes to go to bed, and here there was the blue water, with the white rocks, the sun, the cries of the gulls, But aren't you afraid of sharks? she asked with a grimace, he shook his head, Never with a sandy bottom, the sand in suspension in the water gets in their gills, they were lying in the cove under the overhanging cliff, Sevilla felt as if the sun were drinking him up, it was delightful to go from the cool water to the blazing sun, Why couldn't one simply live the life of the body, free from the cares of professional life and the whole mad rat race, he felt good, he was rediscovering his muscles one by one, putting his hand over his eyes, he turned his head, looked at Arlette, and smiled at her for the first time.

A little later, leaning against the wrinkled rock with their legs flexed and their shoulders touching, they devoured their sandwiches with the avidity of happy animals, the tide had risen, and the last little foamless wave licked their bare feet playfully and retreated with a sucking noise followed, somewhere between two rocks, by a dry *pop* like a bottle being uncorked, a little pink crab walked toward Sevilla's foot, Sevilla wiggled his toes, the crab stood up with his claws extended and waited, on guard like a little boxer, Arlette laughed, Oh, how brave he is, look! he is ready to fight with you, This crab, said Sevilla, is my contemporary, I was born a little earlier, I will die a little later, that's all, I shudder to think of the billions of crabs and the billions of men who came before us, Arlette rubbed her head along his like a horse nuzzling his companion's neck, Let's be like that little crab, let's not think about it, I wish I could, said Sevilla, but there's a mechanism somewhere in my head, as soon as I feel happy I think about death, it's gotten so I'm afraid to feel happy, we should become like primitives, live in the present moment without letting ourselves be tortured by the idea of the future like the white man, but the future is there, it pulls you on, almost as if you needed it, when you're young you're miserable because you don't have a woman, a profession, money, independence, in the prime of life you're tortured by the idea of success, and when you're over fifty it's the worst of all, it's the terror of old age, you feel pushed forward by the years as they speed past, they fall on each other, thin as playing cards, there aren't many left, you've hardly lived and it's already the end, and there's the humiliation of your waning forces, your disappearing vitality, Big bear, said Arlette, it seems to me you're putting up a pretty good fight, he shook his head, picked up a handful of sand, and threw it at the little crab, Yes, he said, his eyes sad, I'm putting up a good fight, but it's a losing one, the pink crab lowered his guard, retreated sideways in haste, and disappeared under a rock.

You didn't tell me you were going to buy a life raft, said Arlette, Sevilla turned his head and looked at her with his serious, dark eyes as if he hadn't heard, You remember the description you gave me of C, well, Adams is a completely different man, sensitive, distinguished, courteous, even human, and yet he's in the same business as C, and what a business, he reproached me, among other things, for making this statement: "If the Buddhists themselves have had enough of us, then all we have to do is leave," frankly, when I was with Adams I couldn't remember saying that, I couldn't even remember thinking it, so I asked him for details and he couldn't, or wouldn't, give them to me, and that struck me as odd since he knows my file by heart, he is capable of telling me that on such and such a day at such and such an hour I said so-and-so to Michael, so I asked myself where, when, and to whom I had made that remark on the monks, But wasn't it to me? said Arlette, Of course! cried Sevilla, I knew I could count on your memory, I did say it to you, and do you know where? On the terrace of the bungalow, you were setting the table and I was sitting in the rocking chair reading *The New York Times*, The bungalow! said Arlette, But that's monstrous, that means . . . she opened her eyes very wide and went pale, her face crumpled and she hid it in her hands, he put his right arm around her and held her tight against him as she sobbed desperately, Oh, what a disgrace, she said between sobs, how loathsome, what contempt for human beings, it's as if they were observing us under a magnifying glass like insects, but did you find the microphone? Rest assured, said Sevilla, his eyes flashing, that I'm not going to start playing detective and feeling the walls to discover the gadgets *de mierda* of those *cobardes*, I'm going to hand in my resignation, I'll never forgive them for humiliating us this way, I'm sick of being spied on, observed, dissected, pretty soon they'll start counting my bowel movements to find out whether my stomach is upset and whether my irregularity is going to affect my loyalty to the United States of America, what an incredible situation, one of the chief reasons I went into research was to get away from this jungle we live in, I wanted to be left the hell alone by politics and politicians, I thought the disinterested search for the truth was the only pure thing there was, and here I am, precisely because of my research, up to my neck in all this shit, forced to have political preferences, my career threatened, and even my reputation, if I am not unconditionally faithful to the Government and its goals, goals I know nothing about, and who does for that matter? since Michael's departure I've started reading the papers and I can find nothing in them but flagrant lies, these people talk nothing but peace and every day they escalate, who knows what the President really intends to do about China, who can truly say, and what does all this have to do with me, I'm not a specialist in international affairs, I'm a zoologist, why am I being forced to enter a field in which I am not competent?

He got up suddenly, waded into the water up to his thighs and dove, he reappeared immediately and turned to face Arlette, she looked at him with a timid, slightly worried smile, Are you coming? she shook her head, he turned over on his stomach, extended both arms in front of him, and began to kick his feet, after a few seconds he raised his head and asked, Am I moving? she suddenly burst out laughing, No, darling, you're not moving an inch, Well, he said, with sudden good humor, that proves that the kicking of my feet is not propulsive, he came out of the water, took his comb out of the back pocket of his shorts, sat down beside her, and combed his hair carefully, You don't know how relieved I am to have made this decision, the hell with my reputation, let Lorensen have the credit, oh, I'm not modest, he went on after a moment, I know it's a great thing to have established communication between the human race and an animal species, it's a great victory for man, a victory full of moral, social, philosophical, and even religious implications, and what a magnificent advance for the dolphin to accede by means of language to human reason, he leaned his shoulder against Arlette's, You're not saying anything, he said after a moment, I'm listening, said Arlette, I wanted to be sure I understood your point of view completely, he raised his thick black brows, Don't you agree with it? Perhaps not, she said, at least not completely, he looked at her, paused for a moment, and went on with new impetus, In my opinion there can never be a good relationship between the scientist and the state, never! their points of view are too different, for the scientist science is knowledge but for the state it is something else, for the state science is power, for the state the scientist is merely a tool which it buys to attain power and naturally it expects from the tool in return for this payment total submission to the goals it pursues, the scientist thinks he is free because he seeks the truth, but actually, without his knowing it, he is regimented, domesticated, imprisoned, well, I'm putting an end to this imprisonment, that's all, said Sevilla, suddenly shouting, there was a silence and Arlette said, But, darling, you're forgetting something, Fa belongs to the lab, to leave the lab is to leave him, you can't do that, Fa is a person now.

● ● ●

December 27, 1970

DEAR MR. ADAMS,

I have thought over your proposition. If I were hiring a lab assistant I would be willing to clear him with you people first, and I could also agree not to dismiss him or accept his resignation without your approval. But I cannot run a laboratory unless I have full initial responsibility for selecting personnel.

Until I hear from you I will regard this as my resignation.

Sincerely yours,

HENRY C. SEVILLA

P.S. I write this from the terrace of a bungalow which you complained was "inaccessible." It had not been inaccessible for several weeks when you made that remark.

December 30, 1970

DEAR MR. SEVILLA,

The proposition contained in your letter of the 27th is entirely satisfactory to us. In view of your magnificent work and the powerful emotional ties you have established with Fa and Bi, Mr. Lorrimer would like you to remain at the head of Operation Logos until such time as the Commission, pending authorization at the highest level, will doubtless decide to announce your work to the public.

Sincerely yours,

D. K. ADAMS

VIII

From a telephone call from Adams on the 15th, which was confirmed by a letter from Lorrimer on the 17th, I learned that the Commission had decided to reveal the results of my studies to the American and international public. Also on the 17th, Adams flew down from Washington to discuss certain questions of security in regard to the press conference which was to take place the 20th. To avoid revealing the location of the lab it was decided that Fa and Bi would be flown under heavy escort to a Florida oceanarium whose equipment was rented for the occasion. At my request the usual number of people present at press conferences was reduced to a hundred, including television, to avoid the possibility that Fa and Bi might be upset by the noise and confusion. For the same reasons the reporters present were asked to refrain from noisy demonstrations, but as will be seen, once the conference started, this instruction was practically ignored.

Adams suggested that Fa and Bi be taken out of their tank during the interview and cooled off, if necessary, by means of damp cloths or washing down, but in my opinion this would have been utilizing them under potentially upsetting conditions, and I rejected the suggestion. I preferred to leave them in their natural milieu, if necessary even filling the tank almost to the top so they could rest their heads comfortably on the lip as they answered questions.

When the press conference opened, not one of the reporters present had the slightest idea what it was about, so well had secrecy been maintained. The lab team and I came into the room along with the reporters, having been provided, like them, with press cards, and sat in the first row of the bleachers, as if to watch an ordinary acrobatic performance put on by dolphins. The security agencies were amply represented on both sides, and Arlette called my attention to Mr. C, sitting modestly in the fifth row, looking exactly as she had described him, plump, blond, jovial, and cold-blooded. Not far from him I recognized, big as life but not quite as lifelike, Mrs. Grace Ferguson who, as soon as my eye fell on her, raised her right hand with the fingers curled over the palm and waved them individually as if she were playing the piano. I suppose her husband is among other things the owner of a newspaper, and that she had managed to take the place of the poor man who had been invited. She was dressed as she imagined a reporter should be, in a white pleated skirt and a simple white sleeveless blouse. I don't know why, but the simplest things looked expensive on her. Before Lorrimer asked me to speak she managed to pass me a note that said, "Dear Henry, I am so happy for you, Grace."

The presence of Lorrimer and the fact that he opened the press conference himself with a short speech showed clearly that the Federal agency intended to have the honor after having borne the burden, at least financially. Realizing how intrigued the reporters must be by a story which they had been promised and about which they knew nothing except that it would be sensational, he amused himself, even as he emphasized its importance, by not revealing it until the very end of his speech, which did not give him any opportunity to expand on it. This was done with a great deal of skill. He began by introducing the dolphins, my colleagues, and myself. He stated that the press conference would be limited to one hour, for Professor Sevilla wanted to spare his dolphins the fatigue that might be brought on by the presence of so many people, the photographers' flashbulbs, and the lights of the TV cameramen. Next, he declared that it was a very great privilege for the reporters to attend a press conference of such importance, for February 20, 1971, was sure to be as memorable a day in the history of the United States and of the world as the day the first experimental A-bomb was exploded at Alamogordo and the day the first man flew in space.

And yet, he added, Professor Sevilla and his team had not perfected any new device or discovered any new substance or combination of substances, and at least superficially their success was not as spectacular as the victories over the atom or over space. However, if it was possible to extend to other dolphins the extraordinary results Professor Sevilla had obtained with Fa and Bi, the significance for man was no less than the imminent achievement of absolute mastery over not only the surface of the seas but their depths as well, a mastery which was every day becoming more vital to the defense of freedom and democracy.

Lorrimer concluded by turning the meeting over to me and by asking me to explain the background of my sensational experiment, for it was I who deserved the credit for being the first man to solve "the problem of the communication of the human species with an animal species by means of articulate language."

Lorrimer uttered this phrase so quickly and sat down so abruptly that there was a kind of commotion, followed by exclamations of astonishment: "What? What did he say? What's it all about?"— people staring at each other in bewilderment as they asked these questions.

As soon as Lorrimer sat down I got up, and turning my back to the tank in which Fa and Bi were playing without ever getting more than a yard apart, I faced the reporters. I was not completely unknown to some of them, having given several lectures which had been reported in the press, but I was certainly much less celebrated a cetologist than Dr. Lilly, who had published his best seller in 1961. The public had concluded somewhat hastily from that publication that Dr. Lilly conversed with his dolphins in English. Actually he had said nothing of the kind, but at least he had the merit of stating that the thing was possible. His book, which was written in a lively and provocative style and embellished with numerous photographs of dolphins, of Dr. Lilly himself, and of his wife (absolutely ravishing), certainly deserved its success. Some cetologists (myself not among them) took umbrage at the book, for they felt that it brought Dr. Lilly a reputation to which his work did not yet entitle him. I suppose some of the reporters present had already boned up on my biography, but others had not taken the trouble, and as I got up, a fat, red-haired fellow of about thirty said to his neighbor in a perfectly audible voice, "Who is this fellow Semilla?"

As I described the genesis of our experiment and the results we had achieved I saw their faces take on expressions of astonishment. The reaction was strongest when I revealed to the audience the fact that Fa could read. This brought on such an uproar that it drowned out my voice. Questions and exclamations exploded on all sides. One of these was eventually taken up by several persons amid laughter: "How does he turn the pages?" I answered, "He could do it with his lateral fins, for he uses them with a great deal of skill, but truth obliges me to say that he turns them with his tongue." (Laughter and exclamations.)

After this, I continued my account and made it as brief as pos-

157

sible, for I was anxious to find out how Fa was going to behave in front of such a large audience. As it happened, I had nothing to worry about. The dolphin's mouth is so sinuous and so turned up that as soon as he opens it he looks as if he's laughing merrily, and Fa really opens his mouth a great deal. Fa is a typical extrovert. Happy, talkative, boastful, aggressive, he was delighted at the opportunity to show off, seemed flattered when his answers made people laugh, and leaped out of the water for joy each time he was applauded.

As for the questions he was asked, they were just what one might have expected: A few were serious, but most tried for the comic effect. All press conferences are alike: They are a terrible mixture of good and bad. As we shall see, the reporters were not always able to distinguish between the first dolphin to speak the language of men and a movie star known for the vagaries of his private life. It is true that Fa unintentionally encouraged this confusion by his sharp answers and his playful mentality.

I should also note that Bi's behavior during the press conference surprised me pleasantly. In her attitude there was no longer a trace of the former timidity which had made her so difficult to approach and which had begun to disappear six months ago when she started to talk, perhaps at the request of her husband. Once she had made up her mind, she manifested a lively spirit of competition toward Fa, and made such an effort that she caught up with him in mastery of the language and surpassed him in quality of pronunciation. She showed the same competitive spirit during the press conference. Without putting herself forward like Fa and without ever answering in his place, she was quite aware that her knowledge of the sea gave her a clear advantage over him, and when the time came she was able to exploit it very cleverly.

•   •   •

PRESS CONFERENCE OF THE MALE DOLPHIN IVAN
AND THE FEMALE DOLPHIN BESSIE
FEBRUARY 20, 1971

(For lack of more precise information, I use the word "Reporter" to refer to any of the various reporters who asked the questions.) *

REPORTER: Fa, how old are you?
FA: Five.

---

* Maggie Miller's note.

[*Fa's shrill, high-pitched, and nasal voice seems to surprise the audience, although in his talk Professor Sevilla has been careful to point out that Fa produces the sounds not with his mouth but with his spiracle*]

REPORTER: Bi, how old are you?

BI: I do not know.

REPORTER: Why?

FA: Bi was born in the sea.

REPORTER: Fa, why are you answering for Bi?

FA: Bi is my wife. [*Laughter*]

REPORTER: Fa, were you born in a tank?

FA: Yes.

REPORTER: Do you miss the sea?

FA: I have never seen it.

REPORTER: There's a lot of room to swim in the sea.

FA: Bi says that the sea is dangerous.

REPORTER: Is that true, Bi?

BI: Yes.

REPORTER: Why?

BI: There are animals who attack you.

REPORTER: What animals?

BI: Sharks and killer whales.

FA: Bi's mother was killed by a shark.

REPORTER: And what did you do, Bi?

FA: Do you mean when it happened?

REPORTER: Fa, let Bi talk.

FA: Yes, sir. Sorry, sir. [*Laughter*]

REPORTER: Bi, will you answer the question?

BI: There was nothing to do. I swam away. It is the big males who chase away sharks.

REPORTER: Could Fa kill a shark?

BI: I do not know.

FA: Show me one, and you will see. [*Laughter*]

REPORTER: Bi, what do you think of sharks?

BI: [*With great feeling*] They are nasty animals, they have a nasty skin. They are stupid. They are cowards.

REPORTER: You say they have a nasty skin. Why?

BI: We are smooth and soft. They are rough. When their skin touches ours, it hurts us.

REPORTER: Fa, is your mother alive?

FA: Pa is my mother. [*Laughter*]

REPORTER: I said your mother, not your father.

FA: I answered you. Pa is my mother.

PROFESSOR SEVILLA: Let me explain. An animal regards the first

159

person he sees after he is born as his mother. In this sense, I really am Fa's mother. [*Laughter*] It was out of respect for human usage that I had him call me Pa.

REPORTER: Mr. Sevilla, I heard your dolphin call a member of your team "Ma." Who is "Ma"?

PROFESSOR SEVILLA: My assistant and colleague, Arlette Lafeuille.

REPORTER: I don't understand. Whom does Fa regard as his mother, you or Miss Lafeuille?

PROFESSOR SEVILLA: Both of us. [*Laughter*] I should explain that a dolphin usually has two mothers, a real mother and a godmother who helps the real mother.

REPORTER: And in the present case, who is the real mother? You or Miss Lafeuille?

PROFESSOR SEVILLA: Your question is not as absurd as it sounds. Since it was I who gave him the bottle during the first weeks of his life, I think it is I who am the real mother and Miss Lafeuille who is the godmother.

REPORTER: Could Miss Lafeuille rise and face us so we could see her?

[*Arlette Lafeuille rises and turns to face the audience. Her physical appearance causes a sensation. Flashbulbs pop*]

REPORTER: Miss Lafeuille, you have a French name. Are you French?

ARLETTE: No, I am American, but my family is from Quebec.

REPORTER: What do you think of General de Gaulle?

REPORTER: Do you buy your clothes in Paris?

REPORTER: Would you like to get into the movies?

REPORTER: Who is your favorite actor?

REPORTER: Are you good at French cooking?

ARLETTE: I'm not French; why should I be good at French cooking?

REPORTER: Miss Lafeuille, can I call you Ma?

ARLETTE: Yes, if you think you're young enough. [*Laughter*]

REPORTER: Ma, does Pa want to marry you?

ARLETTE: Professor Sevilla has not made me any proposal of that kind.

REPORTER: If he did, what would you do?

ARLETTE: I'll decide that when he asks me.

LORRIMER: Gentlemen, I understand and share your keen admiration for Miss Lafeuille, but may I remind you that you are here to interview the dolphins. [*Laughter*]

REPORTER: Fa, do you consider it a privilege to be able to speak the language of men?

160

Fa: I do not understand "privilege."

Professor Sevilla: May I ask that question for you?

Reporter: Certainly.

Professor Sevilla: Fa, are you proud that you can talk to us?

Fa: Yes.

Reporter: Why?

Fa: I had much trouble learning.

Reporter: Why did you go to all that trouble?

Fa: To see Bi and to please Pa.

Reporter: Do animals have a language of their own?

Fa: Dolphins do. I do not know whether the other animals in the sea talk. I do not understand them.

Reporter: Since you started speaking English, do you consider yourself a reasoning animal?

Fa: I could reason before.

Reporter: But you couldn't show it?

Fa: I could not show it as well.

Reporter: Now that you can talk, do you regard yourself as a dolphin or as a man?

Fa: I am a dolphin.

Reporter: They say that dolphins are very friendly toward people. Is that true, Fa? Do you like people?

Fa: Yes, very much. [*He repeats emphatically*] Very much.

Reporter: Why?

Fa: They are good, they are smooth, they have hands, and they can make things.

Reporter: Would you like to have hands?

Fa: Yes, very much.

Reporter: What would you do with them?

Fa: Caress people. [*Laughter*]

[*At this moment there occurs an incident which delights the reporters and gives them material. A fat redheaded reporter from Georgia named V. C. Dumby suddenly gets to his feet in a rage and addresses the gathering in vehement terms.*]

Dumby: This farce has gone on long enough. I find it in the worst possible taste and I will not stand for it another minute! I don't know about you, but I refuse to keep my mouth shut in the face of this disgusting hoax. Never will I believe that a fish is capable of speaking English like a Christian, making misplaced jokes, and talking about caressing us! It's an outrage! Before you know it he'll be asking Mr. Lorrimer for his daughter's hand in marriage. [*Laughter*] You can laugh, but if you ask me, it's disgusting. To

161

think I had to come all the way to Florida to witness this disgraceful fraud! It's obvious that Semilla is a ventriloquist.

PROFESSOR SEVILLA: May I make a few corrections? First, my name is Sevilla, not Semilla. Second, I am not a ventriloquist. Third, Fa is not a fish, he is a cetacean. [*Laughter*]

LORRIMER: Fourth, I have no daughter. [*Laughter*]

DUMBY: Nobody's going to shut me up with jokes! What interest the Government has in lending itself to this deplorable swindle, I can't imagine. But whatever it is, I want no part of it! If Semilla wants to prove his good faith all he has to do is walk away from the tank with his accomplices and leave us alone with his animals!

PROFESSOR SEVILLA: Gladly. [*He rises and walks toward the exit, followed by his assistants**]

FA: [*Half emerging from the tank and crying*] Pa! Where are you going? [*Laughter*]

PROFESSOR SEVILLA: [*Turning around*] Answer the questions, Fa. I'll be back in five minutes.

[*A long silence. Fa looks at the audience*]

FA: Well, who wants to start? [*Laughter*]

REPORTER: You said that you would like to be a man because they have hands and because they can make things. What things, Fa?

FA: TV, for example. TV is a wonderful thing.

REPORTER: You like TV?

FA: I look at it every day. It teaches me many things.

REPORTER: I must say, I find you very optimistic. [*Laughter*]

REPORTER: What kind of movies do you like?

FA: Westerns.

REPORTER: Don't you like love stories?

FA: No.

REPORTER: Why not?

FA: They kiss and it is the end.

REPORTER: You mean it's over too soon?

FA: Yes. [*Laughter*]

REPORTER: While we're on the subject of movies, who is your favorite actress?

FA: Anita Ekberg.

REPORTER: Why?

FA: She is built to swim fast. [*Laughter*]

REPORTER: Would you like to caress Anita Ekberg?

FA: Yes, very much. She must be very smooth. [*Laughter*]

---

* I stayed to record the conversation. (Note by Maggie Miller.)

REPORTER: [*In a loud voice to Dumby*] Well, Dumby, are you convinced?

DUMBY: I am convinced that we are watching a particularly well-executed feat of ventriloquism! If the ventriloquist is not Semilla or one of his assistants, it's somebody else! [*Laughter and protests*]

REPORTER: Dumby, you don't mean that you suspect one of your colleagues?

DUMBY: Don't put words in my mouth. There are other people here besides reporters.

LORRIMER: Personally, I regret to say that I am devoid of all talent as a ventriloquist. [*Laughter*]

DUMBY: I wasn't thinking of you, sir.

LORRIMER: Thank you, Mr. Dumby. [*Laughter*] And now, if everyone is agreed, I propose that we put an end to this interlude and bring back Professor Sevilla.

[*Professor Sevilla and his assistants return to their places in the first row amid prolonged applause*]

REPORTER: Mr. Sevilla tells us that you know how to read. Is that true?

FA: Yes. So does Bi.

REPORTER: What do you read?

FA: *The Jungle Book.*

REPORTER: Do you read any other books besides *The Jungle Book?*

FA: No.

REPORTER: Why?

PROFESSOR SEVILLA: May I answer that question? It is very expensive to prepare a book for Fa and Bi. It requires special paper. Although the book is placed on a desk equipped with buoys, it is impossible to keep it dry.

REPORTER: Why did you choose *The Jungle Book?*

PROFESSOR SEVILLA: There is a certain analogy between the situations of Mowgli and Fa. Each lives on intimate terms with a species other than his own.

REPORTER: Since you could afford to prepare only one book, why didn't you choose the Bible?

PROFESSOR SEVILLA: The Bible is much too complicated a book for Fa.

REPORTER: Fa, I am going to ask you an important question. Do dolphins have a religion?*

---

* The reporter who asked this series of questions was a Quaker, M. B. Frazee. (Note by Maggie Miller.)

163

FA: I do not understand "religion."

REPORTER: I'll ask you a simpler question. Do dolphins believe in God?

FA: Who is God?

REPORTER: Well, that's rather difficult to explain in a few words, but I'll try. God is someone very good who knows everything, who sees everything, who is everywhere, and who never dies. After their death, good men go to live with him in paradise.

FA: Where is paradise?

REPORTER: In the sky. [*A silence*]

FA: Why do good men die?

REPORTER: All men die, good or bad.

FA: Oh, I did not know, I did not know. [*Fa seems profoundly shocked by what he has just learned. A silence*]

BI: May I speak? [*Keen interest*]

REPORTER: Speak, Bi. We will be only too happy to hear what you have to say.

BI: Well, I want to explain something. A long time ago we lived on the land, we ate the things that grow on the earth, and we were happy. Then we were driven off the land and forced to live in the water. But we miss the land and we think about it all the time. That is why we like to swim near the shore and see people.

REPORTER: Bi, I have an important question. Every so often you hear that a school of dolphins or whales has run aground, and when the animals are put back in the water they insist on returning to land to die. Why do they do this?

BI: If we die on land, we will live on land after our death.

REPORTER: If I understand correctly, the earth is your paradise, isn't it?

BI: Yes.

REPORTER: And what about man? Is he your God?

BI: I do not know. I am still not sure I understand the word "God." Man and the earth—for us they are the same. We like man very much, very much.

REPORTER: Why?

BI: Fa already told you: He is good, he is smooth, and he has hands.

REPORTER: You say that man is good. But sometimes he takes you out of the sea and kills you.

BI: We know that he kills us to bring us back to land, so we do not hold it against him.

REPORTER: Fa, you looked as if you were surprised to learn that men die. Were you?

FA: I did not know. It hurts me very much.

REPORTER: It hurts us too. [*Laughter*]

FA: Why do they laugh, Pa?

PROFESSOR SEVILLA: To forget.

FA: You too, Pa? Are you going to die?

PROFESSOR SEVILLA: Yes.

FA: [*Looking at him sadly*] That hurts me very much.

[*Fa's expression impresses the audience and there follows a silence of a quality rarely encountered in press conferences.*]

REPORTER: Bi, I'd like to ask you another question. If dolphins believe that by running aground they will go to paradise, why don't they all run aground?

BI: It takes courage to die. We like to swim, fish, play, and make love.

REPORTER: You are very fond of Fa, aren't you?

BI: Yes.

REPORTER: What would happen if they took Fa away from you?

BI: [*Very distressed*] They are going to take Fa away from me?

PROFESSOR SEVILLA: [*Rising*] Don't ask that kind of question, please!

REPORTER: Bi, I didn't say that they were going to take Fa away from you. I asked you what would happen *if* they took him away from you.

BI: I would die.

REPORTER: How?

PROFESSOR SEVILLA: Don't ask that kind of question!

BI: I would stop eating.

PROFESSOR SEVILLA: [*Very emphatically*] Bi, nobody is going to take Fa away from you. Never! It is I, Pa, who says so!

BI: Do you promise, Pa?

PROFESSOR SEVILLA: I promise. [*To the audience*] I would like to explain my interruption. Dolphins are much more emotional and imaginative than we are. Besides, they do not make the same distinction we do between what is real and what is possible. For them, imagining a possibility is almost the same as having the experience. For this reason you must be very careful. You can ask questions which seem harmless to you and which are in fact needlessly cruel.

REPORTER: I am very sorry. I did not mean to upset Bi.

REPORTER: I am going to ask you a question which certainly will not be cruel. Fa, the French have an expression, "happy as a fish in water." What do you think of it?

FA: I am not a fish. I am a cetacean. How many times do I have to say it? Have you ever looked at the eye of a fish? It is round and

165

stupid. Now, look at mine! [*Fa turns his head to the side and gives the audience a mischievous wink. Prolonged laughter*]

REPORTER: I concede that your eye is neither round nor stupid. But that is not my question. Please answer my question. Are you happy in the water?

FA: Outside the water my skin dries very quickly and I cannot live for long.

REPORTER: You're not answering the question. I asked you whether you were happy in the water. Will you answer me?

PROFESSOR SEVILLA: Please don't bully him. Dolphins are not accustomed to such aggressiveness.

REPORTER: Why won't he answer my question?

FA: I want to answer it, but I do not understand. Where else can I live besides the water?

REPORTER: Fa, since you look at TV every day, I assume you are not completely ignorant of international affairs?

LORRIMER: Gentlemen, I regret to tell you that we have already exceeded by ten minutes the time allotted for this press conference. [*Protests*] Let me remind you of what I said at the beginning. Professor Sevilla feels that this press conference, with the flashbulbs, the questions, and the lights, is a great strain for his pupils and he does not think it should last longer than an hour.

REPORTER: Mr. Lorrimer, I have three more questions. Will you allow me to ask them?

LORRIMER: Very well, ask your three questions, but they will be the last.

REPORTER: Fa, what do you think of the United States of America?

FA: It is the richest and most powerful country in the world. It defends freedom and democracy. The American way of life is superior to all others.

REPORTER: What do you think of the President?

FA: He is a good man who wants peace.

REPORTER: What do you think of Vietnam?

FA: We cannot withdraw. That would encourage aggression.

REPORTER: Fa, in case of war, would you take arms for the United States?

LORRIMER: That makes not three questions, but four. And if you will permit me, I will answer your fourth question myself. Fa cannot take arms, because he has no hands. [*Laughter*] Gentlemen, I thank you for your kind attention, and I suggest that we thank Professor Sevilla and his pupils, Fa and Bi, for their magnificent

166

performance. I am truly proud to have shared this historic occasion with him, with them, and with you. [*Prolonged applause*]

. . .

The Yugoslavian philosopher Marco Llepovič, who was living in the United States in a California university when news of the press conference of February 20 hit the public like a bombshell, was very much impressed by the peculiar state of euphoria and excitement that took hold of the American public, and described it to a friend of his who was a doctor in Sarajevo as follows:

The great virtues of the American people are offset by a few minor defects among which I will mention a tendency toward self-satisfaction and self-righteousness. Both of these qualities are particularly noticeable at this moment in the press, radio, television, and private conversation. Self-congratulation is reaching a degree rarely equaled, even at the time of the great victories in space. As for self-righteousness, it is present, too, although in less conspicuous form. Translated into plain language, the prevailing attitude is something like this: *If we Americans have been the first to make dolphins speak, it is because we deserve it.*

It goes without saying that establishing a fully intelligible communication with an animal species is an achievement of immense significance, and the Americans have a right to be proud of it. But what I find disturbing is that this great scientific advance, or, as they put it in historical-military terminology, this "conquest of a new frontier," seems to them to enhance their claim to world leadership. When they talk about this *fantastic forward leap,* Americans do not fail to refer complacently to the enormous sums which they have been investing for the past ten years (and which they alone have been in a position to invest) in research on dolphins. But at the same time, they regard the success of this research as a gift from the Almighty to the people who are most worthy of it. In making *their* dolphins speak, heaven has obviously confirmed their sense of the world-wide mission with which they are entrusted.

This is the attitude in intellectual circles, but on a humbler level it is most upsetting to observe how often this sensational scientific milestone in the history of the world is immediately interpreted in terms of power and of possible military victory over foreign countries. The taxi driver who brought me back to the university yesterday announced after a few minutes of conversation, "Now that our dolphins can talk, I'll bet you ten bucks none of those

167

damn Russian submarines will dare come near our shores with their fucking missiles." I asked him whether he felt threatened by the Soviets. He answered, "And how! By the Russians, the Chinese, the Viets, the French and the whole fucking bunch! . . ." When one thinks that the United States has in its atomic arsenals the wherewithal to destroy not only all its enemies but the whole planet— itself included—one is surprised by the persistence of so frenzied and chronic a fever in the most powerful nation on earth. This too is an alarming symptom, for the idea of war, even of a war of aggression, may be accepted unresistingly by a population so conditioned, provided it is presented to them as a *preventive* war against an enemy who is *preparing* to destroy them.

It is only fair to add to Marco Llepovič's remarks that the press conference of February 20 did elicit from the American people reactions that indicated much more sympathetic character traits: enthusiasm, humor, and a tendency to be softhearted. From one day to the next, Fa's popularity—which certainly equaled Lindbergh's the day after he flew across the Atlantic—took America by storm.

But popularity is too mild a word. It would be more appropriate to say love and even adoration, so unanimous and powerful was the rush of emotion that the public felt for the two dolphins. Two hundred million reasonable people began to quiver with affection at the mere mention of their idols' names. After the press conference of February 20, the newspapers had hailed them as "the first animals to be endowed with reason." Love of animals mingled with the cult of the rational in the hearts of Americans, and the result was a mixture that was almost explosive. Observers felt the pulse of this great people beating and realized just how far excess of affection could carry them. From one end of the vast continent to the other Fa was simultaneously loved as a pet, admired as an infant prodigy, and extolled as a national hero.

A baseball team named the Lions dropped its name and decided to call itself the Dolphins. Fa fan clubs sprang up, especially among young people, and several pop music stars cut records containing delphinic whistling music. The lyrics of one hit record consisted solely of the words "I love you, Bi" repeated in all registers and all tones of voice, the rest of the record being filled in with whistling that was sometimes languorous, sometimes ardent. A dance called the Dolphin Roll, in which the partners swayed and rubbed their

168

chests against each other while holding their arms behind their backs in an allusion to the dolphin's lack of hands, made its appearance in Minnesota. In three weeks it conquered the United States, Latin America, and Western Europe. Two months later it appeared in Moscow, where it was immediately banned because of its "indecency."

Bi clubs, feminine counterparts of the Fa fan clubs, sprang up in great numbers, especially among high-school girls of fourteen and fifteen. These clubs were based on an identification of the girls with Bi and in certain cases were characterized by a worship of Fa so frenzied that psychologists became alarmed and proceeded to make discreet inquiries. They discovered that at some of their parties, which took place at night in private swimming pools and which had an initiatory quality, teen-agers swam in the nude, straddling rubber dolphins and chanting Negro spirituals in which the Lord's name was replaced by Fa's. Even the slang of these adolescent girls had undergone a transformation. They would say of a boy, Oh boy, he's a Fa, or, on the contrary, He's an anti-Fa, depending on whether or not they felt he had sex appeal. The investigators pointed out that in their opinion the emblem of the Bi clubs—a dolphin with raised head represented in a vertical position—was in reality a phallic symbol.

The business world was quick to exploit this extraordinary popularity. A record containing the highlights of the February 20 press conference sold twenty million copies in a few weeks. A company that bottled nonalcoholic beverages created Dolphin's Drink, which was recommended for its tonic effects on the nerves and muscles. A brand of suntan oil calling itself Dolphinette nourished your skin, effectively filtered out harmful rays, and made your epidermis as soft and smooth as a baby's. Dolphin's Brilliantine (with a lavender fragrance) guaranteed that round-the-clock grooming without which no man could succeed in life. Stores overflowed with objects inspired by Fa and Bi. Drawn, lithographed, engraved, or sculptured, their image was found on cigarette lighters, cigarette cases, silverware, ties, ashtrays, clocks, coatracks, plates, decanters, and even doorknobs (though the latter in no way resembled the stylized dolphins of eighteenth-century France).

Two shows about dolphins ran on Broadway. In one, sixty girls dressed as female dolphins were carried away by sixty dancers dressed as waves, but the main attraction of the spectacle was unquestionably the nuptial ballet, in which a couple of human dolphins performed gracefully and at the limit of eroticism in what appeared to be a giant aquarium.

In the world of toys, the dolphin—in extra-smooth rubber with eyes that moved, a laughing mouth, and a spiracle that emitted the sounds "Pa" and "Ma" when you pressed the dorsal fin—replaced the teddy bear. That summer another version in inflatable rubber, life-size, watertight, and unsinkable, replaced air mattresses on the beaches. Placed on the market by a famous and powerful company, it was the subject of clever billboards, picturing a young boy gaily straddling a dolphin in a stormy sea and bearing the caption: YOU SHOULDN'T GO TO SEA WITHOUT A PORPOISE.*

A house of *haute couture* in New York introduced the Dolphin Look and sent its mannequins to Astoria, clad in sacklike garments of smooth, shiny fabric. The waist was not emphasized, and the dress, after growing narrower at the thighs, ended at the knees in a sudden flare that undoubtedly represented the caudal fin. The announcer advised those who bought the fashion to adopt an undulating walk to create the illusion of the cetacean's graceful movement through the water.

In the daily newspapers, the weekly magazines, the monthly magazines, the scientific reviews for the layman, and in those magazines devoted to nature and animals, which are especially numerous in the United States, the dolphin was all the rage. Most of the articles, the first spate of which had been prepared with great care, were written in the objective tone and with the factual brevity of the European press, without excluding, however, the occasional humorous or sentimental touch that made them palatable.

In some of the lighter publications, of course, the comic element reigned. In the issue that followed the press conference, *Playboy's* cover featured a photomontage of Anita Ekberg in a bathing suit holding Fa in her arms with the caption HE SAYS THAT SHE IS BUILT TO SWIM FAST.

Cartoonists exploited the theme furiously. The drawings with which they inundated the press would have filled several enormous albums. One cartoon showed a dolphin teacher (wearing spec-

---

* Pun taken from *Alice in Wonderland*.

tacles) reading a book, held afloat by a desk furnished with buoys, to a class of dolphins. In the foreground a young cetacean with a bored and stubborn expression feigned disinterest in his instruction, while two of his neighbors exchanged these shocked comments:

"What's wrong with him?"

"He says he wants to learn Russian."

Another cartoon was set in a Florida oceanarium where, just before the show (the public was already hurrying to the box office), some dolphins were filing in front of their worried trainers brandishing signs reading MORE FISH! MORE WATER! and LESS WORK!

Even before Fa zoomed to the pinnacle of popularity the dolphin had made his appearance in the comics with Li'l Abner. It goes without saying that after February 20, he inspired an ever-increasing number of comic strips. Perhaps the most characteristic of these was entitled *Bill and Lizzie* and related the adventures of a male dolphin and his wife. Bill was pictured as a kind of Superdolphin endowed with an enormous chest and an incredible swimming speed, whereas Lizzie, much smaller and more curvaceous, batted her eyelashes coquettishly. The story was full of breathless adventures, especially the kidnaping of Lizzie by a villain named Karsky. (He had a Slavic name but Asiatic features, so that the cartoonist allowed the reader a certain latitude of interpretation.) By capturing Lizzie and abducting her in a powerful motorboat, Karsky tried to force Bill to work for a foreign power (also unspecified), but Bill remained loyal to his American friends. At the head of a platoon of athletic dolphins he caught up with Karsky after a mad race in the middle of the ocean, escaped his machine-gun fire by diving, overturned his boat with the help of his companions, knocked Karsky out with his tail (without killing him), and, bringing him back unconscious on his back, delivered him into the hands of the law.*

.   .   .

Truth obliges us to say that the chorus of praise and love that greeted the dolphins after the 20th of February was not unanimous. Here and there a few discordant voices were heard, and the press

---

* Marco Llepovič clipped out this episode of *Bill and Lizzie* and sent it to his friend in Sarajevo, as an example of the violent fever that was infecting the American people.

immediately played them up, thus satisfying that need for contradiction that lurks at the bottom of the human heart. A certain T. V. Mason, a wholesale hardware magnate who had once run for the Senate in a Southern state, raised some angry questions in a much-publicized speech: "Why," he demanded, "is our dolphin named Ivan? Is Professor Sevilla a Communist? And if he is, will someone please explain why a government agency has entrusted to a Communist the responsibility for teaching our dolphins to read? I have two young children," Mason went on with emotion, "a boy and a girl. I hope that someday they will be good Americans like their father, but not for anything in the world, not even for a million dollars, would I let a Communist teach them their ABC's."

At the request of Adams, who did not take this attack lightly, Sevilla made a statement to the press in which he explained that the night before Fa was born he had seen a movie entitled *Ivan the Terrible*. The next day, after the baby dolphin was born, one of his assistants had remarked that he manifested a "terrible vitality." "In that case," Sevilla had said, "let's call him Ivan." The joke may not have been of the highest quality, but in any case there was nothing to get excited about. Besides, the statement concluded, the recriminations of T. V. Mason were pointless, for Ivan was not known to the public as Ivan but as Fa, a name which he had given himself.

In Congress, there was a rather lively exchange between Senator Salisbury and Senator Spark, nicknamed "the Roman senator" because of his penchant for Latin quotations. Senator Salisbury proposed that Congress set up a fund to enable Soviet dolphins to visit United States oceanariums so that our scientists could compare them with their American brothers. Spark fought this proposal in eloquent language. He declared that even if the Russians were to donate all their dolphins to the United States, he would advise Congress against accepting these gifts. "*Timeo Danaos,*" he declared, "*et dona ferentes*—I fear the Greeks, even when they bring gifts." He violently rejected the idea of inviting subversive dolphins to the United States at the expense of the American taxpayer. In concluding, he described Senator Salisbury's proposal as "indecent and irresponsible."

Paul Omar Parson (nicknamed P.O.P. or, more familiarly, Pop by his friends) carried his negativism much farther than T. V. Mason and Senator Spark by attacking the very principle of dolphin education. Pop had been known to the public at large ever

172

since the regrettable incidents that had marked his campaign for governor of a Southern state. He was a homespun rugged man who liked to take off his jacket and tie when he gave a speech and whose violent and colorful language was a delight to reporters. "My brain," he cried in a speech he gave at a rally in Atlanta, "cannot comprehend why Congress is spending our money to educate dolphins. We made the mistake of teaching our Negroes to read and we already have enough troubles with them without having the dolphins on our back. So let the dolphins stay in their place—the sea—and we in ours, and everybody'll be better off. We live in a world of madmen, cowards, and traitors," Pop went on with vigor, "but as long as I have a drop of blood in my veins, I will rise up against madness, cowardice, and subversion [*applause*]. Personally, like every red-blooded American, I love animals, especially my dog Rookie, but I believe that Rookie's place is to walk at my heels when I go out, and to sit at my feet when I stay home, and not to give me lectures about the so-called advantages of integration [*laughter*]. About these dolphins, I'll tell you what I think, once and for all," he went on, hammering on the desk in front of him with his enormous fist. He paused dramatically and went on in a rising voice: "I believe that the place of a fish is on my plate and not sitting at my table making uncalled-for remarks [*laughter and applause*]! You'll see," he exclaimed in conclusion, "before you know it dolphins are going to start demanding civil rights!" [*Prolonged applause, followed by exclamations of derision and hostility toward dolphins.*]

The fears expressed by Pop found a particularly tragic expression in the vicinity of the most celebrated spot in the United States. On February 22 in Niagara Falls, Mr. and Mrs. Fuller, two middle-aged teachers on a honeymoon trip, committed suicide in their hotel room by taking sleeping pills. They explained their act in a note pinned to their pillow. They said that the news that dolphins could talk had reduced them to despair, for this news marked the end of the supremacy of the human species. The jury rendered a verdict of temporary insanity brought on by travel fatigue and the nervous tension accompanying a honeymoon in persons no longer young.

• • •

It is all to the honor of the American people that at the very moment these negative feelings were being demonstrated men and

173

women of good will were already addressing themselves to the task of defending the rights of dolphins and improving their living conditions.

A group of psychologists who had received permission from the State Department to converse for several hours with Fa and Bi in the Florida oceanarium to which they had been transported, and later had observed their inarticulate brothers in other oceanariums, published a report of which a condensed version appeared in the newspapers and made a profound impression on the public:

From our conversations with Fa and Bi, we conclude that these two dolphins possess the vocabulary, knowledge, and intelligence of the average American teen-ager, except that they do not know slang and express themselves in correct English. The natural intelligence of inarticulate dolphins, judging from their behavior, is just as keen, although obviously they do not possess as many means of expressing it. We have found that relations between men and dolphins, however good they appeared to be in oceanariums, ought to evolve in the direction of greater equality. The affection which trainers and caretakers feel for dolphins is real and often touching, but it contains a hint of condescension which proves that the man-animal complex with its attendant prejudices has not yet been outgrown. In the case of Professor Sevilla, however, man-dolphin relations are excellent. Indeed, it is probably because of his profound humanity and his complete freedom from prejudice that Professor Sevilla has achieved his remarkable results with Fa and Bi.

In all the tanks that we have visited, the dolphins are very well fed. They receive adequate medical care. But their living conditions are far from perfect, for living in a confined space must eventually have an effect on their mental equilibrium. Incidentally, we would like to emphasize that in no case should the tanks be circular, for this causes the dolphins to contract the stupefying habit of swimming around in circles, a habit analogous to the incessant pacing up and down of wild animals in their cages. It would be better to provide them with rectangular tanks at least one hundred yards long, the minimum that permits enough rapid swimming to give them at least the illusion of freedom. But the best remedy for their claustrophobia, in view of the legendary loyalty of dolphins toward their human friends, would be to permit them to make occasional trips to the open sea, which would be comparable to the leaves granted to soldiers.

Almost immediately afterwards, the Association of American Mothers published a group of opinions that struck the same note. "Since dolphins can talk," declared the Mothers, "no one can continue to regard them as animals. Granting this, what right has Dr. Lilly or any other scientist to insert electrodes in the skulls of these creatures? What right have the directors of oceanariums to make them work without salary or time limits, like circus animals? And why must female dolphins have their mates chosen for them instead of choosing them freely, as is certainly the case in their natural milieu?"

.　.　.

As for the reactions of the churches, they were among the most generous in spirit and the most profound in their implications, for they touched upon the future status of dolphins in human society. The first person to raise the point was an evangelist preacher named Leed in a much-discussed article entitled "The Debt of Jonah." Leed pointed out that the dolphin was a cetacean, like the whale (or more precisely, the sperm whale) which had swallowed Jonah. Now, if there was one fact worthy of notice, it was that the whale—to speak traditional language—had not ground Jonah to bits in its terrible jaws. Nor had it reduced him to a pulp by means of the muscles and juices of its stomach. In swallowing him it had provided him with a shelter, not a tomb, and after a few days it had delivered him just as he was, intact, living, preserved for the tasks that awaited him. Mysterious and providential complicity between the cetacean and man!

Leed said that he had had these thoughts when he read the report of the press conference of February 20. It had come to him then that man had a debt of gratitude to discharge with regard to the cetacean, since the cetacean had been marked from the most ancient times as having a special relationship with man. Leed went on to say that he had felt a shock when Fa, in response to the question of a well-intentioned reporter, had asked in his candid and spontaneous way, "Who is God?" What Christian, asked Leed, would not be overcome with painful feelings in the face of such ignorance? The reporter had answered as well as he could, but the only real answer, Leed was not afraid to say, was evangelization: "For the question 'Who is God?' is not an ordinary question to be given a

175

human answer which is, true or false, according to the case. The question 'Who is God?' is in itself an aspiration. If, as everything indicates, Fa is a reasonable creature, he is capable of opening himself to the mysteries of faith."

Leed's daring theory did not fail to encounter opposition and resistance, in evangelist preachers as well as in preachers of other sects. "To be sure," wrote a Baptist preacher named D. M. Hawthorne, "the animals have their place in creation. Like man, they are also God's creatures, since from the greatest to the smallest, from the most useful to the most venomous, He brought them all out of Nothingness. But God placed them on an inferior level in the scale of being by subordinating them to man. God has not granted them the right to love Him, to adore His mysteries, to find their reward in His paradise. I will concede to Leed," Hawthorne went on, "that the dolphin Fa seems to be a reasonable creature. Unfortunately, reason and soul are not synonymous. Do dolphins have souls? That is the question. To be sure of the answer we would need nothing less than a second revelation or, at the very least, a sure and indubitable sign. The evangelization of dolphins is a noble enterprise, but one which may open the way to regrettable liberties, since it tempts us to go beyond the texts that God has given us as a guide. Have we the right," Hawthorne asked in conclusion, "to alter both the spirit and the letter of the Holy Books and to tell the dolphin that the Redeemer died on the Cross to save him?"

It was at this point that Father Schmidt entered the lists. Born in France, probably of Jewish origin, educated in Canada and the United States, Schmidt was a Jesuit with an open mind and far-ranging interests. Doctor of theology, doctor of science, ethnologist, sociologist, numismatist, and archeologist, he knew, in addition to his two mother tongues (English and French), Italian, Spanish, German, Roumanian, and Czech (which, according to Czech friends, he spoke without an accent, a very rare occurrence in a foreigner). He had corresponded with Teilhard de Chardin, Bertrand Russell, Günther Anders, and the Marxist philosopher Garaudy. Now in his sixties, he was learning Russian "in order to read Tolstoi in the original."

Schmidt attacked Hawthorne's thesis with skill and vigor. His first error, he said, was to provide a religious justification for the odious and ridiculous speech P.O.P. had given in Atlanta. This was a danger which Hawthorne himself would have been the first to deplore if he had perceived it. Christianity could not, without running the risk of discrediting itself, seem to side with backward political doctrines. On the contrary, it should strive to maintain contact with the evolution of the world, assimilate advances in thought, and work toward including one way or another the most important discoveries of science. Hawthorne was right, of course, to distinguish between soul and reason. But in the present case, what was his foundation for maintaining, at least by implication, that dolphins did not have souls? What was the soul, after all, if not the creature's capacity to feel the metaphysical anguish of his condition and to free himself from this anguish by a leap of faith?

Schmidt's article continued:

The religious beliefs of dolphins, primitive and crude as they appear in the statements of Bi (press conference of February 20), nevertheless contain the essential elements of the religious impulse: 1) *the notion of paradise lost:* the dolphins were driven off the land at a remote period; 2) *the notion of the beyond:* the land is paradise to which they accede after their death; 3) *the notion of self-sacrifice:* they are ready to lose their lives in order to attain bliss more quickly and more surely; and 4) *the notion of adorable perfection:* they have intense feelings of love for man, who is inaccurately described as supremely good and all-powerful. The French writer Vercors is right in maintaining that the only serious test of the quality of humanity is neither physical appearance, nor language, nor even intelligence, but the religious impulse.

Contrary to what Hawthorne believes, it is not necessary to await a second revelation, for the very fact that we can today conceive of evangelizing dolphins and that we have the means to do it is the revelation. The sure and indubitable sign that Hawthorne demands has already been given to us. It is the miraculous appearance in dolphins of the gift of tongues.

Anthropocentrism, like geocentrism is outmoded. Man is no longer alone on his planet. From now on he will have to accept as his equals those animals which correspond to the criteria by which he defines himself. When he casts aside the conservatism of jealous minds, he will understand that man and the dolphin are a single and identical being called by different names. When this happens it will be possible to say to the dolphin without absurdity that Christ died on the Cross to save him, for by *Man* we must henceforth understand every creature which is endowed with the religious impulse and which can be instructed in the true faith by articulate language.

Returning delightedly to his favorite theme, Schmidt concluded:

Once again, we discover that there is no real opposition between science and religion. On the contrary, science leads us to an expansion of the concept of man which opens our eyes to stirring vistas. Thanks to science, we will now be able to carry the word of Christ into the depths of the ocean.

Following the appearance of this article, several priests belonging to different churches wrote Lorrimer asking him to give them access to Fa and Bi in order to catechize them. Each met with a stiff refusal, couched in courteous terms. The Commission, Lorrimer replied, understood the highly respectable motives that inspired these requests but for the moment did not see how it could satisfy them, since the place where Professor Sevilla instructed Fa and Bi was being kept secret for obvious reasons of security.* Officially, at least, the problem of the evangelization of dolphins had not yet arisen.

A very different problem was engaging the attention of the White House and seemed to demand a swift solution. It was not enough to educate one or two dolphins. If dolphins were to become precious auxiliaries for the United States Navy, arrangements to recruit them must be made without delay. Alerted by his advisers, the President of the United States lost no time: he acted. Remembering the historic decision of President Truman on September 25, 1945, to annex the continental shelf of the United States—a decision which had extended the country's underwater frontiers well beyond its territorial waters—the Government of the United States announced that it regarded henceforth as belonging to the United States all dolphins, porpoises, killer whales, sperm whales, and other

---

* These "obvious reasons" were not the real ones, as Lorrimer later confided to Adams in private conversation. "I don't mind psychologists. But priests! You and I are Christians, David, and it has never prevented us from doing our duty. But God knows how Fa and Bi would react if somebody put the Gospel into their heads! Can you see them as Jehovah's Witnesses and conscientious objectors?"

178

cetaceans whose mating and spawning grounds were included within the limits of its continental shelf. Consequently the fishing for, pursuit of, and capture of the aforesaid cetaceans was forbidden to any boat, ship, or other vehicle, or any fisherman, group of fishermen, or fishing enterprise, whatever its nationality, and fell only within the jurisdiction of the United States Navy.

This document went well beyond the practical considerations which had inspired its authors. Actually it introduced into the evolution of the world a fact of enormous significance. The notion of the *American* dolphin had just entered History.

IX

International reaction to the press conference of February 20 was what might have been expected: polite in the Communist states, admiring in the friendly countries, and admiring but anxious in the nations of the Third World. In the latter, where there was mounting concern over the escalation in Vietnam, the questions asked in hushed tones in diplomatic circles were these: How far will the United States go on the path of industrial knowledge, scientific discovery, and imperial expansion? She has won the Cold War, she has taken advantage of "peaceful coexistence" to advance on all fronts, she has caught up with Russia in the space race; she is ahead of her in all other areas; in Latin America and in parts of Africa and Asia she makes and unmakes governments; Western Europe is at her feet; will she now let her power go to her head and, every time a small nation resists her, send her dolphins to blow up its ports or sink its fleet?

In Parliament, A. C. Crescent, a Member of the House of Commons, asked the Prime Minister how Great Britain, maritime nation par excellence, could have fallen so far behind other countries in research on dolphins. A. C. Crescent was regarded by his own party as an independent, eccentric and slightly mad, but his aggressive, overstated, always explosive opinions were nevertheless very carefully considered. The Prime Minister replied that there surely were some excellent cetologists "in this country," but that Great Britain could not afford to spend hundreds of millions of pounds sterling on cetology alone, and that furthermore she did not have access on her coasts to the warm sea water in which dolphins must be raised. A. C. Crescent asked whether the Prime Minister was so ignorant about the sea that he did not know that there were cold-water dolphins. The Prime Minister replied that Fa and Bi belonged to the species *Tursiops truncatus* and that, as far as he knew, *Tursiops truncatus* lived in warm water. A. C. Crescent declared that in his opinion the temperature of the water was completely immaterial. Judging from personal experience, he did not see why cold water should be an obstacle to literacy [*laughter*]. He asked the Prime Minister what was the point of the considerable sums spent every year by the Royal Navy, when an expensive British aircraft carrier could be sunk in a few minutes by an enemy dolphin whom no sonar could detect [*"Hear! Hear!"*]. The Prime Minister declared that the fears of the Honorable Member were unfounded, in view of the fact that up to the present only American dolphins were operational. The Honorable Member then wanted to know whether the Prime Minister could give assurance that neither Red China nor Russia would ever possess operational dolphins. The Prime Minister said that he could not give such assurance, but that if the occasion arose, the British fleet could call upon the protection of American dolphins under NATO. A. C. Crescent took a deep breath and his eyes began to shine. He had the Prime Minister just where he wanted him.

"In other words," he declared, "we ask the United States to allow us to survive and they grant our request! We ask them to save the pound and they save it! We have no dolphins? Never mind, they will lend us theirs! As Disraeli once said of Ireland in relation to us, our position with respect to the United States is one of 'majestic mendicity [*protests*].' We no longer have an independent economy, a stable currency, or a foreign policy [*cries of "Gaullist! Gaullist!"*]. If loving Great Britain makes a man a Gaullist, then I am a Gaullist [*laughter*]. How can I conceal it? I am profoundly shocked by the deterioration of our prestige in the world and our subservience to the United States. The facts are clear, and it would be hypocritical to turn our backs on them: We are becoming the colony of our ex-colony [*cries of "Shame! Shame!"*]!"

In France, Deputy Marius Sylvain, one of the most brilliant members of the opposition, challenged the Prime Minister in these terms:

181

"You have rightly praised American science, which has just achieved a 'fantastic forward leap' in teaching dolphins to talk This is all very well, Mr. Prime Minister, but it is still not enough. I invite you to go a bit further in your thinking. France possesses no talking dolphins. The United States does. Do you think it was opportune for us to withdraw from NATO in 1966, at a time in history when every military fleet will need these indispensable auxiliaries for defense and reconnaissance [*applause from the benches of the Federation and the Democratic center*]? In short, I invite the Government to look at things as they are instead of taking refuge in dreams of glory inspired by the narrowest nationalism [*protests from the UNR*]. Open your eyes, gentlemen. Economically, financially, militarily, France is a small nation which cannot go her own way [*energetic protests from the UNR, the Independents, and some of the Communist benches*]! Do you deny it [*cries of "Yes! Yes!"*]? In that case, I say that France must choose: Either she must agree to re-enter NATO [*protests from the UNR and Communist benches*], in which case her ships will receive from the United States that protective shield of dolphins without which in our time a fleet of war might as well be sent to the scrap heap [*protests*]; or else France must educate her own dolphins [*cries of "Yes! Yes! Why not?"*]. You say 'Why not?' I agree [*sarcastic cries from the UNR benches: "Then vote with us!"*].

"I, too, say 'Why not?' but I still will not vote with you, and I will tell you why. But first I invite you to consider certain facts and figures. The United States has one hundred and fifty cetologists. Japan, eighty. England and Western Germany, fifteen apiece. And do you know, gentlemen, how many cetologists France has? Two [*exclamations and protests*]! I repeat: two. Gentlemen of the Majority, who have been in power since 1958, in all this time, what have you done for cetology? I will answer for you: Nothing! Precisely nothing [*applause and protests*]! Have you organized cetological research? No. Have you created and subsidized cetological laboratories? No. Have you considered the need for training cetologists? No. Have you captured dolphins in the Mediterranean for the purpose of study? No. Have you even built tanks to accommodate dolphins in the future? Not one. One of the two French cetologists asked you for a small part of an island opposite Marseille to set up a laboratory for dolphins. Did you give it to him? No. And do you

182

know, Mr. Prime Minister, where this cetologist goes to study dolphins? I'll tell you. *He goes to the United States** [*laughter, applause, and protests*]!"

In Italy, as in the other nations of Western Europe, political reaction was not fundamentally different from that of Great Britain and France. Those for and against NATO found in the new success of the Americans new arguments for their respective theses. But it was Italy that produced the most original philosophical reaction in the form of a magazine article that was read and discussed all over the world.

The author was a certain Prince Luigi Monteverdi. He possessed a magnificent Renaissance *palazzo* in Rome full of marble, columns, and statues, liked abstract painting, and was a member of the Italian Communist Party. The comrades from foreign countries whom he sometimes entertained were amazed to wake up in the morning in canopied beds and make their ablutions in marble basins. The prince, slim, elegant, and graying at the temples, was almost six feet tall, but seemed shorter because his features were so delicate and his manner was so free from arrogance.

Raymond Lutin, a member of the central committee of the French Communist Party, who was having breakfast with him one day in the imposing dining room of the *palazzo,* asked, "What's that I hear, Monteverdi? It sounds like chanting."

Luigi Monteverdi waved his hand carelessly. "It's nothing, it's just my aunt and my two nieces having Mass said for them next door by a little *monsignore."*

"And who pays the *monsignore?"* asked Lutin.

"I do, of course."

Lutin began to laugh. "Comrade, you remember what Lenin said: 'Let those who want the Pope pay the Pope.' In my opinion your aunt ought to pay."

"Impossible," said the prince with a little smile. "It's her Mass, but it's my chapel."

In his article, Luigi Monteverdi made a comparison between what he called *the two geneses:* the genesis of the first book of the

---

* Marius Sylvain's criticisms were only partly justified, since the first Pompidou Government had founded a naval center for dolphin research in Biarritz in April 1966.

Bible, and the materialistic genesis of Engels in his *Dialectics of Nature:*

The first genesis invoked a demiurge. God, after creating heaven and earth, created the animals, each according to its species. He fashioned man in His image out of the dust and, blowing in his nostrils, gave him the spark of life and thought. Thus man, a thinking and privileged creature from the moment of his creation, received from God the earth as his kingdom and the animals as his servants.

In Engels, who had based his genesis on the discoveries of Darwin, the hypothesis of the demiurge disappeared. Man was not created, he evolved slowly from the ape. "It was at the moment," writes Engels, "when after thousands of years of struggle the hand was definitively differentiated from the foot and the upright posture was finally established, that man was separated from the ape and the foundations were laid for articulate language and the prodigious development of the brain." In this promotion, Engels insists on the vital role of the human hand. For, once this hand stopped being utilized as a foot by the primate who was our ancestor, it was freed for other tasks. It permitted him to do work, in the course of which the hand grew more proficient, and work in turn increased the need for communication. Out of this growing need, articulate language was born and, with it, the development of the brain.

Thus, in the Bible, it was the hand of God that fashioned man and His breath that gave him intelligence from the first, whereas for Engels it was by his own hand, so to speak, and by the creative work that this hand permitted, that man fashioned his own humanity and was gradually differentiated from the primates.

It was a magnificent thesis, and one that acquired great historical importance the moment it appeared, since by relying on the scientific discoveries of his day, Engels combated with rare effectiveness man's disastrous tendency to explain his actions in terms of ideas rather than in terms of his needs.

However, we must take into consideration the historical, and always historically relative, aspect of knowledge. Science has progressed since Engels, it is progressing still, and its latest developments may well force us to re-examine the role which the great Marxist philosopher attributed to the hand in man's evolution toward intelligence. For after all, here are animals—Professor Sevilla's dolphins, Fa and Bi—who have arrived at articulate language and all the abstract mental operations which it presupposes, and they receive this language from man and understand it by a purely

184

mental effort without any recourse to the human hand, which the lateral fins of cetaceans can in no sense be said to replace. Thus the question arises as to whether Engels, in his desire to oppose the idealism of Christian conception, went too far in the other direction and reversed the terms of the natural evolution. If the example of the talking dolphins shows that the appearance of articulate language is possible wherever the brain arrives at a certain complexity, it is a paradox to say that it is the manual tools of man that have made him think and speak. It would be better to say that it is the brain of prehistoric man which, by developing, has permitted not only all the creative uses of the hand, but the elaboration of articulate language.

After all, the materialism which Engels adopted and which we adopt after him loses nothing from the fact that it is the development and differentiation of the brain cells, and not of the hand, which explains the extraordinary promotion of man in the animal kingdom, just as it explains the recent and sensational arrival of the dolphin at articulate language.

However important Monteverdi's article may have been for all those interested in man's appearance on the planet, it escaped the notice of the United States Navy and State Department. They had their eyes fixed on things they considered more serious. They were waiting with feverish vigilance for Russia's reaction to the February 20 press conference. It came in two stages and after what seemed to the impatient observers a very long wait.

On February 23, or three days after the conference, the Russian Government congratulated the Government of the United States, the American scientists, and the American people in polite language on the "striking advances" they had made in zoology.

A long silence ensued and it was not until March 2 that an unsigned article in *Pravda* again raised the problem of dolphins. Its language was carefully weighed. Soviet scientists, said the author of the article, had been studying dolphins for many years and had achieved striking results.* The author admired the performances of Professor Sevilla's dolphins, but he did not have the impression that Soviet cetology was in any sense less advanced than that of the New World. "It is true," he added, "that comparison is not easy, because

---

* It will be noted that this is the same adjective that had been used to describe the advances of American scientists.

the program for the study of dolphins in the Soviet Union differs both in its goals and in its methods from the program for the study of dolphins in America. Unlike the Americans who, as victims of the individualistic habits of thinking developed in the capitalist struggle for survival, have concentrated their efforts on one or two dolphins and have succeeded in making them perform miracles, our scientists have tried to go directly from delphinic illiteracy to the mass education of dolphins. To a certain extent they have succeeded, for they have perfected a simplified system of communication by means of which they control the movements of some hundred dolphins in the Black Sea. These dolphins are already being used for fishing and they are giving complete satisfaction."

"My God," said Lorrimer when Adams brought him the translation of this article, "we don't know any more than we did before! What do they mean: 'To a certain extent they have succeeded'? And what do they mean by 'a simplified system of communication'? I have a simplified system of communication with my dog, but that's not the same as a language! The damned bastards, their lips are buttoned just as tight as their uniforms!"

● ● ●

Goldstein, whose visit had been announced by Adams on Wednesday, March 6, appeared at the bungalow early Saturday afternoon, he was tall, broad-shouldered, and deep-chested with tufts of red and white hair emerging from his open collar, a muscular neck, strong features, an aggressive chin, and a thick, white, curly mane which made him look like an old lion, he walked a little to one side on the terrace of the bungalow, his big muscular legs seemed to bounce on his crepe soles at every step, his head leaned forward slightly, his big shoulders sagged, his laughing, shrewd little blue eyes were fastened on Arlette and Sevilla, My name is Goldstein, he said in a strong voice, offering Sevilla a large hairy hand, I am the Jewish shark who is going to take ten percent of your royalties from now on, Miss Lafeuille, it's a great privilege to meet you, you are absolutely ravishing, even more magnificent than your photographs, you look exactly like Marie Mancini, you know, the girl Louis XIV adored, Goldstein, said Sevilla, laughing, you can't impress Arlette with your learning, it was *Life* that first compared her to Marie Mancini, and it's no use courting her, I'm going to marry her in a

186

week, you might as well sit down and have a drink, You're marrying her? asked Goldstein, dropping into a white lacquered chair that creaked under his weight, When do you expect to finish your book on Fa and Bi? In six months, I think, Goldstein looked up with a happy and inspired look, his white hair made a glowing halo around his head, Well, *Bruder,* he said, patting Sevilla gently on the shoulder, you'll have to wait and get married when your book comes out, I can see the headlines: PA WEDS MA!

Sevilla and Arlette laughed, and Goldstein howled, What a bomb-shell, they'll love you, Sevilla, you're so famous they expect you to marry money, they'll be moved to tears when you marry a little typist without a fortune, But I'm not a little typist! said Arlette, Far from it, said Sevilla, she's got all kinds of degrees and her father's a big wheel in insurance, I know, I know, said Goldstein, Do you think I didn't read up on your life story before I came here? I'm not telling you the truth the way it is, but the way the papers will tell it, the whole country will weep with joy when they hear that Sevilla is going to marry his secretary instead of some steel heiress, Un-fortunately, said Sevilla, there's no question of waiting until the book comes out, we're getting married in a week, Goldstein shrugged his powerful shoulders and frowned, I didn't mean to be personal, Sevilla waved his hand, Don't worry, he said, laughing.

Good, said Goldstein, and he muttered something unintelligible that sounded like German, Sevilla looked at him in surprise and Goldstein stared back at him, his face serious and tense, Listen, Sevilla, tell me something, are you Jewish or not? I would be very honored to be Jewish, said Sevilla, his head leaning against the back of his chair, looking at Goldstein, his dark eyes twinkling and half closed, That's not an answer, It's the only one I can give you, Look, Sevilla went on, the truth is I don't have any idea, even Mr. C doesn't know, and I really wonder what difference it makes, after all, whether I am Jewish or not, I like to think, said Goldstein, lowering his voice with an emotion that was half real and half put on and which seemed to amuse even himself, I like to think that most of the great men of our time were Jewish: Einstein, Freud, Marx, What racism, said Sevilla, I'll suggest some other names that are more embarrassing: Oppenheimer? Teller? Goldstein roared, We must make a distinction, Sevilla! I condemn Teller, he perfected the H-bomb in peacetime, but Oppie, ah, I defend Oppie, he started

187

work on the A-bomb during the war, when we were afraid Hitler would beat us to it, I know, said Sevilla bitterly, he invented the A-bomb to beat the Nazis and Truman used it against the Japanese, such is the irony of scientific research, Goldstein brought his whiskey to his lips and sipped it, Sevilla looked at his hand enviously, it was broad and muscular with a very long thumb, it did not grasp the glass, it took possession of it, so to speak, it was the hand of a man who moved easily in the world of things, I have lost that simplicity, thought Sevilla.

Goldstein put down his glass, My friend, if I'm going to be nursing your ailing finances you must have confidence in your doctor, Adams tells me you've had fifteen thousand dollars sitting in your bank account for the last two years that you're doing nothing with, it's a scandal, fifteen thousand at ten percent, in two years you could have earned three thousand, or enough to replace your old Buick without touching your capital, Why should I replace my Buick? There you are, said Goldstein, throwing up his broad hands and looking at Arlette as if to call her to witness, I knew it, he's a prophet, we Jews never have a bourgeois attitude toward money, with us there's no happy medium, we're either philistines or prophets, you remember that character in Dos Passos, he becomes a millionaire, he gets brand-new bills from the bank, they crackle, they smell good, they're so beautiful he carries them to his lips and kisses them like a religious fanatic, well, I acted something like that with my first money, when I was young I carried an enormous amount of cash against my chest for a whole day, I was unbelievably excited, I felt as if those dollars were warming my heart through the leather and the shirt, mystics who wear their god against their chests cannot take as much delight in his presence as I felt that day, my dollars made me a new man, my power was increased a thousand-fold, I was alive, I had no desire to buy anything, all pleasures seemed pale in comparison to the power I now had of buying them, and to tell the truth I have never possessed anything since—yachts, cars, houses—the way I possessed those first dollars, I was madly happy, I'm a nut about money, I don't mind admitting it, the way you're a nut about independence, Sevilla, and to be as passionate as I am in the other direction, *Bruder*, you must be of the same blood.

You're amazing, said Sevilla, you're so possessive you even want to annex my origins, look, let's settle this matter once and for all, my father left my mother when I was eight and went to live with a Cuban woman in Miami, come to think of it, it was the best thing he could have done, poor devil, I was fond of him, he was just as gay and affectionate as my mother was rigid, well, he left, or rather he ran away, and morning and night my mother made me say a special prayer to the Virgin for the salvation of his soul and the rest of the day she deluged me with the hatred and contempt she had for him, it was awful, I can still see her—thin, sallow, her hair limp, her eyes implacable—her hatred filled her life, the rest of her thoughts were devoted to religion and psychiatry, strange woman, her hatred was the only real emotion she had, even her laugh was forced, she laughed like this, heh-heh, from the bottom of her throat, with an air of contemptuous superiority, well, when I was twelve my father died, and after that every time I asked about him I came up against a wall, no answer, never, it was the forbidden subject, it was as if my mother made him die a second death by her silence, well, Goldstein, how am I supposed to know whether or not my father was Jewish, I don't know anything about him, not even what he did for a living, all I know is that my grandfather came from Galicia and my father spoke with an accent, "A foreigner," my mother said, "I never should have married a foreigner," there you are, Goldstein, you might as well give up, I am one of those millions of Americans without roots, without traditions, without even a race, take me as I am and stop thinking I'm an anti-Semitic Jew who's trying to pass for a gentile, I never thought that, said Goldstein, he emptied his glass, put it down, and sat silently for a moment, his heavy, leonine head resting on his chest and his two broad hands flat on his knees, then he raised his two hands about a foot, held them in the air for a couple of seconds and let them fall back onto his thighs.

Good, where is the contract Brücker sent you? There, on the table, next to your glass, I got it out when I knew you were coming, Let's see, said Goldstein, he put out his hand, but instead of picking up the paper he looked at Sevilla and raised his eyebrows, You called me a racist, Sevilla, that's an unfair accusation, I'm a Jewish patriot, that's all, you wouldn't criticize an Englishman for being proud that it was an Englishman who discovered the laws of gravity, so why shouldn't I be proud of Einstein? You know as well as I do that a man who defends his country against an invader has a

189

tendency to become a chauvinist, well, Sevilla, what is a Jew but a man whose country is constantly in danger? and besides, in our case there is this unusual aspect, the country of the Jews is their skin, take other nations, the Viets, for example, well, the Viet has the possibility of committing treason, if he goes over to the other side he sells his country but saves his skin, but we Jews coincide with the Jewish fatherland body and soul, the Jewish fatherland is my nose, my mouth, my curly hair, my big eyes, my country is me, so, don't you see, Sevilla, I feel really at ease only with other Jews, away from them I feel surrounded by powerful aggressors, Sevilla put up his hand, If the word "racism" offends you, Goldstein, I withdraw it, do you prefer "chauvinism"? You used it yourself, didn't you? Is that still too strong? Then there must not be a word in the language to describe the symptoms of hyperdefensiveness, You're teasing me, said Goldstein, and what's more, your irony is typically Jewish, Good God, said Sevilla, irony is irony, Goldstein smiled good-naturedly at him and looked at his watch, It's too bad we don't have time to go into it, my plane leaves in an hour, Let's see, he went on, picking up the contract, let's examine this monument of iniquity, even before I read it, I congratulate you on having the good sense not to sign it, he became absorbed in his reading, Good God, what a swindler, he muttered after a moment, A swindler? asked Sevilla, Goldstein laughed, No, no, not literally, don't take me literally, he's a swindler the way all respectable businessmen are, that is, he'll rob you, but within very reasonable limits, and besides, he's a very good publisher, dynamic, daring, you're in good hands, Sevilla, Miss Lafeuille, may I use your telephone? I'll get it for you, said Arlette, she was back in a moment, the long white cord winding behind her on the red tiles, Goldstein looked her up and down, What a pretty little dish, and reliable, serious, she'll be a help to him, Let me call this bandit, he said with a wink, engulfing the receiver in his big paw, a moment passed, a moment without meaning, a void, a wait, a blank period, Goldstein was calling Brücker and that was all, Sevilla looked at Arlette and smiled, she smiled back at him, and Goldstein regarded them both with abstract, expressionless eyes, Sevilla had the feeling that life, with its abundant, uninterrupted flow of emotions, ideas, plans, and anxieties, was secretly pausing at a point that was empty, white, without color or content, Brücker? said Goldstein in a loud voice, and immediately

190

the flow resumed, Brücker, it's Goldstein, I'm calling you about Sevilla, yes, I'm his agent, don't sound so unhappy, old man, not at all, I like you too, we're friends, he'll deliver the manuscript in six months, of course he'll write it himself, he's full of life and spirit, this guy, don't worry, everything's fine on this end, the only trouble is your contract, I'll tell you, we must have all pre- and post-publication secondary rights and all translation and movie rights, what about you? well, you're doing all right, you have American, British, Canadian, Australian, and all other English-speaking language book rights, and that's quite a hunk . . . in the second place, our royalties will have to be a straight fifteen percent, NO, I said fifteen percent, take it or leave it, and the advance has to be a little better than the lousy fifty thousand you're offering, what's that? I said lousy, a hundred? come on, Brücker, let's be serious, I don't care how surprised you are, I don't want your lousy hundred thousand, take it away, I spit on it, I shit on it, if you must know, no, Brücker, you won't get this book with your miserable, lousy, moth-eaten hundred thousand, Brücker, I shit on it, I tell you, what do I want? At last! Bravo! I want two hundred, Goldstein held the receiver away from his ear and covered the earpiece with his other hand, looked at Sevilla, and said in a normal voice, He's screaming like a stuck pig but it doesn't mean a thing, he's already decided to give it to me, he's only protesting for form's sake, Sevilla raised his eyebrows, But isn't that a lot of money? You're kidding, said Goldstein, you'll make over two million in royalties in the English-speaking countries alone, and I don't even dare tell you what Brücker will make, he put the receiver to his ear again, Pardon? No, we weren't cut off, listen, Brücker, you're wasting my time, you're wasting Sevilla's time, and you're wasting your own time, I said two hundred! What? You've agreed? When? Just now? Fine! Send Sevilla a new contract and he'll send it back by return mail, I said return mail, I give you my word, lunch tomorrow? I can't, but Monday if you like, Monday I'd love to, he hung up, laid his palms on his thighs, glanced from Arlette to Sevilla, he looked proud and tired, beads of sweat stood out on his brow, he was panting a little as if he had just been exercising, All that money, said Sevilla after a moment, Goldstein looked at his watch and rose, Sevilla, I'm going to say something and I want you to think it over, I'm serious, as soon as Brücker pays you that advance buy a big house with a big

191

garden and build yourself a fallout shelter, I just built one myself, I have a hunch the world is heading for a big, fat mess.

Right now, said Sevilla, Goldstein is having dinner on the plane, full of himself, he laughed, I like him, said Arlette, I enjoyed his bit on the phone with Brücker, half lying in the rocking chair, Sevilla watched her prepare the evening meal, ham, lettuce, avocado, by an ingenious arrangement the benches that ran along two sides of the table were attached to it, when you lifted the table you lifted the benches too, they were made of thick oak boards blackened by rain and cracked by the sun, Sevilla looked at the table with pleasure, sturdy, rustic, weathered by its long stay in the open air on this terrace where it lived three hundred and sixty-five days a year and where it would end its days without ever having moved more than a few yards to be carried into the shade at noon and into the dying sun in the evening, it's a well-known fact that the oak tree, if it ages well, can live over six hundred years, how many generations! Lord, how brief a man's life is in comparison, we come and go like insects—work, make phone calls, make love—time runs out, second by second, minute by minute, slowly but surely bringing me closer to the moment when I'll be dying in foul sheets, the very idea makes me shudder with panic, it's horrible and incredible, and the most incredible part is that we pretend to forget, we live as if it were nothing instead of screaming with fear, no, we're very good about it, cheerful, efficient, optimistic, we make plans, life belongs to us, besides, it's a well-known fact that it's always other people who die, time passed, he thought with remorse of Michael, Michael in his cell, awaiting trial, sentencing, the destruction of his young life, Big bear, you look sad, No, he said, smiling, I'm thinking about my book, I may have got way ahead of myself when I told him I'd be finished in six months, Dinner's ready! said Arlette, everyone to the table! Sevilla rose and looked at her tenderly, how she loved to repeat the same happy and reassuring rituals, he stepped over the bench energetically, laid his hands palms down on the blackened oak surface, I'm hungry, he said cheerfully.

He cut his salad and his ham into tiny pieces on his plate, A million dollars, he said, what do you do with it, oh, I know, you invest it at ten percent, as Goldstein says, and it brings you a hundred thousand dollars, fine, and then what do you do with the hundred thousand dollars, spend it? a hundred thousand dollars in

192

one year, it can't be done, at least not the way we live, we can meet our expenses very easily as it is, You invest it, said Arlette, smiling, Sevilla raised his knife like a wand, Bravo, that's the height of good sense, you invest it, and next year you have an income of a hundred and ten thousand dollars, at this rate I'll double the million in a few years, and then what will I do with two million? Arlette looked at him, laughing, You keep going, Good, said Sevilla, I keep going and a few years later I have three million, and when I die as all men must, I leave a million to John, a million to Alan, a million to you, and what do you do with your million, my poor little darling, you keep going, of course, accumulating enormous sums you'll never be able to spend, he looked at Arlette and raised his eyebrows, I wouldn't want you to think I look down on money, that's not true, people are always a little hypocritical when it comes to money, they assume poses, the pose of saintliness or the pose of avarice, like Goldstein, actually Adams told me that Goldstein raised six brothers and sisters singlehanded, his father died without a cent when he was fourteen, he supported them all, including his mother, his grandmother and a great-aunt, a whole tribe, he put his brother through college, married off his sisters, established his brother, you could say that his generosity was limited to his own family, but it's a rare and wonderful thing just to have reached the stage of group egotism, most people never get beyond themselves, and Goldstein says he loves money and he thinks I'm a saint because I haven't invested the fifteen thousand dollars in my bank account, but the truth is that I was afraid of losing it, I'm not unselfish, I'm incompetent, actually I've often thought about that fifteen thousand dollars, it has given me a sense of security, and do you think the prospect of a million dollars leaves me indifferent? let's face it, in an industrial society money is the only freedom that isn't theoretical, it's an amazing feeling to know that with that million dollars we can go and live anywhere in the world, tomorrow, and do whatever we like, surrounded, protected by that barrier of gold, yes, there's that, the power and the freedom, but at the same time I'm a little afraid of all that money, I don't trust it, I wouldn't want it to take away my desire to create, to corrupt and soften me, I wouldn't want it to insidiously make me start doing things I don't altogether approve of, to gnaw me from within like a termite.

He turned his head toward the sea and took a deep breath, the sun was slipping down the other side of the cliff and the sea was covered with peaceful, reassuring mauve glints that made you forget about sharks, the water was inviting, the surface very smooth, almost without a wrinkle, actually it was height that flattened out the waves, they rolled without breaking, the way a horse's skin shivers, only the last one broke, picking up the pebbles, stirring them and tossing them aside, the same ones for ten thousand years, the outgoing tide made a terrible sucking noise like the desperate breathing of a dying man, Arlette was clearing the table, he sat alone for a moment with the newspaper in his hand, he was always bored when she wasn't there, when she left the room he had a sensation of cold and abandonment, on page three he ran across an interview with Alan and John, the reporter had managed to track them down in their little New England village, the headline attributed to them the idiotic statement, WE AREN'T JEALOUS OF FA; WE REGARD HIM AS OUR HALF-BROTHER, poor kids, they'd never even seen Fa, I'm going to have to talk Marian into taking them to Europe, they're not safe here any more, one of these days somebody's going to kidnap them for ransom, but try to convince Marian, all I have to do is make the suggestion and she'll be against it, her passion for fighting me always comes before the good of the children, he heard Arlette's step on the terrace, there was a strange silence, he looked up, she was standing in front of him breathing fast and loud, there was an angry little crease between her eyebrows, her black eyes were gleaming like two coffee beans, I don't know whether it's the fame and the money, but I think you're spoiled enough as it is, since February 20 you've been getting ten love letters a day with photographs enclosed, I suppose that's to be expected, but to have Maggie start a special file with the photograph opposite each letter and to bring the file to the bungalow for the weekend to enjoy it in my presence, it's hateful! Sevilla raised his eyebrows, But the file wasn't my idea, it was Maggie's, and the only reason I brought it here was that I haven't had time to read one of those letters, Arlette's eyes shone with anger, when she got angry her voice changed, it became louder and more serious, her body seemed more compact, she gathered herself like a fortress, it took twice as much time for a reasonable argument to penetrate her defenses, Well, if it was Maggie, she said, not at all mollified, I'm surprised at

194

her, and you didn't have to encourage her by bringing the file on a weekend with me, it's hateful and besides, it's in the worst possible taste, he said, Look, don't take it so seriously, I thought it would be amusing to read those letters, Amusing? that muck, she said, shaking with rage, those letters from crazy women who've never laid eyes on you and are proposing marriage to you in more or less veiled terms, and some even say they'll have an affair with you, I quote, "without obligation on your part," Sevilla stared, So you've read them, Yes, she said in a loud voice, the tears sprang from her eyes and rolled down her cheeks, I took the liberty of looking through that . . . harem, that slave market, I even looked at the pictures, those dresses! low-cut, suggestive, skintight—they look as if they were sewn into them, that festival of revolting half-naked women in their clinging or see-through dresses, and the bikinis! and two or three without even a bikini, in artistic poses, oh, don't laugh, don't laugh, I've never seen anything so horrible as this parade of women offering themselves, what a pitiful impression it gives of our sex, the truth is I'm ashamed for them, Stop, said Sevilla in a loud voice, getting up and holding out his arm, half humorous, half imperious, he walked into the living room, strode rapidly to the little table where he had thrown the file when he arrived that noon, picked it up and came back to the terrace, Is this what you're talking about? he asked, showing it to Arlette without opening it, Yes, she said, that's it, he walked over to the railing, brought back his arm, and flung the file into the sea as hard as he could, there was a sudden silence as it opened in midair, scattering its photos, and fell interminably before it hit the water with a barely perceptible plop and was swallowed up in the green foam of the tide, The subject is closed, said Sevilla, he put his right hand on Arlette's shoulder, she relaxed against him without a word, It's curious, he said after a moment, the way success is immediately translated into money and sex, that is, basically, into power, we haven't even emerged from the feudal system, the palace and the harem, the château and the *jus primae noctis,* our civilization is still founded on violence.

Goldstein, said Arlette softly after a moment, said something that impressed me very much, he claimed that we were heading rapidly for World War Three, Oh, I don't know, said Sevilla briefly, I don't know, why don't we take a walk on the beach while there's still a

195

little light left, he said nothing as he preceded her down the steps, carved into the rock, that led to the little creek, some of them were so short you had to put your foot parallel to the rise and go sideways like a crab, there were still rings at hip level in the rocky wall to their left but the rope that served as a handrail had disappeared, Sevilla told himself vaguely for the twentieth time that he really ought to replace it, all he had to do was buy the required length of cord and make a knot at the bottom and a knot at the top to secure it, it really wasn't much to do and yet he knew he'd never do it, in the cove there was a corner where, as a shelter against the north wind, someone, perhaps the children of the former tenants, had built a crude wall of loose stones, it had been done haphazardly and part of it had collapsed but the rest was still standing, Sevilla gave Arlette his hand as she stepped across it, they were sitting shoulder to shoulder, their backs resting against the still-warm face of the cliff, The afternoon Michael gave me his resignation, said Sevilla, he also talked about World War Three, this is how he saw the situation, even if they pour a million troops into Vietnam the United States can't win the war there with traditional weapons, and as the war drags on the hawks will gain more and more support and will succeed in electing a President even more reactionary than Goldwater, at this point the generals who have long been demanding recourse to atomic means in Asia will have their way, people will want to be done with Vietnam and while we're at it, with China before she is too well stocked with rockets, they will stage a provocation of some kind, in the well-planned indignation that will follow they'll drop the first cobalt bomb on Peking, And Russia? asked Arlette, According to Michael Russia will intervene sooner or later, according to him this is the fundamental error of the hawks, they think Russia will let it happen, only too happy to be rid of the Chinese menace on her borders, but actually Russia cannot let the United States get its hands on the vast wealth of Asia, thus becoming masters of the planet in a short space of time and eliminating her once she's isolated, Arlette looked at him with frightened eyes, What do you think? she asked quietly, is Michael right? How should I know? asked Sevilla, throwing up his hands with irritation, when you have a difficult job to do you have to concentrate on it to the exclusion of everything else, as he said the last words he made a little nervous, irritated gesture with his hand as if he were sweeping

196

the phrase far behind him, I must say, though, he went on more calmly, I was impressed by what Michael told me, he swallowed with an unhappy expression, Michael was so intellectually honest, he had put it in the past tense as if he were dead, Arlette opened her mouth to speak but looked at him and said nothing, he was staring straight ahead, his brows knitted, the corners of his mouth drooping.

He got up suddenly, Shall we go back? he said in a nervous voice, Arlette raised her eyebrows, So soon? but we just got here, I'm sorry, said Sevilla, turning his head toward her, and she thought, He's looking right through me, We can stay if you like, he added impatiently, No, let's go back, she said immediately, getting up and smiling at him, I'm sorry, he said again, with mingled embarrassment and irritation, it's this damned bungalow, all we do is go up and down steps, there's no place you can really stretch your legs, Well, we could take a walk on the cliff, she said, there's plenty of space there, there are miles of level space, No, no, he said with a little gesture, let's go back, since you want to, she laughed, But you're the one who wants to go in! he looked at her with an expression that was sad, confused, and impatient, but his eyes softened a little, he smiled wanly and said, Yes, I do, and started up the stone steps.

The architect who designed the bungalow didn't like doors any better than he did windows, there weren't any between the kitchenette and the little dining room, between the dining room and the living room, between the living room and the bedroom, or between the bedroom and the bathroom, as he undressed Sevilla watched Arlette, naked, brush her teeth, so she could see herself in the mirror she leaned over the washbasin, her feet together, her body curved forward, her stomach pulled in, her buttocks prominent, it was a graceful, innocent pose that suggested a good little girl, he smiled, the air rushed vigorously into his lungs, he curbed the rising, almost suffocating rush of joy, not desire, it lifted him, high as a bird, but he knew that in the awareness of joy there was a point beyond which you must not go at the risk of destroying the feeling, he felt light, moved, happy, and at the same time careful not to feel too much, how luminous he felt, he leaped on the young crests of the world in the first hour of the day, the beauty of this body, the gaiety, the hope, the gratitude, he felt his chest dilate to the limit of

197

bearing, all of a sudden his happiness began to race, went beyond the bounds, and almost tumbled, Sevilla began to laugh, yes, you see, he had to laugh, to use trickery, to catch his happiness before it fell by laughing, there was always something to laugh at, something absurd, for example, he was happy because she was brushing her teeth, he laughed, he felt the falsity of his laugh, it was impossible to stay more than a second on the extraordinary crest of life, we are forever going from phase to phase—laughter to flee sorrow, possession to go beyond laughter, tenderness to recover from possession— the second of mad happiness could never be fixed, you were pushed from behind, come on, keep moving, Why are you laughing? asked Arlette, leaning toward the mirror, Because you look like a good little girl, she turned her head and looked into his eyes, a wave of warmth rose through his body from calves to waist, she laughed too, But I am good, she said softly with a little low laugh.

Arlette's head was leaning against his shoulder, his body was bathed in sweat and lying flat, poured onto the mattress, every muscle relaxed, he reached out his right arm and turned off the light, there was a long silence, Sevilla's breathing became so peaceful that Arlette thought he was asleep and yet when he spoke again it was in the most casual, conversational tone, as if he were continuing a dialogue that had only been interrupted for a moment, If the Russians aren't bluffing, he said, his voice ringing out clear and incisive in the silence, if they have reached the stage where they're using a hundred dolphins for fishing, then they must be farther along than we thought in communication between the species, even if we ignore their ranting about individualism and capitalist struggle for survival that has led us poor ugly Americans to concentrate on a single pair, but it's true that teaching two dolphins to talk is nothing, we have yet to extend communication to the entire species or at least to two or three dozen individuals, and I'm damned if I know how I'm going to go about *that*.

．　．　．

INTERVIEW BETWEEN FA AND BI AND PROFESSOR SEVILLA
MONDAY, MARCH 9, 1971, 10:00 A.M.

(*Note by Professor Sevilla:* I had not seen Fa and Bi since I left the lab Friday, March 6, and at the sight of me Fa leaped out of the

198

water, lashed it repeatedly with his tail, and emitted a whole series of joyous whistling sounds. During this time Bi remained a little to one side, mute and distant and barely looking at me.)

FA: Pa! Where were you? Where were you?

SEVILLA: Hello, Fa!

FA: Hello, Pa! Hello, Pa! Hello, Pa! Where were you?

SEVILLA: Hello, Bi!

BI: Hello, Pa. [*Bi is in the center of the tank. She is swimming around slowly in a clockwise direction. She observes me out of the corner of her eye when she passes me, but she is not making any whistling sounds and does not seem to want to approach me. Fa is at the edge of the tank a yard from me, exuberant and affectionate. When I walk over to him he plays his usual joke of splashing me from head to foot.*]

SEVILLA: I left to relax with Ma.

FA: Relax? You mean sleep?

SEVILLA: To relax means to do nothing.

FA: You do not relax here?

SEVILLA: No, not often.

FA: Do you relax there, where you go?

SEVILLA: Yes.

FA: Where is it?

SEVILLA: By the sea.

[*Bi stops swimming around and listens attentively, but does not approach.*]

FA: Here it is by the sea too. Sometimes I hear the waves and when I taste the water, it tastes of other animals.

SEVILLA: I explained that to you: At high tide they open the sea gates and the sea water comes into the tank.

FA: Yes, I know. I did not forget. I never forget anything. I love it when the water tastes of the sea and the animals of the sea.

SEVILLA: Bi, come here!

[*Bi does not obey immediately, and when she does, instead of swimming right over to the edge of the tank, she makes a series of little sideways movements to indicate her reluctance.*]

SEVILLA: Bi, what's the matter? Are you angry?

BI: You did not tell us you were leaving us.

SEVILLA: But it wasn't the first time. Before the press conference I had already gone away twice.

BI: Yes, but you said you were leaving.

SEVILLA: Well, next time I'll tell you.

BI: Thank you, Pa. Is it pretty where you were?

SEVILLA: Very pretty.

BI: What do you do when you do nothing?
[*I laugh, and immediately Fa imitates me, looking at Bi mockingly. Bi bats her eyelashes as if she were annoyed, but says nothing.*]
SEVILLA: I play with Ma, I lie in the sun, and I go swimming.
BI: You ought to take us.
FA: Yes, Pa! You ought to take us!
SEVILLA: I can't, there's no tank.
BI: Where do you go swimming?
SEVILLA: In the sea.
BI: What about sharks?
SEVILLA: Where I am there are no sharks. But you have nothing to complain about here while I'm away, you have fun.
FA: Yes, especially with Ba.* He is very nice. The others are very nice too.
BI: I like Ba very much. He is with us all the time. He swims with us. He plays with us. He strokes us. And he talks. He talks.
FA: He read us articles about us. But he would not explain. He told us, "Wait for Pa."
SEVILLA: Yes, I asked him to do that.
FA: Pa, I have had much pain. There are people who do not like us.
SEVILLA: There are always people who are afraid of new things.
FA: Are they afraid of us?
SEVILLA: Yes.
BI: I do not understand why.
FA: There is a man who said, "The place of a fish is on my plate."
BI: Pa, why did he say that? We are not good to eat.
FA: And we are not fish!
BI: Oh, Fa, do not be such a snob!
[*I laugh and Fa imitates me.*]
SEVILLA: Bi, who taught you the word "snob"?
BI: Ba. Why do you laugh? Is it a bad word?
SEVILLA: It is a very good word. Especially when Fa boasts about being a cetacean.
FA: But I am proud of being a cetacean. The dolphin's brain is as heavy as man's.
SEVILLA: That's good, you haven't forgotten.
FA: I never forget anything.
BI: Are there other articles about us?

---

* Bob.

SEVILLA: We'll see later. Right now I have some things to tell you.

FA: Me too?

SEVILLA: You too. It was you who taught Bi to talk, Fa. Do you remember?

FA: Yes, it was me.

SEVILLA: And now I want the two of you to teach other dolphins to talk.

FA: Why?

SEVILLA: Two talking dolphins are not enough.

FA: Why?

SEVILLA: It would take too long to explain.

FA: Will it please you that we teach other dolphins to talk?

SEVILLA: Yes.

FA: Well, how will we do it?

SEVILLA: I'll bring you dolphins.

BI: Here? In the tank?

SEVILLA: Yes.

BI: Male or female dolphins?

SEVILLA: A female, to begin with.

BI: No, no!

SEVILLA: What do you mean, no?

BI: I do not want it.

SEVILLA: You don't want it?

BI: I will beat her! I will bite her!

SEVILLA: But see here, Bi . . .

BI: I will steal her share of fish.

SEVILLA: But see here, Bi, that would be very bad of you.

BI: Yes!

SEVILLA: You want to be bad?

BI: Yes! I will be very bad, all the time! I will bite her!

SEVILLA: But why, Bi?

BI: I do not want Fa to make an S in front of her.

[*Fa laughs, Bi turns to him and hits him with her tail; he moves aside and does not answer.*]

SEVILLA: Bi, you know that's the way it is in the sea.

BI: It is not the same.

SEVILLA: In the sea a male always has several females.

BI: It is not the same.

SEVILLA: What's not the same? [*A silence*]

BI: Fa and I are talking.

[*I am speechless for a moment, amazed at the implications of this answer.*]

201

FA: Say something, Pa!
SEVILLA: Bi, suppose the other female is stronger than you?
BI: Then I will ask Fa to help me fight her.
SEVILLA: And will you fight her, Fa?
FA: Yes.
SEVILLA: Why?
FA: I always do what Bi tells me.
SEVILLA: Why?
FA: Because I want to. I love Bi.
SEVILLA: What if I put a male dolphin in the tank?
FA: I will fight him. Perhaps I will kill him.
SEVILLA: What if he is bigger and stronger?
FA: Bi will help me.
[*I look at Bi, and Bi nods her head.*]
SEVILLA: Bi, about this female dolphin, why does it matter that Fa and you can talk? Before you spoke English you talked in Dolphinese.
BI: It is not the same.
SEVILLA: What's not the same?
BI: I do not know.
SEVILLA: Before you learned to speak English, would you have accepted another female dolphin in the tank?
BI: I love Fa. I love him the way you love Ma.
SEVILLA: You have noticed that I love Ma.
BI: Yes.
SEVILLA: If I did not love Ma, would you accept another female dolphin?
BI [*Distressed*]: Are you going to stop loving Ma?
SEVILLA: Of course not. I said "if." I already explained what "if" means.
BI: I do not like "if." Fa understands "if," but I do not. A thing is true or it is not true. What is the use of "if"?
SEVILLA: Listen carefully, Bi. Listen to me, it's important. Is it because I love Ma that you don't want another female dolphin in the tank? [*A silence*]
BI: Yes. Maybe.
SEVILLA: Do you want to be with Fa the way I am with Ma?
BI: Yes.
SEVILLA: And if you didn't speak English, would you have noticed that I love Ma?
BI: I don't like "if." "If" confuses me.
SEVILLA: Bi, please try to answer.
BI: I do not know. I am tired.

[*She turns her back on me, swims over to the rubber ring, picks it up with her snout and throws it to Fa, who catches it and throws it back to her. I make several attempts to resume the conversation. She doesn't answer. It is ten twenty.*]

Suzy looked at the team. It was the first meeting since the 20th of February, the chairs were arranged around a table which held a tape recorder, the ritual was always the same, the assistants arrived five minutes ahead of time, Sevilla hurried in last and was the last to sit down, he had replaced Lisbeth with Simon, but whether by accident or by choice, he had not replaced Michael—one replacement, one absence—except for Michael's seat at Suzy's left, everyone was sitting in his usual place, without realizing it Simon had taken Lisbeth's place on Arlette's right, Peter, of course, was next to Suzy, his arm resting on the back of her chair, he wasn't touching her but she felt his warmth against the back of her neck, and Maggie next to Bob, exquisitely dressed, he was doing his best, assuming his most distant manner, he almost had his back turned to her, but he wasn't succeeding in discouraging her comments, with which she was also regaling her neighbor on the left, Simon, so polite and so shy, with his feet hooked under the bars of his chair, he wasn't answering her, but that wouldn't save him, poor thing, on the contrary, for Maggie even silence is consent.

"You are going to hear a conversation I had with Fa and Bi on the ninth of March," said Sevilla. "Please listen carefully, it will be the subject of our discussion."

He turned on the tape recorder, put both hands flat on the table, and sat silently, his eyes fastened on the revolving tape. The shrill voices of the two dolphins took possession of the room.

"Well," he said, when the tape was over, "what do you think of it? For the moment I'm not asking you for practical suggestions, but for an analysis of behavior. On this level, what do you think of it?"

After a moment Suzy said, "In my opinion Fa's reaction is normal. I mean, it is consistent with what we know of the behavior of the male dolphin. He lives alone in a tank with Bi. To introduce another male raises the question of sharing the female and the question of hierarchy."

"In that case," said Arlette, "Bi's reaction is normal. To intro-

203

duce another female into the tank would raise the same problems for her."

"Not exactly," said Peter.

Arlette looked at him. Since Michael had left he seemed more sure of himself, more mature, and more calmly possessive toward Suzy.

"Bi," he went on, "has lived in the sea, which means that she has lived in a school of dolphins, where the couples are not stable and where one male dominates several females in succession. In spite of this, she chooses monogamy."

"You're right," said Sevilla, and Peter looked happy. "It is a deliberate choice."

"And it's even justified," said Bob in his fluty voice.

He was wearing blue canvas shoes, sky-blue slacks, a periwinkle-blue sport shirt open at the neck, and a turquoise-and-black printed silk ascot. Suzy looked at him. It was really exquisite, this symphony in blue, but how could he stand a silk scarf around his neck in this heat?

"To be precise," Bob went on, "I would say that there is a certain ambiguity in her motivation, for Bi has not given one explanation for her attitude, she has given two. First, she speaks our language. Second, she wants her relations with Fa to be like those of human beings."

Sevilla looked at Simon, whose feet were curled under his chair, and asked courteously, "Well, Simon, what do you think about it? Is there an ambiguity in this motivation?"

Simon blushed. He was a tall thin boy, inhibited and conscientious-looking, about whom everything seemed indefinite—age, features, hair color, opinions.

"Perhaps," he conceded prudently, "one might say there is some ambiguity."

Maggie smiled at him encouragingly, and afraid of being rude, Simon threw her a little grimace which could pass for a half smile, Maggie lowered her eyes, poor boy, he's riddled with complexes, he's so shy, how lustfully he looks at me, like an urchin standing in front of a bakery shop, I'm sure he's never kissed a girl, it's almost too bad that things have gone as far as they have with Bob, if I weren't afraid of arousing his jealousy I'd take this boy in hand, I'm sure I could make something of him, after all, he's not ugly, he has

204

very expressive eyes, and a lot of hidden warmth, judging from those sensual lips.

"I don't think there's any ambiguity," said Arlette. "It's true that Bi gave two reasons for her behavior: First, I speak your language, and second, I want my relations with Fa to be like those of humans. But if you look closely these two reasons are really the same. In both cases there is a powerful desire for identification with man."

"Bravo, Arlette," said Sevilla warmly, giving her a quick smile. "Perhaps you remember," he went on, looking his team over, "that during the press conference of February twentieth one of the reporters asked Fa whether he regarded the fact that he could talk as an improvement. In the midst of so much stupidity, it was an interesting question. For Bi, speaking the language of human beings was indeed an improvement. Since she talks, she isn't that different from us. Therefore our type of love relationship must also be hers. By taking the monogamy of the human couple as a model, she is identifying with us."

"That's very interesting," said Peter, "but why is it that Fa doesn't have the same reaction as Bi? If I understood correctly, Fa was not initially opposed to the arrival of a second female dolphin."

"Perhaps," said Suzy, "because the male dolphin—like the male of the human species, for that matter—is more inclined to be polygamous . . ."

There was laughter. It's a good thing Lisbeth isn't here any more, thought Arlette, for her laugh wouldn't have been very pleasant. It's curious how all you need is one hostile personality to spoil everything.

"May I add my two cents' worth?" asked Bob in his mannered voice, putting his right hand on his hip. Once again Suzy admired the facility with which he abandoned his positions as soon as Sevilla had spoken. "Fa also shows a desire for identification, but he shows it in another way. For example, he is constantly saying that he is not a fish, but a cetacean. Why? Because he knows that the cetacean is a mammal, like man; and because he knows that the cetacean called dolphin has a brain that is as heavy as man's. This is what I have called his snobbery. But this snobbery is also a desire to be identified with the human species."

Sevilla indicated his approval by nodding his head, but without his usual warmth. He was annoyed. When Bob agreed with you, he

205

always seemed to be inventing your own ideas. "Well," he asked, "are we all in agreement on this interpretation? Simon?"

"I am in agreement," said Simon, and Maggie gave him a conspiratorial smile.

"I'm not a moralist," said Sevilla, "so I cannot say whether the fact that the first pair of dolphins to speak human language is also adopting the monogamy of Western man constitutes progress or not. But for us this mutation is a serious obstacle and raises a serious problem. How are we to go about extending the knowledge of Fa and Bi to other dolphins?"

The ringing of the telephone filled the air with strident force, Sevilla told Maggie with a little irritated gesture, "I'm not in to anyone," Maggie got up, walked over to the little telephone table and picked up the receiver, Hello? she said in that refined, remote voice she put on to answer the telephone, I'm sorry, it's impossible, Professor Sevilla is in conference, would you mind calling back, I'm so sorry, Mrs. Gilchrist, Mrs. Gilchrist! cried Sevilla, getting up so suddenly that his chair fell over, letting it fall, he strode to the telephone and almost tore the receiver out of Maggie's hands. Mrs. Gilchrist, Sevilla. . . . When? Yesterday afternoon? But that's the maximum! . . . It's monstrous. . . . I don't know what to say. . . . How did he take it? Yes, I know, he's very brave. . . . Don't worry about the fine, I'll pay it. . . . Well, let's call it a loan, he'll pay me back when he gets out of prison. . . . No, no, it's nothing. . . . Yes, I'll write him, yes, of course, tell him I'll come and see him as soon as they give me permission, I'll put in a request today."

He replaced the receiver and turned to face his assistants. He was pale and his expression was blank.

"Michael," he said in a toneless voice, "was sentenced yesterday to the maximum penalty: five years in prison and a ten-thousand-dollar fine."

X

From the California university where he was giving a much-publicized series of lectures on Husserl, the Yugoslavian philosopher Marco Llepovič wrote his friend in Sarajevo as follows:

The Presidential elections which will take place at the end of this year [1972] and about which I will say something later, because of the absurdity of the political context, rekindle feelings I experienced nine years ago at the time of the Kennedy affair. That a great political leader was assassinated as the result of a shady underworld machination was not so surprising: The drama could have taken place in any other country in the world. What I found disturbing was the passivity and malleability the Americans demonstrated on that occasion. For after all, these are people admirable in every way. They are simple, generous, hospitable, full of good will in human relations, disciplined in social relations, very diligent in the exercise of their professions, in short, they possess an enormous savoir-faire in all realms, not to mention their splendid physical appearance, which is the result of sports and the highest standard of living in the world. And yet, politically speaking, these superior people are children. They allow themselves to be manipulated and influenced with disconcerting facility. Let us suppose that in any European country a loved and respected President is killed, that his presumed assassin is interrogated but that no trace of his interrogation exists *(since the local police could not afford to buy a tape recorder)*, that this assassin is in turn killed by a gangster whose ties with the police are well known. Nothing more would be needed to set off immediately a powerful movement of opinion which would have made the

Warren Report's official attempt at suppression impossible from the very start. In the United States not only was the Warren Report born out of public apathy, but it almost succeeded in burying the affair, and if the affair finally has come to light again, though too late—and in my opinion, without any political effectiveness—it is because the members of the conspiracy, in an excess of precaution, removed fourteen important witnesses of the drama, one after the other. It was the accumulation of violent providential deaths that finally aroused public opinion, still to quite a modest degree, whereas in Europe the assassination of the presumed murderer by a gangster-cop would in itself have been enough to arouse the masses.

Today, at the approach of the Presidential elections, I observe this malleability of the American people with the same uneasiness. Right now I am witnessing a phenomenon which would be laughable if it were not also extremely dangerous. There is a campaign going on to *sell* the Hollywood actor Jim Crooner to the American public as a future candidate for the Presidency. I don't suppose that in Sarajevo you have ever seen a film in which this actor played, but here he is very famous. Physically he is a cross between James Stewart and Gary Cooper. Tall, rangy, an athletic fifty, his hair just beginning to turn gray, his smile full of melancholy virtue, he seems to be carrying the burden of the whole human race on his broad shoulders. To American women he is brother, father, and husband all in one, the incarnation of benevolent virility in three persons, an enormous chest to cry on. To everyone else he is the strong man full of resources and know-how who, with a minimum of words and a dash of humor, saves the damsel in distress just as fifty Indians are about to violate her.

Unfortunately, the providential hero is no longer content to save heroines with teased hair in the middle of the desert. He's now going to save the United States of America (and consequently the free world) from the dangers that assail it. It's frightening, because incredible as it may seem to a European, Jim Crooner has a good chance of being elected President. Actually it all began six years ago, in November 1966, when the actor Ronald Reagan, who was advertising a brand of cigars on TV, was elected governor of the State of California. Operation Crooner is the logical consequence of Operation Reagan. I do not know what forces are pushing Crooner to the leadership of the United States, but they must be very powerful to be able to spend the fabulous sums they have been spending on him for the past few months, for this sale is an expensive one. Crooner has behind him a powerful machine—publicity agency, public relations agency, and brain trust. Just as an indication, according to what is said and even printed here, the political film glorifying Jim Crooner cost $150,000, and was carried about forty times on different television channels (which in this country sell politics to the viewers the same way they sell soap) at a price of $7,000 per hour of broadcast time (the film runs about an hour), or a total of $280,000. This is only the beginning; another film is already being announced. In addition, a sumptuous illustrated brochure recalling the life, struggles, and ideals of Jim Crooner has been sent to forty million people to date; printing and postage are estimated to have cost $800,000. The political program in all this? There isn't any, of course. Apart from this splendid physique and his wonderful acting ability Crooner knows nothing, thinks nothing, wants nothing. He is an empty vase waiting to be filled. His speeches, his jokes, his anecdotes, the sob stuff about his penniless childhood, and his dazzling retorts to pseudo-adversaries on trumped-up television debates—everything has been learned by rote. The disturbing thing about Operation Crooner is the choice of a man so devoid of intelligence and political experience to preside over the destinies of the most powerful state in the world. The Presidential function will have undergone a shocking debasement. Kennedy had ideas and courage, he knew how to say no—it may be that it was because of this ability to say no that he was eliminated. And Johnson, in spite of his obvious weaknesses, nevertheless knew the facts of life, he was a professional politician; I like to believe that he first took the path of violence reluctantly, perhaps with a bad conscience. Consider, for example, the moral speeches with which he chose to accompany each new degree of escalation. But if Crooner is elected, the Presidency of the United States will be occupied by a man who will have about as much influence over United States policy as Chiang Kai-shek or Marshal Ky.

That this debasement is desired by those whose ends it serves is obviously the disturbing part, for Jim Crooner will do whatever they want him to—with that kind, fair, responsible manner which is his trademark—including dropping the first H-bomb on China. I hope with all my heart that I am mistaken, but if Crooner is elected, I believe the world will rush pell-mell toward that *major war* in Asia which may lead to World War Three.

•   •   •

Arlette rolled over, stretched out flat on her back, and listened in the warm darkness to the surf battering the island. The sound seemed to come from the tiny harbor which also served as a swim-

209

ming pool, but she knew that it didn't, the channel between the rocks was so narrow and winding that no wave could break that far, it was to the north, behind the head of her bed, behind the wall of the house, behind the enormous reservoir which the last hurricane had filled to the very top, she knew that the sea broke against the girdle of rocks, it was a side of the island where they never went, a stretch of useless land, a little desert of pebbles, not one sandy creek, not one place to swim or even launch the smaller of the two life rafts, nothing but breakers, whirlpools, and mountains of foam, but to the south, where the land was flat, they had brought a little soil from the mainland, enough to grow bougainvillaea and decorate the rambling ranch-style house which had no windows on the north and which Henry called the "blockhouse" because it was constructed out of concrete to withstand hurricanes, the only sound that really came from the harbor was the constant whistling of the rigging of the *Caribee*, its beautiful aluminum mast was so high that it soared over house, island, and rocks, and, like an antenna, was alone exposed to all winds, the *Caribee* had been included in the price of the house, Goldstein must have had a hard time keeping Henry from concluding the deal the same day, that was last year, a year already, and Michael behind bars all this time, the thought of him is like a reproach, how horrible it is to think that he won't be freed until 1976, four years from now, five years of life stolen, at his age, all because he refused to take part in a war he thought unjust, comformity exalted to a tyrannical law, freedom of conscience flouted in the name of freedom, Lisbeth, but I don't want to feel sorry for Lisbeth, she was treacherous, she tried to hurt, the eyes of that girl, the way she used to look at me, I didn't know where to hide, *It's time you realized that you'll never be anything to him but a number in a series,* she was a woman, after all, only a woman can find the remark that really stings, the insidious little turn of phrase that you can never forget, *a number in a series,* Arlette felt her face stiffen, she put out her left hand and groped on the table, it was there, turned over, as always, on its moonlike face, the pretentious, almost illegible numerals gleaming in the half darkness, four twenty or five twenty, why couldn't they use numbers like everybody else, theoretically, an alarm clock is supposed to tell you what time it is, she turned over, he was sleeping, curled up in a ball and breathing noisily, his face like that of a child or a tame

210

lion, the big head lying sweetly on the crossed paws, a surge of tenderness went through her, she ran her hand over the bare shoulder and immediately drew it back, he was such a light sleeper, I'll never ask him for that, there are more important things in his life, you can't use a man like a tool, but why can't I think about it without feeling sorry for Bi and her little stillborn baby dolphin, how sad she was, and what a tragedy if the first pair of dolphins to speak a human language never had any young, I remember how disappointed Henry was a year ago when Bi refused to accept another female dolphin in the tank and how happy he was when Bi became pregnant, *You'll see, you'll see, this baby dolphin will be bilingual,* my God, what a terrible delivery, the hours, if Bi died, Fa would die, everything would be lost, oh, I don't want to think about it any more, and since then, this unproductive period in the study of the whistling language, these extraordinary difficulties, *Bi, how would you say "Throw me that ring" in the whistling language?* I would not say it, Why not? There are no rings in the sea, the incredible number of human things for which they obviously have no equivalent, and some of the whistling sounds almost impossible to reproduce with a human organ, *Well, will we have to invent a machine to whistle in Dolphinese?* Henry so discouraged, so humiliated, *I don't deserve my reputation, I have solved nothing, nothing, two talking dolphins don't make a species, Adams, you must understand that it will take a long time, the research is just beginning, research takes a long time, I can't help it, we're only halfway there, in two years, yes, in two years, maybe, we'll have mastered Dolphinese and then we'll be able to teach English to the whole species,* and it wasn't as if we didn't work like demons after that, the whole team, Bob, Peter, Suzy, Simon, I was so relieved when Henry hired Simon to replace Lisbeth, I was afraid he would choose another girl and fall in love with her, *a number in a series,* that was the time of the album business, I was furious at Maggie, she couldn't believe it, But, Arlette, how could you think that I . . . but it was enough to disgust a satyr, that collection of women throwing themselves at Henry like bitches in heat, what an image, poor Maggie, I shouldn't laugh at her, what a monstrous injustice, a girl like that, it's horrible of us to laugh at her the way we do, but you can't feel sorry for her all the time, she repeats herself ad nauseam—*You see, Arlette, the tragedy about my rela-*

211

tionship with Bob is that I don't want children, the eyes grave, riveted on us, the body straining forward, the noble woman, the embattled intellectual, and a bad actress into the bargain, the voice, the gestures, the expression, she overdoes it, *When she's fabricating,* Henry says, *I notice it right away, it's so badly done,* and perhaps the one most to be pitied is Bob, he spends his time running away from her, he even avoids her eye, he never sits next to her at the table, *I don't even dare ask her what time it is any more, I don't know how she might take it,* he's amusing, I have to admit he's amusing, I've never understood how Henry forgave him so quickly for going to work for that horrible C, but Henry is above all that, his head is in the clouds, he excuses almost everything, perhaps he's influenced by the fact that since Michael's departure Bob has started to work like a demon, always volunteering for everything, consequently he spends hours and hours with Fa and Bi, they dote on him, he has almost taken our place in their affections, I don't like that, I wonder whether Bob is following orders, I'll have to warn Henry, I have no confidence in that little snake, so affected, so effeminate, so narcissistic, I can't stand the way he twists his legs under him when he sits down, perhaps he is simply "one of the American males of the frigid generation," as Greenson puts it, one of the ones who prefer marijuana or LSD to sex, who limit themselves in this area to "quick and easy satisfactions," what an astonishing euphemism, poor Bob, he doesn't even have the courage to be really queer, sometimes I almost feel like telling him so, she seized the alarm clock with irritation and stared for a few seconds at its luminous dial, when you can't sleep the time drags, it passes so fast the rest of the time, week after week after week, two years already since Henry . . . curious that for me the image of happiness is a torrential rain flooding the windshield of a car, the light from the dashboard was shining on my legs, I was afraid he'd seen them tremble, I felt my body melt under his look, a hurricane named Hannah, strange that it killed a hundred and fifty people and that to me it brought life, a real life, before, that feeling for five or six years of stifling in solitude, confusion, and for a year even in idleness, and that foolish, intellectually degrading affair, I felt immobilized, and then all of a sudden when I got my Ph.D., the confidence in myself, the strength, the pride, I knew I would be able to break the spell, Dear Miss Lafeuille, I have read your thesis on

212

the behavior of *Tursiops truncatus* in captivity and I wonder whether you would like to work with me, when I read his signature I leaped with joy, he came to meet me at the airport with Michael, I was almost jealous of Michael, he loved him so much, he really loved him as a son, he had taught him so many things, and now the dominant one is Michael behind his bars, there is a magic in those bars, Henry reads all the papers, he reads and rereads his letters, strange that they let everything Michael writes go through without any censorship, I suppose they must make photocopies of everything, Henry's answers too, and that there is somewhere on Adams' desk, on C's desk, and God knows who else's, an admirably well-organized file with references, notes, analytic index, shrewd comments by the best political psychologists on every remark Henry makes, the file on Oppie before his trial was several yards high, but when I tell Henry that he just laughs, *What do you want, espionage and informing are the mother's milk of U.S. Intelligence,* when you think that the CIA subsidized the National Student Association and that an American university agreed to serve as a cover for a "mission of specialists" to Vietnam, you realize that anything, absolutely anything, is possible, But still, you should pay a little more attention to what you write to Michael, I think you're terribly imprudent, your fame doesn't make you untouchable, remember Oppie, but he'll never listen to anything, when you come near anything that has to do with courage he reacts like a Spaniard, he stiffens and clams up, *I don't want to start by censoring myself, I'd be playing right into the hands of all those cops, that's what they live for—to make you gradually castrate yourself,* and certainly no one can say that Henry underestimates his virility, she laughed soundlessly, put out her hand and touched his shoulder lightly, after a moment she felt his hand closing over hers, and said softly, You're not asleep, will you hold me, can I talk to you?

•   •   •

CONVERSATION BETWEEN SEVILLA AND ADAMS
JULY 22, 1972, ROOM 56–278: CONFIDENTIAL

ADAMS: I'm very happy to see you again. I don't believe I've seen you since the press conference of February 20, 1971. It was very kind of you to send me a copy of your book. I'm told it has done very well.

213

SEVILLA: To my amazement. I didn't put in any of the ingredients that Brücker suggested, only the facts.

ADAMS: I think it is this seriousness that people liked.

SEVILLA: Goldstein has a much more cynical explanation. He claims that the book would have sold anyway, even if I had written it with my feet.

ADAMS: I don't believe a word of it. What you said about Jim Crooner amused Lorrimer very much. I take it you don't like him?

SEVILLA: No.

ADAMS: I don't share your feeling. If Crooner is elected I think he'll put some new blood in our old Administration.

SEVILLA: Let's hope that's the only blood he'll cause to flow.

ADAMS: Do you think him so cruel?

SEVILLA: I think he'll do whatever he's told.

ADAMS: Oh, you are a pessimist! Are you satisfied with Goldstein's services?

SEVILLA: Very much. Frankly, he's become indispensable to me. He's a friend.

ADAMS: I'm delighted to hear it. I hear that your book is going to be translated into twenty-three languages and that Hollywood is going to make a movie out of it.

SEVILLA: Correct.

ADAMS: I also hear that *Look* bought the prepublication rights for two hundred sixty thousand dollars. And that Brücker sold the paperback rights for five hundred thousand and the *Reader's Digest* paid four hundred thousand to condense it. Brücker must be licking his chops.

SEVILLA: It wasn't Goldstein who told you all this.

ADAMS: No. Goldstein is very discreet. The figures were published last week by *Time*. *Time* estimates your total royalties, including movies and translations, at three million dollars. Is that right?

SEVILLA: Bravo for *Time*.

ADAMS: What does it feel like to become a millionaire?

SEVILLA: Among other things, it gives you a sense of freedom.

ADAMS: Freedom?

SEVILLA: Before, I was free, theoretically, to buy a big house on an island in the Florida Keys with a little private harbor and a yacht . . .

ADAMS: Theoretically . . . you have an original way of putting things. [*He laughs*] I'll bet they soaked you for that house.

SEVILLA: No. Goldstein advised me.

ADAMS: You said a sense of freedom, "among other things."

SEVILLA: Yes. I also have a sense of guilt.

214

ADAMS: Guilt? Why guilt? You didn't steal that money, you earned it.

SEVILLA: I feel that I've been overpaid.

ADAMS: What about Brücker!

SEVILLA: I don't care about Brücker. I feel that I've been overpaid in comparison to people who work hard and earn little.

ADAMS: Aha! If it weren't for the yacht I'd suspect you of being a socialist! But see here, those people you're talking about don't have your qualifications.

SEVILLA: Yes, but it's immoral for there to be such a gap between them and me.

ADAMS: Is it because of this sense of guilt that you continue to keep all your money in the bank instead of investing it?

SEVILLA: No, that's different. The idea that my money could work in my place revolts me.

ADAMS: Well, it's working for somebody. Your banker must bless you.

SEVILLA: That's his business. I suppose that's why he became a banker: to make money with money. But my business is to work.

ADAMS: Well, you must give away your millions. [*He laughs*]

SEVILLA: Yes, but to whom? I would like them to be really useful and I don't trust philanthropy.

ADAMS: I was joking. [*A silence*]

SEVILLA: Couldn't we dispense with these preliminaries? You're so nervous you frighten me a little.

ADAMS: I'm not nervous.

SEVILLA: That's the second time you've wiped the palms of your hands with your handkerchief.

ADAMS [*Laughing*]: You can't trust these scientific types. They have a gift for observation. [*A pause*] Well, I like you and I'm afraid what I'm going to say will upset you. I have some very unpleasant things to tell you.

SEVILLA: I had concluded as much from the length of your preamble. But I've already complimented you on your skill.

ADAMS: It's not skill. It's embarrassment.

SEVILLA: Well, out with it! What are you waiting for?

ADAMS: Don't fight me. It's much worse than anything you can imagine. I've received a very shocking order, it's my duty to inform you of it, and I'm very much distressed. As you know, I like you.

SEVILLA: But your liking for me doesn't come before your loyalty to your leaders.

ADAMS: To tell the truth, it doesn't.

SEVILLA: Well, speak. Must I resign from Operation Logos?

215

ADAMS: No, it isn't that. In a way it's worse. [*A silence*] We're going to take Fa and Bi away from you.

SEVILLA: You're going to take Fa and Bi away from me?

ADAMS: Temporarily. Please sit down. Yes, I'm sorry, but it's an order.

SEVILLA: But what are you going to do with them? Where are you going to take them?

ADAMS: I can't answer those questions.

SEVILLA: But this is insane! You don't know what you're saying! Fa and Bi will never withstand this separation! You're breaking emotional ties it took years to establish!

ADAMS: Bob Manning will go with them.

SEVILLA: Bob!

ADAMS: Please control yourself. Do you feel ill? Would you like a glass of water?

SEVILLA: No, thank you. It's nothing. It will pass. [*A silence*] All this is the most monstrous hypocrisy. Adams, I'm going to tell you what I think. For two years you've been nice to me and for two years Bob, on your orders, behind my back . . .

ADAMS: They weren't my orders. I only transmitted them. My responsibility stops there.

SEVILLA: What revolting Machiavellianism! And to what end, I wonder!

ADAMS: I'm going to be frank: We have decided to isolate you from all the practical applications . . .

SEVILLA: You mean all the military applications.

ADAMS: I said practical.

SEVILLA: But Bob is more accommodating. So he'll be allowed to know where you're going to hide Fa and Bi and what insane things you're going to make them do.

ADAMS: Inevitably, since he'll go with them.

SEVILLA: I don't believe my ears! Have you forgotten that Bob is Mr. C's tool?

ADAMS: I don't see how that could be a problem.

SEVILLA: So the noble Mr. C is also mixed up in this business!

ADAMS: Not at all.

SEVILLA: Do you think Bob would lift a finger without informing Mr. C?

ADAMS: That's our problem.

SEVILLA: But where does Operation Logos fit into all this? What's to become of it? It's insane! We're halfway along in our study of the whistling language and you take away our subjects, the only dolphins who can cooperate with us right now! It's monstrous!

216

Think of your responsibility to science if something happened to them!

ADAMS: Nothing will happen to them. The separation is only temporary. Fa and Bi will be returned to you.

SEVILLA: After how long?

ADAMS: I'm not authorized to give you a date.

SEVILLA: Aren't you afraid that when they return they'll tell me what they did with you?

ADAMS: They'll have done nothing that they won't be able to tell you about.

SEVILLA: In that case why not authorize me to go with them?

ADAMS: I've already told you that.

SEVILLA: I don't have the right to see what they do, but they have the right to tell me about it!

ADAMS: That kind of contradiction doesn't bother me.

SEVILLA: I wonder what *does* bother you! Has it ever occurred to you to find out how Fa and Bi feel before taking them away from their family? For we are their family, I hope you understand that. Adams, listen to me, I'm not ashamed to say it: I regard them as my children.

ADAMS: Naturally we have given the fullest consideration to the emotional aspect of the matter. In the first place, Bob has obtained the dolphins' consent to this trip.

SEVILLA: Behind my back!

ADAMS: Bob made it clear that he would go with them. They are very fond of Bob, as you know.

SEVILLA: He made sure of that. The dirty sneak! He has betrayed me twice. Once spying on me for C, and once by winning the dolphins away from me behind my back, on your orders.

ADAMS: It seems to me you're overdramatizing the case. After all, Fa and Bi are only animals.

SEVILLA: You don't understand anything! They can talk. I've been much closer to them than I've been to some people. Fa and Bi are living beings like you and me, and I love them as if they were my own children, as I've already told you.

ADAMS: I didn't take you literally. I'm very sorry. Especially since I still haven't told you the worst. I'm afraid it will hurt you very much.

SEVILLA: You can't hurt me: I'm giving you my resignation.

ADAMS: I must warn you in all loyalty to you—

SEVILLA: I don't believe in your loyalty.

ADAMS: Except toward my superiors: I know. Well, I'm speaking for them. If your resignation is an attempt to force us to abandon

217

our project, you're making a mistake. We won't abandon it. And if, in spite of everything, you insist on giving us your resignation, this time we have decided to accept it.

SEVILLA: You sound as if you'd like me to resign.

ADAMS: Not at all.

SEVILLA: Come now, Adams! You underestimate my intelligence. Do you think I don't understand why my resignation would suit you?

ADAMS: I really don't see why it would.

SEVILLA: Because that way you could be sure that Fa and Bi would not talk to me once their mission was accomplished.

ADAMS: There is no mission.

SEVILLA: Yes there is, and it must be damned important if you're ready to jeopardize Operation Logos, a project on which you have spent fantastic sums for the past ten years.

ADAMS: You're exaggerating. Operation Logos is in no way threatened. Fa and Bi will be returned to you very shortly, without a scratch.

SEVILLA: And will you return them to me psychologically intact?

ADAMS: I don't understand what you mean.

SEVILLA: I'm going to ask you a question. Do you know now how Fa and Bi will react to what you are going to make them do?

ADAMS: I don't understand your question. We're not going to make them do anything abnormal. [*A silence*]

SEVILLA: Aren't you afraid that when I go back to the laboratory I'll talk Fa and Bi out of leaving with Bob?

ADAMS: Yes, we've thought of that. We've taken precautions.

SEVILLA: What precautions?

ADAMS: I said before that I still hadn't told you the worst. Here it is: When you go back to the laboratory, Fa and Bi will be gone. Our men are taking them away right now.

SEVILLA: What a vile trap! You made me come here, and all this time . . . But it's despicable! Words fail me. How can you treat people with such contempt! You have manipulated me in the most cynical manner.

ADAMS: Please try to control yourself. It had to happen somehow. We wanted to avoid unpleasant scenes.

SEVILLA: You've never stopped playing your game behind my back. It's despicable. You've treated me with the most revolting hypocrisy!

ADAMS: I've simply been carrying out orders.

SEVILLA: The orders were unspeakable, if you will allow me to say so.

218

ADAMS: Why don't you tell Lorrimer that? He's the one who gave them.

SEVILLA: Listen, Adams, I . . . [*A pause*] Don't try to provoke me. You'd be only too happy to see me resign.

ADAMS: Nobody wants you to resign. You're suffering from a persecution complex.

SEVILLA: Apart from my psychology, do you have any observations to make?

ADAMS: No.

SEVILLA: In that case I suggest we put an end to this interview. The whole thing makes me sick. I'd like to leave. Frankly, I can hardly stand the sight of you.

ADAMS: Whether you believe it or not, Mr. Sevilla, I am very sorry. Goodby, until we meet again.

SEVILLA: I don't think we'll be seeing each other again.

• • •

August 14, 1972

DEAR MR. SEVILLA,

The Committee met yesterday and they have asked me to inform you of their decisions. In view of the fact that the experiments on the hydrodynamics of the skin which you were conducting in Tank B were interrupted in 1966 to permit you to concentrate your efforts on the linguistic experiments in Tank A, and in view of the fact that the latter cannot be conducted for the moment because of the departure of your subjects—this is the term that we ask you to use in this correspondence—the Committee feels that it cannot ask Congress to renew the appropriation for the operation of your laboratory.

Consequently, the Committee begs you to advise your associates that the compensation provided for in their contracts in case of premature termination will be payable at the earliest possible date. It goes without saying that the same arrangement will be made with regard to you.

The Committee has appointed Dr. Edward E. Lorensen temporary administrator of the laboratory. He will be in touch with you after August 16 and will take all necessary steps for the classification and preservation of the indices, files, recordings, films, and documents belonging to the laboratory. The Committee requests that you do everything possible to facilitate Dr. Lorensen's work, and that you acknowledge receipt of this letter.

D. K. ADAMS

August 15, 1972

DEAR MR. ADAMS,

I have your letter of August 14. My associates and I will be at Dr. Lorensen's disposal after August 16.

Reluctant as I am to ask the Committee for anything, in the interest of my subjects, I must ask for permission to visit them when they are again accessible.

Sincerely yours,

H. C. SEVILLA*

August 15, 1972

DEAR MR. SEVILLA,

As I indicated in my telegram, due to unforeseeable delays, I will not arrive until August 20.

In accepting the position that has been entrusted to me I made it clear that I expect to remain within the limits of my role as administrator. In the event that your subjects should be returned to the laboratory, I have specifically informed the Committee that under no circumstances would I expect to continue your research. Indeed, I hope that in this event it will be possible for you to reconsider your resignation and to finish yourself the job which you have so brilliantly begun.

I imagine that you must be very upset at being separated from your subjects, but that it is a consolation for you that your assistant has agreed to accompany them.

Very sincerely,

E. E. LORENSEN

August 16, 1972

DEAR MR. LORENSEN,

Your letter gives me a great deal of respect for you and renews my faith in human nature, which I must confess does not at this moment appear to me in a very flattering light.

I am afraid that you have been given an inaccurate version of the facts. I gave my resignation orally, while still under the shock of learning that my subjects were going to be taken away from me. But I did not confirm this resignation either during the rest of the interview or in writing. Furthermore, it was without my consent and even without my knowledge that my assistant agreed to accompany my subjects.

---

* This letter was never answered.

In correcting the facts I have no wish for you to reconsider your decision. On the contrary, I would rather have you act as administrator than another researcher who lacked your scruples.

I expect you on the 20th.

Sincerely yours,

H. C. SEVILLA

August 18, 1972

DEAR MR. SEVILLA,

I have been delayed again, and will not arrive until the twenty-fifth.

The information contained in your letter is most distressing. It throws a remarkable light on the role played by your assistant and on the respect for the truth of the bureaucrats who are over us. Having "bought" brains here and in Europe, they seem to feel that they can do whatever they like with them.

I have told Adams frankly that in my opinion it was madness to take your subjects away from you, even temporarily. I can conceive of no practical application that would be important enough to justify the interruption of a piece of basic research.

Very sincerely,

E. E. LORENSEN

•　•　•

In the islands of the Florida Keys I loved neither the swamps nor the mangroves nor the highway, with its bridges from one island to the next on the way to Key West, I wanted an island with rocks, an island worthy of the name, with a girdle of reefs, and when I saw the rocky cliffs of Huatuey with the *Caribee* at anchor in the little harbor my heart leaped, the *Caribee* was a beautiful expensive toy for adults, an adolescent dream come true at an age when you can still enjoy it, and now I have to force myself to take it out, Arlette is reading on the forward deck, if she stayed in the cockpit with me we'd start talking about Fa and Bi again and I'd get lonely, silent, and withdrawn, steering the *Caribee* calms me, she knows it, she must be suffering too as she pretends to read, from where I am all I can see is the brim of the enormous straw hat that protects her head, she must have taken off her bikini to tan the pale areas of her skin, even thinking about her body no longer gives me pleasure, strange how mental suffering erases desire even when love remains intact, it is as if there were in suffering a diminution that impels you to

221

diminish yourself all the more, a mutilation that demands further mutilations, it is false, totally false, that there is some magical virtue in suffering, suffering is defeat, paralysis, humiliation, nothing good ever came of it, it must be overcome, and what I do to overcome it is play with the *Caribee*, this boat is my drug, its rolling motion soothes me, I leave myself behind, my hands on the tiller, I take the southwest wind on the quarter, leaning to port, into the wind, my side rises at regular intervals to take the long swell that hits me broadside, I follow my course toward the open sea, before me lies the vastness of the ocean without a trace of human life, behind me the land, diminished, hazy, its odor of leaves and smoke gradually fading into the salty air and the smell of new varnish, behind me the wake, not straight but curving to starboard with the drift of my course, I cut through the water throwing back foam on both sides of my bow, my swelling blue mainsail without a wrinkle from top to bottom, the bright red genoa jib vivid as a balloon, the mast bending with the strain, the starboard stays taut and vibrating like violin strings under the incredible force of the wind, it may get even stronger but there's no danger, no need to worry about taking in sail or running for shelter, a fine day, dazzling, insolent without a cloud, the sun still high, the sea a reassuring color, a fine, deep, benevolent blue, wind and tide holding back, letting you feel reserves of strength, like a tiger purring gently while the terrible muscles roll under the skin, like waves that lift the water without breaking, I curl my fingers around the tiller for the pleasure of caressing the polished mahogany, but I don't need to steer, the *Caribee* sails steadily without swerving, luffing, or slipping, gliding silently, or rather, with the light, muted, soothing sounds of which silence is made: the tearing of silk as the water is cleaved by the prow, the lapping of the waves on the side of the hull, the whistling of the breeze through the taut rigging, the gull cry of the pulleys, the groan of the hull as it falls back into the hollow and its sudden shudder as it rises again with the wave, half bird, half fish, one red wing, one blue, and its beautiful round, glossy, polished, sleek body gliding through the sea.

It doesn't really glide, Fa glided, without a wake or an eddy, it was a joy to watch the way he cut through the water, his friendly and mischievous eye fixed on me as soon as he turned around, as if to say, Pa, don't go away, Pa, stay a little while longer, Pa, you're always leaving, eight years already since he sucked the bottle, pressing himself against us anxiously, he'd start to whistle and squeak as soon as he felt lonely, we were exhausted from staying up with him at night, it was then that I found the two little polyester rafts between which he would sleep and which replaced us to a certain extent, at least at night, what a place he occupied in our lives for so many years, our only care, our only concern, our only work, what a time we had teaching him the first five words, and afterwards, what a fantastic acceleration with Bi, a hurricane named Hannah, Oh, to relive every second of these past six years, full to the brim with work and happiness, the first time in my life I have lived without one part of me being sacrificed to another, without feeling deprived and mutilated, free from that senseless cycle of arid and loveless little affairs, like the one with Ferguson, Arlette and I, the dolphins, the team, Michael, what a rich, full, creative life, let's try it again, let's try it again, the fatigue, the endless questioning, the infinite re-examining, I can't get rid of these thoughts, they gnaw at me like rats, always the same, they go round and round as in a delirium, in maddening repetition, Lisbeth, Adams, Bob, above all Bob, the least motivated of the three, inching his way slowly toward the goal he had been assigned two years ago, eating with us, drinking with us, friendly, smiling, hard-working, I know, *one may smile and smile and be a villain,* but the incredible absence of any motive, he didn't even hate us, nor did he act out of a spirit of vengeance like Lisbeth, or out of obedience like Adams, pure, gratuitous evil, a mystery even to the person who does it, I remember his amazement when he heard me say one day that I loved Fa, You love Fa? Of course, does that surprise you? But, after all, he said, Fa will never be anything but a subject, like a guinea pig, a rat, or a dog, we all looked at him speechless, horrified, even Maggie, but Bob—let's see, it's been so many years—he pulled himself together, he laughed, he made a joke of it, but there, in a flash, was his insensitivity, his profound inhumanity, his incurable callousness, I should have paid more attention and been more suspicious, but the moment he became C's informer he became taboo, even now I can't get it through my head that I may never see Fa and Bi again, I remember when I left Marian I used to wake up at night, soaked with sweat, terrified at the thought that I would no longer live every day with the two boys, it was like a dagger thrust right to the heart, I was paralyzed by a pain which I couldn't imagine ever stopping, and yet at the time I was seeing them two or three times a week . . . something clicked inside of him, he looked at his watch, two hours already that he had been sailing the *Caribee* toward the open sea, it was time to turn around, he wanted to get back before dark, it was impossible to find the way in the dark, he didn't even have buoys. He freed the mainsheet, pulled in the boom, put the tiller over, the *Caribee* luffed, the boom swung to the right, he uncleated the jib sheet and made it fast to the starboard cleat, I could have helped you with the jib, cried Arlette from the front deck, he waved his hand, hauled in the mainsheet, and made it fast too, I'm burned to a crisp, said Arlette with forced cheerfulness, jumping into the cockpit, I'm going to get dressed, she disappeared into the cabin and reappeared a minute later in a striped sailor's jersey, she leaned against Sevilla's shoulder and said in a dull voice, I couldn't concentrate on my book, I'm so depressed, apart from losing you I can't think of anything worse that could happen, remember how happy we were when we bought the house, and now everything is spoiled, ruined, I can't believe it, I keep wanting to go back in time, like a film being played backwards, back to the laboratory, Fa and Bi in the tank, the study of the whistling language, I feel as if I've lost my children, my reason for living, I want to cry all the time, he put his right hand on the back of her head and drew it against his neck, Yes, he said, it's not just Fa and Bi, it's the work too, after eight years of research, it's terrible to find your hands empty, with nothing to do but go over the past, two poor unemployed people with a mountain of money, he smiled bitterly, the *Caribee* scudded toward the house they had loved, the four hours on the sea had been only an interlude, they were going back to the emptiness of their life, without the dolphins, without the team, without a purpose, Listen, said Sevilla, we can't go on this way, we'll go mad, we'll leave, I've been thinking that you might like to see Spain, tomorrow I'll call a travel agent, we could be gone by the end of the week.

• • •

DEPARTMENT OF STATE, WASHINGTON, D. C.

Professor H. C. Sevilla
Huatuey Island
The Florida Keys
Florida

We hereby inform you that, by a decision of the Department of State on August 24, 1972, your passport and that of Mrs. H. C. Sevilla are revoked.

●　　●　　●

CONVERSATION BETWEEN H. C. S.,
VISITOR, AND PRISONER C. B. 476,
SING SING PRISON, DECEMBER 22, 1972, ROOM R. A. 74.612
CONFIDENTIAL

VISITOR: As you know, I would have come to see you sooner if I had received permission.

PRISONER: I must say, I'm amazed to be meeting you in such quiet and comfortable surroundings. It's highly irregular.

VISITOR: I suppose they want to record our conversation.

PRISONER: Your deductive faculties seem to be intact.

VISITOR: It's not a matter of deduction but of experience. You seem to be in good form.

PRISONER: Nobody can accuse me of not leading a regular life.

VISITOR: How's your morale?

PRISONER: The worst is over.

VISITOR: Has it been hard?

PRISONER: At first, yes. I had trouble with the other prisoners. They didn't approve of my views. You have no idea of the conservatism of the criminal classes.

VISITOR: What kind of trouble?

PRISONER: They interpreted my refusal to serve in Vietnam as cowardice. They thought I was a "nervous Nelly." I had to fight one of them.

VISITOR: What happened?

PRISONER: Eight days in solitary for each of us. I told them I started it. So did my adversary. Here, as you know, we have a high idea of honor.

VISITOR: I suppose after that your reputation improved.

PRISONER: Yes. I was no longer a coward but a nut. And here it's not so bad to be a nut.

VISITOR: Let's talk about our letters. I've received twenty-seven all together.

PRISONER: I counted the same number. So none were lost.

VISITOR: And none were censored.

PRISONER: Neither were yours.

VISITOR: Hurrah! We live in a free country.

PRISONER: That's what they tell me. Have you found out why they revoked your passport?

225

VISITOR: Yes. Although my relations with "persons politically suspect" have been criticized, I am not a "security risk," and I have always been "loyal to my country." However, if I were to go to a foreign country I could not be assured of "adequate protection."

PRISONER: Bravo. They acted in your best interest, then. Have you made public the revoking of your passport?

VISITOR: No. Goldstein advised against it.

PRISONER: Do you think he was wrong?

VISITOR: I don't know. Goldstein was fantastic. He outdid himself. He had no reason to take so many risks for my sake. Goldstein thinks that announcing the cancellation of my passport is a weapon we ought to keep in reserve.

PRISONER: Hasn't Goldstein advised you to see less of "persons politically suspect"?

VISITOR: Absolutely not.

PRISONER: I'm grateful to him for that. But I must say—

VISITOR: Don't say anything. You'll say something silly.

PRISONER: All right, I won't. If you'll excuse the liberty, you seem to be in good form too.

VISITOR: We had a very hard time when they took Fa and Bi away from us. It lasted two months. Then I bought a dolphin, a female, and set up a private laboratory with my own money.

PRISONER: Where do you keep your dolphin?

VISITOR: Below the house on the island. I have a little private harbor.

PRISONER: Don't you close it off?

VISITOR: Yes. I stretch a net between the two breakwaters from the surface of the water to the bottom. But it's almost useless. After a few weeks, Daisy—that's the name of my dolphin—learned to leap across the net and play in the open sea. But she doesn't swim away except when I go out in the boat myself, and she always comes back at night. She likes to sleep against the side of the *Caribee*. I suppose she thinks of the yacht as a kind of super-mama dolphin which accords her its protection. At night I stretch the net between the two breakwaters again as a security measure against sharks.

PRISONER: Tell me about Daisy. When I think that it's two years since I've seen a dolphin!

VISITOR: Do you want me to send you some movies? Do you think you will be able to run them?

PRISONER: Oh yes. We have everything here—a discotheque, a cinema, a theater, and even a room where you can get a tan with ultraviolet lamps, but only when you're approaching the end of your term.

VISITOR: Why only then?

PRISONER: So your neighbors will think you've just come back from a long trip to the tropics. [*He laughs*] Sing Sing is not what you think. We care about what people will say.

VISITOR: I admire your detachment. Does a person get used to prison life?

PRISONER: No, you don't get used to it. Never. You live your life between parentheses. You know the cliché, time hangs heavy: Never have I understood it so well. You have no idea of the length of time here. It's incredible. The days seem like weeks and the weeks like months. [*A silence*] Tell me about Daisy.

VISITOR: Well, she's gay, mischievous, affectionate, and not at all shy, the way Bi was in the beginning.

PRISONER: How old is she?

VISITOR: Judging from her weight and size, she must be about as old as Bi was when she became Ivan's wife. About four, I'd say.

PRISONER: How do you run your laboratory?

VISITOR: I've hired Peter, Suzy, and Maggie.

PRISONER: And you're paying them out of your own pocket?

VISITOR: Yes.

PRISONER: You'll go bankrupt.

VISITOR: Oh, there's a margin. And when the money's gone, I'll stop. Meanwhile it's going very well. We're making progress.

PRISONER: There's something I don't understand . . .

VISITOR: I'll explain it to you: Lorensen has given me copies of all my tapes.

PRISONER: Lorensen must have had his troubles.

VISITOR: That's putting it mildly.

PRISONER: What happened?

VISITOR: Nothing, in the end. I have all the tapes of Fa and Bi, and now those of Daisy.

PRISONER: What stage are you at?

VISITOR: We're making progress.

PRISONER: You don't care to tell me any more?

VISITOR: No. [*He laughs*]

PRISONER: I didn't expect to see you like this after your last letters. You've recovered all your vitality.

VISITOR: Let's talk about you for a while.

PRISONER: It's not a very interesting subject. [*A silence*] I'm here, and I'm waiting.

VISITOR: Are you just as pessimistic as ever about the international situation?

PRISONER: More than ever. But I'm optimistic, too, when it comes to the long view.

VISITOR: I'll admit I was relieved when Jim Crooner was beaten and Albert Monroe Smith elected. Smith is the lesser of two evils.

PRISONER: I don't think so. Smith will do exactly what Crooner would have done in his place. American democracy consists in giving the voter the illusion of choice. When voting for Congressmen, he has a choice between two parties, both of the right; for President, between two candidates who are equally reactionary, but one of whom manages to give the impression that he is more liberal than the other.

VISITOR: Oh, you're exaggerating! I don't think Smith and Crooner belong to the same category.

PRISONER: I'm not exaggerating. Do you want a few examples? In 1960 you voted for Kennedy because you thought he was more liberal than Nixon, and Kennedy gave the green light for the invasion of Cuba and the massive augmentation of our "military advisers" in Vietnam. In 1964 you voted for Johnson to stop Goldwater, but once in office, Johnson got us started on the same path of escalation advocated by Goldwater.

VISITOR: So you think Smith is just as capable as Crooner of getting us into a war with China?

PRISONER: Yes. With a few moralizing speeches thrown in.

VISITOR: That's depressing.

PRISONER: Not really. You see, elections don't matter. They're rigged from the start. It's public opinion that counts.

VISITOR: Yes, I know. That's why you chose to go to prison. Repression has scored some victories. The number of conscientious objectors has decreased.

PRISONER: Yes. And sometimes I feel discouraged.

VISITOR: But through your imprisonment you have had a profound influence over all the people you know. I don't want to mention names, you understand why, but you've opened my eyes to certain problems.

PRISONER: If that's true, it's worth being here.

VISITOR: It is true.

PRISONER: You make me very happy. I thought I'd detected a new tone in your letters for the past few months.

VISITOR: I've decided to pay no more attention to photostats and tape recordings . . . I think it is very bad to censor oneself in advance. I am more determined than ever to say what I think.

PRISONER: Is it possible that I have had a share in this decision?

VISITOR: Certainly, a large share.

PRISONER: I can't tell you how happy I am. And how modest you are! After all, I am only your pupil.

VISITOR: That's irrelevant. When you're looking for the truth you can't bother with considerations of that sort.

PRISONER: It's very generous of you to say so. [*A silence*]

VISITOR: It's almost time, I think.

PRISONER: Wait. We still have five minutes. Tell me about Peter and Suzy.

VISITOR: Well, as you may have heard, they're married.

PRISONER: She wrote me about it. Suzy is a magnificent girl. You know, I might have fallen in love with her myself if Peter hadn't gotten there first.

VISITOR: She speaks of you with a great deal of affection.

PRISONER: Yes. I'm very fond of her too. I often think about you all. [*A silence*] It wasn't easy to leave you.

VISITOR: We're waiting for you. You'll come and work with us again.

PRISONER: In three years. [*A silence*] In three years the whistling language will hold no more secrets for you.

VISITOR: There'll be other problems.

PRISONER: Well, in three years, then.

VISITOR: I'll come and see you again, if they let me. It's time, I think.

PRISONER: Goodby. Write to me. Thank you for coming, and thank you too for . . . well, thank you.

VISITOR: Goodby, Michael.

•   •   •

SAIGON, Jan. 4, 1973 (U.P.I.) —The U.S. cruiser *Little Rock* destroyed by atomic explosion off Haiphong. No survivors.

229

XI

Like a giant who has gone to sleep in the serene certainty of his strength and is awakened by a treacherous blow, the first reaction of the United States to the destruction of the *Little Rock* was stunned amazement. Indignation did not appear until twenty-four hours later, as if it had required all this time for an appropriate emotion to traverse this great body. But the fury that possessed it then was on a scale commensurate with the most powerful nation in the world. From one end of the vast continent to the other a surge of anger was discharged that submerged one hundred and eighty million Americans like a tidal wave. On the radio, on television, in the newspapers, ordinary words seemed too weak to express the horror inspired by this outrageous act. A race of omnipotent gods attacked on their Olympus by an inferior species could not have been more surprised, more horrified, more disdainful, or more certain of annihilating their assailants in short order.

For the reporters who described this state of mind, only bestial metaphors seemed to convey the contempt in which their compatriots held their adversary. In the press, where headlines appeared that had not been seen since Pearl Harbor, Communist China was commonly compared to a "mad dog" that must be either punished or put to death.

The tragedy of the *Little Rock* had left no survivors and had had no witnesses. After analysis of the air and of the debris gathered, the authorities of the Seventh Fleet concluded that it had been caused by "an atomic device of unidentified origin." But in spite of the

230

cautiousness of these conclusions, there seemed to be no doubt in the minds of the commentators about the guilt of the Chinese leaders. Most of them remarked that by her "surprise attack" and her "cowardly aggression," China had banned herself from the international community. She had been the first to break the "balance of terror." The only way to re-establish this balance was to "punish the aggressor by means of immediate reprisals," the more moderate specifying that these be directed at Chinese atomic munitions plants, and the others at the "vital centers of Red China." They said vital centers instead of cities because the word "city," being much too concrete, had the disadvantage of suggesting the millions of people who lived there.

In the press the protest was based on questions of law and morality; but private conversations had a different tone. Another motivation could be discerned in the nicknames given to the adversary. The word "Chinese" was little used: People preferred Chinks, yellowbellies, slants, Charleys, or, more politely but with no less hostility, Asiatics. From what was said in the street, in bars, and in offices, it was obvious that for the speakers the existence of seven hundred million Chinese was defined by three fundamental sins: They were yellow, they were little, and they were Communists. Apart from these sins, their virtues were turned into vices. Their intelligence was merely guile. Their patience was ambition, their economy avarice. Their ingeniousness was diabolical. In reality, God had given the world to the big white men, together with the wisdom and power necessary for its exploitation. It was true that these little yellow monkeys imitated Western science rather well, but the creative aptitude was missing. Besides, their numbers were offensive. They pullulated. They swarmed like ants. The bestial metaphor progressed from the dog to the monkey, and from the monkey to the ant—and the last image was the most dangerous of all, for it evoked all too well the boot of the hunter, ill-humoredly stamping on an anthill he had tripped over.

Because of their long experience as prudent professional politicians, most members of Congress understood before anyone else did the enormous wave of anger that broke over the Union. Their alignments were quick, astute, and patriotic. Senator Burton Murphy, who until then had been one of the most confirmed doves, and who only the day before in an interview had deplored the in-

231

terminable war in Vietnam, learned of the catastrophe of the *Little Rock* at five P.M. while buying gas at his neighborhood service station. He hurried home and phoned the White House to assure President Albert Monroe Smith of his unconditional support.

In Congress in the days that followed, the last outpost of doves, which had been undermined by recent elections, finally fell. In the end two-thirds of them passed over to the hawk side. They did so with an alacrity that proved how happy they were to have found an unassailable patriotic excuse to revise opinions which had brought them nothing but grief. The other third said nothing. They were not convinced of China's guilt in the *Little Rock* incident, but did not have the temerity to say so. Even so, they were not resigned to "run with the hare and hunt with the hounds."

If Senator Burton Murphy astonished political circles by the speed of his conversion, most of the alignments that occurred after the destruction of the *Little Rock* did not occasion any major surprise. They attracted attention, however, because of the prominence of the people involved.

The actor Jim Crooner, ex-candidate for President, was scheduled to give a televised talk on the future of women in the United States at seven thirty P.M. on January fifth. He announced personally that due to the gravity of the situation he would not discuss that subject, but that instead he wanted to address a few words to the nation. As he spoke his presence filled the little screen. With his serious and determined expression, his graying temples, and his face seamed by the many furrows of experience, he had that decent, unpretentious, and responsible manner which quickened the hearts of a hundred million American women. He expressed himself in that completely nonintellectual style which so well suited his physical appearance and which his brain trust had perfected for him at the beginning of his campaign. He spoke with unaccustomed slowness, even with effort, as if he were struggling valiantly with an emotion he could master only with difficulty. "I don't know what the President will say to you tomorrow," he declared, "and naturally I'm not going to say anything tonight that might embarrass him. I know what I'd do if I were him, but he's the guy at the wheel, so he's the one who has to get the car back on the road, I ain't a guy to indulge in back-seat driving. That could only bother him. The duty of all Americans," he went on gravely, "yours and mine alike, is to unite in the face of this attack and trust in the wisdom and strength of the Government of the United States."

On the same day at ten P.M. Cardinal Minuteman was scheduled to give a radio talk on "The Spirit of the Gospel in Modern Times." The prelate represented a unique phenomenon in the annals of the country: Without having served in the Army, he had received the highest military decoration of the United States. Apparently the armed forces had decided that he alone was worth a division. A few years earlier, on a visit to South Vietnam, he had tried to rekindle the faith of the boys by inciting them to achieve "final victory over the Viets." The command was grateful to the prelate for his frankness, for in their public announcements, especially at each new degree of escalation, Johnson, McNamara, and Rusk talked about nothing but peace. Naturally, the necessities of diplomacy were not lost on the generals, but on the other hand, all this talk about "negotiation" and all these promises to leave Vietnam after the peace did not have a good effect on the GI's.

The cardinal was very upset by the tragedy of the *Little Rock,* but at the same time he was of the opinion that it proved the justice of the "hard line" he had always taken toward atheistic communism. With characteristic impetuosity he changed the subject of his talk and at the last moment chose as his text Genesis 19:24–25. "In these days of mourning," he said, "when the American nation has been knifed in the back by cowardly assassins, now more than ever, it is the duty of Christians in this country to regard themselves as the missionaries of Christ and to draw the inspiration for their action from the sacred texts." He then alluded to the above verses of Genesis and recited them in a powerful voice: "The cry of the abominations of these peoples [the prelate emphasized "these peoples" in an angry voice] rose louder and louder in the face of the Lord. . . . 'Then the Lord rained upon Sodom and upon Gomorrah brimstone and fire from the Lord out of heaven; And he overthrew those cities, and all the plain, and all the inhabitants of the cities, and that which grew upon the ground.' "

In a more succinct and less evangelical style, General George C. Curry declared that night in the Washington *Post:* "After this, there's nothing to do but bleed them white."

Paul Omar Parson, Pop to his friends and "Deep South Babbitt" to his enemies, didn't mince words. He spoke his mind freely

233

to a reporter from Atlanta. "You'd have to be a real bonehead," he said, in the picturesque style which had done so much for his popularity in the Southern states, "not to have expected this. Nobody can say I didn't warn the State Department. For years I've been asking them, How long are you going to put up with the insolence of Castro? The bluster of Nasser? The aggression of Charley in Asia? And the insults of Red China? If you forget all that baloney about peaceful coexistence, the truth is that America has been much too patient. But she must be getting a little tired of turning the other cheek and getting kicked in the butt in return for all the dollars she hands out all over the world for the under-developed countries. Underdeveloped, my ass. All those people want to do is rip our guts out, first chance they get. Witness the *Little Rock*. Well, let this be a lesson to us. If we don't get China now, she'll get us later. Don't get me wrong: I have nothing against the Chinese. If they want to come over here and open laundries and wash my dirty clothes, I have no objections. But I do object to letting these little monkeys wander all over Asia with H-bombs. It's a tough world. You've got to be tough to survive in it. Well, the time has come to show China who's boss. Now, I'm not a blood-thirsty man, but I won't sleep peacefully until our rockets have turned Communist China into one big parking lot."

On January 6 at one P.M., as had been announced the day before, President Smith delivered a short speech on television. Although his message was couched in lofty language and invoked some very noble ideas, his implicit conclusions did not differ essentially from those that Pop had set forth. The only discernible difference was that Pop had made no allusion to divinity, whereas Albert Monroe Smith conformed scrupulously to the great White House tradition: He enlisted God, morality, and the heavenly hosts in defense of the Union. In moments of crisis no American President before him had failed to do this—not in vain, moreover, since each time God had responded to the call. Never had the territory of North America been invaded or bombed, and never, since its founding, had the United States lost a single one of the wars it had declared.

When Albert Monroe Smith appeared once again on the little screen it was easy to see how he had managed to triumph over Jim Crooner in the favor of the masses. Although he had already occupied some very high positions, Albert Monroe Smith still had the physical charm that had done as much for his success as the fame of his ancestors. His swinging stride, his muscular athletic neck, and his candid and charming smile made him look—at forty-five-plus—like a college boy, but this juvenile air was offset by the gravity of his alert, deep-set gray eyes. The distinguished columnist Malcolm Munster said of the new President that he had managed to combine two kinds of sex appeal: that of youth and that of maturity.

Staring gravely at the televiewer, the President spoke without the slightest gesture in a calm, controlled, and even suave voice which gave his message a vaguely clerical quality. "America," he said, "has always been a fundamentally peaceful nation. She remains true to this tradition today and does not seek to conquer any territory or new wealth in Asia. But with the help of God, she is determined to defend freedom and democracy wherever they are threatened by Communist aggression. I repeat, our armed forces seek no selfish advantage on land or on sea. On the contrary, they are in Asia in order to allow peoples oppressed by subversion to choose their own destiny freely. This is our mission and our pride. [Here he paused and his expression became more somber.] You are all aware that on January 4, 1973, a day which will forever bear the brand of infamy, in the Gulf of Tonkin, the United States was the object of a brutal and deliberate attack. There is not the slightest doubt about either the nature or the origin of the device which destroyed the U.S. cruiser *Little Rock*. Even if it was manipulated by Vietnamese hands, it was manufactured in the atomic munitions plants of China. Therefore, Communist China bears the entire responsibility for first resorting to this atrocious weapon and for organizing against the United States an act of aggression which, if not in its magnitude, at least in its cowardice, treachery, and cruelty, recalls the attack on Pearl Harbor on December 7, 1941. America cannot remain indifferent to the insult she has suffered. Naturally, we would be the first to applaud if Communist China were to concentrate her vast energies on improving the living conditions of her population. But when she does not hesitate to resort to a weapon of terror to serve her subversive ends, we are forced to intervene. If America were to tolerate such an odious act of aggression against herself without answering back, before long the nations of the world would settle their differences by force. Then we would see

235

the great nations, those possessing atomic weapons, blackmailing the small nations that do not possess them. The Government of the United States, aware of its responsibilities toward the American continent and the free world, has called upon Communist China to dismantle her atomic munitions plants under international control. She has given China eight days to do this. After this date, and in the event of a negative response or no response at all, the United States will take all necessary measures to assure her security."

* * *

For a week after the President's speech the United States was in a strange situation. The country was not yet at war, but it was no longer at peace either. Generally speaking, people had difficulty emerging from everyday life and adjusting their mental universe to the great event that was impending. When men discussed the situation, they resorted to athletic metaphors. For example, they described the act of aggression in the Gulf of Tonkin in terms of football: China had scored a goal by means of cheating and treachery, but she didn't have what it took, and once the United States got into the game, China would soon realize that she was in for a shellacking.

At the same time, that aspiration to devote oneself to the common good which is an essential component of the American character was aroused, but because it did not immediately find an appropriate outlet, it was frustrated. Thousands of people telephoned the White House, either to offer their services free of charge or to give the authorities advice on world strategy. The students at Vassar College, which numbered within its walls, in the words of the American Communist McGregor, "the richest, most elegant, and if not the most beautiful at least the cleanest girls in the United States," met to take stock of the situation. After two hours of discussion they passed a resolution stating that they were prepared to offer the country the benefit of their special talents. Nobody ever learned exactly what they meant by this, for the authorities did not follow up their generous offer.

At ten thirty P.M., on the night of the day that Albert Monroe Smith delivered his speech on TV, a policeman arrested and took to the police station Seaman Joe MacClyde, U.S. Navy, and Sally Shute, thirty-four, prostitute, who were fighting in a state of intoxication on the sidewalk of a street in Hoboken. According to Sally's statement she had brought MacClyde to her room, saying, "Sailor, after what those bastards did to the *Little Rock*, I'll give you a good time for nothing." But MacClyde left her after about half an hour, taking with him a silver compact which he intended to give his sister for her birthday. Sally followed him into the street. Joe MacClyde, twenty, six feet, hailing from San Angelo, Texas, told the judge, "It wasn't until she screamed 'Go get your balls shot off by the Chinese' that I started beating her up." The judge made MacClyde pay a fine and gave him a reprimand, but acquitted Sally Shute. However low she may have sunk in her private life, the judge remarked, she nevertheless preserved a keen sense of patriotism, as witness her naïve proposition to Seaman MacClyde.

In a completely different setting, and also obeying a need for dedication, although in a different way, Mary White, thirty-six, unmarried, editorial secretary, joined a Puritan sect in Indianapolis which had given itself the name the Sons of Mary.* When Mary arrived, ten minutes late, at the meeting scheduled for nine P.M. on January 6, she found the members of the sect in the midst of a debate. The issue was whether, as a reprisal for the blowing up of the U.S. cruiser *Little Rock,* an atom bomb should be dropped on Peking. The discussion became heated and even violent, and Mary White was rather astonished; she did not see what influence the decision of the Sons of Mary of Indianapolis could have on the White House. Finally a vote was taken and the resolution to bomb Peking was rejected, twelve to nine. The majority motion, which was communicated to the local papers that evening, explained that it would be immoral to eliminate the three million Chinese of Peking to avenge the death of two hundred American sailors. It concluded: "After all, we are a nation of lofty ideals." Although Mary White had found the debate somewhat unrealistic, she felt deeply satisfied with this conclusion.

Elderly persons who had been through the Second World War took a less abstract view of the situation. Ernst Rosenblum, fifty-two, a German Jew who had emigrated to the United States in 1939 and was now a tailor in Lexington, Kentucky, listened to the President's

---

* As opposed to the Sons of Martha. See the Gospel according to St. Luke, Chapter 10.

televised address with mixed feelings. Although he did not have very definite ideas about Vietnam, for some time he had been inclined to think that the country should "give them everything we've got and get it over with." When he had heard about the catastrophe of the *Little Rock* he had been highly indignant and had told his wife, "I hope the President will take a hard line." And now that the President had taken a hard line, Rosenblum felt a strange mixture of relief, pride, and dread. His wife Gerda was curled up beside him on the sofa, her feet tucked under her, her face gentle and tired. She looked like a big cat that has grown old by the fire. After the President's speech she looked up at her husband and was surprised at his pallor. He looked back at her, his eyes blazed, and he said in a low, angry voice, *"Und jetzt sind wir wieder in der Scheise."*

• • •

An article that appeared in the January 8 issue of *Izvestia* carried the first official reaction of the Soviet Union to President Albert Monroe Smith's speech. The anonymous writer first pointed out that the material damage and loss of human life caused by the destruction of the *Little Rock* could not be put in the same category as the catastrophe of Pearl Harbor with which President Smith had compared it. At the time of Pearl Harbor the American fleet was riding at anchor and a state of peace reigned in the Pacific, whereas for several years now in the Gulf of Tonkin the Seventh Fleet had engaged in continuous acts of aggression against North Vietnam, which had been bombed day and night without previous declaration of war, with total contempt for human rights. Furthermore, in the absence of either a survivor or wreckage capable of being analyzed, there was no proof of Chinese or Vietnamese guilt for the blowing up of the *Little Rock*. Under the circumstances it was conceivable that the atomic device that had destroyed the *Little Rock* had been on board the ship itself and had been set off by mistake.

In reality, *Izvestia* observed with regret, the State Department gave the impression that it was exploiting the *Little Rock* affair as a *casus belli*. The Soviet Government, added *Izvestia*, had warned the United States of the extremely grave consequences for world peace

---

* And now we're back in the shit again.

of an act of atomic aggression. "The Washington warmongers," concluded the author of the article, "cannot expect us to sit idly by while American rockets devastate the cities and factories of a country bordering on the Soviet Union."

State Department experts had long been divided on the question of what attitude the Soviet Union would adopt in the event of a conflict between the United States and China. The article in *Izvestia* confirmed both opposing views. The first group concluded from it that sooner or later the Soviet Union would throw the weight of her arms into the conflict. The second group found confirmation of its belief that despite the firmness of her tone, Russia would go no further than verbal protestations to the United States or material aid to China if the war were prolonged. But this possibility was ruled out, for the Pentagon had announced that it needed only two hours to wipe China off the map.

On the same day that the article appeared in *Izvestia* the New China Agency published the longest and most dramatic communiqué in its history. The Agency began by issuing a categorical denial to the "lying fabrications of the imperialist Yankee bandits." Communist China had had nothing to do with the destruction of the United States cruiser *Little Rock*. It had given no atomic weapons to North Vietnam, nor had it used any itself. China remained true to the promise she had made following each of the experimental explosions she had carried out: "She would never be the first to use the atom bomb, but if attacked, she would reply in kind." The destruction of the *Little Rock* was simply a "vile and criminal provocation" contrived by the Americans themselves for the purpose of addressing to China an "insolent ultimatum" which the Chinese Government could only refuse. Moreover, in order to carry out their "diabolical plan" in the Gulf of Tonkin, the Yankee pirates had chosen meteorological conditions such that the radioactive particles, instead of falling back on their own fleet, must necessarily fall on Chinese territory.

And indeed, this is what actually happened. About an hour after the blowing up of the *Little Rock* the Chinese town of Peihai had received a radioactive shower lasting forty-five minutes, in the form of a cloud of white dust. Almost all of the fifty thousand inhabitants of Peihai were now gravely infected, and the reservoirs that provided the city with fresh water and the marshy farmlands that sur-

239

rounded it were contaminated. The Chinese Government had provided an airplane for foreign correspondents from Peking who wanted to visit the town and study the situation at first hand. It was not Communist China who ought to dismantle her atomic munitions plants but the United States, the New China Agency concluded, who, after her abominable attacks on the Asiatic cities of Hiroshima and Nagasaki in 1945, had just committed a third crime against Asia by condemning the fifty thousand inhabitants of Peihai to a hideous death.

It is a tribute to American democracy that even on the eve of world war freedom of the press continued to be exercised without any restrictions in the territory of the United States. An American reporter, James Bedford, who had gone to Peihai on Tuesday, phoned in to *The New York Times* that evening a long article which was published the next day, confirming the contamination of the Chinese city. Accompanied by doctors and interpreters and dressed in the same kind of protective medical garment they wore, Bedford had visited the different sectors of the city and questioned the inhabitants. At noon on the fourth of January, they had seen a blinding light in the southern sky. This glow, whose glare was intolerable, since it was more intense than the sun, lasted three minutes. An hour later the sky, which had been perfectly clear until then, suddenly darkened, and a fine white glittering dust rained down on the city. Its resemblance to powdered sugar was so close that a considerable number of children had gathered this powder and tasted it. These children were now suffering from horrible burns, and they were already condemned to death, since their intestines had stopped functioning. But all the inhabitants of the city were contaminated in varying degrees, some because they had received the fallout on their heads, hands, and legs, others simply because they had drunk radioactive water from the reservoir.

James Bedford had been able to see and question a great many sick people. In most cases parts of the body that had been exposed to the terrible white rain had taken on a blackish coloration, hair fell out in tufts, and small hemorrhages occurred which could not be stopped. Results of blood tests confirmed the disaster. In some cases a cubic millimeter of blood showed only thirty white corpuscles instead of seven thousand, and six hundred platelets of coagulation instead of two hundred thousand. The diagnosis was clear. The bone marrow of these patients had lost the ability to produce white blood corpuscles. The prognosis was no less pessimistic: Given the incredibly high number of persons afflicted, it would be possible to attempt the grafting of healthy bone marrow in only a very small number of cases, the great majority of the sick being condemned to a slow death which could take weeks, months, or years.

Bedford's article was all the more impressive because it was written simply and did not try for the sensational. But in spite of the attention it attracted abroad, it had no perceptible effect on American opinion. In the week that followed its appearance a Gallup poll showed that the percentage of people who believed that China was responsible for the destruction of the *Little Rock* had risen from seventy-two to seventy-eight. As for the advocates of immediate atomic reprisal, the percentage of these had risen by ten percent. Commenting on these figures, the Yugoslav philosopher Marco Llepovič wrote, "Newspapers, billboards, radio, television— the force of pro-war propaganda is such that it can erase half a dozen pacifist articles without leaving a single trace. Freedom of the press is quite real, but it is ineffectual. In a country where all the news media are in the hands of money, the still small voice of truth is quickly drowned out by the powerful organs of falsehood and confusion."

Outside the United States, however, James Bedford's article reinforced a growing skepticism about Chinese guilt. The great Japanese newspaper *Asahi,* although it refrained from choosing between the American version and the Chinese version of the incident (an impartiality which irritated American diplomats in Tokyo, because it amounted to discrediting the official line of their country), deplored the radioactive contamination of an Asiatic town in scathing terms and called for an immediate meeting of the countries belonging to the Atomic Club.

The Secretary of the United Nations regretted that he could not submit the matter to the Security Council, for since Communist China had not been admitted to the U.N., she could not even be present to make her defense. But he too favored the idea of a vast confrontation of powers, and the Pope made a similar statement a few hours later.

On the afternoon of the eighth the State Department announced categorically that there had been no atomic device on board the *Little Rock* or any other ship of the Seventh Fleet. Therefore, an accident was impossible. Moreover, the State Department repeated verbatim its accusations against Communist China and reiterated that the American ultimatum to China would expire at noon on Monday, January 14. The fact that the word "ultimatum" appeared in the communiqué alarmed the chancelleries, for this word had not appeared in President Albert Monroe Smith's televised speech of January 6.

This stern communiqué from Washington only increased the moderation and reticence of international opinion. In France, the January 10 issue of *Le Monde* expressed this view with a clarity that would have impressed even the Americans if they had attached any importance to either the information or the opinions given in the European press. But American newspapers quoted only other American newspapers or, at the most, British newspapers, in their columns.

The *Monde* article, solidly based on historical precedent, was written in that balanced, careful, and competent style that gave readers of that newspaper such a pleasant sense of personal superiority. It began by reminding them appropriately that this was not the first time in the history of the United States that the destruction of a U.S. warship had caused the White House to issue an ultimatum. On February 15, 1898, the American battleship *Maine*, at anchor in the port of Havana, blew up and sank beneath the waves with all its crew. The Government of the United States had immediately accused Spain of planning this crime, disregarded its desperate denials, declared war on her, and sent troops into Cuba. The least one could say was that Spain had nothing to gain by perpetrating this crime. She had for years been waging a very difficult war against the Cuban rebels, she was almost ruined, she was on the verge of defeat, and what she feared above all was precisely United States intervention.

Like the sinking of the *Maine,* continued *Le Monde,* the explosion of the United States cruiser *Little Rock* was no doubt destined to remain one of those historical puzzles that never find a solution. For if you looked closely, neither of the two current theories was at all acceptable from the point of view of good logic. For how could one accept the idea that the Government of the United States could conceive the criminal plan of sacrificing one of its ships and drowning its own sailors as a pretext for declaring war on China? On the other hand, how was one to believe that China, turning her back on the extreme caution she had heretofore exercised in her relations with the United States, could suddenly have committed such a stupid provocation as to attack an American cruiser that was already outmoded and whose disappearance would in no way diminish the offensive potential of the Seventh Fleet? An action of this kind could be effective only if it also attacked important units like the atomic aircraft carrier *Enterprise* or the missile-launching cruiser *Long Beach*. Strategically speaking, it made sense only if it served as a preface to a massive attack by the Chinese land army on American positions in Korea and North Vietnam. Finally, could anyone imagine for a moment that China, assuming she wanted to destroy the cruiser *Little Rock,* would choose a time when the wind, which had been blowing in a northerly direction for twenty-four hours, would infallibly carry the atomic fallout to her own territory instead of dropping it on the Seventh Fleet?

•   •   •

A few hours after the second communiqué from Washington the world learned to its shocked amazement that Stockholm had been the scene of a serious panic brought on by an exercise in passive defense. Disregarding her neutrality and the fortunate circumstances that had enabled her to remain at peace for one hundred and fifty years in a world often torn by war, Sweden, with admirable prudence, had created on her territory a system of fallout shelters. Everything had been anticipated. In Stockholm, for example, as soon as war broke out, part of the population was to leave the city by car and get to the country as quickly as possible. The rest were to take refuge at once in the magnificent air-conditioned underground shelters that had been constructed at great expense twenty years before in the heart of the capital. Successive governments had continued to maintain them with the most attentive zeal, taking care to habituate people, especially children, to spending long hours in them at work or at play. Miracles of intelligent foresight defying the unforeseeable future, these shelters were designed to assure the survival of eight million Swedes in the apocalyptic world of World War Three, in which three hundred million Westerners would be annihilated in a devastated Europe.

Exactly what happened in Stockholm on the evening of January

243

8? The order to go to the shelters to take part in a passive defense drill was given at eight thirty-five P.M., or five minutes after the communiqué from Washington containing the word "ultimatum" had been translated over Swedish radio and television airwaves. Was the order given in too realistic a manner? Or did it take on this quality because it came on the heels of the alarming bulletin from Washington? Whatever the answer, the fact remains that instead of calmly obeying instructions, the most disciplined nation in the world was suddenly seized by a collective delirium. It was one of those confused, inexplicable situations in which one group of people, not knowing what is happening but alarmed by their very ignorance, imagines the worst from the behavior of other groups and immediately imitates them, so that the madness gradually spreads to more and more frenzied mobs.

Ill fortune decreed that just as large numbers of private cars were leaving the city as instructed, some Swedish jets were flying overhead. There was a series of sonic booms which led some drivers to believe that their vehicles, immobilized by the heavy traffic, were going to serve as targets. Panic-stricken, they abandoned their cars and began running blindly through the streets, screaming that bombs were falling. As a consequence the tie-up became hopeless, panic became universal, and thousands of individuals, the majority of them men, rushed into one of the vast fallout shelters of Stockholm, which was already filled to its capacity of twenty thousand persons. Horrible scenes followed—women were trampled, and children died of suffocation. Some policemen who tried to intervene were attacked, and one was lynched. Others had to use their guns in self-defense. The all clear sounded without changing the situation at all, the calm was not restored until early the next morning. The incident left a profound sense of horror and shame in the hearts of the Swedish people. The toll of this senseless panic came to one hundred and twenty-six dead and nine hundred and thirty-two wounded. By a terrible irony of history, these unfortunate people were the first victims of a war that had not yet broken out.

The Stockholm panic of January 8 was not without repercussions elsewhere in the world, and especially in the United States, where public opinion, which had been lulled for years by a sense of overwhelming superiority, suddenly awoke to the apprehension of danger. Although everything had long stood in readiness to launch

244

devastating attacks against the enemy, what was known about the anti-missile system that the United States had organized when China had exploded her first H-bomb was not reassuring. However costly it had been, the barrier, according to the experts, was still thin. It was not impermeable. The Washington *Post* recalled the experience of the *Nautilus,* which in the course of a very realistic maneuver in the Atlantic had come within a few miles of Boston without being picked up by sonar. Its plan had been to follow at a depth of thirty yards in the wake of a cargo ship whose propellers drowned out the hum of its turbines. The conclusion was obvious: What an American submarine had done, Chinese submarines could also do and, in a few undetectable moves, wipe out several cities.

There was no use deluding oneself. In the event of war, the United States Government could bury itself under several dozen yards of rock, concrete, and steel in a great metropolis, but what shelter had been provided for the American people? None. Only the rich had been able to build fallout shelters for their families in their back yards or on their ranches. But for lack of land and money, the great mass of poor people were condemned to death. Americans discovered to their amazement something they already knew: the power of the dollar was infinite. Everything could be bought, including life.

A deluge of vehement letters, telegrams, and phone calls inundated the White House. "If World War Three breaks out," columnist Malcolm Munster wrote bitterly, "a man will be safer in a submarine cruising under five yards of ice in the Arctic Ocean than he will be lying in his own bed in his home in the suburbs."

Starting on the 4th of January, well before news of the Stockholm panic, a suicide epidemic of unprecedented proportions broke out from one end of the United States to the other. The percentage of suicides for the single day of January 5 was seventy-five percent higher than the percentage for January 5 of the preceding year. Stationary on the 6th, it rose on the 7th and 8th in such alarming proportions that the authorities asked the newspapers to stop playing up the cases that came to their attention in order to avoid the effect of contagion. Generally speaking, this recommendation was followed, but in spite of this, the percentage continued to soar on the 9th, 10th, 11th, and 12th, and it was a week before the curve began to level off and then to drop. "The historian," wrote Professor Marco Llepovič, "will wonder someday for what mysterious reason so many educated, happy, and well-fed Americans preferred to end their lives for fear of losing them, while in underdeveloped countries hundreds of millions of people endure daily the terrible suffering of undernourishment without even thinking of putting an end to their torment."

At the same time criminality, notably deliberate homicide and rape, also reached a record figure in the history of the United States. The majority of these crimes were committed by first offenders, who left many clues and sometimes even turned themselves in and confessed of their own free will. Several of them explained that they had experienced an "irresistible urge" to kill and that the choice of victim was actually a matter of chance. But perhaps the most revealing insight into the motivation of these crimes was provided by Roy Creighton, twenty-two, unmarried, store employee, without previous record of crime. Between Monday the 6th and Thursday the 9th, Creighton, who was regarded as a steady, hard-working boy, committed a series of rapes of the most revolting sort upon minors of twelve to fourteen. After his arrest he freely admitted the facts. He added calmly that he "had always wanted to do things like this" and that he had decided to "indulge his desire" when he realized that there was going to be an atomic war and that we would "all be in the same boat and end up in the same hole."

Fear mounted every day and violence, fanned by fear, sometimes assumed a mask of patriotism. People began to speak in hushed voices about the fifth column and the role played by the Chinese living in America, who were all seemingly friendly but in reality were secretly won over to the Communist cause. In various cities in the United States Chinese restaurants were looted and their personnel insulted and abused. In Washington an attaché at the Japanese Embassy who was buying shirts in a store was called "yellowbelly," and as he tried to explain to the crowd that he was Japanese and not Chinese, the insults redoubled and he narrowly escaped being lynched.

On January 10 at eleven P.M. half a dozen teen-agers drove into Chinatown with all their windows down and began to fire at pedestrians at random, killing four people and wounding a dozen. Then they abducted two Chinese girls who were walking home from the movies, took them to a deserted wharf, and there, after beating and raping them, threw them into the icy water. When one of the girls tried to swim back to the dock, they shot and killed her. The other managed to hide behind a small boat until the gang had left.

The newspapers, radio stations, and television channels went wild. In the more serious periodicals writers estimated how many megatons were necessary to destroy China, and one expert showed that it would take thirty thousand. "We have them," concluded the expert, "and then some." In railroad stations, post offices, subway stations, and on the enormous billboards that lined the highways, huge signs began to appear. One simply read: REMEMBER THE LITTLE ROCK. Another had the word REMEMBER at the top, the words THE LITTLE ROCK at the very bottom, and, in between, a sea filled with wreckage and bodies. The water, which glowed with a strange sulfurous light, seemed to be seething, and in the foreground, facing the public, a sailor, his eyes blinded, his face blackened and burned, his mouth twisted in a desperate appeal, was pulling himself out of the water, his charred left hand on the "i" of LITTLE and his right hand on the "c" of ROCK. He was painted so realistically that he seemed to come right out of the sign to cry vengeance on his assassins.

* * *

On the night of January 8, the Secretary of State and the Secretary of Defense conferred with President Albert Monroe Smith at the White House until two o'clock in the morning. After they had gone the President sat motionless for a long time in his chair, he felt empty, exhausted, inert, he rose with difficulty, his shoulders drooping, his legs heavy as lead, but it was above all his soul that was weary and without courage, he took his private elevator to the second floor, in his room he felt a little better after he had taken off his shoes and put on his bedroom slippers and changed from his charcoal-gray jacket into his old tweed jacket with leather patches at the elbows, he wasn't sleepy, he was too tired to sleep, he pushed the door of Vic's room open a few inches and stood listening for a few seconds in the warm and perfumed darkness, how amazing and pathetic was the infinitesimal respiration of a human being, that complicated machinery operating smoothly, that obstinate, unbroken movement, nerves and muscles running themselves in the

247

little death of sleep, Smith closed the door softly, crossed the hall, pushed open the door of Lolly's room, which was always ajar, she was sleeping on her side, through the white muslin curtains her straight profile was clearly visible under the little blue night light at the head of the mahogany bed, at twelve she still had to sleep with a night light, he looked at her, the full, freckled cheek leaning on the plump hand, the peaceful lashes, and the short, full, curved upper lip which gave her the innocent animal-like look of a Renoir adolescent. Smith shook his head, he felt almost guilty at his emotion, heavily he walked down the long corridor and into the Oval Room, turned on the chandelier lights, and sank into the huge green leather armchair behind the desk, never had he felt so exhausted, even during his Presidential campaign, even during Kennedy's, what times they had had together, the dark circles under John's eyes, his grave, rather sad expression as he dropped into the seat across from me on the Pullman that took him from town to town, Why don't you go to bed, John? he shook his head, motioned toward the table and the notes for the speech that he had to give the next day, and recited Frost's lines, "But I have promises to keep/ And miles to go before I sleep/ And miles to go before I sleep."

The eyes tired, the smile full of gallantry and goodness, the first "sleep" pronounced lightly, and the second in a low, deep voice veiled with melancholy, Well, you're sleeping now, John, they got you three years later, almost to the day, they were much too afraid of you to let you live, what they need are docile Presidents like Chiang Kai-shek, like Ky, like . . .

The Oval Room was an orgy of yellow: the damask walls, the big oval rug, the two sofas, the Louis XVI armchairs, all this gold rather overpowered the Cézannes hanging on the walls, it was all too rich, too luxurious, Smith selected a cigar, lit it, and paced up and down, his steps muted by the rug, he looked at his watch, at this hour everyone is asleep except me and the cops, thirty-eight cops, count them, stationed in every corner of the house, cops on the grounds and cops at the gates, what a nice subject for a picture, the President of the United States surrounded by his cops, spending his night in meditation on the eve of the Third World War, his throat tightened, the President! the omnipotence of the President! the quasi-dictatorial powers of the President! yes, but the subtle, power-

248

ful, constant pressures, the rut dug in advance so my wheel will fall into it, the states within the state, the Pentagon, the State Department, the financial circles with their military ties, and the police forces, the FBI, the CIA, the lobbies, the pressure groups, the President as prisoner, the President as instrument, the President as hostage, a Gulliver among the Lilliputians! apparently the strongest, actually the most helpless, the single point at which a complex group of forces converges, my speech of January 6 was after all if not the best, at least the least bad, the least dangerous, I *could* give, I could do no less, and those bastards, two days later, deliberately making things worse behind my back by using the word *ultimatum*, I am tied, tied, tied, to manipulate me all they have to do is give me a problem and distort the facts, intoxicate me with false information, as they did to John in April '61 during the Cuban crisis, I'll never forget how the big pundits, the oracles, the experts of the CIA, the Pentagon, the State Department, gave him all that crap about the sure success of the anti-Castro invasion, "The plan is excellent," said General Lemnitzer, "it can only succeed," and Dulles: "It will be even easier than Guatemala," and Bissel: "When the anti-Castroists get off the boat the Cuban people will welcome them with open arms," but at dawn on the seventeenth of April in the Bay of Pigs the Cuban people fell on them with guns, tanks, and cannons, and crushed them in less than seventy-two hours, my God, are they about to do the same thing to me with the *Little Rock?* Smith froze, petrified, the ash at the end of his cigar curled, he took a step, carefully reached for the nearest ashtray, but the ash broke off and fell, scattering on the rug, he shuddered, after a few seconds he noticed that his hand was trembling, he straightened his shoulders, one mustn't see signs everywhere, he dropped into a chair, he must have dozed off for a few seconds, for his right knee relaxed automatically as if he were falling through space, he started, If there's one thing a President can neither reform nor control it's his own political police force, they are the real rulers, since it's they who give him information, he got up and began pacing again, after a moment he noticed that each time he crossed the room he was careful not to walk on the ashes, I'm sure the CIA knew that the Bay of Pigs would be a failure, I'm sure the plan was to confront John with a setback so serious, a loss of face so terrible that John would send the marines to Cuba, and John came close to doing it,

249

such a disaster at the beginning of his Presidency, he was so morti-fied, so humiliated, so upset, but he pulled himself together, he said no, he knew how to say no, no to war against Cuba, no to war against China, no to segregation, they killed him because he knew how to say no, send him to Dallas and we'll take care of the rest, in Dallas we have policemen who can slice a cigar in two at thirty yards, murderers with a Soviet-Cuban pedigree into the bargain, and murderers of murderers who carry out their own sentences by inoculating themselves with cancer.

Smith plunged his hands deep into his pockets and thought with pain, I kept my mouth shut, but I had to choose, either I said the Warren Report is the biggest bunch of lies in the history of the United States, and my career was finished, or I kept my mouth shut and someday I could carry on John's torch, he stopped pacing, time passed, he thought with shame, I kept my mouth shut, he walked over to the window, lifted the heavy drape, and pressed his forehead to the pane, at once a man walked away from a tree and came toward him quickly, looking up, Smith waved him back, the man disappeared, Smith's glance lingered on the magnolia tree that President Jackson had planted, it was enormous and gnarled, behind it the birches seemed frail, naked and vertical, like a drawing by Buffet, illuminated like a movie set by the beams of the security floodlights, when spring comes I'll have to remember to have Johnson's sonic anti-aviary devices removed from the branches, We, Lyndon Baines Johnson, hereby forbid birds to enter the White House grounds, they offend our dignity by soiling the lawn, Smith looked at the funereal silhouettes of the birches, it was enough to make you weep, even through the windowpane there was an odor of rotting dampness, And what did I do when he fell, his head full of holes, drenching Jackie's suit and stockings with his blood, amid the hatred and hypocrisy of Dallas, but he was dead and it wasn't possible to avenge him, to accuse without proof, and whom could I have accused?

At the very least, gentlemen, we can assume a kind of hypocritical and tacit complicity, You bring him to Dallas and we'll take care of the rest, perhaps not even in so many words, or so clearly, or so consciously, Our good city of Dallas awaits him, look, be just a little imprudent, bring him to us, because these bastards have to go on respecting themselves, their souls are complex, and under the com-plexities, hints and halftones, unstated hatreds . . .

If I had spoken they would have passed me off as insane, the enormous machinery would have gone into action, I would have been politically finished, pulverized, without helping anybody, not even John, for what? but of course, to declare war on China, who put this time bomb under my chair? oh, I know, our oracles and experts are categorical, polished and infallible, as always, in two hours we crush all the atomic arms plants and launching pads in China, Russia doesn't move, China is incapable of striking back, and we have a century of peace, but suppose it weren't true? with Cuba too, the CIA had stated, first, that Castro's aviation was "quasi nonexistent," and second, that it had been "destroyed" by surprise ground attacks on Sunday morning, and when the landing began the "nonexistent" and "destroyed" aviation of Castro brought down almost all the B-26's and sank half the invading fleet, and today no matter whether they're deceiving themselves or deceiving me, if one atomic submarine, just one, can slip through our defense network and destroy New York in less than a minute, what good does it do to have a hundred times more rockets than the Chinese? Smith turned out the enormous chandelier, walked down the endless hall to his room, the bedside lamp was burning, he took off his bedroom slippers, untied his tie, turned out the light, and fell, fully dressed, on the four-poster bed where Johnson used to take his three-hour naps, nobody had ever seen a President sleep so much in the afternoon or look sleepier the rest of the time, Smith cursed, I hate to lie down on it, he dozed off but awoke with a start with a cramp in his stomach, My God, to get out of this mess with honor, to prove that there's nothing in it but a vile provocation, an idiotic trap, it smells to heaven, a little Pearl Harbor that couldn't be more clumsy or moth-eaten, all the allies reticent, even those who are so faithful when it comes to lining up for handouts, and Japan! the polite smile, the impenetrable eyes, It is most unfortunate, Mr. Ambassador, that it is always Asiatic towns, our embassy in Tokyo besieged night and day by crowds yelling Peihai! the Secretary of the United Nations openly hostile, the Pope issuing statement after statement, all the churches against us, the worst combination of circumstances for a declaration of war, the moral contest lost in advance, the diplomatic maneuver reduced to nothing, Smith turned over, he was lying on his back in the dark with his legs stretched out, his hands flat on the bed, he felt inert, empty, and helpless, on board a runaway train that was rushing through space

251

at a vertiginous speed, his head began to turn, he felt as if he were falling through space, his nails dug into the bed and he thought, Lord, I would give my life, listen to me, Lord, I would give my life . . .

XII

On January 7, the day after President Albert Monroc Smith's televised address, Sevilla left the house before breakfast (it was seven o'clock in the morning) and walked down to the little harbor where the *Caribee* and the larger of the two life rafts were at anchor. When he was about six yards away he saw, or thought he saw, Daisy playing around the life raft, and he whistled to her. There was no answer. Instead of coming up to him as she usually did and laying her head on the dock to be petted, she turned her back on him, dove, and disappeared. Sevilla walked out on the float that separated the yacht from the life raft. He saw nothing around the raft and nothing around the *Caribee* either, and whistled again. After a few seconds, the long, undulating, pale gray form of Daisy appeared in the water beside the *Caribee*, her head emerged, and she fixed her laughing eye on Sevilla.

"The first time I called, you didn't answer," said Sevilla in the whistling language.

Daisy made a noise that sounded like a chuckle. "The first time, it was not me."

"What do you mean, not you?"

"Another dolphin."

"Don't talk nonsense," said Sevilla.

"I am not talking nonsense."

Some days he couldn't get a thing out of Daisy. Either she pretended not to understand his whistles or her answers didn't make sense. What a difference from Bi's seriousness! Sevilla turned his back on her and walked away, annoyed.

"Where are you going?" cried Daisy behind his back.

"To the house, to eat."

"Talk to me!"

Sevilla said over his shoulder, "You talk nonsense."

"I do not talk nonsense. There is another dolphin in the harbor."

"There's a very silly dolphin named Daisy in the harbor."

"I'm not silly. Look."

She dove. Sevilla watched her, backing up a few steps because the hull of the *Caribee* was in the way. Just as he reached the float he distinctly saw two curved backs emerge from the water at the same moment and disappear. He froze, astonished. He really had seen two backs. Just then they reappeared a little farther on. Daisy and her visitor were swimming in a circle. Daisy was swimming on the inside and trying to push her companion toward the float, evidently without much success. Sevilla whistled. Daisy stopped swimming, dove under her partner's body, reached the dock with three flicks of her tail, emerged, laid her head on the boards, and looked at Sevilla.

"Who is that dolphin?" asked Sevilla.

"He is mine!" said Daisy triumphantly.

Backing up, she leaped out of the water and landed close enough to Sevilla to splash him.

"Daisy, stop that!"

"Am I silly, Pa?"

"No."

She gave another leap and splashed him again.

"Now stop, Daisy. So he's yours," he went on, looking at the dolphin. "He's magnificent."

Daisy chuckled.

"When did you find him?"

"In the sea. Last night. I swim and I swim. Suddenly in front of me I see a dolphin, a dolphin, and a dolphin. They stop. They look at me and they talk."

"What do they say?"

"They say, 'Who is it?' A big male swims over and swims around me. I say nothing, I do nothing, but I am afraid. He is very big. He says, 'Where is your family?' I say, 'I have lost my family. I live with men.' The big male goes away and talks to the other males. They talk and they talk. Then all the males swim over together and surround me. I am afraid. This is the way they kill sharks. They

254

swim over and surround them. But the leader says, 'It is good. You may return to the men or stay with us.' I say, 'I will return to the men but I will play with you.' The leader says, 'Good. You will play.' The females come over. They are nice, except one very old one, she tries to bite me. But I snap my jaws and she goes away."

Daisy stopped talking.

"Well?" said Sevilla.

Daisy chuckled. "A big dolphin comes. He chases the females away and wants to play. He is big and strong. He is beautiful."

"Do you play?"

"I play, but the whole school is around us. So I bring him here."

"Why?"

"So we can be alone."*

Sevilla laughed and went on: "Is he the leader?"

"No. He is a big male. He is very big. Give him a man's name!"

"Later."

"Give him a man's name!"

"Jim."

"Jim!" She laughed. "Jim!"

"Tell him to come over."

"He is afraid."

"Tell him when he is here he plays with you and talks with me. Tell him."

She laughed. "Perhaps you speak and Jim does not understand. You whistle badly." She laughed.

"Stop your foolishness, Daisy. Tell him."

"Tomorrow I tell him."

"Perhaps tomorrow he will not come?"

Daisy made a sound that was joyous, triumphant, and not very ladylike. "Jim!" she said, emerging almost entirely from the water in an upright position. She backed up, very erect, waddling self-importantly, her caudal fin lashing the water powerfully. "Jim comes tomorrow, tomorrow, and tomorrow! He is mine!"

• • •

---

* The mating of dolphins, a delicate operation at best, is hindered by the presence of boisterous young males who follow the operation, making numerous whistled comments and showing obvious signs of excitement themselves.

255

Bruder, said Goldstein, if you insist, I'll be glad to share your humble breakfast, Arlette's coffee is so aromatic, it's your fault, not mine, *Bruder,* if I land on you at this early hour, actually I should have gotten here last night, in my innocence I imagined that having committed the folly of buying a house in the Florida Keys, you would at least have had the elementary good sense to choose one of the islands that are connected to the mainland by the Key West highway, instead of this godforsaken, windy little rock surrounded by reefs, I tried in vain last night as it was getting dark to bribe two ancient mariners to take me to you, No sir, no sir, I'm not going to risk my tub taking you to see those nuts at night—very interesting and talkative, these ancient mariners, after two or three drinks pearls of wisdom began dropping from their beards and I heard the saga of the blockhouse you live in—have you heard it, *Bruder?* Yes, said Sevilla, but tell us anyway, there are two sides to every story, he looked at Goldstein with his dark, attentive eyes, on the surface all that glib, aggressive, irritable energy, on the façade the skepticism, the cynicism, the opportunism, and behind the façade and beneath the surface a man with a truly generous heart, and I'll be damned if I understand why he came here and why he went to so much trouble and wasted so much time when he could just as well have called me.

Well, Goldstein went on, for your information, the man who built your blockhouse is the famous actor Gary James, Famous? asked Arlette, Goldstein turned his blue eyes toward her and shook his white mane, Young woman, he said severely, don't remind me of what an old codger I am, Gary James was famous twenty years ago, and twenty years goes by very fast, you'll see, in short, James read *Walden,* or said he did, for *Walden* is the heaviest, most pedantic book ever written, Maggie looked up and said in a pious and shocked tone, I don't agree, it's a masterpiece, I'm so sorry, said Goldstein with a shrug, but any man who chooses to live *alone* in a cabin for two years is a monk, impotent, or a . . . Don't be crude, said Arlette, laughing, In short, Goldstein went on, he was a little touched, but to get on with it, Gary James read *Walden,* decided to go back to nature and "live naked and alone on an island," okay, he buys his godforsaken rock, builds a harbor, a reservoir, this blockhouse you call a house, installs electricity and telephone by cable from the mainland, for such was his conception of the return

256

to nature, and this done, moves in, stays three days, and never sets foot here again for the rest of his life [*laughter*], Goldstein smiled at Arlette, Baby, can I have another cup of coffee? If this house weren't a blockhouse, said Sevilla, built out of solid concrete and even rounded at the corners to resist the wind, a hurricane would have blown it away long ago, we're right in the path of the hurricanes when they come up from the Caribbean, nine times out of ten they angle in on the Florida Keys, perhaps you don't know that there used to be a railroad connecting the islands as far as Key West and that it was destroyed by a hurricane, but I like the house the way it is, I admit it's rather terrifying, even without a hurricane, when the sea is rough and the wind blows you get waves that cross the reefs, come right over the house, and land on the terrace like a waterfall, and even though the little harbor is under the wind and well protected you still have to triple the moorings of the *Caribee* and seal the windows of the house with those enormous shutters you saw when you came in, frankly, for a few hours you feel as if you're living on board a submarine, I'm sure there are waves that completely cover the island, you can hear them landing on the concrete roof, How intoxicating, said Suzy, opening her blue eyes very wide and panting a little, her lips half parted, it gives me such a delightful sense of isolation and intimacy, I hope one of these days we'll have a hurricane, a real one, forty-eight hours of wind at ninety miles an hour, Peter extended his long arm and laid it on Suzy's shoulder, And water in the reservoir, he said, with a resounding laugh, a good warm torrential rain for forty-eight hours, that's what we need, *Bruder*, said Goldstein, placing his hands flat on his large thighs, I suggest that we ditch these young salts and that you take me to see the *Caribee*, Sevilla glanced at him, and finally got up. There was a red concrete ramp leading from the terrace to the little harbor, and on either side of this path, making it look like an absurd attempt to introduce a temporary human order into the general confusion, lay a desert of coral rocks. Beside him Goldstein walked energetically in spite of his great size, he looked like a mammoth, his big legs seemed to bounce on the cement path, his eyes were small and shrewd, his shoulders broad and round, his heavy jaw thrust forward, his grayish-white mane, like that of an old lion, shining in the sun, he stepped over the ropes into the stern with heavy agility and dropped onto the seat of the cockpit, *Bruder*, he said, it's marvelous, but don't make me go into the cabin, the cabin of a sailboat is always bleak and sad, the bunks are so narrow you couldn't even consider making love in them, I find that depressing, but it's marvelous, he went on, looking at the *Caribee* admiringly, a marvel of chrome, mahogany, brass, and polish, and on top of that she's so pretty, so cute, so well built, if I had the time I'd ask you to take me for a little ride, with a thing like this it would be a cinch to get to Cuba, Sevilla smiled, For that purpose I'd prefer the big life raft with the Mercury outboard, I could reach the coast of Pinar del Río in less than four hours, I say four hours because of the powerful currents that come up from the Gulf of Mexico toward the Atlantic, the boat sits low in the water, so I'd have a much better chance of getting by the U.S. warships and the Cuban coast guard ships, especially the latter, I suppose with all our plotting the Cubans must be hot on the trigger, Well, he went on, turning to Goldstein, what do you have to tell me? Anything new to report on my passport? Goldstein shook his head, The State Department has other fish to fry, you can be sure of that, they're much too busy pushing us into World War Three, I have the impression that the country is going mad, it's charging headlong, blindly, into an atomic conflict, over a point of honor, unconsciously, stupidly, submissively, it's not to be believed, never have we had the sense of being less governed and never have we known less about who was governing the country, certainly not poor Smith, he looks like an overgrown college boy, I found his speech very painful, you could feel so much uncertainty under the apparent firmness, I know him well, you know, I had occasion to work for him during his campaign, I wonder what there is inside of people that makes them want to kill each other, and anyway, what the hell are we doing in Southeast Asia in the first place, can you tell me that? Goldstein glanced around him, I assume I can speak, they haven't managed to plant microphones in the *Caribee* yet? Sevilla smiled, You know from your own experience that the island is inaccessible at night and during the day there's always someone puttering around the harbor, Goldstein leaned over the ropes, But I don't see your dolphin, Right now we only work after dark, Daisy is away all day long and doesn't return to the fold until evening, but she comes back every evening, she's attached to us, but even more so to the *Caribee*, when it gets dark she comes and snuggles against it like a child clinging to its mother, Sevilla broke off, sat up straight and looked at Goldstein, Well, he said, what are you waiting for? Goldstein blinked, looked away, and said, Adams wants to see you.

Sevilla got up, leaned both hands on the steering wheel and turned it a few degrees to the left as if the *Caribee* were under sail and he wanted to make a turn, Never, he said, without raising his voice, but his fingers, clenched on the wheel, went white, Never, he said in a flat voice, between his teeth, I've had it with that bunch, he looked at Goldstein and Goldstein looked back at him, a silence fell and thickened, immobilizing them both in the same positions, Goldstein sitting down with his head jutting out like a turtle cautiously inspecting the road ahead, and Sevilla standing behind the wheel with his legs apart, his eyes staring at the stern, his neck stiff, suddenly he looked taller, more compact, and tougher, as if all the angers and resentments he had ever felt were welling up in him to the bursting point, I've had it with that bunch, he said in the same flat, controlled, barely audible voice, It's all over, thought Goldstein, he's not going to blow up, he's not going to get rid of his anger, he's going to hold it in and make it worse, Goldstein lifted his two big hands and let them fall back on his thighs, *Bruder,* he said in his grating, aggressive, jovial voice, that's your business, the reason I left everything to come and beard you in your den is that Adams came all the way from Washington yesterday to see me, and he succeeded in convincing me that it was, and I quote, *terribly important,* at first I refused, but I've never seen a man so upset, I won't say he went down on his knees to me, but almost, I've never seen Adams in such a state, usually he's cold as a fish, in short, I agreed to give you his message, and now my job is done, if you reject his request it's your own business, I couldn't care less, I understand your point of view completely, those *mamzers* treated you in the most—I repeat, I'm simply giving you his message, word for word, *Tell him it is terribly important,* his voice trembled, I have a thick hide, but I can tell when a man is on hot coals, he repeated at least ten times, *it's terribly important,* well, I've said my piece, now I can go, again he slapped his thighs with the palms of his hands, and as if the gesture had triggered a reflex movement in his knees, he sprang to his feet, Sevilla let go of the wheel, turned to him, thrust his hands in his pockets, and said, On two conditions, the first is that the interview take place here, the second is that Fa

259

and Bi be given to me, not just temporarily entrusted to me again, but *given*, as my exclusive and personal property, and I refuse to discuss these conditions, they are the preliminary terms, Well, said Goldstein with a short laugh, I'm glad to see you can be a tough businessman when it's not a question of money, if you can talk your young salt into taking me over the reefs in the life raft, I'll pass your preliminary terms on to Adams, he's waiting for me on the mainland, and if he accepts your proposals Peter can bring him back to the island at once.

•   •   •

Peter returned less than an hour later with Adams and a young man Sevilla did not know, The life raft is a little soft, called Peter, it has a small leak, I think, if you'll help me get it out of the water and carry it to the terrace I'll repair it right away, I'd like you to meet my assistant, Al, said Adams, in a nervous, staccato voice, Sevilla made a vague gesture of welcome but said nothing and did not come forward, Adams went on, We can help you if you like, there were two rubber handles on each side of the boat and the four of them carried it up to the terrace without difficulty, but when they turned it over at Peter's request they drenched their shoes and trouser bottoms, I'll make a fire in the fireplace so we can dry off, if you'll allow me, said Adams, meanwhile Al will make a tour of the house to see whether they've installed a mike somewhere, I'd be amazed, said Sevilla, the reefs make the island inaccessible, the only entrance is the channel that leads to the harbor, it isn't even marked with buoys, it's very difficult to avoid certain rocks, you saw for yourself, this is our third puncture in a month, a high flame, red at the base and pale pink at the top, leaped up in the fireplace, licked the pine logs, crackled, sparks flew, Adams unlaced his shoes, took them off, laid them on the hearth, and leaned back in the white lacquered rocking chair, holding his feet to the fire, Have you ever left the island since you bought it? Sevilla shook his head, There's always someone here, Still, said Adams, one or two frogmen at high tide on a clear night, coming through the roof, Sevilla shook his head, The roof is concrete, the only opening is the chimney, and nowadays we have a fire almost every day, Al appeared in the doorway with a leather case in his hand and a pair of powerful binoculars around his neck, his face wore a childish and sullen expression,

260

Where can I find a ladder? There's one in the garage, said Sevilla, ask Peter.

I'm going to put my shoes back on before the soles begin to shrivel up, said Adams with a faint smile, he was pale, his smooth face with its regular features was hollow-eyed and tense, there was a silence, they waited for Al and watched the fire, Sevilla leaned forward, grabbed the tongs, picked up a blackened, unburned branch, and wedged it between two glowing logs, nothing happened for what seemed to Sevilla an abnormally long time, then suddenly the branch burst into flames along its whole length and the two logs began to burn with a cheerful crackling sound, We're dry, I think, said Sevilla, we can let it die, anyway it feels very good, Al appeared, his mouth pouting, his dark, severe eyebrows running across his forehead, his manner sober and competent, Everything's okay, he said, the electrical circuit is intact, nothing suspicious, and nothing on the horizon either, not even a fishing boat, but just in case, while you talk I'll go back and watch from the roof, Leave your shoes here, said Sevilla, they're drenched, Peter will lend you another pair, It doesn't matter, said Al, with a severe and puritanical air, he closed the door behind him, Thank you for seeing me, said Adams, staring at the fire, he drew back his rocking chair without looking at Sevilla, You don't have to tell me what you think, I know, well, he went on with effort, I phoned the higher echelon, your conditions have been accepted, Fa and Bi will be delivered to you today, your personal and exclusive ownership of them will be guaranteed in writing, I must warn you, however, that right now possession of the two dolphins involves certain dangers, Sevilla turned his head quickly, What kind of dangers? without looking at him, Adams said, For them and for you, but if you like we can leave a security guard on the island, No, thank you, said Sevilla with bitter irony in his voice, my island is a strictly private laboratory, nobody subsidizes me, nobody controls me, and nobody protects me, Adams pushed his chair back another yard from the fire, I had anticipated your reaction, well, let me explain what little I can, Fa and Bi have carried out a mission, we don't know what it was, there were two commandos, Commando A—our people—brought Fa and Bi to the site, and there they were turned over to an operational commando which we'll call Commando B, We might just as well call it C, Sevilla said with a short laugh, I don't know anything

261

about it, said Adams in a flat, mechanical voice, his eyes still staring at the fire, I'm not making any hypotheses, I'm just stating the facts, we know nothing about Commando B, neither its origin, nor its composition, nor its goals, under the previous Administration we received an order from the highest echelon and we carried it out, to continue, at H hour, Commando A turns Fa and Bi over to Commando B in the open sea and immediately returns to its base. Twelve hours later Commando A receives a message from Commando B: Have lost all trace of Fa and Bi, have you seen them? After that, every hour, we receive the same message from Commando B. At H hour plus twenty-six, to everyone's amazement, Fa and Bi return to our base on their own, visibly exhausted, we conclude that they've been swimming since H hour, twenty-six hours of continuous and rapid swimming. Bob questions them. Excuse me, said Sevilla, where was Bob after H hour? Adams shook his head, Bob didn't leave Commando A, to continue, Bob questions Fa and Bi, silence, total silence, and even the most open hostility toward Bob, a surprising, amazing attitude, given his good relations with them, we are very intrigued, mission accomplished or not, why didn't Fa and Bi return to Commando B? how did they find our base again? and finally, what is the explanation of their attitude toward Bob? We report immediately in code and we receive two orders, the first, not to tell Commando B that Fa and Bi have been recovered, the second, to send Fa and Bi home. Well, since the return of the two dolphins we have questioned them constantly, always without success, they are silent and hostile, refuse to be petted and snap their jaws menacingly when anyone comes near them, Adams stopped talking, Sevilla was surprised by his altered expression and his defensive tone, he looked at the fire, to his surprise, it was still keeping itself alive with the little wood that remained, it was glowing frugally, without spending itself in flames, but without smoking either, without that sickening smell of rubbish and ruin that it leaves behind, Sevilla sat up straight, put his hands on the arms of his chair, and looked at Adams: I suppose you're giving me Fa and Bi so I'll make them talk and you can find out what happened, Yes, said Adams without moving, And from your warnings I conclude that there are people who might take the greatest interest in . . . Yes, said Adams, Well, you tell too much and too little, there are gaps in your story, you've talked about H

262

hour but you haven't located the theater of operation nor given me the date of D day, Adams shook his head, I've told you all I can, Sevilla looked at him but Adams refused to return his look, Sevilla got up and thought immediately, Why am I getting up? Is it the need to act or a reflex of flight? He forced himself to stand still, one hand resting on the chair, but his legs trembled beneath him, looking down, to his amazement he saw his left leg quivering convulsively from hip to toe, he pressed his foot to the floor but he couldn't stop the trembling, he sat down again, his legs were still trembling, he felt weak, exhausted, bloodless, all he could see of Adams was his profile, and suddenly he felt like screaming, Look at me, Adams, look at me, why are you afraid to look me in the eye?

. . .

Adams got up. "May I use your telephone?"

"Of course."

He walked stiffly to the desk, picked up the receiver, and dialed a number.

"Hello, Herman here. . . . Let me talk to George. . . . George, please send me two cases of beer, a case of Coca-Cola, and a bunch of bananas. Thanks. You have plenty of room to land." He hung up and turned to Sevilla. "A helicopter will bring them here in an hour and take me right back."

"I understood the two cases of beer," said Sevilla, "but not the Coca-Cola or the bunch of bananas."

Adams smiled. "In view of your pacifist ideas, I don't suppose you're armed."

"No."

"The Coca-Cola will take care of that. And I'm adding a little radio set."

"I see."

"Do you know how to use light infantry arms?"

"Nineteen forty-four. Arromanches."

"That's right, what's the matter with me? As if I didn't know your biography."

There was a silence and Sevilla said, "Would you like a cup of coffee?"

"I'd love one."

He led Adams to the dining room, where the three women were sitting.

"Although you've never met them," said Sevilla, "I suppose there's nothing about them you don't know. Arlette, this is Herman."

"Mrs. Sevilla," said Adams gravely, "it's a great privilege to meet you. Your husband has a terrible sense of humor. You know my real name."

"How do you do, Mr. Adams," said Arlette coldly.

Adams greeted Suzy and Maggie from a distance. They nodded back, but did not approach.

"Maggie," said Sevilla, "is there some coffee for Mr. Adams and me?"

"Of course," said Maggie.

They sat down on either side of a long table with a blue Formica top. The telephone rang. Sevilla picked up the receiver, carried it to his ear, and said, "Sevilla here. . . . Who? George? George who?"

"It's for me," said Adams, holding out his hand. "Hello, Franklin? . . . This is Nathaniel. . . . What? . . ." Adams went pale and his hand clenched on the receiver. "Bertie is on the premises? . . . Well, tell him to call me and report."

He hung up and looked at Sevilla with tired, hollow eyes. He seemed breathless, as if he had just made a violent effort.

"Bob has been killed in an automobile accident. His body has just been found in a ravine."

Someone screamed, and Adams started violently. Sevilla looked up just in time to see Maggie run out of the room holding her head in her hands.

"Go to her, Suzy," said Sevilla.

"What's the matter?" asked Adams.

"It's Maggie. She was in love with him."

"I'd forgotten," said Adams, passing his hand over his face. "But God knows . . ."

"Excuse me," said Sevilla.

He hurried out of the room, caught up with Suzy on the terrace, and whispered in her ear, "Before you go to Maggie, tell Peter to keep an eye on Al."

Sevilla came back into the room. Arlette was setting a cup of coffee in front of Adams.

264

"Thank you," said Adams gratefully.

"Would you like something to eat?"

Sevilla looked at her. She spoke with icy hostility. She hadn't forgotten the spying on the bungalow.

"No, thank you," said Adams, "I'm not hungry." He turned to Sevilla. "What kind of a driver was he?"

Sevilla looked at him. "Very cautious."

Adams stared at the blue Formica, brought the cup to his lips, and drained it greedily.

"Would you like another cup?" asked Arlette in a neutral voice.

"Thank you."

The telephone rang, Sevilla picked it up, listened, and passed the receiver to Adams.

"Bertie? . . . Ernest here. . . . I can hardly hear you. . . . Nothing? What do you mean, nothing? . . . Nothing but ashes?"

•   •   •

Maggie was lying face down on her bed, her face buried in the pillow, her shoulders shaking with sobs, Suzy closed the door behind her, sat down beside her, and sighed, Here we go, once again I'm going along with it, I'm associating myself with the fiction, I'm lying too, but just how aware is she that she's lying, nobody knows, not even her, Suzy looked at Maggie's heaving shoulders and thought with remorse, After all, laughter may be a mask, but pain, even if it has no object, is always real, Maggie turned around, gripped her hands hard and looked at her, her eyes swimming with tears, There, there, said Suzy in a sweet, patient, sympathetic voice, calm yourself, don't put yourself in such a state, just then Suzy caught sight of herself in the mirror over the couch and thought, My God, this sticky sympathy, this insipid, confidential manner, all these lies, it's enough to make you vomit, she heard Maggie say, You see, Suzy, in a broken voice and she thought with exasperation, Here we go again, what a ridiculous farce, this hodgepodge of sentimentality and sex, I don't know whether to laugh or cry, You see, Suzy, said Maggie in a broken voice, the awful part, the part I'll never forgive myself for, is that it was I who killed him, no, it's true, I was so changeable, so inconsistent, so unconsciously cruel, she sobbed harder than ever, her incredibly ugly face made even uglier by tears, I reduced him to despair, no, it's true, first of all by

265

refusing to marry him, but you know all about that, I know it may sound absurd, abnormal, even monstrous in a way, but I don't want to have children, I don't like them, I know it sounds horrible to say a thing like that, but I can't help it, I am what I am, listen, I want to make a confession, there's something worse, much worse, I have to tell you, the truth is that I treated Bob abominably, since I didn't want to marry him, Suzy, you're such an honest person, you'll agree, I should have discouraged his advances, and God knows he made them, in a way, I tell myself, that's my excuse, for never has a woman been more courted, more pursued, more hounded, even, of course with Bob it wasn't crude or obvious, it was delightfully subtle, it showed itself in a thousand little ways, for example, the furtive way he would avoid my eye at the table, it was his way of saying My love, I cannot look at you, or everyone will know, oh, he was adorable, what manners, what refinement, listen, Suzy, I'm going to tell you everything, this confession is hard for me, but I think it will do me good, surely you remember that Friday when the two of us left for the weekend in his car, No, said Suzy with controlled exasperation, no, I don't remember, and immediately she thought, What's the use, it's like trying to stop a flood with one pebble, Well, said Maggie, I don't remember the date, it doesn't matter, anyway, it was in March, I'm sure of that, we left together, you remember, he had just bought his Ford coupé, the interior was leather, red leather, he could never stand plastic, well, that day he begged me so hard, with real tears in his eyes, that I gave in and let him take me to a motel, at the desk he registered me in his own name, poor darling, how happy he must have been to give me his name, if only for one night, don't misjudge me, Suzy, I'm not trying to exonerate myself, well, even there, in that little room beside the sea, I remember, the view was magnificent, we were almost on the beach, even there, he was so good, so sensitive, he wouldn't have touched me if I hadn't wanted him to, and it was me, Suzy, it was me, she hid her big red tear-streaked face in her hands, Look, said Suzy, don't think about it any more, you'll make yourself sick, But you don't understand! cried Maggie, how could I have been so cruel as to give myself to him and then refuse to marry him, it's hateful, I can't stop thinking about that night, we didn't sleep a wink, as you can imagine, it was a beautiful night, there was a magnificent moon, we could hear the waves breaking a few feet away, he looked

266

at me, in his eyes was a mute, desperate question, and I, I said nothing, I did not say the yes he was waiting for, I said nothing, I had that terrible courage, I had given him my body, but nothing more, oh I remember! he lay beside me, not moving, even now I can see his profile on the pillow, it's like a hallucination, it stood out against the moonlight shining through the window, so beautiful, so delicate, almost feminine in its delicacy, and his large open eyes staring into space with unfathomable sadness, oh, Suzy, how could I have been so cruel, it's all my fault, it all began that night, in that motel, do you think Bob would have agreed to work for those people and go with Fa and Bi if I had consented to be his wife, and now they come and tell me he's dead, that he died in an automobile accident, he who drove like an angel! he hated speed, you remember, he used to say that a car should glide over the road like a boat over the water, the truth is that he killed himself, no, Suzy, I don't want to run away from the truth, even if it hurts twice as much, he killed himself because he couldn't stand to live alone, without me, without hope, without the child he wanted me to give him, how can I ever forgive myself for my cruelty, my insensitivity, my unawareness, for after all, Suzy, I rejected him, the poor darling, just as I rejected Sevilla, but I didn't really hurt Sevilla, he's an instinctive man, a primitive even, after me, he pounced on the first woman who came along and satisfied himself with her, poor Arlette, she's nothing but a substitute, I wonder how she'll take it when she realizes it, and then Sevilla, though he's certainly a great intelligence, is a rather frightening man, don't you think, those eyes, that mouth, that hairy chest, just between us, Suzy, I would have been terrified to give myself to Sevilla, it would have been like being ravaged by a patrol of marines, well, Sevilla is what he is, I don't blame him, he's a man, that's all, but Bob, she went on, the tears streaking her mottled cheeks, Bob wasn't a man, Suzy, he was an angel, a kind of Shelley, so pure, so tender, so disembodied, he had a profound spiritual need of me, not of my body, of me, me as a human being, Take these, said Suzy firmly, pouring some pills into the palm of her hand and offering them to Maggie, come on, take them, now drink, in a moment you'll be asleep, she took Maggie's hand in hers and held it tightly until the girl began to drop off, she looked at the red, graceless features, like the face of a boxer who has lost a fight, and that's what had happened, after all, poor Maggie,

267

beaten in the first round of the battle of the sexes, doomed from the start to hunger, horrible sexual hunger, not the worst form of suffering but the most humiliating in a world of people who eat, Suzy brought her left hand to her face and ran it lightly over her own features, but everything was as it should be, well distributed, the young skin firm over the delicate bones, the nose finely chiseled, the small ears, the dimples, the seductive mouth, oh, it wasn't fair, who had doomed Maggie to hunger and, with her, millions of lonely human beings who can think about nothing else? Maggie was asleep, Suzy gently withdrew her hand, she walked out of the room, took a deep breath, and ran into the garage where Peter was kneeling and puttering with the motor of the outboard, Hold me, she said, But my hands are dirty, he got up and looked at her with his tender, laughing eyes, I don't care! she pressed herself against his chest, warm, plump, sweet-smelling, he held her with his elbows, his hands in the air, No, no, she said, not like that, hold me, hold me tight, she was panting, her eyes shone with tears, she put her arms around him and pressed herself against him frantically, as if she wanted to enter his body to protect herself from life.

"I hope," said Adams, "that you now admit the necessity for protection on the island."

"Not at all," said Sevilla, looking up and meeting his eyes. "I categorically refuse. My point of view is unchanged."

"See here, Sevilla, I must insist. After what has just happened it is clear that if Fa and Bi are turned over to you, you will be in great danger."

Arlette opened her mouth to speak, but her gaze met Sevilla's and she remained silent.

"Mrs. Sevilla, did you want to say something?"

"No," she said coldly. "Nothing important."

Adams studied Sevilla for a moment. "In that case," he said slowly, "I don't know whether I can turn the dolphins over to you. Without a detail of guards on the island the minimum security conditions do not seem to be met."

"Don't turn them over to me," said Sevilla curtly. "I don't want any favors." He added, "I didn't ask to see you, either."

There was a silence. Adams looked at the floor, his hands in his pockets. "You're a strange man. A few months ago, I remember clearly your telling me that you regarded Fa and Bi as your own children."

Sevilla's face closed. "I may have exaggerated my feelings."

Arlette looked at Sevilla, again seemed about to say something, and changed her mind. There was another long silence.

"Allow me to summarize the situation," said Sevilla in a crisp voice. "If, after thinking it over, you decide not to turn Fa and Bi over to me, you will cancel the helicopter and Peter will take you back to the mainland. If you do turn them over to me, you will acknowledge my personal ownership of them in writing. For my part, if they speak, I promise to record their statements and send you the tape. But under no circumstances will I accept a detail of guards on the island. If you want to set up a maritime observation post at a suitable distance from the island, that's your business; I see no objection to that. Nor do I see any objection to your giving me guns as well as a shortwave radio to communicate with your post. On the other hand, I don't want any aerial surveillance or planes flying over the island."

Adams kept his eyes lowered. He waited a few seconds and then said, "My turn. If you get a story out of Fa and Bi a tape recording won't be sufficient. I'll have to hear it from their mouths."

"Agreed," said Sevilla. He corrected Adams immediately: "From their spiracles."

"Excuse me?"

"Not from their mouths, from their spiracles."

"I'd forgotten," said Adams with a strained smile. "In the second place, I think it is indispensable that Maggie, Suzy, and Peter be left out of all this."

"Agreed," said Sevilla. "As a matter of fact my wife and I have done that by tacit agreement so far. This is what I propose: Your helicopter lands on the terrace and delivers the guns, the radio set, and the dolphins. Your men take the dolphins down to the harbor and put them in the water without our being present. Then the helicopter picks up you and Al, and leaves. After your departure Arlette and I make contact with the dolphins."

"I suggest a variation," said Adams after a moment. "I could be present when Mrs. Sevilla and you make contact with Fa and Bi."

"No," said Sevilla. "Absolutely not."

"Why?"

269

"Must I say it again? This laboratory belongs to me: Nobody subsidizes me and nobody supervises me. Adams," he went on ill-humoredly, getting up, "if you spend all your time questioning my conditions, we'll never be done. Make up your mind. As far as I'm concerned the negotiations are finished."

"But I agree," said Adams with an offended air. "If you don't mind my saying so, you drive a hard bargain."

Sevilla looked at Adams with his dark eyes and said nothing. Then he waved his hand and said, "With your permission, I'll leave you alone for a few minutes so you can confirm in writing the fact that you are giving us Fa and Bi."

Sevilla motioned to Arlette. They walked out of the room and went into the garage. As soon as he saw Sevilla Peter got up, scrawled a few words on a page of his notebook, tore it out, and handed it to him.

Arlette looked at Suzy. "How's Maggie?"

"She's sleeping. I gave her a sedative."

"How is she taking . . ."

"The way you'd expect: It's her fault. She broke Bob's heart, that's why he committed suicide."

"Poor girl. I don't know why, I always feel guilty about her."

"Me too."

"Do you know that your dress is all dirty in back? You must have leaned against the motor."

"I guess so," said Suzy, smiling. In a sudden burst of affection she took Arlette's hands in hers and squeezed them hard.

Sevilla handed Arlette Peter's note. She glanced at it: *Al installed a mike in the house, but he didn't go near the harbor.*

"How are you coming with your repairs?" asked Sevilla in a loud voice.

"The big life raft is fixed, but I'm not going to put it in the water until tomorrow. I'm cleaning the motor of the little one."

"Good. I'll leave you. Arlette and I are going to put the net back across the entrance of the tank."

When they reached the dock Arlette turned to Sevilla and said in a low voice, "Why didn't you accept the protection Adams wanted to give you?"

"I didn't like his insistence. Protection of that kind is a two-edged sword."

"Do you really believe that?"

"Yes, I do. I sensed an ambiguity in Adams' attitude. He wants to know the truth, I'm sure of that. But why? To pass it on to the 'higher echelon'? Maybe. And maybe also simply to have a hold over B. I don't trust him."

"Do you think he or his leaders might decide to suppress the truth?"

"Yes, I do."

"In that case . . ."

Sevilla looked at her with his dark eyes. "In that case, we are in the way."

XIII

Adams handed the paper to Sevilla, who read it carefully, folded it twice, and put it in his wallet, Adams looked at his watch, They'll be here any minute, when I landed this morning I didn't see your dolphin, it's a female, isn't it, won't there be a problem with Bi? There will be a slight difficulty, said Sevilla, you have a good memory, Bi won't tolerate the presence of another female around Fa, but in the present case I don't think it will be very serious, the tank is open, Daisy is in the habit of coming and going, if the tension between her and Bi becomes too great she'll leave, he was about to mention Jim but changed his mind, somewhere there was the shrill hum of a motor, Listen, there are our men, said Adams, going over to the window, he opened it, leaned out, and looked up at the sky, If you will allow me, said Sevilla, I'm going to close it again, you know our agreement, your men are to put Fa and Bi in the tank and none of us is to be seen by the dolphins until you leave, Well, said Adams, I wish you luck, his voice was almost drowned out by the deafening roar of the approaching helicopter, It is terribly important, I don't have to tell you that, he looked at Sevilla with his tired, hollow eyes and Sevilla looked back at him, it was amazing, he seemed sincerely upset, but in the end it didn't mean a thing, he was one of those people who can erase their identities as soon as they receive an order, It is also very important to work fast, Adams went on quickly, breathlessly, As soon as they talk, if they do talk, call me by radio, I'll be staying in one of the watchtowers, I'll come at once, the din of the helicopter cut him off,

272

he caught his breath, looked at Sevilla, and unexpectedly held out his hand, Sevilla looked down, always the same ambiguity, the perversion of human relations, friendship, respect, nothing was false, nothing was real, the handshake or the bullet in the brain, everything was subject to orders, Adams had put his conscience in the hands of his leaders, everything was decided elsewhere, it was the hand of an absent man, I'll do everything I can, said Sevilla without moving, I think I know what's at stake, Adams walked to the door, as soon as he opened it the room was invaded by the inhuman din of the machine that was landing on the terrace together with a violent blast of wind, the door slammed behind Adams as if he had been snatched up by the wind, I'm terribly excited at the idea of seeing them again, said Arlette, I wonder what kind of a welcome they'll give us, Sevilla put his arm on her shoulder, I was wondering the same thing, anyway, it will be a joy to have them here, let's sit down, he went on, I'm exhausted, I can't stand that man, he thought, what I just said is on tape, he began to laugh, Why are you laughing? Nothing, nothing, I'll explain, they sat down side by side, he leaned his shoulder against hers, she was wearing white shorts and a light-blue linen blouse, her tanned neck and fine head rose gracefully from the collar, which was turned up in back, she looked at him with her soft eyes, her gleaming, curly hair formed a black halo around her smooth, flushed face, her gentleness, her marvelous gentleness, a minimum of claws, and then only in a state of jealousy, she had the most important quality in a woman, she was sweet, and it wasn't just a surface sweetness, she was sweet inside too, her very being was benevolent, at this moment he no longer thought about the danger, the war, he had Arlette, he was getting Fa and Bi back, a new life was beginning, he felt light, buoyant, he looked at Arlette, she was fragrant and tender, she looked like a fruit, a flower, a colt in a meadow, a ray of sunlight in a clump of birches, What are you thinking? she asked, he smiled at her, Nothing, nothing, he didn't want to say anything to her, right now he didn't want to speak, even to her, he wanted to savor her image by himself, to let her melt in his mouth like honey, Remember when we gave Bi to Fa? she said, he splashed me, I was tired, drenched, and so happy, I came to help you keep the time, I gave you the seconds and even the tenths of a second, you teased me about my precision, we started laughing and all of a sudden I felt so

273

close to you, he ran his hand behind the collar of her shirt, took her by the back of the neck, and brought her head to his, it was maddening, the volume of noise that these machines could produce, even with the doors and windows shut the din went right through your head, you couldn't hear yourself think, They're flying away, said Arlette, getting up and going over to the window, they're flying away like angels, she went on with a little mocking laugh, it's extraordinary how relieved I feel, I felt as if the island were occupied, he went over to her, opened the door, went out on the terrace, the helicopter was flying off at an angle with that strange, awkward, crablike flight, like that of a clumsy insect weighed down by its big-bellied body, Sevilla strode rapidly to the garage, opened the door, I'm going to ask you to stay away from the harbor today, he told them, I want to be alone to renew contact with Fa and Bi, Suzy and Peter looked at him for a moment, surprised and hurt, Okay, said Peter stiffly, and handed Sevilla a page of his notebook on which he had scrawled *Shall I kill the mike?* Sevilla shook his head, grabbed the pail of fish intended for Daisy, and, motioning to Arlette, walked rapidly down the red concrete path that led to the harbor, he walked out on the little wooden jetty where the *Caribee* was docked and saw the two dolphins circling the tank side by side, his heart pounded, he called Fa! Bi! they froze five or six yards away and looked at him, leaning their heads first to one side and then to the other in order to study him with each eye. They considered him this way for over a minute, keeping afloat by lightly flicking their caudal fins and not exchanging a single whistle with each other, Fa! Bi! Come here! cried Sevilla, but nothing happened, nothing but this mute, suspicious inspection, no leaping out of the water, no gaiety, no mischievous splashing, it was their silence that affected Sevilla the most, It's me! he cried, it's Pa! you remember Pa! and taking a fish out of the pail, he knelt on the jetty and held it out toward them, nothing unusual happened for several seconds, they looked from the fish to Sevilla, then suddenly, with one accord, as if they did not need to consult each other to come to an agreement, they turned around, swam away, and started circling the tank again, throwing Sevilla and Arlette the same scrutinizing, indifferent looks each time they passed, It's all over, said Sevilla, his throat tight, oddly enough, at this moment he no longer felt like an adult, he was regressing to a much earlier situation, he felt like a little boy who has been rejected, without knowing why, by companions he loves, a sense of injustice compounded his humiliation, he could hardly keep back his tears, he set the pail on the jetty, threw the fish he was holding into it, and straightened up, Arlette touched his arm, Aren't you going to go in the water and try to approach them? No, he said after a moment in a toneless voice, that would be a mistake, they'd be even more stubborn, for the moment there's only one thing to do, leave them alone, come, let's not stay here, he pivoted on his heels and walked up the cement pier, Arlette walked at his side, her eyes full of tears, suddenly the slope ahead of her seemed steep and arduous, he stopped and turned around just in time to see Fa emerge from the water, lay his body on the jetty, and with a jerk of his head, exactly like a goalie defending his goalpost, sweep the pail of fish into the water, this done, he gave a whistle of triumph, dove, reappeared with a fish in his jaws and swallowed it, then Bi dove, they devoured the contents of the pail with incredible rapidity and greed, Sevilla looked at them rigid with sorrow, he felt rejected, excluded, humiliated, They didn't want to take anything from my hand, he said in a low voice with something like shame.

· · ·

"Have you mastered this gadget?" asked Sevilla wearily.

Peter looked up at him. He was surprised at his tone of voice.

"No problem. But you can't talk in 'clear.' There's a code."

"Please call Adams and tell him that the first contact is not encouraging. Silence, hostility. They won't even accept a fish from my hand."

Peter's face darkened. "As soon as I can put that in code, I'll call him."

"Thank you. Suzy, will you tell Arlette that I won't be coming to lunch? I'm going to lie down."

Suzy looked at him with her clear eyes. "Are you ill?"

"No, no. A little tired, that's all."

"I want you to know how sorry I am."

He made a gesture, turned on his heel, left the room, and went out into the hall. All the rooms in the bungalow had two exits: a French door onto the terrace, and a regular door onto a hall. This hall, which was located on the side the wind came from, had no window, and its only illumination was provided by a triple row of

275

glass bricks at eye level. For the first time since he had bought the house Sevilla found this hall gloomy. He entered his room, drew the curtains, and fell on the bed. Then he got up, took his dressing gown, and lay down again, placing it over him. He slipped the sash out of the loop and laid it over his eyes. He was lying on his left side, curled up, facing the wall, both hands under his chin, like a shriveled leaf, he wasn't cold, the dressing gown gave him a sense of security, time passed, he could neither fall asleep nor think, the same image passed endlessly before his eyes with exhausting monotony: Fa and Bi, five yards away, turning their heads to the left, then to the right, looking at him.

The door opened and Arlette's voice said very softly, Aren't you asleep? No, he said after a moment. He turned around, the sash that was covering his eyes slipped off, and he saw Arlette standing in front of the bed holding a tray, You brought me something to eat, he said vaguely, sitting up in bed, she placed the tray on his knees, he took a sandwich and began to chew, his eyes absent, when he had finished she poured a can of beer into a glass and handed it to him, he drank a few swallows and handed back the glass, Do you want the other sandwich? he ran his fingers through his hair and shook his head, she put the half-full glass and the remaining sandwich on the bedside table, she looked at him, whenever he felt unhappy he was ashamed of it, he wanted to be alone, he went to bed, at first she had been shocked, Do you know why you are shocked, dear? Because I'm reacting naturally, I have a horror of all this Anglo-Saxon cant about virility at any price, when I feel weak I don't pretend to be strong, I curl up into a ball and wait until it goes away, and it was true, it always went away, in a few hours he would recover his courage, his *joie de vivre*, she leaned over and stroked his cheek, he submitted silently, his face sad, his eyes dull, she always had the feeling that he exaggerated, that he overdid it, that he couldn't be as depressed as he seemed, but perhaps the theatrical element was part of his therapy, perhaps he experienced his depression almost as a caricature the better to banish it, I'll leave you, she said, he gave her a joyless smile, then lay down again, turned over on his side, heard the door close, felt for and found the sash of the dressing gown and put it over his eyes again, immediately the images of Fa and Bi appeared, endlessly leaning their big heads first to the right, then to the left, staring at him inscrutably.

276

He felt as if he had dozed off for only a few minutes but when he looked at his watch he saw that he had slept two hours. He sat up in bed, his dressing gown slipped off, he was cold, he opened the French doors, came back to the bedside table and got the second sandwich and the glass of beer and walked down to the harbor, the sun immediately beat down on his head, the back of his neck, his back, the calves of his legs, he felt better, when he reached the wooden jetty he walked out to the end, set the glass on one of the boards, and sat down, his legs dangling over the water, the sun relaxed him, he sniffed the sandwich and suddenly it was as if he had long since forgotten the smell of bread and ham, he redis-covered it with joy, as if after a long illness, the saliva flowed in his mouth, he bit into the sandwich, the mouthful flooded his palate with pleasure as it dissolved and he restrained the brutal desire to swallow it, he forced himself to eat slowly to prolong the sensation, but greed, haste, gluttony had their pleasures too, when he had finished he drank the rest of the beer, it was warm, but it had a clean, good-natured, honest flavor, he wiped his mouth and hands with his handkerchief and looked at Fa and Bi, the idiots! the damned little idiots! they were snubbing him!

He sat up and whistled vigorously in Dolphinese, "Fa, speak to me!"

Fa turned his head to the right and to the left and said, "Who is whistling?"

"It's me! It's Pa!"

He swam over. "Who taught you so well? You did not whistle well when we left."

"Some dolphins. Some other dolphins."

"Where are they?"

"You'll see them. They will come here."

Bi swam over. "Male or female?"

"A male and a female."

"I do not want them," said Bi.

"Why?"

"I do not want them."

"They were here before you."

"I do not want them."

Sevilla turned to Fa. "Fa, why wouldn't you take a fish out of my hand?"

277

There was a silence, and then Fa turned his head away.

"Answer, Fa."

There was another silence and Bi said suddenly, "You betrayed us."

"I?"

"You let Ba take us away."

"Bob took you away behind my back. I did not agree to it."

"Ba told us, 'He has agreed to it.' "

"Bob told you the thing that is not so."

"Ma was there when Ba took us away. Ma did not say anything."

"Bob told Ma, 'Pa has agreed to it.' "

After this there was a long silence. Bi and Fa looked at him, neither friendly nor hostile. They did not come any closer. They stayed several yards from the jetty. They no longer refused to talk, but they still refused to have any contact.

"Well, Bi," said Sevilla, "don't you have anything to say?" He addressed her again because he knew she was the tougher one of the pair.

She cocked her head on one side. "Maybe Ba said the thing that is not so. Maybe you say the thing that is not so. How do I know?"

"I," said Sevilla, "say the thing that is so. I love you. Remember, Bi: Pa brought up Fa. Pa gave Fa to Bi."

"But Pa put a wall between Fa and Bi."

Sevilla looked at her, dumfounded. She still held that against him! The tenacity of feminine resentment! "Look here, Bi, that was only to teach Fa English. Afterwards I took it away."

There was a silence and Bi said, "Now I do not talk any more. Now I swim."

"Say something in English."

"No."

"Why?"

"I do not want to speak the language of men any more."

"Neither do I," said Fa suddenly.

"Why not?" asked Sevilla, turning to him.

Fa did not answer.

"Why, Bi?"

Bi looked at him first out of the right eye, then out of the left.

"Why, Bi?"

Several seconds passed before Bi replied. Curiously enough, she

278

did not whistle her reply. Without regard for the apparent contradiction, she gave it in human language. No doubt she meant to emphasize that it was by choice, and not because of a bad memory, that she would henceforth refuse to express herself in English.

In a voice that was shrill, nasal, and perfectly understandable, she said, "Men are not good."

So saying, she turned her back and began to circle the pool with Fa at her side.

. . .

Sevilla looked around, Arlette was standing beside him, he realized that she must have been there from the beginning of his conversation with the dolphins, she looked at him reproachfully, You didn't tell me you were coming down to the harbor, he smiled and put his arm around her, she leaned toward him, nestling her head against his neck, and left it there for a moment, A believer adores his god, in his eyes the god is all goodness, all truth, all nobility, and suddenly he discovers that his god is base, lying, and cruel, he waved his hand at Fa and Bi, that's what happened to them, Still, said Arlette, they opened up to you, you were able to talk to them, that's progress, Sevilla shook his head, They opened up only to close again, all I can say is that I don't have the right to give up, they've had a terrible shock, they've suffered the worst possible trauma, remember, man is good, he is smooth, and he has hands, in short, man is God, and now I can't even open my mouth without their immediately suspecting me of lying, and I must convince them of my good faith in a language I've only half mastered and knowing that they may put an end to the conversation at any moment, "Now I do not talk any more, now I swim," you know Bi's trick, how many times has she used it on us, she sails off like a queen and of course that big boob of a Fa follows her immediately, he fell silent, Adams called, said Arlette, he wanted to know how things are coming, Please tell him that there's nothing new, I don't like the idea of this communication through the air, anyone can break a code, Arlette ran her fingers down his arm and took his hand, Maggie is awake, she's waiting for you in your office, she wants to talk to you, Good God, said Sevilla.

She was sitting rigid in a chair, her hair wild, her eyes swollen, her face scarlet, her manner serious, strained, *problematische*, Sevilla dropped into his desk chair, his body felt like lead, he took a pencil and a sheet of paper, focused on a point in space over Maggie's head, and said in a neutral voice, Well, Maggie? at once it was as if he had opened a floodgate, a tide of words rushed, bubbling, over him, he submitted to it, his eyes lowered, his face attentive, the point of his pencil pressing on the paper, it had been years since he had listened to Maggie, his ear had become selective, it let through only the facts, the information, the objective data, as soon as the delirium began it closed, he drew a circle, and in the circle a square, I wonder what my ear does to act as a filter, how does it know that there is no point in listening before I am fully aware of it, he forced himself to pay attention to Maggie, he dove into the flood of her words like a dragnet sinking to the bottom of the sea to bring up a sample, *He registered me in his name, poor darling, how happy he must have been to give me his name, even for one night,* well, the sample answers my questions, what guides my ear is the voice, Maggie has two voices, the clear, well-modulated voice of the secretary who keeps functioning at a high level of professional efficiency, and the voice of delirium, a shrill, high-pitched, artificial voice, the voice of the adolescent who had sexual fantasies about all the men around her, and who has been having them ever since, he raised his head and looked at Maggie, She obviously doesn't care that I'm not listening to her, she doesn't really need someone to talk to, she isn't talking to me, she's talking at me, she doesn't need a person but the fiction of a presence in order to talk about herself, and the reason she needs to talk about herself is to give substance to her fantasy, so she can believe in it herself, *remind you of your responsibilities,* Excuse me? said Sevilla, starting suddenly, my responsibilities? what responsibilities? You see, said Maggie in her crisp, well-modulated secretary's voice, you haven't been listening to me, but that's nothing new, you never listen to me, I always feel as if I'm talking to a blank wall, I beg your pardon, said Sevilla, embarrassed, I'm a little tired, Maggie looked at him and a wave of tenderness went through her, it was true that he looked tired, and besides he was adorable with that look on his face, like a little boy caught misbehaving, of course, Arlette is not at all the kind of woman he needs, too sensual, not tender enough, she brings out the ape in him, the orangutan always ready to jump on you brandishing his sex, this Latin priapism revolts me, I remember the first year, he gave me terrible nightmares, every night I used to see him in the corner of my room, naked, hairy, erect, he comes toward me, devouring me with his dark eyes, I melt with terror, his brown hands tear off my pajamas, my naked breasts appear, he crushes me with his weight, I am so afraid I don't even resist, You were talking about my responsibilities, said Sevilla, there was a silence, he looked up, she looked at him breathless, her eyes a little haggard, the sweat stood out on her forehead, *You can't deny,* she said suddenly in a shrill, high-pitched voice, *that you did everything you could to come between me and my fiancé, oh, I don't blame you, I fully understand the primitive feelings that drove you,* the sound of her voice receded, crossed a threshold, became faint and vague, Sevilla drew a square in the center of the smallest circle and crosshatched it carefully, poor girl, the neurotic narrowing of the field of consciousness, the endless repetition, the inability to think about anything else, there they were, five days before the thirteenth of January, five days before the turning point of the century, millions—hundreds of millions—of people might die, the planet was on the brink of war and perhaps of destruction, but for Maggie none of this was real, she was trapped inside her own skin, walled in by her obsession, tortured by her sexuality, there was a gentle tap at the door, Arlette's head appeared, Would you come, darling, Daisy and Jim are back and things aren't going well with Fa and Bi.

· · ·

Sevilla looked at his watch. Six o'clock: another hour of daylight. By all outward appearances, nothing was happening in the harbor. Daisy and Jim had retreated to the side of the *Caribee*, Fa and Bi were on the other side of the pool. The two couples were facing each other, motionless. From time to time one of the two females would give a shrill whistle which the other would echo.

Sevilla turned to Arlette. "Were you there when Daisy and Jim arrived?"

"Yes. Without preliminary warning, Bi attacked Daisy and bit her. Daisy fought back and bit Bi. This battle of the females was interrupted by Jim, who gave Bi a few whacks with his tail but didn't bite her. Bi withdrew."

"What about Fa?"

"Fa didn't move. He stayed in his corner and when Bi came back, he gave her a scolding."

"And since then?"

281

"The females have been exchanging whistles. Each of the two accuses the other of invading her territory. It looks like a battle over territory, but in reality, only Daisy is attached to the pool, or, more precisely, to the *Caribee*. Fa and Bi have just arrived, they don't feel at home yet. As for Jim, being a 'wild' dolphin, he feels like an intruder anyway. The real problem is Bi. Her accusation that Daisy has invaded her territory is pure hypocrisy. She doesn't want Daisy around, that's all."

"A shrewd interpretation of feminine behavior, Mrs. Sevilla," said Sevilla with a smile.

He looked at the two couples facing each other, each unmoving in its corner. The whistling had ceased. He went on: "We could leave things the way they are, but in my opinion that would be unwise. As long as the battle is limited to the ladies, it won't go very far. But if the two males got into it, it would be very dangerous. They're about the same size and weight, in fact you could almost get them confused, and they could do each other a lot of harm."

"What are you going to do?"

"Suggest a compromise."

He walked to the end of the wooden jetty and whistled. "Fa! Bi! Listen!"

There was a silence and Fa said, "I am listening."

"During the day," said Sevilla, "you will stay in the pool. At night, you will leave the pool to the other two."

There was a barely audible exchange of whistles between Fa and Bi. Then Fa came a few yards closer to Sevilla and said, "And where will we go at night?"

"I'll show you a grotto not far from here."

Fa went back to Bi and again there was an exchange of whistles. Sevilla listened, but the sounds were so low that he could not catch what they said.

Fa turned away from Bi. "Fa and Bi agree."

Then, as if he wanted to be sure he understood the conditions: "During the day the tank is ours. At night it is theirs."

"Yes."

"Will you bring us fish?"

"Yes."

Fa turned around and looked at Bi.

"Well," said Bi, "let us go."

Now that she had accepted the proposed solution she seemed very impatient to carry it out.

"I'll go and get a little boat," said Sevilla, "and I'll show you the way." He walked up the cement ramp. He was walking so fast that Arlette could hardly keep up with him.

"You're not afraid to leave Fa and Bi in the open sea?"

He shook his head. "Absolutely not. Did you notice Fa's reaction: *And where will we go at night?* There was anxiety in that question. They no longer love man, but they don't know how to get along without him yet."

"Yes," said Arlette. "I think you're right. I was very much struck by Fa's question, *Will you bring us fish?* That is surprising. I mean that Fa, born in captivity, has never had the opportunity to learn to fish, but what about Bi?"

Sevilla pushed open the door of the garage. "Peter," he said, "can we use the small life raft?"

"For how long?"

"A good hour."

"It'll hold out for an hour. But could you bring it up here after you're through with it? The air is low. I think one of the valves must be leaking. Or one of the seams."

"Of course."

Sevilla turned to Arlette. "Will you wait for me a minute? I want to say something to Maggie."

He left them and went to his office. Maggie was sitting motionless with her hands on her knees. The door creaked as it opened. She turned her head and looked at Sevilla, and her eyes gave a bizarre impression of solitude.

"Maggie," said Sevilla quickly without coming into the room, "I'm sorry but I haven't time to talk to you right now. But I want to tell you what I decided while I was listening to you just now. You will leave tomorrow morning to stay with your aunt in Denver for a few days."

"I have a lot of work to do," said Maggie.

"Forget the work."

"It's always the same," she said in a bitter voice. "You don't realize it, but you're going to be lost without me."

"That's my problem. You need rest." He added firmly, "It's settled."

She lowered her eyes and said in a submissive tone, "Okay. After all, you're the boss."

There was a pause, she straightened in her chair, looked up, and, staring into space, said in a shrill, high-pitched voice, "You're like an ostrich. You get rid of your problems by refusing to face them. As long as I've known you you've always acted this way. You put me on a shelf and you turn your back on your own happiness."

The door slammed, he was gone. Maggie put her hands to her temples and the tears sprang from her eyes.

"He doesn't listen to me," she said out loud with a convulsive sob. "He's never listened to me!"

. . .

Sevilla drew in his right oar and backwatered with his left. The nose of the small life raft missed the jetty, the right side came alongside the dock, and Arlette jumped out. He hadn't wanted to attract the attention of the watchtower by using the motor, and he had rowed to the grotto, a good half hour of effort each way. They took the boat out of the water, carried it a few yards up the cement ramp, and came back and sat on the boards of the jetty. It was getting dark, but the air was as hot as ever.

"Do you intend to tell Adams how they're doing?"

"No."

"Why not?"

"I've decided to tell him as little as possible."

"What about Peter?"

"If things don't work out, it's better for him to know nothing. I say Peter, but of course I include Suzy. Maggie doesn't count, I'm sending her to Denver tomorrow. It's curious, I feel almost guilty about her. And yet I have nothing to reproach myself for. Except," he added with a little laugh, "my extraordinary patience."

Daisy advanced majestically between two waves, her head emerged, and she fixed her affectionate eyes on Sevilla. Jim followed two yards behind her. Evidently he was growing bolder.

"Who is that female?" asked Daisy. "What was she doing here?"

"She has belonged to me for a long time. She went away, then she came back. The male too."

"She is bad."

Sevilla shook his head. "She is jealous."

284

Daisy meditated on this and said, "But I have a male. I have Jim."

Since Sevilla shrugged his shoulders without replying she went on: "She told me that she spoke the language of men. Is it true?"

Arlette began to laugh. "What a snob that Bi is!"

"Is it true, Pa?" repeated Daisy. "Is it true what she said?"

"It's true."

"But I am not stupid."

"No, Daisy, you are not stupid."

"Tonight I want to learn the language of men. Tonight, Pa."

Sevilla began to laugh. "To learn will take tomorrow and tomorrow and tomorrow. And tonight I am tired."

"Don't you want to whistle?"

"No. I am tired."

"But at night you whistle with me."

"Tonight I am tired."

There was a silence and she said, "Are you going into your house?"

"Yes."

"It is early!"

"Yes."

Daisy half emerged from the water and put her enormous head on the jetty between Arlette and Sevilla. They began to stroke her. Their caresses were vigorous, but they avoided touching her spiracle.

"I love you, Pa," said Daisy, closing her eyes.

"I love you too."

"I love you, Ma," said Daisy with a sigh.

"I love you too, Daisy," said Arlette.

Every night for four months Daisy had been making the same declarations, and every night for four months Arlette had felt moved. It was the same feeling—the throat a little tight, a sudden wave of tenderness, a sweet sadness and—she did not know why— underneath, the fear of death. Neither did she know why, at these moments, she felt so sorry for Daisy. There was nothing pathetic about Daisy. She was young, vigorous, full of health. Arlette lifted her shoulders as if the weight of the world were crushing them. What a planet, what men, what a mess! God knows why these animals love us so much. There's nothing lovable about us. No, no,

285

she told herself immediately, I shouldn't say that. I'm making the same mistake as Fa and Bi, I'm putting all of humanity in the same category.

An inhuman roar shattered the air, it seemed to come from behind the house, they looked up and just then a helicopter appeared and flew over the little harbor about fifty yards above the water, the slow and powerful report of a heavy machine gun broke out, Sevilla grabbed Arlette around the waist and covered her body with his own, but it wasn't they who were being fired at, he distinctly saw the tracer bullets shoot up from the sea and flank the machine with long dotted lines of fire, the helicopter rose, turned, and disappeared into the twilight.

"Come on," said Sevilla, "we're going to find out what this is all about."

They ran up the cement path. Just then Peter appeared and yelled, Adams is calling, Sevilla caught his breath as Peter decoded the message, pencil in hand. When he had finished he tore the sheet out of his notebook and handed it to Sevilla: *B knows. Danger tonight. Demand you accept protection on island.*

Sevilla took the pencil out of Peter's hand and wrote, *You gave yourself away when you fired.*

Peter translated this into code, transmitted it, received the answer, decoded it, and handed it to Sevilla: *Warning shot necessary. B could have blown up harbor. Repeat proposition.*

Sevilla wrote, *No. Will provide own protection.*

Peter put this into code, transmitted it, and got up. "I was in the garage. I thought they were firing at you."

"So did I," said Suzy.

Sevilla did not answer. On the back of the last message he scrawled *Kill Al's mike* and handed the paper to Peter. Peter nodded and disappeared.

Sevilla turned to the two women. "No one may use the telephone and no on may turn on a light. Where's Maggie?"

"In her room," said Suzy.

"We'll leave her there for the moment. We'll have a cold supper on the terrace and we'll all sleep on the roof. Bring blankets, the concrete is not comfortable."

"I'll make the sandwiches while there's still some light," said Suzy.

As soon as he was alone with Arlette, Sevilla took her by the arm and led her down the cement path that led to the harbor.

Arlette said softly, "Shouldn't we have Peter guard the harbor?"

"We should, but I don't dare. These people are specialists. They're capable of spotting Peter and killing him before he even sees them."

"Would they kill him?" asked Arlette in a flat voice.

Sevilla looked at her. "They killed Bob. Why not Peter? Why not us? A human life means nothing to them. Not one, not two, not a hundred. They'll do anything to keep Fa and Bi from talking. And us along with them. Before the thirteenth of January."

"Before the thirteenth of January?" repeated Arlette, her eyes wide with horror.

"The ultimatum expires on the thirteenth. Once war is declared, the truth will no longer matter. That means we have five days to make Fa and Bi talk."

"You talk as if you already knew what they're going to say."

Sevilla looked at her. "I don't know, but I have my suspicions." He added, "And so do you."

"So do I," said Arlette with effort. A chill went down her spine, her scalp tingled, sweat was running down her back and at the same time she felt her hands go cold. She started to rub them together and noticed that they were trembling. She hid them behind her back, straightened her shoulders, and said in a choked voice, "Is it really a good idea to station ourselves on the roof?"

"I think so. Once we've pulled up the ladder they can't take us by surprise. The concrete rim will protect us from an ambush. And if we have to fire ourselves, it's a dominant position."

"Very good, Captain Sevilla," said Arlette with a smile. But she felt drained, her knees were weak, she was ready to pass out. Sevilla looked at her attentively, put his arm around her shoulders, and held her tight against him. She went limp, buried her face against his shoulder, and said in a small voice, "Oh, Henry . . ."

"Come on," he said, "let's get ready. Let's not give way to fear."

A little later the whole team was sitting around the table on the terrace eating silently as darkness fell. Maggie was slumped in a chair. Peter and Suzy had not asked any questions. They had withdrawn into a silence that meant, Since we are no longer in your confidence and since we don't even have the right to see Fa and Bi, don't tell us anything, see if we care. Sevilla could hardly make out the white blobs of their faces in the gathering dusk. He looked at them fondly. Suzy, Peter—how important they were to him. He felt guilty about them, not for keeping them in the dark but for subjecting them to the danger, they who were only starting to live. He thought about Michael, Michael in prison. Paradoxically, he might be the only one who would survive.

"Peter," he said in a low voice, "what have they given us in the way of weapons?"

"An automatic rifle, a submachine gun, four M 16's, and some grenades."

"Who knows how to shoot?"

Peter, Suzy, and Arlette raised their hands.

"Suzy, would you be able to fire a gun?"

"I've used a telescopic rifle to fire at targets."

"So have I," said Arlette.

"The principle is the same. Peter? The automatic rifle or the submachine gun?"

"It makes no difference."

"Well, let's say that the man on guard will have the automatic rifle. Is the searchlight working?"

"Yes."

"We can use it. Wear dark clothing. Bring blankets, two apiece, flashlights, something to drink, field glasses, raincoats, and, of course, the radio."

There was a silence.

"When shall we take our positions?"

"When it gets dark."

•　•　•

Sevilla felt somebody shake him, he opened his eyes and saw nothing, the night was black, Peter's voice said in his ear, It's four o'clock, it's your turn, everything's okay, there was a silence and the low, barely audible voice went on, If you're really awake I'm going to go back to sleep, it's almost impossible to keep your eyes open in the dark, give me your gun, the automatic rifle is in firing position in front of the life raft, Take me there, said Sevilla, I'm afraid I'll lose my way, he felt beside him, took his gun, put his left hand in the direction where his ear told him his assistant should be and

288

encountered only space, reached out his arm, swept the air, met Peter's shoulder, moved his hand down, and closed his fingers over Peter's, he felt himself being drawn forward and counted six steps before his right foot bumped against the inflatable mattress, Sevilla felt Peter's breath against his cheek as he spoke, The automatic rifle is propped against the edge, be careful, the safety catch is off, the searchlight is on your left, about a yard away, within arm's reach. Sevilla let go of Peter's hand, he swayed slightly on his feet, Peter continued his explanations in a low voice, the faint murmur of his voice was the only thing that connected Sevilla to the world, he had a bizarre sense of unreality, he felt as if it were not he but someone else who was living this moment, In a few minutes, said Peter, you'll think you see the *Caribee*, a gray shape against the black, but it's pure illusion, I noticed that rather quickly, are you sure you're really awake? Sevilla lay down on his stomach on the inflatable mattress, Go and get some sleep, Pete, I'm fine, he heard Peter's footsteps retreating, then a slight rustling of blankets and that was all, the silence closed around him again and suddenly the night seemed even blacker than before, there wasn't a breath of wind, the sea was so calm you couldn't even hear the incoming tide beat against the jetty, the air was mild, it was the eighth of January, he was lying motionless in the night in a pair of flannel trousers and a pullover, there was a touch of dampness in the air, but the cement of the roof still retained its diurnal heat, the air smelled of iodine, salt, and the dry, inhuman, dead smell of the rocks, the night before had been just like any other night in his life, if he lived to be eighty then he would still have, let's see, well over nine thousand days and an equal number of nights, few enough even at the most optimistic estimate, but now everything had changed, the die had been cast yesterday when he had realized what an extraordinary risk Goldstein had taken in agreeing to serve as intermediary, that was when he had decided to say yes, and that evening, after the appearance of B's helicopter, he had gone without transition from an ordinary day in his life to a night which might be the last, Well, after all, I don't really mind that much, the important thing is not to live at any price but to know why one dies, if I am killed tonight will my life be a success or a failure, who will say? who is the witness? what is the criterion? fame? but fame rewards crooners without voices, actors without talent, politicians without genius,

289

scientists without principles, of course I can say that at least I have accomplished something, I am the man who taught the animals to talk, but I suppose Prometheus was pleased about giving fire to men before he found out what they were going to do with it, in *The Tempest* Caliban tells Prospero, "You taught me language, and my profit on't is, I know how to curse," I remember the effect that passage had on me, it leaped out of the page with terrifying force, the whole of human destiny was there, man corrupting everything, soiling everything, turning the best into the worst, honey into gall, bread into ashes, and I too can say, "Lord, I have taught the animals to speak, and the only profit man has derived from it is a new weapon for his destruction," Sevilla's right hand was resting on the butt of his rifle, the barrel was propped against the edge of the roof, but if he heard a disturbing sound, what would he aim at? what would he fire at? he could turn on the searchlight, of course, but then he would reveal himself, he would become a target, it was utterly absurd, without a light he could do nothing, if he turned on the light he was dead, the night was of truly frightening opacity, without a glimmer, without a light area, without even a suggestion of light-gray or dark-gray forms distinguishable from the jet-black, so this is the way the world looks when a hundred and eighty million Americans are asleep, black, void, formless, a good prefiguration of the post-atomic universe, emptied of its turbulent human life, the thought was barely imaginable, the planet Earth without human beings, without even one man to remember the magnificent things that men had done, the religions in which they had believed, the massacres they had committed, like the one that was being prepared, a world without history, since there would be no more historians, what a dreadful idea for the Christian, God creating man and man destroying himself, depriving God of His creature, for the nonbeliever an irrevocable squandering of the earthly hopes of man, personal death, after all, is nothing, in any case it is a thing one can accept, as the Vietnamese accepts it to defend his land and his dignity, or even as the United States Marine accepts it, without ideology, as a professional risk (thus showing what a low opinion he has of his own life), but the total destruction of the species, without anything left behind, neither work nor descendants, is an unbearable idea, a negation which no man is capable of conceiving, and indeed that is the danger, nobody believes in it, even those who are pushing us into war are incapable of imagining their own end, for them death is always the death of others, Sevilla put his left hand under the edge of the roof and with his right hand lit his flashlight for a split second, the face of his watch appeared in a blinding, painful flash of light, he squinted, Five o'clock, they won't come now.

He must have dozed off for a few seconds or even minutes, he started, he had just heard a sound that was like the light lapping of a small wave against an obstacle, perhaps it was a breeze, perhaps simply Daisy or Jim in the harbor, the sleep of dolphins is always rather restless, they don't stop swimming even when they're asleep or half asleep, they are constantly moving on a vertical axis too, since they come up to the surface at regular intervals to breathe, Sevilla strained his ears but it was almost impossible to locate the source of a sound without the aid of sight, he heard the sleepers breathing beside him on the roof, he realized that he had been hearing their breathing all along but that he had rejected it from the outset as a sound which had no interest for him and which he had to ignore, but now that he was listening as hard as he could the confused and unrhythmical cacophony of their respiration burst upon his ear without warning, as loud and annoying as interference on a radio set, once again there was a light, almost imperceptible splash, but he could not tell whether it came from the harbor or from somewhere on the island, where all around him the sea could beat, and where the slightest cavity in the rock and the slightest movement of the water could produce an infinite explosion, Sevilla put out his left hand, found the searchlight, and groped until he felt the switch under his fingers, But no, if they aren't in the port, but behind my back, behind the house, one flash of the searchlight and they spot me, they see me without my seeing them, and then all they need is one well-aimed grenade, Sevilla felt the tension mounting in him, his nerves vibrated, the palms of his hands were sweating, but at the same time he felt calm and lucid, he kept the index finger of his left hand on the switch, he listened, it was not the breathing of the sleepers that bothered him but a sound that was closer, louder, and more rhythmical, the beating of his heart, whose dull thuds shook his rib cage and reverberated in his temples. There was no transition, in a few seconds the night lifted, became less black, and this time without possible illusion he made out the shape of the *Caribee* with its dark gray mast standing out against the shadows, he distinctly heard two rather loud splashes, one after the other, where did they come from? behind him? on the jetty? behind the *Caribee?* his finger remained on the switch, he could not make up his mind to turn it on.

Then the harbor was illuminated by two enormous, blinding columns of flame, and there were two explosions of such violence that Sevilla felt the house tremble beneath him, he felt something strike his left hand and that was all, he turned on the searchlight, the *Caribee* had vanished, he heard voices behind him and without turning around he yelled, Don't get up! Crawl to the edge! he began firing long volleys just over the end of the jetty, What are you firing at? Peter yelled in his ear, not letting go of the trigger, The channel! They have to leave through there! he yelled, On his right, between two volleys, he heard the quick, short, sharp reports of the M 16's, day dawned with surprising rapidity, Sevilla saw Arlette on his right, Maggie on his left, Maggie, stand by to turn out the searchlight, just then the clatter of a heavy machine gun broke out, the first tracer bullets landed beyond the entrance of the narrow channel and began to work their way up the channel in a zigzag pattern until they reached the near end, Adams was going into action, Aren't we bothering him with our searchlight? cried Peter, Sevilla relaxed the pressure of his finger, No, I don't think so, but call him, he motioned to Suzy and she stopped firing, anyway it was no use, the heavy machine gun was painstakingly crosshatching the channel, the dotted lines of fire were tracing methodical diagonals backward and forward, but was it really effective? Below what depth would the bullets lose their force of impact? He felt a twinge in his left hand, it was bleeding, it was swollen and painful, Are you wounded? asked Arlette anxiously, No, he said, looking around, he reached out and picked up a jagged piece of wreckage, it's nothing, he said ironically, a fragment of the poor *Caribee,* behind him Peter yelled, Adams says to turn out the light and take a look, what shall I do? Go ahead, said Sevilla wearily, in any case the danger was over, but what was there to see? Nobody spoke until Peter came back, the mist was rising along with the sun, the night seemed to be breaking into dark, cottony shreds, after a while Peter's tall form reappeared on the cement path, he was walking slowly, when he reached the terrace he raised his head and looked up at Sevilla, his face looked pale and defeated in the gray dawn.

He said in a broken voice, "Fa and Bi . . ."

"Well?"

"Torn to pieces."

Arlette sat up straight. "But Fa and Bi weren't . . ."

Sevilla pressed her wrist hard and she stopped. "Inform Adams," said Sevilla.

XIV

Adams was standing on the jetty with his hands in his pockets, looking over the edge. He hadn't bothered to shave and his chin and cheeks looked dirty. Under the water and on the water, what had once been the *Caribee* was nothing but a pile of fragments. The explosion had been capricious. It had blown the mast to bits, but the aluminum kitchen unit lay three yards down, as intact and shiny as the day it was installed. Two divers with gloves on were busy gathering from the bottom, and laying on a piece of canvas on the jetty, all that was left of the dolphins. Although the sun had just risen and the air was still fresh, the stale, sweetish smell that emanated from this debris was almost unbearable. The men who were fishing them out of the water were trying to reconstruct the two bodies as if they were solving a puzzle. When they made a mistake, Peter, who had put gloves on too, would lean over and correct them. His white smock and the gauze mask he wore over his mouth made him look like a surgeon.

"I see only two bodies," said Adams after a moment. "Where is Daisy?"

Sevilla squinted. "Last night when she came back to the harbor, Bi attacked her and bit her."

"And she went away? That bite saved her life. But she must have been terrified by the explosion. You won't be seeing her for a while."

Sevilla nodded his head without answering. After a moment he said, "I suppose the job was done by frogmen."

"Come on," said Adams. "Let's not stay here."

294

They took a few steps in the direction of the house. Adams stopped and said, "What do Peter, Suzy and Maggie think about all this?"

"They don't understand anything and so far they haven't asked me questions. Maggie is leaving this morning for Denver."

"Perfect. It's better to keep them totally in the dark." He went on: "We've found the bodies of the attackers. There were two of them."

Sevilla shuddered. "You found their bodies! I hope it wasn't we who . . ."

Adams gave a faint smile which made his ill-shaven face look thinner and harder. "Rest assured, they were our bullets, not yours." He added in a low voice, "When I think about it, what extraordinary courage! They knew we were guarding the channel. Once they'd done their job they had very little chance of getting out alive." He paused. "Toll for the first battle: two dolphins, two men."

"It's monstrous," said Sevilla, clenching his teeth.

"It's absurd. And the most absurd part about it is that B is just as convinced as we are that he's serving his country. To him, we are traitors. And to us, he's a madman: We think he wildly underestimates the striking power of the Chinese."

Sevilla looked at him. "Even in the absence of the testimony of Fa and Bi, you could inform the President of your suspicions about the role they were forced to play."

"We have done so."

"And of the attack on Fa and Bi, since it corroborates those suspicions."

"We'll do that too, but it won't be very useful to him. Politically speaking, a suspicion is not a weapon. The President is subject to terrifying pressures right now, and he has *nothing* with which to resist them, not even public opinion. Have you heard about the latest Gallup poll?"

"No."

"They discussed it last night on TV. Fifty-eight percent of the American people accept the idea of a war with China."

"That's frightening."

Adams gave another of his faint smiles. "There's no lack of candidates for corpses."

"I'd like to ask you a question," said Sevilla, looking at him attentively with his dark eyes. "Is your attitude toward all this shared by the other people in your agency?"

Adams hesitated noticeably. "Far from it. There are two tendencies in our organization, even in the highest echelon, and one of these two tendencies sympathizes with B's point of view."

"So it is not out of the question that B was kept constantly informed about Fa and Bi by persons in your entourage?"

"Unfortunately, no," said Adams, lowering his eyes. He raised them after a moment and glanced at the little harbor. The divers were climbing up onto the dock, their job done. He sighed. "Anyway, it's all over now."

Sevilla looked at him. Adams seemed weary and bitter but, at the same time, curiously relieved. World peace was lost, but he, at least, could make his little personal peace with B. Two dolphins, two men, that didn't count: minor damage incurred in a minor dispute between agencies. Now that B was winning, Adams would be able to go over to the majority opinion—behind his leaders—in all good conscience.

"Should I call the police?" asked Sevilla after a moment.

"By no means," said Adams emphatically. "The disappearance of Fa and Bi must remain a secret." He paused. "Besides, I have already contacted them and explained the shots. We came upon a team of Castroist saboteurs who were trying to infiltrate the Florida Keys, and we wiped them out."

Since Sevilla said nothing, he went on: "Of course, this means you won't be able to collect insurance on the loss of the *Caribee*. But I suppose our agency can indemnify you."

Sevilla looked at him loftily. "I'm not asking for anything."

"You're as quixotic as ever, Sevilla." Since Sevilla did not reply he went on: "I'm going to have some photographs taken of the dead dolphins before I go. Do you want to keep the guns?"

"As you like."

"Well, keep them, at least for the time being, although in my opinion you are no longer in danger."

"Are you going to withdraw your security net from around the island?"

"Certainly. In my opinion, this job is over." He added after a moment, "As far as protection goes, if I had your island and your money, do you know what I'd do? I'd build myself a fallout shelter, right here, surrounded by rocks. No matter what happens, you'd have a very good chance of surviving."

Sevilla looked at him. How cynical this way of thinking was! And how natural it seemed to Adams! A hundred, a hundred and fifty, two hundred million Americans die a hideous death, and I survive because I have money. I have the right to do what I like with my money; for example, devote it to saving my own skin amid the general slaughter. What's more, all America would approve of me, in the name of individual liberty and free enterprise.

"Shall I have the bodies removed?" asked Adams indifferently.

Sevilla closed his eyes briefly. "No."

"What do you intend to do with them? Put them in the water?"

"No."

"Why?"

"Sharks. I wouldn't want them to be eaten by sharks." He added, "I'll soak them with gasoline and burn them."

"Like the Buddhist monks," said Adams with a little laugh.

Sevilla looked away.

"I beg your pardon," said Adams. "I'd forgotten how attached you were to those animals."

•   •   •

With what logs were left in the sitting room (everything had to be brought from the mainland, even wood) Peter built a bonfire to leeward of the house, all the way to the other end of the island, where nobody ever went, for there was nothing but sharp rocks and reefs where the water churned constantly when the sea was rough, leaving in their crevices mountains of dirty white foam that looked like crude cotton, they had to make several trips with the metal wheelbarrow to get what was left of the two bodies and shovel them onto the wood, Sevilla, pale, teeth clenched, emptied two jerry cans of gasoline on the pyre and set fire to it by holding a long pine torch to the base and dropping it immediately, the flames exploded with terrifying force and rose fifteen feet in the air, the oil sizzled with extraordinary intensity, globs of burning fat were thrown for several yards, Peter and Sevilla stepped back, the fire gave off an enormous cloud of black smoke, thick scrolls mottled with oily blue, although the wind was blowing the other way, their mouths and

297

noses were filled with the nauseating odor of burning flesh and fat, Sevilla saw Peter moving his mouth and looking at him but he could not hear a sound, the crackling of the flames and the sputtering of the grease drowned out his voice, Sevilla closed his eyes, time fell away, Captain H. C. Sevilla, U.S. Army, assigned to the Nuremberg Trials as interpreter, listened, horrified, to the statement of the witness. An *SS Sturmbannführer* from Culmhof had discovered, by trial and error, the optimum arrangement of the wood and the ideal dimensions for the ditches, fifty yards long, six yards wide, three yards deep, at the bottom of the ditches he had drains dug so the animal fat could run into a vat, the yield was colossal, eight thousand bodies in twenty-four hours, which was, despite the crude simplicity of the arrangement, far superior to that of the giant crematorium of the mother house, the great modern death factory of the Birkenau-Auschwitz compound, where at peak moments, when it was necessary to reduce four hundred thousand Hungarian Jews to smoke as quickly as possible, the strictly timed production line (not a single dead period from the moment two thousand Jews entered the gas chamber until forty-six minutes later, when they went up in smoke, leaving to the factory by-products which were methodically recovered along the line: clothing, rings, gold teeth, hair, and grease destined for the manufacture of soap) , the production line was supplemented, but only *in cases of extreme urgency,* by half a dozen ditches copied from Culmhof, but reluctantly, with a bad conscience, because of the professional waste of the by-products, *SS Obersturmbannführer* Rudolf Hess, Commandant of Auschwitz, looked at the president of the tribunal with empty eyes and said in a colorless voice, On the thirtieth of June 1941 the Führer ordered the final solution of the Jewish problem, personally, Mr. President, *I gassed only a million and a half Jews,* but if you count the small, supplementary extermination camps, Culmhof, Wolzek, and Treblinka, you arrive at a total of six million noncombatants, including women and children, arrested, tortured, stripped, starved, gassed, reduced to ashes from 1941 to 1945, transports of Jews destined for Auschwitz had priority from one end of the Third Reich to the other, they even took precedence over transports of food and munitions to the troops on the eastern front, Hitler had granted absolute priority to the greatest genocide in history, Sevilla's chest tightened and a flood of shame overwhelmed him, But we're going to do better, much better, an H-bomb exploding at an altitude of twenty miles gives off a heat so intense that everything within a radius of sixty to eighty miles is burned to a crisp, four H-bombs exploding simultaneously at the same altitude eliminate all forms of life over an area of one hundred square miles, the radioactive cloud from a single cobalt bomb can transform a region three times the size of Great Britain into a desert, according to our calculations, gentlemen, we need only thirty thousand megatons to eliminate seven hundred million Chinese.

Come, said Sevilla, laying his hand on Peter's arm, let's not stay here, Peter put the shovel in the wheelbarrow, turned his back to it as if he were harnessed to it, and began to pull it behind him over the rocky ground, before they reached the house he stopped, straightened up, and looked at Sevilla, May I ask you some questions? Sevilla looked back at him gravely, If they're the ones I'm thinking of, don't ask them, I'm not in a position to answer them, you know very well that it's not lack of confidence in you, it's to protect you, you and Suzy, believe me, it's better for you to know nothing, But what about you, said Peter, are you in danger? Sevilla made a face, Adams doesn't think so, he thinks that it's over, that they'll be content with the dolphins, but I'm inclined to think he's mistaken, Peter squared his shoulders, Well, in that case, why shouldn't I share your dangers? Sevilla raised his hand, Without sharing them, you might be able to help me escape them, How? asked Peter fervently, By doing what I ask without asking questions, Ah, you've got me there! said Peter, but isn't that the way it's been all along? Sevilla put his hand on Peter's shoulder and smiled, Precisely, keep it up, listen, Pete, time is short, if you want to help me here's what you must do, he dropped his hand, First, take the life raft, take Maggie to the mainland and put her on a plane, Suzy will go with you, second, while you're there, watch to see whether you're followed, keep your eyes open, these people are specialists, masters in the art of tailing in shifts, third, I'll give you a check in your name which you'll deposit in your bank, Peter raised his eyebrows, Why a check in my name, why not a check in your name with your own endorsement as usual, Because your account certainly isn't being watched, Pete, because I'm afraid mine is, because I have no confidence in the discretion of banks, and because the check is a very large one, does that answer your question?

· · ·

As soon as Sevilla left the channel to go to the grotto he shipped the oars, put one of them in a notch in the rear platform and began to scull, in the front of the small life raft Arlette stood by with the second oar, ready to keep the prow away from the two rocky walls between which the boat was gliding, it got stuck irritatingly no matter how little it swerved, Sevilla covered about twenty yards this way, then he yelled in a loud voice, Backwater! and Arlette backwatered vigorously in front, he worked his oar fast and furiously, pivoting the boat almost in a hairpin turn, against the current, it entered a dark, vaulted, winding passage, seemingly without an outlet, a damp wall covered with shells and mold rose in front of her, blocking their way after about a dozen yards, but before they reached it Sevilla made another hairpin turn, this time to the left, and entered a narrow passage with so little headroom that they had to crouch, at this stage it was no longer possible to scull, Arlette turned on a powerful flashlight, Sevilla put out his arms and, by pushing as hard as he could with both hands against the lateral walls, moved the boat forward amid the splash of tiny waves, the inflated tubes occasionally scraping against uneven places on the walls with an alarming sound, Sevilla slowed down, he was afraid the boat would get wedged between two rocky projections, Arlette heard him panting in the half-light, it was the most difficult moment and the most dramatic, then Sevilla muttered, Here we are, and suddenly the boat emerged into the grotto, whirling as if it had been expelled by the passageway, it was a round, low, spacious chamber that resembled the dungeon of a fortified castle, the ceiling was a perfect arch except for a few cracks which let in a blue-green light, the grotto was separated from the channel by the thickness of only one wall, yet it took over half an hour to reach it through the maze of passages, Sevilla replaced his oar while Arlette ran her light slowly over the surface of the water, neither Fa nor Bi was visible, all was darkness and silence, aside from the small concentric ripples which the motion of the boat was still sending to the sides of the grotto the water was calm, black, silky, Fa! Bi! called Sevilla anxiously, his voice hung in the air and bounced off the vault, then silence closed in again, a silence disturbed only by the sound of water dripping from the oar.

It's not possible that they've left, Sevilla said, I can't believe it, even if they were afraid, Arlette turned to him, she was still aiming her light at the water with her arm held out to the side, Sevilla saw her as a slender, dark shape two yards away, and on his left as a monstrous shadow cast on the wall, You don't think they could have been killed by the frogmen? No, said Sevilla, how could the frogmen have found the grotto? it's not known, it's very hard to get to during the day, and on a dark night it's inaccessible, But Fa and Bi might have ventured as far as the channel during the night, said Arlette, Sevilla shook his head, It's not likely, he said after a few seconds, even if they had they would have spotted the frogmen with their sonar from quite a distance, whereas the men would have had no way of knowing they were there, besides, those frogmen were carrying out orders, they must have been given a precise and limited objective—Destroy everything in the harbor—they weren't looking for anything else, Well, said Arlette, Fa and Bi must have been afraid, the explosion terrified them, and they left, there was a long silence, it was very cool in the grotto, moisture fell on Sevilla's back and shoulders, he said in a strangled voice, I hope not, my God, I couldn't bear it, he said nothing for a long time, there was something funereal about the silence in the grotto, Sevilla was lost in thought, it was curious that at this moment he was thinking less about the fate of the world than about the fate of the two dolphins, Remember, he murmured, those nights when we used to take turns on the polyester rafts so Fa wouldn't be lonely? Yes, said Arlette, we'd hang our hands in the water and after a moment he'd nuzzle them and early in the morning he'd put his big head on the raft, a little to one side, and look up at us, what nice eyes he had, so round, so lively, Sevilla listened to Arlette's voice and thought, And now we'd better leave, it's all over, no use staying in this hole, but with his hand on the oar and the prow of the boat pointed toward the passageway he couldn't make up his mind to leave, his heart was heavy and he had the paralyzing sense of having suffered a fantastic impoverishment, as if a large chunk of his life had disappeared all at once, something he had cared about every day for years, the mad anxiety when Fa and Bi refused to eat, the endless hours of study, the constant effort of attention, observation, and identification, even at play, even in idle moments, Let's go, he said out loud, there's no sense staying here, I feel as if I've been buried alive, the daylight will do us good, Arlette aimed her light at the entrance to the passage, but Sevilla didn't move, his right hand rested limply on

301

the oar behind him without grasping it, he looked over his shoulder at the prow, time passed, he thought bitterly, How bizarre, this morning I was so sure I was going to make them talk that I even brought my tape recorder, the only thing I didn't think of was that they'd leave, and now it's all over, including the hope of stopping the war, how absurd for the fate of the world to depend on what went on in the brains of two dolphins, on the idea they formed of the event when the explosion took place, on the conclusion they drew from it, and now, the crowning irony, B's going to try to get us because he's afraid they had time to talk to us, Let's go, he said for the third time and his hand closed around the end of the oar.

In front of the prow of the boat, fully lighted by Arlette's flashlight, his enormous shadow instantly leaping to the top of the arched vault, a shape leaped out of the water, jovial, squeaking, whistling, followed by another, smaller shape, Fa! Bi! cried Sevilla, beside himself, then the great leaps began, the splashing, the shrill squeaking that sounded like laughter, the backward dancing with three-quarters of the body out of the water and the caudal fin thrashing the water vertically, Henry! cried Arlette, overjoyed, this time there was no mistake, it was the frenzied welcome of the old days, the boundless affection, the inexhaustible joy, the love that could never be fully expressed.

"Fa! Bi!" cried Sevilla. "Where were you?"

"Here!" cried Fa in his high-pitched voice. "We are here all the time. We listen."

Arlette leaned over and touched Sevilla's arm and said in a whisper, "Darling! He's speaking English!"

It was true. He was speaking English, he had forgotten nothing!

"What do you mean, you were here?"

"Here," said Bi. "We do not move. Our spiracles in the air, our bodies in the water."

"But why, why?" said Sevilla.

Fa laid his head on the side of the rubber boat. "We say to ourselves, maybe they come to kill us. Maybe they are friends, maybe not."

So that was it! Mistrust, doubt, the profound ravages of human falsity in creatures in a state of innocence.

"But we love you!" said Sevilla.

"I know," said Bi. "I hear. I hear you talk about Fa."

302

"I hear" for "I heard"; "talk" for "talking": their English had certainly deteriorated in the six months they had been away. As with conquered peoples whose language is no longer taught in schools, the words had held out, but the syntax had suffered. There was now something infantile about the construction of the sentences, and the pronunciation was more dolphinlike than ever.

Bi made a prodigious leap into the air and fell back close enough to the boat to splash Sevilla.

"Stop it, Bi!" cried Arlette. "It's too cold in here to play."

"I hear," said Bi, laughing. "Ma talks about Fa, but not about Bi."

"I love you, Bi," said Arlette.

"Ma forgets Bi," said Bi, and Arlette's flashlight revealed a malicious gleam in her eye.

Fa had stopped talking. He had laid his head on the side of the boat and closed his eyes and he was letting Arlette stroke him.

"Bi," said Sevilla, "tell me how it is you have not forgotten the language of men."

"When nobody listens, Fa and I talk. We do not want to forget."

"Why not? Since you did not want to talk to men any more."

"To keep it. And," she went on after a moment, "to teach the children."

Quietly Sevilla took the battery tape recorder out of his jacket pocket, turned it on, and unhooked the microphone. Curious logic: Man is bad but his language is good, provided it is not used to communicate with him, an acquisition valid in itself, a thing to keep and even to pass on, indeed, even a social advantage, about which Bi had boasted to Daisy the day before.

"Bi," said Sevilla, "do you love Pa and Ma?"

"Yes."

"And other men?"

"No. Other men are not good."

Sevilla brought the microphone closer to the side of the boat. "Why? What have they done?" he asked, leaning toward Bi.

"They lie. They kill."

Excellent résumé, thought Sevilla. The whole history of the human race in four words. From the beginning to 1973, to the day when humanity, grabbing itself by the throat like a comedian, inadvertently strangles itself.

"How do they lie?" asked Sevilla.

Fa turned his head and looked at him. "At first, with Ba, it was fun. But after the airplane, they lie, they kill. They even try to kill us."

"Explain, Bi," said Sevilla.

"No, me!" said Fa eagerly. "At first, with Ba, before the airplane, they make us wear harnesses. On the harnesses are mines. They show us an old empty boat, very far away. We swim and swim. Near the boat we dive, we come very close, we turn around, the mine goes on the boat—"

"Wait, Fa, not so fast. When it touches the ship the mine comes off the harness and sticks to the ship?"

"Yes."

"How does it stick?"

"Like a shell on a rock."

"And what do you do then?"

"I swim. Far, far."

"Me too," said Bi. "I have a harness and a mine. The mine goes on the ship. I swim with Fa." Bi began to laugh.

"Why do you laugh?"

"At first Ba says Bi will put the mine on the ship, but I say no. I say Fa comes, or I do not go. Then Fa will go all alone, says Ba. Bi comes, or I do not go, says Fa. The men are very angry. They say, Bi in one tank, Fa in another. I do not eat. Fa does not eat. In two days, the men give up."

"Fa," said Sevilla, "where on the ship do you put the mine?"

"In the middle."

"And you, Bi?"

"In the middle. Next to Fa."

Obviously the second mine was a dud. It was only there to satisfy the dolphins' demand not to be separated.

"Then what?" asked Sevilla.

"We swim and we swim. And the ship goes *bang*. Very loud, like last night. Another day Ba says, See the boat, catch it. And the boat swims fast, very fast; but Bi and I catch it, put the mine on it, and come back."

"And does the ship explode?"

"No. Never when we catch it."

"In your opinion, why doesn't it?"

304

"Because there are men on it."

"What else do you do?"

"Every day," said Bi, "we race with a boat that has two big motors."

"What kind of motors? Motors like you see in the back of boats?"

"Yes. It is fun."

"Why?"

"The boat goes fast, very fast, much faster than all the other boats." She went on triumphantly: "But we win."

"Is the race long?"

"That depends: half a length, one length, a length and a half, two lengths. But we win. The men on the boat are very happy. They yell. They whistle."

"Another day," said Bi, "there is a submarine. The submarine picks us up, takes us out to sea, far from shore, and leaves us. Ba says, Swim south one hour and come back to the submarine."

"How do you know when you've swum an hour?"

"We know. We are trained. Half a length: half an hour. One length: one hour. Two lengths: two hours."

"Don't you ever make a mistake?"

"No."

"And you always come back to the submarine?"

"Always."

"How?"

Fa said, "Ba asks us that too. But we are not sure. We taste the water."

"You taste the water?"

"When we swim," said Bi, "we open our mouths a little and we taste the water."

"And where the submarine has been the water has a different taste?"

"Yes."

"Sometimes," said Fa, "it is not the submarine that we must find again, it is the base. That is more difficult."

"Why?"

"We must know the coast around the base."

"When you don't see land, how do you find it?"

"By the taste of the water."

"And when you see land, how do you find the base?"

"With my sonar. And when I am close enough, with my eyes."

First, taste. Next, hearing. Finally, sight—the least useful of the three.

"Can you find the base at night?"

"Yes. But first I swim all around the base with my sonar. We must know the coast well."

And make readings in every direction of all the irregularities of the underwater terrain, and store these thousands of readings in a prodigious memory, and have all these readings accurately in mind when you navigate without visibility. But for Fa, it was very simple.

"All right," said Sevilla. "Let's get to the airplane."

"A long trip," said Bi.

"What was it like?"

"We lie on stretchers. I am hot. I am very dry, I suffer. Fa too. Ba puts damp cloths on us. After the airplane there is a base. I swim in the base and I swim around the base. But not much. Fa comes with me."

"The water has a funny taste," says Fa.

"Then what?"

Fa went on: "Ba takes Bi and me on a boat. Ba says, A submarine waits for you. You go in the submarine. I do not go. A man tells you, Do this, and you do it. I say to Ba, Why do you not come? He says, It is an order."

"How does Ba look when he says this?"

"Not happy. We stay on the boat."

"How long?"

"When I do not swim, I do not know how long."

"A short time or a long time?"

"A long time."

"What happens when you meet the submarine?"

"Ba puts us in the water and we swim to the submarine. The men take us on board."

"Isn't it hard for you to get into the submarine?"

"Yes. Very hard. But the men are gentle. I am afraid anyway. In the submarine it is very hot. I am very dry, I suffer."

Bi went on, "In the submarine the man tells us—"

"What man?"

"The leader."

"Is he in uniform?"

"No."

"What does he look like?"

"Short, blue eyes, not much hair."

"What does he say?"

"He shows us a little gray boat with guns which he holds in his hand. He says, Look well. I put you in the water, you find this boat. You put a mine in the middle and you come back to the submarine."

"How long do you stay in the submarine?"

"A long time. We look well at the little boat."

"Is this the first time they ask you to identify a real ship by showing you a model?"

"No. At the base Fa and I do this very often."

"Do you make mistakes?"

"At first, yes. Later, never."

"Good. What happens next?"

"The men put harnesses on us."

"The same kind as usual?"

"No. Different ones."

"What about mines?"

"No, not yet. The frogmen help us get out."

"Under the water?"

"Yes."

"How?"

"They put us in a room, they close the door, water comes in the room. The room opens into the sea. We go out. The frogmen hold our harnesses. They swim with us."

"For a long time?"

"No. They stop and fasten the mines to the harnesses."

"Then what?"

Fa answered, "We swim north."

"How do you know it is north?"

"By the sun. When we leave the submarine it is the middle of the morning. We swim fast."

"How long?"

"A length and a half. I find the ship. I swim close to it. There are men on it. I say to Bi, This is no fun. No *bang!*"

"No explosion?"

"Yes. I think, There are men, no *bang*. Bi says, I will get there

307

before you. So I swim and I swim, Pa, I swim like a bird flies! I get there before Bi, I turn around, the mine goes on the ship, but I am on the mine!"

"You mean that the mine is attached to the ship, but it is still on the harness?"

"Yes!"

"You are stuck to the ship?"

"Yes! I am afraid! I cannot breathe! I will drown! I call for help, Bi! Bi!"

"With my teeth," said Bi, "I cut Fa's harness under his stomach. He is free. I do not touch the ship."

"You don't plant your mine?"

"No."

"Listen to me, Bi: You don't plant your mine?"

"No. I am afraid. Fa is afraid too."

Sevilla's hands began to tremble. "What do you do with your mine?"

"I tell Fa, Cut my harness with your teeth. He cuts it. The harness and the mine fall down."

Sevilla looked at Arlette. His hands were trembling. The lives of hundreds of sailors had depended on this tiny quirk of fate: It was on Bi, and not on Fa, that the frogmen had fastened the dud.

"So the harness and the mine fall to the bottom of the sea?"

"Yes."

"Then what?"

"I swim back to the surface with Fa, I breathe, and I swim south. I swim fast, fast. I am afraid."

"What direction does the ship go?"

"North."

"And you go south?"

"Yes! And the ship goes *bang!*"

"Do you see it?"

"There are men on it, and the ship goes *bang!*"

"Do you see it?"

"I hear it. I am far away in the water, but I see the light. I hear the noise and I feel the shock in the water. I dive, I swim, I am afraid!"

"How long do you swim?"

"A length and a half. I taste the water. The submarine is gone."

"What do you do then?"

"I look for it. Fa too. But it is gone. A long time ago. The water has no taste."

"Then Bi and I understand," said Fa.

"What do you understand?"

"The men on the ship die. Fa and Bi die with them, on the hull. The man in the submarine says, Very good, they are dead, no need to wait."

"Well?"

"I say, Men are not good. Let us stay in the sea. Bi says, No, we must go back to the base."

"Why?"

"To tell Ba."

"To tell Ba what happened?" Sevilla asked, making an effort to control his voice.

"Yes. Because Ba is our friend. But the land is far away. I swim, I find the land, but I do not find the base. I do not know the coast well. I swim the rest of the day and the whole night. I do not eat, I swim, I am very tired."

"Oh, I am so tired!" said Bi. "With Fa, I swim and I swim. Finally in the morning I see the base. Ba is standing on the pier. He sees us. He dives into the water with his clothes on. We are happy."

"Then what?"

There was a long silence.

"Then what?" repeated Sevilla patiently.

"I tell Ba."

"You tell him what happened?" said Scvilla, barely able to speak. He squeezed Arlette's hand hard.

"Yes."

"Everything?"

"Yes."

Silence again.

"Then what happens?"

"Ba looks at us. He is very white. He says, It is not possible. It is not true. Bi, you are lying. You must not say that. Do you hear, you must not say that. He is very white. He shakes."

"And what do you say?"

"I say, it's true, it's true, it's true!" said Bi with despair. She fell silent again.

"Then what?" asked Sevilla.

"Then I understand that Ba is not our friend. We say we will not talk any more with Ba. We will not talk any more with men."

Sevilla turned off the tape recorder and looked at Arlette. "Well, now everything is clear. Bob told B's men everything he knew before he was eliminated. And how could they believe that Fa and Bi haven't talked to us?"

"They *know* they haven't," said Arlette after a moment. "Don't you think they intercepted all those radio messages yesterday between Adams and you?"

"And interpreted them as a smoke screen."

"Well, suppose they do interpret them that way. Suppose they think Adams is now in possession of a tape containing the dolphins' confession. In that case we are out of danger."

"On the contrary, as far as they know, the dolphins have been eliminated. For this tape to be valid evidence we must be alive to authenticate it."

"Pa!" said Bi. "We want to talk."

"Just a minute, Bi," said Sevilla, putting his hand on her head. "Pa is talking to Ma."

"Bi next?"

"Bi next."

"So you think B's men will come back?" asked Arlette.

"Yes, I do," said Sevilla in a low, distinct voice. "They'll be back tonight."

There was a silence and Arlette went on: "If you think that, Adams must think so too. So why has he withdrawn his protection?"

Sevilla pressed his hands together and shrugged. "Oh, Adams! Adams has played a double game." He went on, making an effort to control his voice: "Adams' position has been ambivalent from the beginning, because he is acting in the name of an agency in which some believe in the truth and some in suppression. First Adams gambled on the truth. Now that Fa and Bi are 'dead' he thinks that the side of truth has lost, and now he is gambling on silence."

"Fa and Bi are *not* dead," said Fa.

"Of course they're not," said Sevilla.

"You said 'Fa and Bi are dead.' "

"It is the bad men who say that."

"But it is not true!" said Fa anxiously.

310

"No, Fa, it is not true."

Sevilla looked at Arlette and remembered the terrible reality that words had for dolphins. You had to be very careful.

"You said that Adams was gambling on silence," said Arlette. "What did you mean?"

"There was a moment this morning when Adams gave himself away. That was when he suggested that I keep the guns. Why should he leave them with me if he thinks I'm out of danger?"

"He's a monster!"

"No," said Sevilla, "not altogether. He is not completely lacking in feeling for us and he still has a spark of humanity. The proof is that at the last minute he couldn't bear the idea of leaving us to B's men without guns. He gave us a chance."

He added with a short laugh, "A very small chance."

.   .   .

Sevilla pulled in the stern oar, laid it on the bottom of the life raft, took the flashlight out of Peter's hands, and aimed the beam at the dolphins, Fa! Bi! he called in a loud voice, they emerged halfway from the water and laid their heads on the side of the boat, Be quiet, Sevilla told them, I have to talk to Peter, Peter stared, speechless, from one to the other, Fa and Bi! he said in a flat voice, but who was the big male this morning? A wild dolphin that Daisy had tamed, Peter shook his head, I'm beginning to understand, Sevilla directed the pencil of light at him, Peter squinted, he lowered it to the level of his chest, and suddenly Peter's blond, open, innocent face, lighted from below, took on unaccustomed strength and maturity, even the dimples at either side of his mouth looked severe now that they were accentuated, the prominent chin, the neck tendons standing out like those of a straining athlete, the whole chiseled, virile face, even the eyes, which looked more deep-set than ever, had become less childlike, Peter, said Sevilla, the main reason I brought you to the grotto was to show you that Fa and Bi are alive, I want you to be able to testify later, if necessary, that you saw them alive on the morning of January 9, that is, the day after the explosion that destroyed the *Caribee*, I apologize for taking you away from Suzy the minute you got off the boat, but I wanted to talk to you quietly, in the grotto, without fear of long-distance electronic

311

espionage, now that Adams has left the field open for them these gentlemen are going to deploy all their talents, first question: were you followed? Yes, said Peter, Starting when? On the sea? When you hit the mainland? Peter shook his head and announced happily, almost excitedly, No, they were very astute, they knew that once on land my first thought would be to pick up my Ford at the parking lot, well, when I get there my Ford is inaccessible, hemmed in by an incredible jumble of cars, it takes the attendant half an hour to get it out, the manager has plenty of time to phone the proper authority, as I leave I notice a black Dodge behind me, behind the Dodge is a blue Oldsmobile, then an old dirty Chrysler no particular color, then another Dodge, oh, I forgot, let's go back to the parking lot, I looked around for your Buick, it was just as inaccessible as my Ford, although you'd left it there only two days ago, as you instructed, it had just been washed, water was still dripping off the doors, the boys must have gone out of their way to stick it in the farthest corner after they washed it, it was almost funny to see your spotless Buick surrounded by a bunch of filthy jalopies that hadn't budged for months, that was when I began to see the light, Sevilla looked at him, he was so young, so gay, so proud of his talents of observation, it was a lucky thing they hadn't kidnaped him and Suzy on the mainland, They're so sure they're going to get us all tonight, Peter, he said in a grave voice, the time has come for us to separate.

Peter stared at him, open-mouthed, overcome, No, Peter, don't ask questions, nothing could give me more pain than to have to leave you but it's absolutely necessary, we are all four in danger of our lives, we must run away and hide, we don't have much time, when it gets dark we'll leave the island, you in the small life raft, for the mainland, and I in the big one, I'm not going to tell you where I'm going, but this is what you'll do, you and Suzy, you'll take only the bare necessities, plus the tapes of Daisy's whistling, all our work on the island, you will also take two letters, one for Maggie, telling her that she must go into hiding too as fast as possible, and the other, very important, for Goldstein, as soon as you're sure you're not being followed you must mail these two letters, but I'm getting ahead of myself, when you get to the mainland under no circumstances are you to go to the parking lot, go to the nearest service station and there you're bound to find some "fantastic bargain," buy it, Peter raised his eyebrows, I'll give you all the

312

money you need, said Sevilla, you'll drive all night, in the morning I advise you to sell this car, at a loss if necessary, buy another one in another garage, and repeat the whole operation at least once, all right, you reach Canada, and from Canada you go to Europe, I don't think getting out of the country will give you any problem, it's not the FBI that's after you but an agency that certainly doesn't share its secrets with the FBI, I know what you're going to say, Peter, but I owe you some compensation for breaking your contract, and after all the work we've done together the least you deserve is a quiet year of sabbatical somewhere in Europe, I'd like to point out, said Peter, that no such compensation was mentioned in my contract, Sevilla smiled, Well, that was an omission, I want to make up for it, anyway, what am I supposed to do with all this money? Peter looked at him for a long time without saying anything, I'd like to ask you one question, should I take a gun? That's a question you must answer for yourself, said Sevilla, I don't know how far you carry respect for life, Peter squared his shoulders and looked Sevilla in the eyes, I'll put my question another way, if they catch up with us do you think they'll torture us to make us talk? I think so, Suzy too? Peter gasped, Sevilla raised his eyebrows, Believe me, they won't make any distinction.

• • •

No light had been turned on in the house, the doors and windows were closed, they used flashlights, and then only for a few seconds, in the sky over the terrace a ceiling of huge black clouds hung motionless, stifling, without a chink of gray, the night promised to be just as dark as the one before, Sevilla had a sense of unreality, the four of them in the gathering dusk, dressed in dark colors, the two women in slacks, moving back and forth from the house to the terrace, from the terrace to the harbor, soundlessly making preparations to leave, walking barefoot, occasionally whispering in each other's ears words that were barely audible, four shadows, less and less distinct in the deepening night, gliding toward each other, separating, passing, coming together, moving away, at first Sevilla recognized his companions by their silhouettes, Arlette the shortest, Peter the tallest, Suzy in between, but even this difference was blurred and disappeared as the forms were erased and consumed by the darkness, their movements became slower, the sound of breath-

313

ing informed him of a presence, a hand touched his chest, he took it, it was Peter's, a voice murmured in his ear, We're finished, it's time, Peter, said Sevilla in a whisper, I saw you take a revolver, one word of advice, take grenades instead, if there are several armed men coming out of a car only a grenade . . . Arlette's voice against his neck, Suzy wants to say goodby to you, a hand touched his shoulder, it was Suzy, she murmured in his ear with extraordinary feeling, Good luck, Henry, it was the first time she had called him Henry, he felt her take his face in her hands, he leaned down, she pressed her lips to his cheek and whispered again with the same intensity, Good luck, Henry, the hands dropped, there was a brief stifled sob, he realized that the two women were embracing, Sevilla felt a surge of joy—good will, concern for other people, profound affection, man was these things too, Peter's hand glided along his arm, he seized it and pressed it hard, Pete, he said in a low voice, his mouth to Peter's ear, I'm going to borrow the little boat and get Fa and Bi, he took two steps, someone was beside him, the perfumed hair, the cool hands, it was Arlette, her ears were amazing, a yard away she had heard, she leaned against him and whispered in his ear, I'm coming with you, Henry.

They entered the winding passageway, it was almost unnecessary for Arlette to use her flashlight, it was the third time today Sevilla had been through this passageway, he knew it almost by feel, like the unlighted hallway of the house you grew up in, as they went farther and farther into the rock he experienced a deep sense of relief and security, he understood what prehistoric men felt when they discovered a winding cave on the side of a hill, yes, even if they had to chase the bears out before taking refuge there, axes and spears against teeth and claws, it was worth confronting a herd of giant *Plantigrada* to steal their warm, dark, deep, and inaccessible lair where, jammed together in a pile of warm humanity, the future lords and destroyers of the earth felt as safe from the terrifying dangers of the outside world as if they were in their mother's womb, You can keep the flashlight on, said Sevilla out loud as he pushed with both hands against the rocky walls of the last tunnel, it was a new joy to talk out loud and see clearly, Fa! Bi! he called in a loud voice, the dolphins appeared around them, joyous, boisterous, leaping, No, no, don't splash, cried Sevilla, we have to make a long trip tonight in an open boat, we'd be cold if you got us wet, listen, once in the

314

channel and in the sea don't say a word, not a single word in the language of men, talk only by whistling, in front of us the enemy, to the right and to the left the enemy, Arlette began to laugh, it was the first time in two days, Darling, she said with nervous, irrepressible gaiety, you sound like a general, and you have secrets like a general, the most incredible is that I don't even know where we're going, Cuba, he said, I've thought about it so much since yesterday, I thought I'd told you, it's only ninety miles from Key West to Marianao, the closest foreign country and the only country in Latin America where not having a United States passport is a recommendation in itself, also the only one from which we can easily get to Prague, perhaps with Cuban passports, our goal is to get to some European capital with Fa and Bi before the thirteenth of January to reveal the truth, if Goldstein hasn't received my letter by then, or hasn't succeeded in convincing Smith by playing him this morning's tape, I think this tape and news of our presence in Prague with Fa and Bi would be enough to make Smith put the machine in reverse, I wouldn't like to have to call a press conference and say terrible things about the secret services of my country, it would be enough for Smith to announce that the commission investigating the *Little Rock* incident had concluded that the explosion was an accident.

In the channel again, with the two life rafts side by side in the inky blackness, their motors pulled up, their oars parallel to their sides, speech again reduced to almost inaudible murmurs, Sevilla re-experienced the anxiety he had felt a few hours before when he had learned from the dolphins that Bob had known everything, he waited for Peter to finish stowing his bags in the smaller of the boats, the waiting was almost unendurable, his nerves were jangled, his temples throbbed, the sweat streamed steadily down the sides of his body, he could hardly sit still, Arlette took his hand, he immediately pulled it away, it was moist, Peter still wasn't finished, he was always so meticulous, so finicky, a wild impatience overcame Sevilla, half anger, half panic, he opened his mouth but immediately checked himself, he moved to the front of the life raft and stopped, fascinated, the luminous face of the ship's compass was staring at him, a friendly presence in a sea of darkness, the only fixed and reassuring point in a hostile world, all of a sudden he remembered Normandy, the summer of 1944, behind a hedge, during a night attack, the luminous hands of his watch appeared, standing out against the hostile dark, he felt relieved, lucid, his mind began to function again, Todd, take ten men, go and reconnoiter the stream in the bottom of the valley, and if you have to fire don't fire at each other, that nightmare feeling of advancing blindly, falling into trap after trap, the terrible hedges of Normandy, behind each one a German machine gun, admirably camouflaged, waiting in absolute silence, my forward guard cut down every time, they knew how to fight, he felt Arlette's cool hand on the back of his neck, her lips on his ear, Peter's ready, Well, let's go, said Sevilla, something snapped, as if a veil had suddenly been ripped, no, it was madness, entering the channel surrounded by fog, without being able to see anything or know where anything was, Wait, he said, tell him to wait, he leaned over the side of the boat, slapped the water twice with the palm of his hand, in an instant his hand was raised by a warm, smooth mass, they were both there, he whistled softly in Dolphinese, Fa! Bi! it was curious how the whistle blended into the sighing of the wind and the splashing of the water against the rocks, what must they be thinking out there, their ears glued to their headphones?

"Fa, Bi, swim through the channel until you reach the sea."

"Then what?"

"Maybe there is a ship. Maybe there is a frogman. Come back and tell us."

There was a silence, and Fa whistled, "There is a frogman, he swims toward us, what do I do?"

"You knock him out."

"Oh, no," said Fa. "I knock him out, he goes down and he dies. Oh, no."

"You don't knock him out, he kills us."

There was a silence, and Bi whistled. "I cut his air pipe with my teeth. He comes up for air. I get behind him and push him on the rocks."

Admirable rejection of violence: She puts him out of commission, but saves his life.

"Good," said Sevilla.

They disappeared and he imagined the two of them gliding through the black water, preceded by the beep of their sonar which gave them as clear a picture of the obstacles ahead as if they had seen them, long, streamlined, streaking like arrows, propelled by the supple and powerful movements of their caudal fins with marvelous economy of effort, without noise, without eddies, without cavitation, as fluid as the water itself, flashing through the water without disturbing it, one with the water, their weight alone a terrible weapon at this speed, under the sheath of their elastic skin, three hundred and fifty to four hundred and fifty pounds of muscle commanded by a brain as clever as man's but controlled by goodness.

A few seconds later Sevilla felt their noses under his hand.

Fa whistled. "A boat like yours, made of rubber. Bigger."

"Is the boat moving?"

"No. Anchored. At the entrance."

Lying in wait, barring their way. B's men must have understood from what they heard, or rather from what they did not hear, on their radio that they were preparing to escape.

Sevilla reflected. Arlette's lips clung to his cheek. Peter said they should go and attack them with grenades. Sevilla whispered in Arlette's ear, No. Tell him no. To throw grenades, you have to be able to see. And if there's a fight people will die on both sides. Ours too. He sat silent, time passed, the palms of his hands were wet.

"What do I do?" said Fa.

"How is the boat anchored?"

"A rope and something at the end."

"A rope? Are you sure? A rope, not a chain?"

"Yes."

Sevilla sat up straight. "You dive. You cut the rope with your teeth. And you push the boat gently, gently."

"Where?"

"To the right. There is a current. You must find it."

"Bi will find it," said Bi.

They disappeared. Arlette's mouth was against his cheek again. When the boat moves they will feel it, Sevilla ran his hand over Arlette's face, brushed aside a lock of hair, found her ear and said in a whisper, No, dark night, no landmarks. He ran his right hand through the water and thought, They'll notice, but it will be too late, they'll be on the rocks, not knowing where they are, at best with a few punctures.

He leaned to port and groped with his left hand until he found Peter's, he felt Peter lean over, Peter, if Fa and Bi pull it off, when you get out of the channel row for an hour to your left, then turn on the motor, use it five minutes, stop it, listen, turn it on again and so forth, there was a silence, Peter said, If they're stranded why not take advantage of it right away and turn on the motor full steam? No, said Sevilla emphatically, there's certainly a mother ship somewhere, they'd alert it by radio, it would pick up your motor on its sonar and be on you in less than a minute. As you know, there are very few fishermen around here at night.

"Pa," whistled Bi, "where is your hand?"

Sevilla put his hand in the water. She waited for him to pat her before talking.

"It is fun," she said. "The boat moves, they do not know."

"Are they talking?"

"No," said Fa. "They do not talk. The boat moves. They do not talk."

Bi chuckled. Sevilla leaned to port. Peter, he said in a whisper, goodby, and suddenly from one boat to the other in the night without a word four hands groped for and clasped each other hard for several seconds, Sevilla swallowed, his heart beat violently, strange, the present moment was so intense that it vanished before it was even over, these few seconds already belonged to the past, a moment which he already looked back on.

"Go, Pete," murmured Sevilla.

He heard him shove off and put his oars in position.

Bi whistled, "I will help him."

Sevilla positioned his own oars and began to row cautiously, but after a moment he drew them in again: Fa was pushing him from behind. He whistled, Not so fast, Fa. He freed one oar, handed it to Arlette, and said, Check the wall on your side, and I'll do mine. But Fa pushed the boat straight on its axis, correcting its course himself precisely as if he could see clearly.

As they came out of the channel Sevilla received the sudden cool blast of the south wind and the boat began to dance, he plied the port oar until the needle of the compass pointed steadily to the south, he whistled, Fa, can you keep the course to the south? Of course, said Fa, Call Bi, I'm here, said Bi, the boat started to go faster, Bi must be pushing too, Sevilla stowed Arlette's oar in the bottom of the boat but kept his beside him, he sat down, he felt Arlette leaning against his shoulder, her hair was sweeping his face, Bi whistled, Pa, why don't you turn on the motor? he leaned over,

318

he could see nothing, he couldn't even hear them, they swam so silently, they must be pushing the boat on either side of the motor in the place where the inflatable tubes joined the body, he whistled, Later, Bi, we're still too close, they have machines in the water that can hear motors, are you tired? Bi gave a whistle that sounded like a laugh, followed immediately by another, it was a long time since Fa and Bi had been so happy, to push the six hundred and fifty pounds of the boat, its occupants, and the motor through the water was nothing, it was a game, and the best game of all, this long un-expected journey through the open sea at night with Ma and Pa, they understood the importance of their mission, they were helping the good gods escape from the bad gods, everything was clear again, Sevilla asked, How long can you push? there was an exchange of whistles and Fa said, A length and a half, Sevilla looked at the luminous dial of his watch, ten thirty-five, let's say an hour, allow-ing for Fa's boastfulness, at eleven thirty-five he would start the Mercury and the most dangerous moment would begin, he would send Fa two miles ahead and Bi two miles back, the sonars of the two dolphins would detect suspicious movements of ships but for the moment, skimming over the sea in the dark night without making a sound, he was as hard to spot as a fish, except perhaps by the network of sonar buoys of the U.S. Navy, which were so sensitive that they could spot the spout of air and vaporized water made by a whale from miles away, but anyway, thought Sevilla, the intensity of that sound is not comparable to the respiration of dolphins, he leaned over, he let his right hand dangle over the side of the boat, he felt the power of its forward movement with his fingers and said in a low voice, It's marvelous, we're doing at least ten knots, Arlette did not answer, the silence lengthened, he realized from the move-ment of her body that she was weeping against his neck, he put his arm around her and waited, suddenly he thought, Yesterday, it was yesterday that Goldstein arrived on the island, how long the time seemed, how short it had been in reality, a day, a night, a day, and in the middle of the second night they had lost everything, the *Caribee*, the harbor, the house, the island, and even their country, and I don't really care, this is no time to cling to one's own nest, if there is an atomic war everything will be taken away from us, including the earth itself, the desperate absurdity of it all, when animals fight it is for food or to defend their territory, but never

319

have they conceived the plan of destroying an entire species or the earth they walk on, Arlette's voice whispered in his ear, Darling, do you think we have a chance? he answered in a reassuring voice, Yes, I think so, he was sitting behind the wheel on the inflatable seat, Arlette was beside him, his eyes were fixed on the compass, his left hand held the oar, ready to correct their course, but it was not even necessary, how did the dolphins do it, they kept the boat going due south in spite of the bumping, the swerving, and the long waves that caught them sideways, Arlette sat up straight, I'm not afraid to die, she whispered, I'm just afraid we won't make it, We'll make it, he said vigorously, actually he was far from sure, the chances were still very uncertain, he was not naïve enough to think that a cause triumphs because it is just but he could not afford the luxury of being pessimistic, there was no alternative but hope, they carried with them the truth that could keep the world from destroying itself, Fa and Bi had carried it before them, out of pure affection, through twenty-four hours of exhausting swimming, to Bob, Bob had not wanted it, and this night, this moment, in the Caribbean Sea, was man's last chance, Sevilla was aghast at the importance of the stake, he had never formulated it so clearly, just then, as if she had followed his train of thought, Arlette said in his ear with a quaver, If we succeed it will be because of us that the earth, she did not finish her sentence, he repeated to himself, Because of us, but he had a sense of doubt, as if, being a man, he participated in spite of himself in human irrationality and cruelty, even while opposing them, he listened to the water splashing against the rubber tubes, each time the front of the boat fell back into the hollow of a wave, the jointed wooden floor cracked beneath his feet at the impact, the air was warm and so was the sea, when he put his hand in the water it did not even feel cold, it lay around them, dark, its depths rich with life and presences, with enough fish, surely, to feed the Indians and the whites for centuries, if one group had not decided it more convenient to exterminate the other, he heard nothing of Fa and Bi except the rhythmic sound of their breathing when their two spiracles returned to the surface and decompressed, Because of us, he murmured doubtfully, or because of the humanity of the dolphins?